DEMONMACHY
Messiah of death saga
Volume one

Brant Danay

I

The blood in the giant bong bubbled and swirled, emitting a sweet-smelling steam as it heated throughout the labyrinths of the monstrous Satanic pipe. A furnace the size of a torture chamber, an altar of sacrifice the size of a temple, an incinerator the size of a crematorium, the Bloodbong nearly consumed the capacious inner sanctum of meditation which housed it. Hells within hells within hells, like the universe itself.

The Bloodbong's endless mazes of tubes and chambers were woven into hypnotic patterns and mandalas, flowing endlessly into and unto themselves while filling its hollow, translucent effigies, caryatids, and telamones with hot vermillion plasma. Twisted like catacombs and intricate to the point of psychedelia, the sinister device was yet as controlled as a circulatory system, a mechanical tapestry of capillaries, arteries, veins, and organs that pulsed and beat like those of a living creature. Through the transparent, scarlet-fogged, rune-carved glass the blood could be seen pumping back and forth, rushing upwards, cataracting downwards, and swirling in crimson maelstroms, driven by the same powerful necromancies which had spawned the Bloodbong eons ago. Flames churned upwards from the interdimensional portal at its base, burning at light speed through an abyssal, roiling wormhole leading to the underworld, heating the Bloodbong with the very fires of Hell.

The center of the bong was huge and shaped like a living heart, its four contracting and expanding sections filled with a tangled mass of naked, screaming bodies, immersed to their necks in boiling blood. Some of the blood was their own. Some had belonged to their ancestors. Some was the blood of their children. They clawed at the sides of the bong's heart-chamber, their faces contorted into raw-meat animal masks. Nearly the last of the universe's dwindling population, they were not near to being the last of the Necrodelic's own personal supply of flesh. Victims, prisoners, and slaves he had, imprisoned throughout the demonium of his living spaceship. Evil he had. Power he had. What he craved, now, was enlightenment.

Chariah, the Death Addict, the Necrodelic, sat with his legs crossed in the ancient, often lethal, black lotus position, his wrists upon his knees, his thumbs and forefingers joined. Gently, he wrapped his lips around the mouthpiece of the Bloodbong. Chariah inhaled, the deep, slow breath of the succubus. Smoke billowed and filled the chamber, filled his black lungs, his black flesh, his black soul. His jet hair and ebon claws grew longer; his red eyes glowed with a hotter shade of crimson. Veins bulged like black mambas across the chiseled muscles of his caliginous figure. His blood quickened and fevered, as did his gonglike heartbeat, his meditative thoughts, and his sin-laden astrosome.

The bodies in the bong began to disintegrate, their flesh pulling apart and transmogrifying into red-tinged fumes. The thin screens surrounding the nexus of the gargantuan hookah like pericardium drew the fumes into the tubes of the pipe. Chariah exhaled, the deep, slow breath of the incubus. The clouds of smoke suffocating the chamber began to take on mystical formations. Death screams resonated like hideous mantras, then mutated into visible wraiths in rushes of synesthesia.

The Necrodelic smoked his victims alive. His plasmoptic and pyroptic powers now heightened, the Necrodelic gazed through the blood and the smoke as though it were boiling Lethe and crystalline steam. He watched with drugged fascination as the skin of his victims fell to float in the blood of the bong, as chunks of muscle dropped away like the flesh of immolated lepers, as raw gleaming organs were slowly exposed, loosened, and freed, then dissipated into gory flotsam. He watched as bones began to separate, as charred skeletons unhinged, as entire bodies were reduced to wet ash, their fresh ghosts free-falling like his drifting consciousness, and then he himself was floating like the gruesome detritus in his pipe, floating downwards into a grave, the grave of the astral plane, where Mother Chaos awaited, pink flesh beckoning, purple hair streaming on psychic vibrations.

The touch of Mother Chaos was as that of a shadow or an ebony sunset, ephemeral as the blind eye contact of the null-demons which inhabited the black holes littering space. Her mouth and vagina were two of those black holes, it seemed, sucking Chariah's tongue and penis through the pink death that was her flesh, through the limits of love and beyond, to salvation or damnation, nirvana or Hell, their astral sex a microcosm of their apocalyptic spiritual war.

Cursed with omnisentience, Mother Chaos felt all the suffering throughout the universe simultaneously, as well as all the suffering which had gone before and all the suffering yet to come. The pleasure and pain of every spirit in existence, living or dead, resonated within her omnisentient astral body, an infinity of torments which only the love of her demon devotee could assuage.

The Necrodelic pretended he was Satan, his wrathful and ultimate master, as he made love to Mother Chaos. He could feel Satan watching as they writhed through time; he was Satan, now, horns bleeding, veins and arteries wrapped in an interdimensional labyrinth around the exterior of his crimson body, barbed penis leaking fiery semen. He breathed omniscience like a drug, sighed omnipotence an eternity later.

As the Necrodelic and Mother Chaos made love, spirits rocketed through the astral plane from above, the severed souls of those whose bodies Chariah had smoked. They screamed at him as they were drawn inexorably downward.

"...bastard Necrodelic...by bloody karma, Satan will have your soul as well...you will never become the Jh'a'vyraa..."

The white cataract of souls came to a blazing finale as they dropped out of sight, soon to be repossessed by Hell, probably never to be born again, for universal moksha, the terminus of all reincarnation, was imminent. Even now, reincarnation was attained by only the most highly evolved demons, for the gauntlet which preceded it grew more arduous by the moment, in direct relation to the proximity of the end of time and the velocity with which it approached. For most, to die in this age meant an eternity in Hell, their spirits plucked from the endless orbits of their samsaric cycles like planets being devoured by a black hole.

Chariah knew this, and, thinking of such universal armageddon, asked Mother Chaos, "Will I be the Jh'a'vyraa?"

"... you will be the Jh'a'vyraa...my Jh'a'vyraa...together we will escape Satan...and attain the final enlightenment beyond...you shall become the Messiah of Death...and the salvation of the Jh'a'vyraa shall be ours..."

Chariah kissed Mother Chaos and made love to her anew, her long purple nails vibrating along his back, her amethyst wings fluttering. Chariah's astral body quivered as they floated.

"Who is to be my next victim?" Chariah asked of Mother Chaos, his words running like ichor in the pulsating atmosphere.

Mother Chaos kissed Chariah on the forehead, and from her damson lips words came like slow worms, using his astral body as a conduit to embed themselves in his brain.

"...you will seek out Morpheus Rex...the Oneirophage...on the planet Grystiawa...he is a powerful demon with intricate and deadly designs on becoming the Messiah of Death...of attaining the Jh'a'vyraa...the devourer of dreams represents a serious threat to your destiny...his wise and ancient mind contains many dreams which he has ingested over the eons...dreams which you must smoke from his skull...tonight, we sail to Grystiawa, upon this dark jihad..."

The words maggoted through his mind, sensuously massaging and painfully lacerating his optic lobes, creating gory visions of the words' true meanings, and then the womb of Mother Chaos was shrinking, tighter and tighter, squeezing the blood and oxygen from his engorged phallus until it became bruised and disfigured like the throat of a strangled corpse. The Mistress of Entropy pulped his member for several moments before finally constricting her thighs and womb one final time, like a boa constrictor with its prey.

Mother Chaos' erotic quietus, their last act of tantric sadomasochism, brought the Necrodelic to Dark Orgasm, sexual death, his ceremonial gateway back to the physical plane. Blind as a grub, senseless as a corpse, helpless as an embryo, the Necrodelic drifted in an existential cosmos where nothing existed except void and orgasm. The sexual nihilism drained the thoughts from his mind like a sinkhole, then through his unfeeling body to be released with the smoke and the space that he invisibly ejaculated into the vacuum. Visions, dreams, and prophecies took the place of thoughts, only to be forgotten in the moments following their psychic flashpoints, and then the void became the orgasm, the orgasm became the void, and he was floating, floating upwards through a grave, the grave of the astral plane, back to the universe he must rape, back to the races he must slay, back to the smoke-filled, sperm-splattered meditation chamber of the living spaceship, and back to the body he must escape, ascending to the ultimate state of consciousness and freeing the tortured soul of Mother Chaos, his soulmate and guardian angel.

Awakening with newfound evil enlightenments, Chariah exited the meditation chamber through a living door that automatically dilated before him and constricted behind him. Chariah made his way to the womblike cockpit in the center of his bestial spaceship, where hanging forests of umbilical cords writhed and curled as they dangled from the ceiling. Likewise, living jungles of umbilical cords swayed and reached out like tentacles from the floors and walls. Chariah stepped inside, and a pink umbilical cord extended slowly from the ceiling and attached itself, on one plane, to his forehead; on another plane, to his third eye. A hundred more followed, joining their flesh to his with wet sucking noises at a hundred different points, pulling his body in a hundred different directions. The Necrodelic was raised toward the ceiling on umbilical stalactites, while umbilical stalagmites simultaneously fought to drag him back down to the floor. Tautening tentacles from every angle suspended the cruciform demon in midair, where he floated as though upon very slow winds. Through these umbilical cords Chariah connected with the ship's nervous system and telepathically guided it toward the Tyterviax system, where the planet Grystiawa spun and the Oneirophage dined upon feasts of dream.

A pair of telescopic umbilical cords attached themselves to the rims of flesh around the Necrodelic's eye sockets, then stretched and bifurcated throughout the bestial spaceship to the myriad eyeballs scattered across its exterior. These scrying tubes allowed the Necrodelic to observe the universe from deep within his living vessel. He gazed with wonder across the dead and dying galaxies, graveyards of space once teeming with life, now laid to waste by armageddon and extinction. He contemplated the passing cosmos, its vastness as black as his billion lifetimes.

As Chariah navigated the universe, he meditated upon love and death, and throughout the entire journey to the Tyterviax system, and throughout his entire meditation, he was haunted by Satan's blood-red stare, poking like hot torture irons through the myriad planes which separated the two of them, voyeur and demon, father and child.

2

Grystiawa's sunset was a bloodletting, a bloodletting Morpheus Rex felt in his flesh. Lounging on his vast, rose-colored bed, surrounded by bloodstains and blankets, he watched the sunset through the giant window that comprised the western wall of his bedchamber. Scarlet rays sprayed the firmament as though from a thousand severed carotid arteries. The clouds of evening absorbed the infinite shades of darkling red and hung like blood-soaked bandages across the wounded skies. Crepuscular crimson sunbeams flowed profusely over the planet, as if the jugular veins of Satan himself had been slashed asunder. At the nexus of this ensanguined twilight the red sun Tyterviax beat like a dying heart, sinking deeper and deeper into a lake of its own blood, twitching like the scattered shrapnel of daylight surrounding it as it drowned.

The spill of crimson light from the setting sun was not only reminiscent of a bloodletting, but symbolic of one as well, for it was a harbinger of the violent deaths which were as inherent to the Grystiawan nocturnes as black skies, red moons, and golden starlight. With eyes like flaming prisms Morpheus Rex gazed upon the shadowy, blood-colored wastelands of his realm. Grystiawa was dying in pieces, a little more with each victim he killed. The bloodletting sunset was the signal of temporary safety for those few who had escaped his clutches thus far, those still roaming the crimson deserts, badlands, moors, and mountains outside his castle. It was the signal of doom for the fourteen demons chained against the wall across from his bed. Their final day had ended. Their final night had commenced.

For the devourer of dreams, the sunset was a soulletting, as well. As the day died, so too did his diurnal persona. As Morpheus Rex, the Dreaming Predator, he had stalked the badlands of Grystiawa since dawn, walking with deafening silence, running at blinding speeds, and fighting with mind-numbing ferocity upon the lower body of a bipedal demon. With the thighs of a tiger and the tattoos of a serial killer he had hunted, crippling and subduing his prey with Prismsword, Spectrumhammer, and Rainbowspear, leaving his victims bloodied, wounded, and maimed, but never dead. Dreams were a drug most potent when imbibed from the flesh, blood, and brains of the living. Thus, the sacrificial dreamers never knew death until their slayer had satiated his addiction.

Until such time, their vanquished bodies were stored in the Darkprism, a sable, pentagram-shaped talisman which he wore around his neck while he hunted, a tiny black hole from which neither light nor souls could escape unless summoned. Thusly were his prey and their dreams preserved until he returned home to Phantasmagorika, his mighty, glittering, sparkling castle which had been carved from a single gargantuan prism, an ephemeral oneiromancer's palace which disappeared every evening and reappeared in a different part of Grystiawa every morn.

As the last vermillion rays of sunset laced his bedchamber window like veins and arteries, the diurnal persona of Morpheus Rex began to retreat. The sun and the skies, the clouds and the land, gradually turned black by degrees of crimson. Grystiawa reddened itself into darkness. The pellucid window transformed into stained glass, a multi-colored grotesquery that displayed new images every evening, like some species of sentient artwork perpetually inspired to reinvent itself by a Satanic muse.

The sound of Phantasmagorika's heliotropic gateways closing for the night reverberated and echoed across the planet. They did not close to keep intruders out. They closed to keep victims in. In one silent moment nightfall covered Grystiawa. The soulletting of Morpheus Rex followed within a nanosecond. The flesh between his thighs welded itself together and his legs transformed into the tail of a giant snake. Like a male lamia he hissed and slithered, the alpha naga, a demon from the waist up, a serpent from the waist down.

The change was one of inner metamorphosis as well, a psychic transmutation of self, a nocturnal enlightenment, a spiritual vivisection, a soul transplant. As his brain slowly filled with blood like a living sponge, the bestial psyche of Morpheus Rex was conquered by the demonic psyche of the Oneirophage. Oestrus became sadomasochism; torture and suffering became meditation. Hunger and thirst became vampiric cravings for blood, flesh, and dreams; shamanic cravings for drugs, enlightenment, and power. Totemic religion was conquered by devil worship. Psychedelic synesthesias of blood assailed him from every possible sensory organ. The thrill of the hunt mutated into perversions of evil, fetishes for murder and mass destruction, a lust for apocalypse and eternal damnation. Death was revealed as the ultimate reality, the meaning of life, his raison d'etre. The entire universe was his hunting grounds, and total genocide was vital to his survival.

The nocturnal transformation was complete. Carnivorous beast had evolved into genocidal demon. Morpheus Rex had metamorphosed into the Oneirophage. The familiar, black enlightenments known only by highly evolved demons, powerful deities, and almighty Satan himself permeated his mind, body, and soul for another night.

The last changes were minor, final adaptations of the flesh to the spirit's metamorphosis. Externally, his large, round, kaleidoscopic, prismatic eyes began to glow from within, rather than reflecting and refracting the light around them. Heat-vision gave way to night-vision and dream-vision. Internally, the cravings began. Like a vampire's bloodlust, dreams were the only substance that could sustain his nocturnal flesh and evil soul. He craved dreams, needed dreams, was addicted to dreams like a drug. His brain was starved, throbbing with stabbing hunger pangs, so many hunger pangs that they left him room for only one thought at a time, a single mantra that repeated itself, over and over, inside his pain-wracked mind:

I would die for dreams.

Since appendages often became repositories and escape routes for dreams, the feast of the Oneirophage had to be properly prepared. So, as he did every night, he herded his shackled victims into the Amputator, the gargantuan, imposing, iron limbing machine in the southern wing of the bedchamber. Fourteen prey, Morpheus Rex had captured for him. Fourteen skulls worth of dreams the Oneirophage would eat and drink this night.

With death's own gaze the prism-eyed Oneirophage prepared his prisoners outside the mechanical jaws of the Amputator. The sacrificial demons were laid prostrate upon a lengthy, gem-encrusted surgical table, then bolted down by iron collars that fit around their necks and abdomens. The long adamantium chains that had bound them to the floor, ceiling, walls, and each other were hooked to iron rings on either side of the limbing machine's innards. The chains held their captives tautly spread-eagled, arms and legs extended like living pentagrams, horizontally crucified. The fourteen pentagrams of flesh were bound in a straight line upon the elongated, jeweled, bloodstained platform, which now looked eerily like the feasting tables in the dining halls of cannibal emperors.

The Oneirophage slithered to the giant wheel protruding from the side of the Amputator. He gripped the wheel with both hands and slowly turned it, grinding the gears of the mutilation machine. The surgical table bearing the captives lurched and began moving inexorably into the bowels of the Amputator. Four guillotine blades fell simultaneously, followed by the wet thud of four severed limbs striking the floor. The screams of the dismembered demon tore the night air as it was borne further into the sadistic device. As a second demon was dragged beneath the guillotines, the first was conveyed past two walls of open flames that cauterized the wounds on its shoulders and hips, preserving both life and dreams. Finally, at the Amputator's exit, a giant scraping device lifted the limbless body from the table and deposited it in an obsidian cage.

The Oneirophage listened to the severing mechanisms of the Amputator as he operated it. The sound of terrified screams, the smell of naked flesh, and the taste of blood in the air made the Oneirophage's dream-cravings even more intense. His prismatic eyes gleamed with lust and his three forked tongues licked his dripping fangs and rainbow lips. His chiseled, bulky muscles stood out against his skin as he toiled, bringing the tattoos which covered his entire body to life. Death's heads and demon faces smiled and snarled, incubi and succubi copulated and battled, torture devices shifted and churned and excruciated their victims. A thousand images writhed as the sinews beneath them moved, tinged with the pale blood the Oneirophage sweated as he operated the Amputator. His tattooed lips shimmered like banded coral snakes. Incarnadine perspiration soaked his long, brown, prism-plaited hair and beard, and ran down his body as his cravings deepened and his withdrawals intensified. One by one the victims were limbed, cauterized, and collected. After mere minutes, the ceremony was complete.

The Oneirophage gathered up his dismembered prey,

grabbing handfuls of hair and fistfuls of genitals and tossing the amputees onto his roseate, gore-stained blankets in a pile of flesh. Upon his bedside table, whose legs were caduceus staffs and whose surface was engraved with arabesque, serpentine bas-reliefs, and whose wood was so splotched and stained with vermillion that it seemed the table had been carved from a giant piece of driftwood fished from a river of blood, lay the Umbilicus. A hollow, strawlike wand, capable of infinite permutations and rhabdomancies, the Umbilicus performed a myriad of surgical and sorcerous functions for the Oneirophage. Reaching between the prism goblets and chalices scattered across the table, he grabbed the Umbilicus and held it to his lips.

Gripping the Umbilicus with his manicured right hand, each long fingernail painted with sigils and mandalas, he observed the victims writhing on his bed, their still-sizzling armholes and legholes sticking to the blankets and leaking black pus. He leaned over a pale green female, her naked, limbless torso twitching like a large invertebrate, her breasts swinging back and forth as she wormed and writhed. He placed the straw between her emerald lips and drank, sucking dreams of romance through her mouth and into his, down his throat, and into his bloodstream. Dreams of succubus lips and Satanic kisses blossomed in his brain, of vaginas and oubliettes opening and closing like mouths. The Oneirophage licked his rainbow lips with each of his three forked tongues and sighed.

He shoved the straw into the ear of a blue-skinned male and sucked again. Dreams of comets shooting up from Hell hit him in the teeth and tongues, slamming into his heart and taking him deeper into trance. Switching the Umbilicus into a triple-curled, six-pronged straw, he cleaned the blood from around the mouth and ears of the two dream-robbed husks, vacuuming up any remnants of dreams they might carry, then inserted two of the tube's tips into the eyes of a yellow-skinned male. Dreams of Satan came bubbling; he watched them travel up the straw with drugged fascination. He dreamed that he was Satan, swimming in an ocean of blood, amidst crimson mermaids whom he made love to, swimming to a heart the size of a planet. Fascinated, he placed the straw in the yellow-skinned male's nostrils, hoping to tap these archetypes again. The ocean of blood returned, he dreamt he was Satan, the red mermaids beckoned, and then the dream faded and was no more.

Allowing the dreams to flow, for they could become lethal if he did not, the Oneirophage turned his attentions downward. He raped a pink-skinned virgin succubus with the Umbilicus, plunging it into her vagina, perforating her hymen with a spray of blood, and lodging it deep inside her womb. Pretending the pink demoness was Mother Chaos, the Oneirophage breathed in sexual fantasies and sadomasochistic phobias. The Oneirophage dreamt that his two penises were ejaculating pink, perfumed semen. Not yet satisfied, he stabbed the straw into the urethra of a purple-scaled incubus and shoved it all the way back to his diaphragm. He performed fellacio upon the Umbilicus, sucking all the sperm and blood from the incubus' testicles, then all the wet dreams and erotic nightmares from his brain, a mixture which influenced the Oneirophage's thoughts toward the coming of the Jh'a'vyraa. Feeling as if his mind's eye had become infinitely more focused, the Oneirophage dreamt of becoming the Jh'a'vyraa, the Messiah of Death, and attaining that state of bliss beyond rebirth, where Satan could not terrify him with excruciating nightmares, fear injections, venereal paranoias, primal instincts, and suicidal tendencies. As the Jh'a'vyraa he would torture himself eternally, masturbate eternally, and dream eternally. The euphoric dark enlightenments of pain, sex, and evil would be forever bound to his soul.

For hours, the Oneirophage drained the limbed bodies of their dreams, imbibing most of their blood, and eating some of their flesh and organs as well. His final dream-visions were of the Necrodelic, and he knew that he would soon meet the Death Addict in battle. He watched the Omnibeast soar through space, then peered inside the Omnibeast and observed the Necrodelic himself. The flesh-smoker was breathing death from his Bloodbong. The Oneirophage gazed across his black form, his chiseled muscles, his vaguely catlike features, his tapering face, his vampire fangs, his slanted crimson eyes that glowed like tilted abacinating irons, his hair that cascaded in an Acheronic cataract down his back and nearly touched the floor while he sat in the black lotus position. He dreamed of scalping the Necrodelic, creating a bloody oracle upon his glistening, gory skull. He peered through the crown of the Necrodelic's head and watched the dreams flow through the Death Addict's black brain. The dreams were memories of past slaughters and prophecies of massacres to come. The Oneirophage observed the flesh-smoker's fighting methods through his dreams of war, noting his tendencies, his strengths, his weaknesses. He saw that the Necrodelic received his powers from death itself.

Dreams of Mother Chaos filled the scalped-skull oracle now, and the Oneirophage saw that she was the Necrodelic's soulmate. Mesmerized by their second dream encounter of the night, the Oneirophage drifted once more into a concatenation of erotic fantasies, a sexual reverie that bore him past the threshold of midnight and into deeper slumber.

As sperm, blood, and venom fountained from his two erect penises, splattering his unconscious body in the name of the Mistress of Entropy, the Oneirophage's astral body arose from the sanguinary, corpse-laden covers and projected into the night. For a time he soared over the maroon wastelands of Grystiawa in his nightly travels, scouting the living and haunting the newly dead, escorting them downward, ever downward, to the boundaries of Hell. He observed the prey that he would stalk the following day, singling out the weak, the sick, and the old, forming battle-strategies for the coming dawn, when he would once again assume the role of the hunter and the beast, the Dreaming Predator, Morpheus Rex. He dreamt also that, in the near future, he became the hunted.

His brain turgid with dreams, the Oneirophage slept, his wandering soul soaring wistfully through realms of ephemera and phantasmagoria. Above Grystiawa, Tyterviax shone on, and space continued to grow blacker and blacker with evil and death. Elsewhere, somewhere, or perhaps nowhere, beyond everything Satan had ever created, salvation awaited the conqueror of the universe, for the last entity or pair of soulmates left alive at the end of time would become the Jh'a'vyraa and attain infinite peace. Every other soul in existence would be tortured in Hell for all eternity. Of this, the Oneirophage dreamt until waking.

*

The crimson dawn was like surgery, the red sun Tyterviax a bleeding tumor excised from the flesh of night. Beams of morning light revealed the badlands of Grystiawa like scalpels and daggers exposing inner organs. Red dunes and pieces of desert opened like wounds before the stabbing illumination.

Mountain ranges glistened like exposed spines. Like surgery, the seasons changed, the eons passed, the stars and planets revolved in orbit, and so too did the Grystiawan night pass once more into day.

Surgical, as well, was the psychic mutation of the Oneirophage. The rebirth of Morpheus Rex, and the limbo of the Oneirophage, were samsaric surgeries, a metamorphosis of the spirit, like the cycles of reincarnation that stretched from the genesis of the universe to the end of time. The soulletting was instant, at the exact nanosecond of sunrise, and the diurnal destroyer, the bestial slayer, the Dreaming Predator, Morpheus Rex, had arisen again.

He awakened in a mass grave, the carnage of the Oneirophage's nocturnal rituals strewn across the bed. A cannibal's breakfast surrounded him, and he nourished himself with raw demon meat, tearing chunks of flesh apart with his sabretoothed cobra fangs, swallowing inner organs whole with his anaconda throat, and lapping up blood and other bodily fluids with his three forked tongues. Upon finishing his morning feast, Morpheus Rex licked the gore from his rainbow lips and prepared for battle.

Fully awake, his instincts razor-bladed and saw-edged for the hunt, Morpheus Rex tossed back his long, prism-plaited hair, placed the Darkprism around his neck, and inserted the Umbilicus in a tiny sheath of flesh carved in his wrist. He exited his bedchamber, which now resembled a golgotha, walked down the hall, and entered his weapons gallery. He removed his Prismsword and Spectrumhammer from their weapons rack and slung his Rainbowspear over his shoulder, then left the room and descended the sparkling stairways of his palace to the bottom story. With rainbows carving the air up like lasers, the Dreaming Predator stepped into his entrance hall.

Phantasmagorika's seven heliotropic gateways had been unlocked and opened by the rays of dawn. Morpheus Rex navigated the labyrinthine egress of double-doors, swinging doors, trap-doors, ceiling-doors, hidden doors, and irising portals, then passed under the sparkling spikes of the heliotropically raised portcullis and over the heliotropically lowered drawbridge. The bridge led Morpheus Rex safely across a psychedelic moat of brain-destroying liquid hallucinogens and into his hunting grounds.

Raising high both Prismsword and Spectrumhammer as he stood outside his resplendent palace, with the colors of his weapons reflecting and refracting all around him, and his grotesque and sinister tattoos glowing and shimmering across his bulky, bulging muscles, Morpheus Rex let ring his piercing battle cry.

The hunt had begun.

3

The Necrodelic's bestial spaceship skimmed the crimson cumulus of Grystiawa's atmosphere, its shadows falling not only upon the clouds, but into the clouds, as though they had mass and weight, or were composed of antimatter. The shadows dwelled inside the clouds like gargantuan parasites, their bodies visible through the layers of mist like ticks nestled in flesh, or spiders gestating in translucent egg sacs.

The nearly tangible nature of the spaceship's shadow was a dark testament to the raw, pure power of the vessel and its master, as well as an ominous sigil which augured the extreme evil of the invader. Like a black hole moon, the writhing spaceship orbited the rim of the planet, dropping its shadows into the clouds, across the scab-like deserts, and onto the maroon mountain ranges. With the deliberate slowness of a predator, the bestial spaceship circled closer and closer to the surface, until the creatures fleeing across the wastelands could make out its sinister features with their naked eyes.

The hideous vessel seemed an amalgamation of every species that had ever lived, joined together by surgery and sorcery. Appropriately named the Omnibeast, the soaring monstrosity was the result of several millennia of conquerment and enslavement, subjugation and domination, breeding and mutation, vivisection and necromancy. Large, triangular dragon scales protruded from the ship's outer skin, vertical and diagonal mountain ranges that often converged to protect the ship's vital parts. Several of these vital parts were the Omnibeast's crimson eyes, which were now blinking open to gaze across the Grystiawan landscape. Humongous, black, open-mouthed nightworms with rings of sabretooth fangs, some of which dripped venom, protruded from the exterior of the mammoth vessel. Hundreds of eyestalks extended from the spaceship as well, ending in swiveling bloodshot spheres that looked about in all directions. If followed into the vessel with X-ray vision, one would see those same nightworms and eyestalks flowing seamlessly into the hundreds of umbilical cords that were ubiquitous throughout the ship. Those umbilical cords controlled the Omnibeast like the multi-tipped whips of a hecatoncheire dominatrix. They looped, mazed, slithered, and burrowed through glands, nerves, organs, oracles, and altars of sacrifice, ultimately converging in the nexus of the vessel. Inside this central cockpit the Necrodelic's body was attached to the umbilical tubes, and through them he controlled the nervous system, circulatory system, digestive system, endocrine system, and every other aspect of the living spaceship, sometimes giving it coordinates for flights across the universe and sometimes commanding it in cataclysmic battles and apocalyptic space-wars. The umbilical cords pumped thousands of drugs and hormones, hypnotic suggestions and Satanic chantings, black electricity and sacrificial blood, into and out of the Omnibeast's consciousness. They were the chains of the dungeonkeeper, the reins of the dragonrider, the whips of the beastmaster. They were lifelines in the grip of the Necrodelic, and through them Chariah possessed the Omnibeast in much the same way he often possessed the minds, the flesh, and the souls of the innocent and the damned. Through the umbilical cords, Chariah was at one with his sentient, intergalactic monstrosity. The bestial spaceship was an extension of the Necrodelic's dark spirit, just like a possessed victim, just like his own physical body.

Extending from the Omnibeast's carapace like turrets were the eight Hydratowers, rearing back on hundred-foot long necks in a circle around the center of the spaceship's roof. Each severed but still-living hydra head faced in a different direction, equidistant from one another, like the points of a compass. The eight legs of a gargantuan spider protruded from the ship's underbelly to form the Arachniotics, the vessel's landing gear. The Omnibeast also possessed four giant, living figureheads: the Overdragon, Scythetooth, War Mantis, and Darkworm. Each behemoth had been embedded in the ship and bonded to its nervous system. The Overdragon was breathing fire from what was currently serving as the front of the spaceship, and it was before his fiery maw that the inhabitants of Grystiawa now fled. Its fanged mouth breathed the very flames of Hell from its interplanal lungs, and was capable of unleashing the fiery tornadoes and hurricanes of the infernal underworld, as well. It could destroy or devour a moon or a small planet within a matter of hours.

The Overdragon's head extended from a long, thick neck, adorned by plates and spikes, that seemed perpetually arisen for battle. Above its crimson eyes and crocodilian snout the horns of Satan crackled with black electricity, sometimes oozing blood from their tips during combat. They were strong enough to trigger supernovas and sharp enough to cut through the very fabric of space and time. The Overdragon's horns had been bestowed upon it by Satan himself, for the Overdragon had once been the high priest of a race of devil-worshipping dragonmen. It had been conquered by the Necrodelic in an ancient, bygone age, and after the Necrodelic had genocided its species, he had made the Overdragon into a living sacrifice. Subjugated to Chariah's necromancy, and bonded by a blood debt, the creature had been used as the basis from which the rest of the bestial spaceship was grown. Its slanted eyes still burned red in their sockets with the wisdom of its eons of existence, but they were enslaved to their demon master, and the Overdragon had very little hope of becoming the Jh'a'vyraa. Its titanic body was now nothing more than a steed and a slave for its possessor.

The Overdragon breathed tsunamis of flame across the badlands, searing the flesh off of various monsters and demons in less than a nanosecond, and leaving mushroom clouds and billowing smoke in its wake. Charred skeletons stood amidst the conflagrations for several moments before collapsing to the singed and smoking ground. Deserts of maroon sand transformed into plains of black glass as the Overdragon scorched the planet's surface with Hellfire.

Deep inside the Omnibeast, Chariah watched the devastation through telescopic umbilical cords. The smell of roasted flesh wafted into the cockpit in sooty clouds of oily smoke, transported to the chamber directly from the killing fields and exhaled by the various umbilical cords which dangled and swayed from the floor, walls, and ceiling. The Necrodelic breathed in the smoked flesh and was soon suffused with the pleasant sensation of necrodelia. Though far less powerful than smoking flesh from the Bloodbong, it nonetheless heightened his senses, sharpened his instincts, and created a feeling of tranquility. The umbilical cords exhaled puffs of smoke like mouths, and the cockpit soon grew murky and became covered with a fine silt of ashes.

Rhythmically breathing in and out, as though deep in meditation, Chariah telepathically flew the Omnibeast across Grystiawa, spreading genocide and coming a little closer to becoming the Jh'a'vyraa with every murder. With umbilical cords attached to his eyelids, he searched for Morpheus Rex. The ground and sky blurred past at supersonic speeds. Far below, the little creatures ran and died, and even the tallest anakim and largest nephilim seemed like insects as the flames struck them. He caught a few winged spiders in mid-air with fireballs as well. Some of the spiders exploded, while others crashed like flaming meteors to the ground. Others the Omnibeast swallowed whole. Mountaintops whizzed by and the Overdragon assailed them with barrages of Hellfire. Giant black tentacles reached out from the Omnibeast and snatched organisms from caves and peaks and valleys, to be absorbed into the vessel through one of its myriad orifices and borne through its veins and arteries into Chariah's dungeons.

Once past the mountain range, Chariah directed the spaceship east, and momentarily glimpsed the flashing colors of Morpheus Rex's Prismsword. Chariah could smell the dreams of his enemy from afar, and as he breathed in their mixture of perfume and decay, the Oneirophage's dreams from the previous night played like reveries in his brain. His mind's eye watched the Oneirophage metamorphose into Satan and swim through an ocean of blood where mermaids played and a beating heart the size of a planet churned the waters with a hypnotic rhythm. Chariah hissed as he observed the Oneirophage divining from the oracle of his own exposed brain, with a sensation that was like being in an interdimensional labyrinth of broken mirrors. He snarled and flexed his claws as he observed the Oneirophage's desire for Mother Chaos, and the wet dreams wherein the dream-eater raped Chariah's soulmate.

Detaching himself from the umbilical cords as the Omnibeast landed, Chariah left the cockpit and made his way through the labyrinth of his vessel. A few minutes later, the jaws of the Overdragon opened, its fangs raised like a portcullis, and the Necrodelic emerged from its corridor-like throat to stand within its dripping maw, his long, black hair streaming behind him, surrounded by clouds of sulfurous smoke.

"Drakhus," he spoke. The dragon's tongue elongated and lowered its master to the ground several hundred feet below.

The Necrodelic stood as dark, as silent, and as still as outer space, making his descent with stoic evil. His black mane billowed behind him, fluttering and floating on the downward breezes. As he stepped onto the surface of Grystiawa, the soul of the planet shuddered like a submissive bitch. With Hell in his eyes, Chariah gazed across the blood-red badlands, his enlightened demonsight drinking in every detail of the new battlefield for thousands of miles around.

The Necrodelic focused his crimson eyes upon his prey. His demonsight isolated Morpheus Rex several miles in the distance, hunting beyond the horizon, stalking the badlands adjacent to a mountain range. Chariah watched as Morpheus Rex battled, subdued, and captured a Grystiawan demon. He observed the Dreaming Predator's strengths and weaknesses, his fighting techniques and tendencies, his massive muscles and psychedelic tattoos. For one eternal moment, the Necrodelic spied upon Morpheus Rex the same way Satan spied upon the universe: from beyond. Then, in one timeless instant, from miles away, the Necrodelic gazed directly into Morpheus Rex's eyes.

The Dreaming Predator felt the Necrodelic's flaming eye contact before he saw it. It was like being telepathically abacinated. When he raised his eyes to meet the Necrodelic's, two infrared beams formed across the wastelands, locking the warriors together with eye contact as tangible as fire, eye contact that pierced like branding irons, the eye contact of bellipotent demons destined to do battle since the beginning of time.

The infrared eye contact drew the Necrodelic across the vast expanses of desert to combat Morpheus Rex. Chariah could no more unlock his gaze than he could gouge his own eyeballs out. Morpheus Rex's eyes had likewise been impaled, as surely as if incandescent spikes had been driven through them and then drilled through his entire brain, emerging from the back of his skull and pinning his head to a wall of brimstone. With hot blood running down his face, he watched the Necrodelic come. The infrared beams grew shorter as the Necrodelic approached. Chariah strode with the purpose of a panther, then came to a catlike stop a mere foot from his prey. His black claws glinted, his dark muscles rippled. They were his only weapons, but they were among the deadliest in the universe. His only armor was his skin, his chiseled physique, his healing powers, and his immense capacity for physical damage. The Necrodelic fought naked, for he was practically immortal, and his threshold for pain was nearly indomitable. His sorceries were as deadly as his claws, and as cruel as Satan himself. An infinity of necromantic spells were stored within his charred brain and scorched soul. The flesh-smoking demon palpably radiated death.

Morpheus Rex raised his Prismsword and Spectrumhammer, reflecting the infrared eye contact across the badlands like the veins and arteries of Grystiawa's sunsets. Morpheus Rex gazed upon the Necrodelic with bloody-rimmed eyes, thousands of colors flashing inside them every second, like prisms spinning beneath a solar flare.

"I've been dreaming of you," hissed Morpheus Rex, his voice the susurrus of a serpent, his three forked tongues flickering in and out of his mouth. "I've been dreaming of you every night. I've been dreaming of you making love to Mother Chaos. Dreaming of your extinctions of entire species, your genocides of entire races, your detonations of entire solar systems. I've been dreaming of your Bloodbong, your Omnibeast, your necromancies. Soon, I will be eating your dreams and drinking your blood. Soon, I will be haunted by your ghost in my bedchambers. When I sleep, I will dream your dreams, grow wet with your fantasies, and scream from your nightmares. After tonight, Necrodelic, you shall dream nevermore."

Chariah watched Morpheus Rex's three forked tongues slither back and forth. They darted in and out of his rainbow lips while he spoke in the sibilant language of serpentkind. Morpheus Rex rose up and swayed like a cobra while he talked of dreams and threatened death. Like a cobra he paused, and then, like a cobra, he struck, Prismsword curving through the air in a rainbow arch aimed for the Necrodelic's neck.

Sparks flew as Chariah deflected the blow, and then, with razor-sharp claws pressed against razor-sharp blade, Chariah leaned in close to Morpheus Rex's face, bared his fangs, and snarled, "You'll be dreaming in Hell tonight."

Their eye contact materialized again, redder and hotter than before. Morpheus Rex's eyes were welded to the Necrodelic's stare like cauterized flesh. His eyelids were immoveable, adhered like roasted skin to lenses and sockets alike. Sparks filled the air between the two demons, and then the fires of Hell came roaring through Chariah's soul, through his incandescent eyes which had been forged in those very fires, and the space between Morpheus Rex and him exploded.

Flames reached a thousand feet into the skies, thunder shook the ground and air, and the explosion of Hellfire threw the Dreaming Predator a mile into the distance. Chariah stood peacefully amidst the roaring fire and black smoke, calm and serene in his natural habitat, a pleasant rush of pyromania flowing through his body.

The same glowing eyes which had brought Hellfire to Grystiawa watched Morpheus Rex blow backwards through the red-hot air and into the distant wastelands. Seconds later, Morpheus Rex landed on his feet in a battle stance, holding the Prismsword at a diagonal angle and the Spectrumhammer over his head. Chariah did not hesitate, but charged at once from the wall of fire. One demonic leap landed him nearly atop the stunned Morpheus Rex, but he came down with the Rainbowspear firmly driven through his thigh. The Necrodelic had barely twisted enough, at the apex of his flight, to avoid being castrated in mid-air by the ensorcelled projectile.

Four sable claws slashed four lines of scarlet across Morpheus Rex's face as the Necrodelic dropped from the skies like a bird of prey. The wounds gushed immediately, leaving Morpheus Rex awash in his own blood. The Necrodelic pulled the Rainbowspear out of his thigh and hurled it over the horizon.

Morpheus Rex licked the blood matting in his prism-plaited beard with his three tongues. As he moved his mouth, Chariah peered through the hole that had been torn in the Dreaming Predator's cheek. Just before it was once again obscured by dripping ichor and hanging flaps of skin, the opening briefly revealed the inside of Morpheus Rex's mouth. Within, the Necrodelic glimpsed the glistening of just-summoned venom on the tips of his fangs, like dripping hypodermic needles connected to syringes of liquid cyanide.

Even though Chariah saw the poison drip from Morpheus Rex's fangs before he opened his mouth, he was barely able to avoid the supersonic cobra strike. Morpheus Rex's fangs closed upon air as Chariah sidestepped his attack. Droplets of venom spattered the sands like raindrops, where they would continue to sizzle for hours afterward.

Chariah backslashed his claws across Morpheus Rex's exposed throat. One claw severed his jugular vein, the other his carotid artery. The third clove his esophagus in half. The fourth ruptured his larynx. The blow would have decapitated a lesser demon. It would have decapitated ten lesser demons, standing in an executioner's row. Morpheus Rex, however, was a highly evolved and enlightened demon, and could not be destroyed so easily.

As Morpheus Rex staggered backwards, blood pouring down his chest from his ruined throat, and jetting outward in streams from his mutilated jugular vein and carotid artery, the Necrodelic leaped towards him, his right arm extended over his head to deliver another blow. Morpheus Rex raised the Prismsword, tilting it towards the sun so that it reflected a multitude of colored beams at the Necrodelic. The strings of color tangled with the demon's long talons, stopping them in mid-air. A second later, Morpheus Rex pulled Chariah towards him with a jerk of the blade. A swinging overhand blow with the Spectrumhammer met the Necrodelic halfway, smashing him in the chest, crushing his sternum, shattering his ribcage, and slamming him to the ground.

Chariah rose with black ribs protruding jaggedly from his side, their ebony edges tipped with crimson. The claws of his right hand were still caught in the rainbow webbing of the Prismsword. He countered by sinking his fangs into the side of Morpheus Rex's skull.

The Dreaming Predator tried to swing the Spectrumhammer again, but their close quarters prevented it. Morpheus Rex unleashed his serpentine powers of hypnosis instead, his prism eyes transforming into kaleidoscopic mandalas that paralyzed Chariah's eyeballs within their very sockets and momentarily halted his every thought process. Within that instant, Morpheus Rex struck, burying his fangs in the Necrodelic's neck, even as the Necrodelic's fangs remained lodged in his own skull.

Venom coursed into the Necrodelic's carotid artery. The poison burned, but the Necrodelic seemed immune to the pain. Its paralyzing chemicals seemed ineffective, as well. Enraged, Morpheus Rex drove his fangs even deeper into the side of Chariah's neck, into his throat, injecting yet more venom into his bloodstream. Chariah swung his right hand, claws still entangled with the Prismsword, in a sweeping arc through the air, forcefully unsheathing Morpheus Rex's fangs from his throat, breaking the rainbow strands of color around his talons, and flinging the Dreaming Predator far into the distance, to land with bonebreaking force amidst the now flickering-out fires of Chariah's pyromancy.

Chariah caught his breath and refocused upon his enemy, prepared to attack again, but Morpheus Rex was already halfway across the desert, and an instant later, had completely disappeared. He raked his demonsight across the planet, but could find no trace of the Dreaming Predator. Neither his sense of smell, his echolocation, nor his psychic powers could determine where Morpheus Rex had gone. He had obviously cast some sort of warding spell with his oneiromancy to prevent the Necrodelic from tracking him.

The Necrodelic's sculpted pectoral muscles heaved up and down as he struggled to breathe with broken ribs. A winged spider briefly attacked him. Chariah slashed his claws in a glittering black blur through the air, and the flying arachnid fell to the ground in four oozing, spasming pieces. Silently, Chariah turned and walked back to his ship. Directly behind him, the crimson sun Tyterviax was setting in a brilliant bloodbath to rival the one it had just witnessed, and Chariah's imposing silhouette stood black as night and deepest outer space before its sanguinary corona. Casting long obsidian shadows which were not quite as dark as his flesh, the Necrodelic strode away from the setting sun, his silhouette growing larger while the red sun behind it grew smaller.

He returned to the Omnibeast, whispered "Drakhus," and

rode the Overdragon's tongue back into his lair. Minutes later, the Omnibeast rose into the sky and soared away. The night, which was another of Chariah's natural habitats, had just begun, and so too had his battle with Morpheus Rex, the Oneirophage.

4

Leaving a sigmoid trail of blood in his wake, the Oneirophage dragged his wounded body through Phantasmagorika. Torn flaps of snakeskin dangled from his face and chest, and half-clotted scabs obscured his elaborate tattoos. Just navigating the mazes and slithering up the rampways of his palace was excruciating, the injuries he had suffered in combat against the Necrodelic alive with pain. Though Morpheus Rex had desired to continue his battle with the Death Addict, the were-mechanisms in his brain had been triggered by sunset, rendering him a zombie and hypnotically forcing him back to his lair with a primal force as irresistible as gravity.

He briefly visited his weapons gallery and hung the Prismsword and Spectrumhammer on their rack. The Rainbowspear had been summoned back to his open hand as he made his retreat and, like an obedient familiar, had launched itself from whatever unknown region of Grystiawa it had been flung to by the Necrodelic, flying like a heat-seeking missile to its waiting master. He placed it on the weapons rack with its two brothers, then headed for his bedchamber.

Once inside his nocturnal sanctum, he hissed a serpent mantra, and a pile of nine bodies tumbled from the Darkprism to the floor, writhing like a mating ball, legs and arms protruding at strange angles from the living heap. The chains and shackles along the southwest wall automatically shot out with the celerity of amphetamine-saturated cobras. They straightened in mid-air and quickly cuffed and fettered the captives, roughly disentangling the mass of bodies while simultaneously dragging it across the floor.

The Oneirophage bound his victims to the Amputator, then lurched to the wheel of the limbing machine. While dismembering his victims, he assessed his injuries. He was halfway decapitated, his head bobbing on slashed tendons and ligaments as though he were floating underwater. His face had four deep gashes, slanting diagonally from his left temple to his right mandible. One of his forked tongues was flickering through a hole in his cheek. The right side of his head had been partially chewed off. He had too many burns and broken bones to count, and he was losing blood at a violent velocity.

The Amputator finished its work, and the Oneirophage flung nine limbless demons onto his bed. Twirling the Umbilicus in his long-nailed right hand, he rearranged the sorcerous apparatus into a ten-tipped straw, nine to be inserted into his victims and one to be suckled like a teat by his torn mouth. The nine bottom tips of the straws were plunged simultaneously into the nine chests of the amputees, driven directly between their ribs and into their hearts. The Oneirophage immediately began to suck, imbibing the blood of all nine at once, swallowing greedily like a hedonist swallows wine, to replenish the copious amounts of plasma he had lost.

The heartbeats of the doomed ennead quickened with terror and pain, causing their collective vitality to pump more rapidly through the Umbilicus, aiding the Oneirophage's voracious consumption. Excruciatingly impaled through the hearts, their chests became empurpled with internal hemorrhaging. Strings of tiny air bubbles surged through the Umbilicus. Its tips puckered the perimeters of skin at their insertion points, raising large, circular, pinkish welts upon the breasts of those it skewered. As their lifeblood was being drained directly from their hearts, their veins and arteries excruciatingly dried out and shriveled up. Heartbeats began to slow, running out of blood to pump, atria and ventricles grinding painfully against one another like crepitating bones, the periods between systole and diastole growing exponentially longer with each pulsation. Heart attacks went off like bombs, one after another, a chain reaction, exploding the pain-swollen teats of the females and disintegrating the cracked ribcages of the males. The shrapnel of exploded breasts decorated the floor, walls, and ceiling with astrological charts of ensanguined milk, vermillion ichor, severed nipples, and gobbets of fatty tissue. The force of the concussive heart attacks dislodged the Umbilicus. The ninefold straw spurted gore from every tip. Spinning jets of blood spattered the walls and ceiling with spiral galaxies of red dwarfs, forming thick nebulae and supernovas when combined with the gory debris of the pyrotechnic-like exploding mastectomies from the moment before.

All the while, the Oneirophage began to heal, drinking blood like a vampire and gradually mixing in dreams as he grew stronger. A kaleidoscope of images were already flashing through his brain, and he relaxed as his oneiromantic drugs assuaged his suffering. He looked on with drugged fascination while his ninefold prey suffered their successive heart attacks. In his ensorcelled mind the hearts and breasts exploded in slow-motion. They looked and sounded like roses blossoming, and the spraying blood was as beautiful as summer rain.

The Oneirophage closed his spinning eyes and dreamed of hydras sprouting new heads every time they were decapitated. He dreamed of the hymens of a ravished succubus regrowing in her thirteen vaginas. He dreamed of lizard demons losing their tails in battle, and growing them back, then being castrated by their lovers, and growing their genitals back. He dreamed of phoenixes eating entire gardens full of drugs, overdosing to the point of neurological annihilation, then regenerating new brain cells and nervous systems with their powers of neurogenesis. He dreamed of the Plaguepossessor, come to eat his diseases and ease his suffering. He relived his every crucible in the living, interdimensional gauntlets of the Reincarnatron and the Reincarnatrix, the churning, grinding torture-mazes which were the apotheosis of the samsaric cycle, the sentient labyrinths of reincarnation that he had traversed a billion times. He dreamed of becoming the Jh'a'vyraa and freeing his soul from the endless circle of life, death, and rebirth. Then, finally, the Oneirophage slept.

*

The Oneirophage awoke at midnight, the deep wounds in his flesh still burning and dripping pus. Many had adhered to the sheets and blankets of his bed while he slumbered. The corpses of the night's nine victims were strewn all around him, the Umbilicus still stuck in their shriveled hearts like the nine-way blood catheter of a voluntary sacrifice, an autobloodletter, a hemagogue addict, or a hematophiliac onanist. Bloodless husks, pale and limbed, the dead bodies looked like gargantuan grubs with death's heads. Still weak, the Oneirophage withdrew the Umbilicus from their lifeless chests, rearranged it, and drank the cold dreams from their curdled brains. He drifted once more into slumber, still suckling upon the Umbilicus, its nine tips now driven through an eyeball, a nose, a mouth, an ear, a suture, a fontanel, a penis, a vagina, and a rectum.

The Oneirophage dreamed of orchards whose trees bore living heads on their branches. He dreamed of cannibals binging and purging on demonflesh, eating hundreds of bodies at a single feast, vomiting after each one was consumed and then eating another, and then lapping up the vomit when the feast was gone. At one point, the Oneirophage dreamt he was one of the gluttonous cannibals; at another, he dreamt it was his own flesh being torn away, chewed, swallowed, digested, regurgitated, and lapped back up. He dreamt in succession that he was devouring males, females, children, fetuses, and embryos, and then drinking sperm from their hollowed out skulls. He then dreamt this same dream in reverse order, first imbibing the sperm from severed heads, and then eating embryos, fetuses, children, females, and males.

An hour later, the Oneirophage woke once more. He had stopped bleeding, but was still scorched and ripped. He had not only lost a lot of blood, but a lot of flesh, as well. The Oneirophage spun the Umbilicus in his fingers until it became a singular straw again, this time with two wide ends like those of a vacuum. He attached one of the tips to a carcass beside him and the other to a long gash on his chest. The laceration wrapped itself around the Umbilicus like a pair of lips, and then the wound itself began to suckle, just like a mouth. The Umbilicus trembled and vibrated, vacuuming up the skin, flesh, muscle, and organs from the bones of the corpse and redepositing it upon and inside the Oneirophage. For an hour, the Dreaming Predator used this gruesome technique to repair his injuries, his every wound a suctorial organ. The surgical Umbilicus performed skin grafts and flesh transplants, reducing the mass grave of demon amputees to an ossuary, their bones sucked as clean as if they had been devoured by starving cannibals who hadn't eaten in centuries.

Exhausted, the Oneirophage closed his eyes and slept once more. He dreamed of eating Satan's penis, its barbs tearing holes in his cheeks and catching on his three forked tongues. Satan's blood and sperm were like lava in his mouth and throat, and his crimson flesh tasted like raw meat panaceas and flaming hot ambrosia. Satan watched the Oneirophage's sadomasochistic communion fantasy in Hell, spying upon the ophidian demon's dreams, laughing in his brimstone lungs and exhaling clouds of black smoke.

"Serpentling..." spake Satan, with a voice like a supernova, "Sweet slitherer, you are my slave...Soon, you will be mine in Hell, and I shall cut you apart and make a penis of your lower half, you who would devour mine..."

The Oneirophage lifted his face from Satan's crotch. Blood dribbled and dripped through his prism-plaited beard. Rearing back like a cobra, the Oneirophage gazed upon the half-eaten phallus of his Satanic master. Its left side had been chewed to the groin, and the entire tip was gone. Where crimson skin pulled back from scarlet pulp, blood and sperm dripped unevenly, like froth from the broken jaw of a rabid wolf. Satan laughed again as the Oneirophage pulled farther back into the shadows, the smell of brimstone and the echoes of madness following him long after Satan himself was out of sight. Finally retreating all the way back to his bedchambers, the Oneirophage fell into the healing sleep of a shaman. Satan's presence remained in the room with him for the rest of the night, hovering over his body and watching him dream like a voyeuristic eidolon.

*

The Oneirophage awoke just before dawn. Raising himself from his gore-stained blankets, he glanced around his bedchamber and gazed upon his skeletonized prey. Their skulls and bones were scored with straw-marks similar to the teeth marks left on skulls and bones by ravenous carnivores. Even their organs had been devoured. He would have to take his breakfast from the Flesh Reservoir, a small slaughterhouse within Phantasmagorika where he kept a supply of extra victims for emergencies.

Despite the closure of his wounds and the renewal of his vitality, many of his tattoos were tattered, old skin hanging from new flesh like cobwebs, or sometimes in entire sheets of disconnected epidermis. Following his visit to the Flesh Reservoir, he would have to visit the Alcoves of Exuviation and the Tattoo Laboratory.

Grabbing his Darkprism, the Oneirophage traveled through

a bloodstained labyrinth of carved prism. Every color of the spectrum flashed through the air, but many now had a reddish tinge to them, for the half-clotted blood left upon the floor the previous night was like a trail of gelid rubies, little jewels reaching with red shafts of light into the shimmering air.

The Oneirophage made his way to the Flesh Reservoir, a long, rectangular chamber on the top story where thick rows of meathooks hung on adamantium chains. Five of the meathooks held demons, each impaled through a different body part. The Oneirophage slithered into the abattoir. A bald ogre, dangling upside-down from a gaping wound in the middle of its back, became the Oneirophage's first victim. The Oneirophage's jaws unhinged like a boa constrictor's, his mouth opening to a grotesquely large size, completely enwombing the head of his prey. He swallowed the ogre whole, leaving only a rustling chain and a dripping meathook behind.

He glided to the next victim, an azure and black succubus hung by the vagina, and devoured her piece by piece, in seven massive bites. His stomach grew warm with the fresh meat and blood, alive with a pleasurable nausea as it rapidly digested whole carcasses in minutes, completely absorbing their every cell. Digestive fluids being the basis from which venom had evolved in serpents, their efficacy was often reflective of the toxicity of their owner's poisons, and those of the Oneirophage were akin to corrosive acid.

The dreams of his victims were coursing pleasantly through his head as he finished his breakfast, consuming another succubus, this one tiger-striped and suspended in mid-air by the gold rings in her twenty nipples. He swallowed a wailing infant impaled through the fontanel and, lastly, ripped the genitals from a purple incubus dangling by its cervix and devoured them, then drank the blood that came pouring forth. Now fully nourished, the Oneirophage left the rest of the still-living, freshly-castrated demon to be eaten at a later time.

The Oneirophage prepared to shed his skin. He exited the Flesh Reservoir and made his way down the hall to the Alcoves of Exuviation. He gathered a handful of diamond nails from a secret compartment next to the door, then slithered into an octagonal chamber adorned with seven upside-down crucifixes. Each cross had been carved from a single jewel and represented a different color of the spectrum. An eighth inverted crucifix, one of obsidian, hung upon the door. The room consisted of a large platform whose edges ended a couple of feet from the walls, with another room visible below. A catwalk extended from the door to the platform. The Oneirophage slid across this catwalk to the upside-down emerald cross in the alcove directly ahead of him. The crucifix had four emerald chains as well, one from every end, bolted to the floor, the ceiling, and the stained glass walls slanting from the back of the alcove. The stained glass was alive with artwork, depicting the violent and sexual acts of several species of demons. Taking the lengths of green chain in his hands, the Oneirophage lowered the emerald crucifix onto the octagonal platform and placed it horizontally upon the floor, then lay down upon it in a supine position.

He placed the diamond nails inside the Umbilicus, point-first, one after the other, then assumed a cruciform posture, shoulders, arms, hands, and fingers stretched out upon the crosspiece. The opposite end of the Umbilicus divided into three parts and snaked across his body, until two of its circular tips pushed firmly against his flattened palms and the third pressed into the bottom of his tail. The Oneirophage blew into the Umbilicus, and an instant later his left hand had been impaled by one of the diamond nails. He exhaled again and his right hand was likewise skewered, and then a third time, driving the final nail through the tip of his tail. The Oneirophage spoke a susurrating mantra through the Umbilicus, and the emerald crucifix lurched and raised back off the ground, to hang upside-down from the ceiling while the other three chains secured it to the floor and held it to the stained glass walls..

Crucified on an upside-down cross, streams of blood descending from his tail to his torso, the Oneirophage began to wriggle his serpentine body. The small ridges and facets of the crucifix caught against the grooves of his scales, and by catching his flesh against them he was able to shed the snakeskin of his lower half, writhing until it had completely detached. The demonskin of his upper half followed as he slithered in place on the cross. He slid down the entire length of the crucifix, his face, shoulders, and chest disappearing behind the ledge of the platform and penetrating the chamber below. With continuous thrusts his head drew closer to the floor. The shed skin hung above him in sheets, like the multicolored parchment of a necronomicon written on serpent vellum. His palms dragged themselves through the diamond nails, ripping free with rivulets of blood that formed helices around his outstretched arms. He slipped down several inches at a time. The force of the descent pulled the skin of from his face. The tip of his tail disappeared from the octagonal chamber, snaking down the final length of the cross. As though emerging from a womb or a caul, the Oneirophage left his skin behind him like hanging afterbirth, and gracefully slithered, upside-down, into the Gallery of Snakeskins below.

The Oneirophage removed the Umbilicus from his mouth, then pulled his shed skin from the upside-down cross. Its removal triggered a shift in the Alcoves of Exuviation, each crucifix moving to the left so that the topaz cross now occupied the wall he had descended from. Holding his warm, dripping peelings in both hands, the Oneirophage glanced around the mazelike basilica of the Gallery of Snakeskins, the convolution of hallways, vestibules, foyers, rotundas, and antechambers wherein all the snakeskins the Oneirophage had ever shed were displayed like paintings. Several eons' worth of decortication were exhibited in this labyrinth, a visual akashic record chronicling the dream-eater's entire existence. The Oneirophage hung his new, fresh, dripping piece of artwork upon one of the walls, then slithered from the Gallery of Snakeskins to the Tattoo Laboratory across the hall, to repaint the agrippa of grotesqueries, baberies, and arabesques that was his flesh.

The Tattoo Laboratory, like the Flesh Reservoir, housed a small number of living demons to be utilized when necessary. Four victims, chained to walls, floor, ceiling, tables, and each other, were hooked up to vast syringes by gargantuan hypodermic needles. These needles, in turn, were interlinked with other strawlike devices to form one continuous network throughout the chamber, designed to draw forth pigments, toxins, and inner liquids simultaneously. The lengthy and humongous needles were inserted at various points upon each victim's body, to siphon specifically colored bodily fluids. Needles were driven into hearts, jugular veins, carotid arteries, aortas, wounds, and menstruating vaginas for red blood. They vertically penetrated the urethras of penises for white sperm and the nipple-holes of breasts for white milk. Vertebrae were pierced for white spinal fluids; bones and skeletons for brown and yellow marrow; livers and stomachs for green bile. Heads were impaled through eyes, ears, nose, mouth, and various parts of the skull, tapping the brains inside for the rainbow colors of dreams. Hollow dragon dildos were inserted in vaginas to siphon amnion, afterbirth, and the drippings of venereal diseases through the artificial urethras in their scaly glans. The Tattoo Laboratory was a menagerie of torture.

The Oneirophage stood between two rows of syringes in the nexus of the chamber, ceremonial mask in hand. A diabolical, dark green sculpture configured to create artwork with the expulsions of the gore it absorbed, the mask consisted of a long drilling needle in the form of a lizard's tail, topped by a five-headed serpent in the form of a pentagram. The fanged mouths of the serpent formed the points of the upside-down star and jutted beyond their shared circle of coils. The snakeheads, in turn, surrounded the pentahedral head of a dragon, which wore them like a crown. The dragon's snout extended forward into a mouthpiece, with hooked teeth and a tubular, forked tongue between its adjustable jaws. Two large syringes of pale, transparent jade formed lungs on either side, pulsating like gills, air bladders, and air sacs. Tentacles protruded and dangled in all directions from its bottom, forming needle-tipped tendrils capable of being joined with all the various tubes in the room, interlinked with the Umbilicus, or used individually. When attached to the Oneirophage's face, the contraption was an exact replica of a symbiobaena, the chthonic, reptilian, face-eating parasite which had inspired its creation, and whose power the mask invoked when adorned by the initiated.

The Oneirophage wore the ceremonial mask like a breathing device. The five snakes which formed the points of the pentagram were equipped with barbed forked tongues that hooked into the skin of his face. Two embedded themselves in his scalp, two more bit down around each ear slit, and one clenched its maxillae and mandibles together in the soft flesh under his mouth, between chin and throat. From their five-sided nexus protruded the mouthpiece, the crocodilian dragon head that opened on jawlike hinges to engulf his nose and mouth like a respirator. Its forked tongue reached halfway down his throat in a manner like tantric ophidian fellatio, one bifurcation inserted in his esophagus, the other in his trachea.

Gazing through the two pyramid-shaped holes formed by the straight coils of the twin serpents biting his upper forehead and hairline, the Oneirophage breathed through the dragonhead, and the lung-syringes bubbled around him. He twirled the Umbilicus into a three-dimensional labyrinth with a hundred tips, then connected it to the needles at the tips of the mask's tentacles and the various tubes, straws, syringes, and victims throughout the Tattoo Laboratory. The gigantic hypodermic needle in the form of a long, slightly curled lizard tail began to vibrate and drip colors. Rhythmically breathing in and out through the device, the Oneirophage repainted his body, inhaling gore and exhaling tattoos.

The Tattoo Laboratory gurgled and churned as the organic warpaint was ritually extracted, and the screams of the tormented were thick in the air as the Oneirophage imbibed their plasma, glandular secretions, and bodily fluids. The myriad syringes bulged and roiled, and it was as though the Oneirophage meditated in the middle of an apothecary's pleasure chamber. All the vital fluids of life and death had been mixed in infinite combinations to create the right tinctures and shading. With dark voodoo instruments, lungs like Siamese twin creatrixes, and three dexterous forked tongues, the Oneirophage orally tattooed his body, inhaling mutilation and exhaling artwork. Black horned skulls were drawn upon each of his shoulders, embuing him with the power of a two-headed, hermaphroditic devil he had slain in a past life. Spiderwebbing stretched all the way down his left arm, with various, multicolored prey struggling in its deadly mesh. His left had resembled a spider, completely black except for the crimson hourglass upon his palm and the eight red eyes along his knuckles. His right arm bore a red incubus simultaneously fighting and fornicating with three green succubi, the demonesses wrapped around their lover's thighs, torso, and throat just like the tattoo itself wrapped around the Oneirophage's wrist, forearm, and bicep. His bottom penis was tattooed like a serpent, with diamondback patterns of emerald, ruby, and obsidian, and ended with the head of a green mamba whose forked tongue was etched in scarlet on the underside of the Oneirophage's glans, as though it were flicking in and out of his urethra. His upper penis was entirely covered by a dark red tattoo of Satan that frequently shifted like a sentient creature. Sometimes the underside of the Oneirophage's phallus bore the face; sometimes the top. No matter its position, the tattoo of Satan was eternally looking on with glowing eyes and glinting fangs, horns wrapped around the glans and wisps of smoke adorning the small urethral opening, muscular arms diagonally crossed, claws slanting above his shoulders, his barbed phallus leaking fire and lava below. The lower half of the Oneirophage's body was a mosaic of mandalas and camouflage, the scales of a thousand different species of serpents at once. Satan's lambent eyes, looking on from the penis above, had the visual effect of fire, making the patterns flicker and flash.

The tattoo that covered his entire chest, abdomen, and back was a psychedelic monstrosity, a single, continuous image of a great, gruesome, malformed, mutant, sadistic machine that did the work of an entire torture chamber at once, a mechanical nightmare christened Torturoth by the Oneirophage, who had dreamed of its incarnation every night since birth. For now just a vividly lifelike tattoo, Torturoth was a seamlessly conjoined labyrinth of suffering, an intricate, sentient, amalgamated torture device that performed its own punishments, inquisitions, bondages, sadomasochisms, rapings, and executions. Each part was connected to all the others like organs and flesh. Torture racks flowed into iron maidens, which streamed into garrotes, which cascaded into gallows. Masticators with dripping jaws gave birth to guillotines, which grew into torture wheels, which copulated with crucifixes. Flesh ovens bubbled like tumors, whips and chains stretched like scars, impaling devices erected like phalluses, scavenger's daughters constricted like vaginas. All were filled with writhing, screaming beasts and demons that he had conquered and slain over the millennia, their ichor running and dripping through the twisted mechanism and forming its own circulatory system. Every machine and victim shared each other's blood, and all was as one, a communal utopia composed entirely of torture chambers.

As the first rays of dawn filtered through Phantasmagorika's skylights, the Oneirophage completed the ritual and twisted the

Umbilicus back into a single straw. He shuddered as his reinvigorated tattoos conducted the power of Satan through his flesh, his blood, and his soul, electrifying him with the dark energies of evil and the red-hot enlightenments of Hell. The Oneirophage exited the Tattoo Laboratory and made his way to his bedchamber. Through the window he watched the tiny orb of Tyterviax rise like a single droplet of blood welling from a puncture wound on the tip of a phallus. Phantasmagorika had reappeared somewhere in the southern hemisphere of Grystiawa, and the time to hunt had come once again. The Oneirophage could feel Satan watching him as he made his diurnal metamorphosis. A moment later, it was Morpheus Rex who felt the hot stare of Satan, watching him while he, in turn, watched the vermillion sunrise, the crimson badlands beneath it, and all that the blood-red sun portended.

5

Bearing the red traceries of war upon his skin, the Necrodelic stepped into his meditation chamber. Black ribs jutted through the flesh in his side, dripping blood from their jagged tips like feasting nightworms that drooled ichor while they satiated their carnivorous appetites. The crepitus of his broken ribs was loud inside the still sanctum, and sounded as through someone was skinning a basilisk with a rusty saw. Chariah walked across the room to the opposite wall, and from his movements and invincible aura, it would have been impossible to detect that he had suffered even the slightest of injuries.

He grasped a bone lever on the wall near the Bloodbong and slowly pulled it down. Immediately, the interplanal portal beneath the giant pipe opened and unleashed the fires of Hell into the sinister sanctuary, illuminating the labyrinths of rune-carved tubes and chambers, and the rivers and oceans of blood inside them. Chariah took hold of a second bone lever and pulled again. This time, the portal in the ceiling above the Bloodbong's heart-chamber opened, and a large mass of demons tumbled into the scalding blood below. After a few moments, Chariah raised the lever back up, and the portal closed. A succubus who had only slid halfway through the irising gate when Chariah closed it was cut in half, her thrashing legs and dilated vagina plummeting to join the rest of the victims, her upper half left to die in the dungeon above.

The Necrodelic seated himself in the black lotus position and began to meditate. The Bloodbong's mouthpiece snaked its way to his lips, curving and rising through the air until it was between its master's fangs. Chariah inhaled for five minutes straight, using the deep concentration and pranayama breathing techniques he had acquired over centuries of practice, just like deathmonks and other various mystics did. The others, though, breathed air. The Necrodelic breathed flesh and blood. The Necrodelic breathed death.

Mesmerized, Chariah watched the bodies dissolve into a gory soup of organs. A virgin screamed as she died. The echo of her voice traveled through the pipe and into Chariah's mouth as he inhaled. As the Necrodelic breathed in, the ribs jutting from his side withdrew into his body like sentient creatures retreating into their burrows or dens. The flesh they had torn through began to visibly heal itself, and a moment later, it was as though he had never been scratched.

He inhaled again, gazing inside the Bloodbong as faces floated off of skulls, as heads floated from bodies, as brains floated out of mouths left hideously agape from a simultaneous combination of terrified screaming and instant rigor mortis. As he breathed in, one demon's limbs were ripped from his torso, leaving him writhing like a dying merman in the hot ichor. The severed legs of the bisected succubus were twisted apart at the vagina and floated to the roiling surface, where they lurked like excorticated crocodiles until all the flesh had been smoked from them and their bones drifted back down into the swirling morass. A loose hand floated past, and behind it a winged spider drifted forth and pressed against the glass. Chariah inhaled more forcefully, and the winged spider exploded into black splinters, leaving behind a million tiny bubbles, which the Necrodelic pondered one at a time while savoring the taste of smoked spiderflesh. Spiderwebs continued to float through the Bloodbong for hours, long after even the last bones had become sodden dust. They were all that remained of the dead arachnid. Of the slain demons, there were no remnants whatsoever.

Chariah's soul slowly fell away from his body as he entered

a deep state of necrodelia, floating downward, downward into a tomb, the tomb of the astral plane, where Mother Chaos greeted him.

"...the first steps on the stairway to salvation have been taken...you make me proud, my devotee..."

Chariah floated in a vibrating mirror of space, just above Mother Chaos. His erection pulsed and glowed. Mother Chaos whispered enlightenments beneath him.

"...Satan watches, even now...his fury breeds flies and black holes...wormholes to Hell and rocketing maggots in the corpse of space...we must be strong...take me now...we will fight Satan with sex..."

Mother Chaos' vagina constricted around Chariah's engorged member. Mother Chaos kissed him with spectral lips and then her vagina turned into a mouth, her mouth to a vagina. Chariah's tongue became a penis; his penis, a tongue. They writhed together for an eternal instant, and then the Dark Orgasm came to both of them, black hole supernovas nullifying their minds for an infinite moment, embracing them with nirvana and bringing the stench of vibrating death and twisted immortality.

The power of their Dark Orgasm inadvertently drew Satan forth. The malevolent father of the universe tantalized them with doom.

"Sweet meat, you are dying even now...To limbo with thee, to black judgment days in the inferno...Even now I feel the vibrations of your ghosts-to-be...You are no Jh'a'vyraa, neither one of you..."

Chariah and Mother Chaos fell deeper into the Dark Orgasm, driving Satan away with their black ecstasy. Satan drifted back to his fire-wombs and charred caverns in Hell. The touch of nirvana was as poison to him.

The Necrodelic could hear his mistress calling to him through the transposed mouth in her crotch. "...return now, beautiful one...to the planet of the dream-eater...go forth, my dark champion...and show the Oneirophage why you shall be the Messiah of Death..."

With that, the rapture of the Dark Orgasm faded, and the astral bodies of Chariah and Mother Chaos, with genitals and oral organs reversed, began to regrow around the reversed body parts, faces growing around transposed mouth and tongue, legs sprouting from transposed genitals. Chariah felt like he was being turned inside-out on a crucifix.

Chariah rose through the astral plane to the Omnibeast. As he prepared for battle, Mother Chaos massaged the vestiges of his astral body which had remained in her arms to comfort her, black wisps of soul like the mists of Erebus. Satan in Hell laughed at Mother Chaos' small solace.

The flames of Hell had died down to lambent embers in the interplanal portal. The blood in the Bloodbong moved sluggishly now, tepid, gelid, and clotted. Chariah reached up and pulled the mouthpiece from his charred lips with one hand, then rose from the black lotus position and exited the meditation chamber.

Chariah flowed like shadows through the living labyrinth of the Omnibeast's innards. He entered the nexus of the spaceship, attached himself to a dozen umbilical cords, and searched Grystiawa for the Oneirophage's lair. The Necrodelic found no trace of either the dream-eater or his ensorcelled palace, and it would be several hours later when he finally glimpsed Morpheus Rex. Upon a dawn-lit mountain range, with the rising sun swelling like a sore behind their pyramidal silhouettes and then bursting like a blister pricked upon their crimson peaks, spraying blood-red morning across the planet, he spied the Dreaming Predator.

The Omnibeast spun in mid-air so that the Overdragon faced north, pointed in the direction of Morpheus Rex's glittering figure. With a telepathic command through the umbilical cords attached to his skull, Chariah flew his spaceship towards Morpheus Rex, weaving between sharp peaks and narrow passes as he descended into the mountain range. As the Dreaming Predator looked up from his fallen prey, the Overdragon opened its jaws and unleashed a fireball.

Morpheus Rex gazed upon the looming Omnibeast with kaleidoscoping eyes. His left hand held up the slumping form of a paralyzed demon with the marks of a snakebite upon his throat, while his right hand held the Prismsword aloft. As the gargantuan spaceship sped towards him, Morpheus Rex could make out the form of the draconian figurehead breathing fire in his direction. Swinging the Prismsword in an arc, Morpheus Rex created a forcefield of flashing colors that deflected the fireball into a nearby mountain. Three more fireballs followed, each reflected and refracted away by the protective spectrum cast by the Prismsword. The final one ricocheted into the spaceship itself, scorching the flesh beneath the Overdragon's head. The Omnibeast soared past Morpheus Rex with the effect of a sonic boom, echoing throughout the valleys and mountain ranges and triggering several avalanches. The narrow pass upon which Morpheus Rex stood trembled as he held the five points of the Darkprism toward his paralyzed prey and absorbed the stiff body with a black spiral flash.

Thunderous reverberations vibrated through his serpent's glands as the bestial spaceship pivoted in mid-air, changed direction, and approached again. This time a mammoth mantis figurehead served as the Omnibeast's front, ramming the opposite side of the mountain with its genetically and sorcerously hardened head. The entire mountaintop instantaneously turned into rubble. Pebbles, rocks, and boulders sprayed through the air, then rolled or plummeted to the valleys below.

Morpheus Rex sensed the incoming blow with his serpent's glands and leapt from the mountainside mere moments before impact. Holding his Prismsword and Spectrumhammer in his outstretched arms, the Dreaming Predator hurtled through the thin air, an explosion of rocks, dust, and debris following right behind him. Avalanches erupted as the spaceship crashed through the mountaintop. Morpheus Rex looked back to see the mantis head breaking through concentric circles of destruction, surrounded by tiny asteroid belts and small meteor showers that had been a mountain just seconds before.

Morpheus Rex landed upon the ground fifty thousand feet below. He watched the skies as he began to wind his way through the caverns and valleys at the base of the mountain range. The Omnibeast made a few more passes over the mountains, casting fireballs as it flew and setting entire mountainsides aflame. After a few minutes, eight giant spider legs unfolded from its underbelly and it landed on one of the mountaintops. Morpheus Rex wondered to himself why the Necrodelic didn't just destroy the entire mountain range in an attempt to murder him, then realized with a chill that it was because the Death Addict wanted to smoke him alive.

Hissing, the Dreaming Predator began to stalk the Omnibeast, creeping upwards toward his mammoth prey, winding his way along a spiraling mountain path into the skies. He climbed sheer cliff faces like a lizard, skulked through caverns, and prowled silently across catwalks, his serpent glands probing the air for movement, heat, and premonitions. Halfway between the jagged ground and the Omnibeast's perch, Morpheus Rex hid in the shadows of a small cavern and unslung the Rainbowspear from his back. Hefting it in his right hand, he used all of his ophidian senses to aim the projectile, then launched it in a spectral arc toward the seemingly torpid spaceship. At the exact same instant, a black tentacle burst from the bowels of the cave behind him and wrapped itself around his chest. The smell of the dark tendril, its temperature, and its vibrations were unmistakable. The tentacle belonged to the Necrodelic's bestial spaceship. It had descended from the vessel and slithered through the mountain range to capture him. As the Rainbowspear struck the ship's underbelly with a wet thud, the tentacle quivered sympathetically. Morpheus Rex used its momentary undulation to loosen its grip upon him, then hacked at it with his Prismsword. Bits of black flesh fell writhing to the ground, sometimes wriggling off the side of the mountain like suicidal nightworms. Morpheus Rex spun himself around in the tentacle's grip, then severed its tip by pinning the length of the tendril to the wall of the cavern with the Spectrumhammer and chopping through it with the Prismsword. The mutilated tentacle screamed through the red mouth of its wound and retreated back into the caverns, up through the mountain to the spaceship, leaving a trail of blood behind.

Morpheus Rex unwound the amputated tentacle from his waist and threw it from the mountainside. Little black pieces of flesh were still milling around his ankles, and beginning to attach themselves to his skin like burnt leeches. One by one, he flicked them over the edge of the mountain with the tip of the Prismsword. The Rainbowspear was still buried in the sentient hull of the intergalactic behemoth above, its path a perfect rainbow from the center of Morpheus Rex's palm. Gripping the spectral tip, Morpheus Rex pulled upon the Rainbowspear to bring it back to his hand, as he had so many times before. This time, however, the Rainbowspear bore a passenger.

The Necrodelic perched like a raven upon the thin shaft of the Rainbowspear, balanced like a feline deathmonk. No muscle moved upon his body as he rode the projectile down its arching path, his hands raised in a fighting stance, his fingers spread-eagled, his dark claws whistling as they dismembered the air, his biceps tensed as he prepared to deliver a deathblow. Just before the Rainbowspear returned to the hand of its master, Chariah pounced, soaring through the air like the shadow of a horde of bats, tenebrous, silent, fluid, and ominous.

As he flew past, he grabbed Morpheus Rex by the hair with one hand and impaled him with the other. Morpheus Rex felt as though a portcullis had been dropped onto his chest. The momentum of Chariah's flight carried them both backwards. As they toppled, the Necrodelic drove a hard knee into Morpheus Rex's diaphragm, then rode him to the rocky floor of the cavern. Chariah landed atop Morpheus Rex, driving the air from his lungs with an explosion of blood from mouth and nose alike. The pressure of the Necrodelic's knee prevented any oxygen from returning. His four talons were still driven like spikes through the Dreaming Predator's chest, and were now anchored several inches deep in the mountain stone below.

Morpheus Rex gurgled, vomiting blood. Chariah drove his knee deeper into his guts, as far as he could, choking off and paralyzing his ruptured diaphragm. More ichor sputtered from Morpheus Rex's rainbow lips as he began to choke. Three of the four claws had impaled him through vital organs. Two had crucified him by the lungs, and the other had spitted him through the heart.

Chariah crouched over his fallen prey and snarled. Kneeling upon his victim, the Necrodelic twisted his claws, grinding the pain and the death into Morpheus Rex. His hand flexed back and forth, excruciatingly corkscrewing through Morpheus Rex's vitals, drilling through his lungs and heart, further enlarging the already gaping wounds.

Morpheus Rex knew he would die moments after the Necrodelic withdrew his claws. He had to muster an attack before that. With prismatic eyes spinning hypnotically, spiral mandalas beckoned Chariah inward, downward. Like a cobra with its prey, Morpheus Rex paralyzed the gaze of the Necrodelic and through that fixed stare paralyzed his body. The

Necrodelic stiffened as though with rigor mortis, ceasing to twist his claws, blink his eyes, or even think. Morpheus Rex brought forth a toxin to his fangs that would leave the Necrodelic paralyzed even longer, then sunk his venom-drenched incisors into the flesh-smoker's jugular vein and carotid artery. A moderate amount of blood was injected, too, both from the blood he had been regurgitating and the blood which had seeped into his venom due to his internal injuries. Morpheus Rex struck twice more, until the Necrodelic was motionless, no more than a heavy statue pinning Morpheus Rex to the ground, his claws turned to stone in Morpheus Rex's chest.

The Dreaming Predator embedded his fangs in the Necrodelic's throat one final time, pumping him full of a nerve toxin that would leave him in excruciating pain once the paralysis wore off. Morpheus Rex called forth the Umbilicus. Using it as a basic, singular straw, Morpheus Rex plunged the Umbilicus into the Necrodelic's forehead and through his skull, deep into his blackened brain. Coughing up blood, Morpheus Rex imbibed the burnt dreams of the Necrodelic, suckling upon the taste of scorched memories, necromancer's meditations, ashubha, and thanatopsis.

The violation of his mind, however, brought the Necrodelic back to life. He ripped his head free of the umbilical cord-like straw, leaving a jagged crimson gash over his eye. Snarling, the Necrodelic began to chew Morpheus Rex's face off. Then the pain toxins kicked in.

Writhing in agony, the Necrodelic withdrew his fangs from Morpheus Rex's orbital bones. While the Necrodelic was incapacitated by the extreme torment, Morpheus Rex was able to shove and peel and leverage him from his decimated body, casting him into a corner to twist in his own suffering. Morpheus Rex himself collapsed against a wall of stone, four sucking wounds in his chest opening and drooling blood with every heaving breath. Staggering onto his hands and knees, Morpheus Rex again grasped the Umbilicus and plunged it into the wound in the Necrodelic's skull. The Dreaming Predator drank more dreams from the Necrodelic, ingesting the raw, brutal suffering of his own nerve toxins as they coursed through the flesh-smoker's system, as well. Immune to his own poisons, he enjoyed feeling their effects upon his prey with a strange empathic masochism, sympathetically experiencing the torture without the suffering, just like Satan himself, the all-seeing voyeur, the omnipotent sadist, reveling in the torment of the universe he had created.

As he imbibed the burnt dreams of the Necrodelic, his wounds began to close and heal, until finally he had the strength to fight once more. The Necrodelic still lay upon the ground, spasming as if in the throes of death. Morpheus Rex raised his Prismsword to finish his wounded prey. He struck a decapitating blow that should have separated the demon's head from his body. Instead, he found the Prismsword between the fangs of the Necrodelic, who had summoned enough strength to lash out like a rabid werewolf and catch the blade in his teeth. Morpheus Rex struggled to free the Prismsword from the Necrodelic's mouth. The edges of its blade carved holes in his mouth and throat, and its multicolored laser beams opened surgical cuts all over his face and chest as he thrashed. Still, the Necrodelic would not release his animal grip on the weapon.

With his left hand free, Morpheus Rex gathered up his Spectrumhammer and started bashing the Necrodelic's head and ribs. The sound of bones cracking split the air asunder, yet somehow, the attack seemed to be empowering the Necrodelic. The pain toxins rendered the blows of the Spectrumhammer ineffective; the Necrodelic could not even feel them through the intensity of the agony he already suffered. His crimson eyes glowed and fixed upon the kaleidoscope eyes of the Dreaming Predator. The Necrodelic wielded eye contact like a weapon. Like blood-red gravity wells, they held the eyes of Morpheus Rex fast in their sockets, then seared them with a blinding heat that intensified until Morpheus Rex felt his eyeballs burst into flames and begin melting down his face, leaving red scars like the paths of boiling teardrops on his cheeks.

Blinded, rainbow-colored smoke curling from his eye sockets, Morpheus Rex was easy prey for the slashing blows of the Necrodelic. Two successive strikes flayed his chest open again. He narrowly avoided a third strike to the throat before using his serpent's glands to dodge the blow and guide him, fleeing, from the cave.

Morpheus Rex exited the cavern, but instead of leaping to

the valleys below or seeking distant shelter, he immediately climbed onto a small ridge over its entrance. Here he doused the fires that ravaged his eyes with his three forked tongues and a splash of venom. When his serpent's glands detected the vibrations of the Necrodelic approaching, he crouched above the entrance to the cave and waited with cold reptilian patience. His vision was damaged, so he relied on his other senses to locate the Necrodelic, then vomited all the venom in his body with one violent paroxysm, to pour down upon the Necrodelic in a cataract of poison and pain.

The Necrodelic felt the presence of his attacker too late, turning just in time to feel the tsunami of toxins strike his face and douse his entire body in acid. His black skin melted and peeled away, revealing black muscle, black tissues, black organs, and black bones. The neurotoxins seeped into his bloodstream and nervous system, spreading paralysis and agony. A chain reaction of venom went off inside his body, bringing terror, blindness, fever, seizures, hallucinations, and nightmares. Organs failed, vital fluids changed their composition, his entire body chemistry was disrupted and destroyed, leading to an infinite barrage of torture. Morpheus Rex possessed hundreds of types of venom in his serpentine glands, and he had vomited every last drop of every single one of them in an ultimate assault upon the Necrodelic.

Chariah stood fast as poison drenched his body in a bath of death, delivering a counterattack within the brief moment that he was still capable. Channeling his powers of pyromancy Chariah again called forth the Hellfire, which would render the day's combat a deadlock. An instant later, Morpheus Rex spontaneously burst into flames, and, having used up nearly all of his bodily fluids in his venomous attack, burned like dry kindling, a living immolation, fires raging through his flesh as though he had been resurrected upon his own funeral pyre.

The Omnibeast released several of its tentacles to retrieve the Necrodelic, bearing him back to the ship blinded, excruciated, paranoid, fevered, convulsing, lost, hallucinating, and nearly comatose, his flesh half-eaten away from the libation of venom. His adversary, Morpheus Rex, had to travel for miles across the desert like a fleeing, heretical suttee, his entire body aflame, to the nearest oasis, where he doused his burning flesh.

As Tyterviax began to set, Morpheus Rex dragged himself back to Phantasmagorika, burnt beyond recognition, raw red wounds dripping hot pus, pieces of his flesh dripping off and left sizzling and smoldering upon the ground in his charry wake, coughing ashes from his blackened lungs, his eyelids, nostrils, earslits, and urethras cauterized shut, and smoke rising from every single inch of his scorched body into the twilit, crimson skies.

6

The tentacles of the Omnibeast carried their unconscious master into his meditation chamber, then gently set him down and guided him into the black lotus position. While one of the tendrils removed the umbilical cord which had been serving as a lifeline and respirator from his mouth and replaced it with the mouthpiece of his Bloodbong, two other tentacles simultaneously pulled down the levers of bone that released flesh from above and Hell from below, activating the Satanic pipe. As the bodies started to fall and the flames began to rise, the myriad tentacles withdrew in a caliginous mass through the irising doorway, looking for a moment like the blossom of the black lotuses their master emulated, then shrinking away into the inner darknesses of the Omnibeast.

The Necrodelic's eyes were shut as though he were sleeping, a weakness he had forsaken long ago. Black sweat drenched his body. His flesh looked as if it had been immersed in lava, then washed clean with ethanol and dried by coriolis storms. Snakebites covered his shuddering body, and his mouth continually bled from having clenched the razor-sharp Prismsword in his fangs. His head had been split to the brains in a wound above his left eye. Chariah looked and felt half-devoured, his flesh eaten by corrosive acid, his dreams imbibed through the hole in his skull. With venom coursing through his arteries and veins, agony in every nerve, and countless afflictions resulting from the myriad poisons of Morpheus Rex, the Necrodelic smoked death to bring himself back to life.

The Necrodelic breathed in, and his crimson eyes opened, burning like the bubbling volcanoes in Hell. He breathed in a second time, without exhaling, and every snakebite closed like a sphincter muscle. Chariah inhaled again, and the cuts in his mouth healed themselves while the red tunnel in his forehead grew smaller and smaller until it disappeared. For a full hour, the Necrodelic drew one continuous breath, smoking the flesh off of hundreds of skeletons, gesturing towards the bone lever and telepathically pulling it whenever he had finished one hecatomb and was ready for another. Over the course of the hour, his acid-eaten flesh repaired itself, growing, healing without scars, restoring the Necrodelic's demonic body to the perfect incarnation of evil which it had been.

Only after inhaling for an eternity, after all his physical wounds were healed and his strength restored, did the Necrodelic finally breathe out, and when he exhaled, he expelled all the snake venom from his body in one acrid cloud of green smoke. Chariah watched the venomous mist dissipate amongst the roiling black smoke of the chamber as he exhaled for another hour, releasing all the toxins from his body and using his powers of necromancy to build anti-toxins within his glands and bloodstreams to render the Dreaming Predator's venoms less effective in the future.

After completing his hour-long exhalation, the revitalized Necrodelic resumed his normal breathing patterns. All the flesh he had smoked had left him in a deep, tranquil trance, reflecting upon the battle that was and pondering the battles yet to come. His eyes closed peacefully, this time of their own accord, and Chariah drifted downward into the astral plane, where Mother Chaos embraced him and kissed him, speaking even as she kissed him, even as her pink tongue sought out the smoothness of his fangs and its own black counterpart.

"...you grow stronger every day, my demon lover...your soul darkens as your mind deepens...like death itself you are, my pet...my champion of the apocalypse..."

Mother Chaos caressed Chariah's long hair with her purple fingernails and pink fingertips as she slid her vagina over his engorged penis. The flaring opening on the tip of Chariah's phallus glowed with a crimson light. Mother Chaos healed the damage to Chariah's soul with her sex, absorbing the wounds of sorcery and the karmas of war, bestowing hitherto unknown powers and enlightenments upon his darkling spirit as they made love.

Chariah could feel himself melting into Mother Chaos with every movement, further and further with every thrust, twisting until he had turned around and lay within her astral body as though he were floating on his back in a pool of water. He kissed her mouth from the inside out, his penis protruding now from her vagina as he made love to her from within.

"...frustration I sense in you, my love...frustration in your war with Morpheus Rex, the Oneirophage..."

Mother Chaos' voice came from all around him, from every ripple and wave in the pool of her essence, where he floated like a fetus in a womb, a womb which was the size of the entire mother, which stretched, in fact, through the mother's entire body, a labyrinth womb, a pleasure womb...

"...a womb for a demon prince... " Mother Chaos whispered, "...my demon prince..."

Chariah drifted inside Mother Chaos as though she were a cosmos unto herself. Galaxies floated by outside her translucent body as Chariah watched through the windows of her flesh. Infinities later, the two soulmates slowly flowed in and out of each other until their spirits had separated. Just before Chariah ascended to the physical plane, Mother Chaos cradled him to her pink breast, and bade him drink a droplet of amethyst elixir from her purple nipple, within which, she whispered, were the battle plans he craved. Chariah swallowed the tiny bead of liquid amethyst, which tasted at once like perfume made from milk and wine made from roses, and then the Necrodelic found himself rising through the astral plane, with the purple droplet inside him the way he had been inside the soul of Mother Chaos, and the hypnotic instructions of Mother Chaos inside the purple droplet the same way, a womb within a womb within a womb.

*

Morpheus Rex awaited the Necrodelic upon a revolving crucifix thousands of feet tall, his tattooed arms draped over the giant cross as it spun above the abandoned temples of the snake lord, Serpentikal. He had completed his hunt in the morning and had been waiting ever since. After another rigorous night of dreams, surgeries, and parasitism within the scintillant Phantasmagorika, he was once again completely healed, and he knew instinctively that the Necrodelic was, as well. He had left his weapons on an altar of sacrifice below, amongst the looming ophidian stone effigies of extinct religions. The only sentient creature in the entire badlands, and the only sentient creature to visit the vast, sprawling temples of Serpentikal in centuries, Morpheus Rex spent the day in contemplation, riding the pillar-like crucifix like a masochistic stylite. His tattoos gleamed in the sunlight as the enormous crucifix turned him like a piece of meat on a spit. He used his own flesh as bait, displaying his brightly colored body in the barren, maroon expanses of surreal rock formations, an act designed to attract his nemesis.

His three forked tongues flickered in turns from his tilting head as it lolled back and forth, rising and falling with his tattooed chest as he breathed the labored breath of the crucified. The ancient cross revolved from an axis within the temple, allowing Morpheus Rex to spy upon the entire badlands for hundreds of miles around. With the black patience of the demonic and the cold patience of the reptilian, the Dreaming Predator waited for his prey.

The Necrodelic found Morpheus Rex, just as the Dreaming Predator had intended, but not until the late afternoon. The Omnibeast rose from the distant red horizon like the black antithesis of the sun Tyterviax, growing larger and larger as it flew closer and closer, until Morpheus Rex could see the outlines of the Hydratowers arising from its carapace. The crucifix turned, and when it had borne Morpheus Rex around again, the two flanking figureheads of the insectoid War Mantis and the mammalian Scythetooth could be seen jutting from its sides. Another revolution of the cross, and Morpheus Rex could detect the ubiquitous waving tentacles of its underbelly. The spinning crucifix revolved again, and when it finished its next rotation, the Omnibeast was upon him.

The mammoth vessel stopped just short of its target, hovering over the decrepit temples, its heavy shadows quickening the decomposition of the ruins, felling walls and statues and breaking chunks of stone into rubble. The shadow of the Omnibeast also fell upon Morpheus Rex as the crucifix once more spun in place. It was as though a heavy blanket composed of antimatter had been draped over him, contouring around him, its gravity palpable and magnetic. The Omnibeast lowered itself from the skies. More pillars and serpent statues toppled and burst into dust as the bestial spaceship drew closer. When next the crucified form of Morpheus Rex faced the Omnibeast, the living figurehead of the Darkworm was mere inches from his face, its black segments glistening around its rings of fangs, its mouth wide open. Morpheus Rex gazed into its seemingly bottomless scarlet gullet, at the end of which he caught glimpses of the spaceship's inner corridors and chambers. Morpheus Rex revolved again while the Darkworm hovered and hissed in mid-air. The crucifix turned, and Morpheus Rex spun back to the Darkworm's abyssal maw, this time finding himself face to face with the Necrodelic, who had emerged from the vermian figurehead's throat and stood now upon the tip of its black tongue, its fangs surrounding him like a cylindrical iron maiden.

Morpheus Rex lashed out with his clawed feet even as the Necrodelic leapt from the mouth of the Darkworm. His muscular legs wrapped around the Necrodelic's torso, catching him in mid-flight and squeezing him in mid-air as the giant cross revolved. Morpheus Rex flexed his thighs, breaking the Necrodelic's ribs and forcing the air from his lungs with a spray of blood. Chariah struggled and twisted in Morpheus Rex's viselike grip, then unleashed his excruciating eye contact. Morpheus Rex's eyes began to bleed, as if daggers were being repeatedly driven through his sockets and into his cerebrum. Chariah pried the Dreaming Predator's arms from around the crosspiece, maneuvered them to the front of the crucifix, and buried the claws of his index fingers in Morpheus Rex's palms, drilling them into the iron bar and crucifying Morpheus Rex with his talons. The looming crucifix spun onward, with Morpheus Rex's hands impaled by the Necrodelic's claws and the Necrodelic caught in the constricting grip of Morpheus Rex's legs. Chariah could see his opponent readying a cobra strike, which he countered by pressing his forehead against his, their close quarters preventing the assault. As the crucifix turned the Necrodelic unleashed a barrage of rapid-fire headbutts, smashing the back of Morpheus Rex's head against the cross and fracturing the Dreaming Predator's skull.

Chariah's forehead split open, splattering the temple roofs with crimson. The blood lubricated the flesh between the Necrodelic and the Dreaming Predator, allowing Chariah to slither free from Morpheus Rex's serpent-thighed grasp. Dangling limply, Morpheus Rex could only watch as the

Necrodelic wriggled his way out of his crushing embrace.

With one graceful motion, Chariah pulled his claws from Morpheus Rex's palms, leaving torn and gaping stigmata rhythmically spurting arches of blood into the sky. The Necrodelic leapt onto the crossbar and grabbed Morpheus Rex by the hair. With one hand he dragged Morpheus Rex into the air and dangled him for a few seconds, then hurled him from the spinning crucifix to crash through the roof of a distant temple, not only thousands of feet below, but thousands of feet away, as well.

Chariah raised his arms over his head, reaching towards the sky with both hands, then brought them down abruptly in a pyromancer's gesture. A bolt of black lightning struck the base of the revolving crucifix as he dropped his arms. A moment later the giant cross stopped spinning and toppled into the temple ruins.

Chariah rode the plummeting crucifix as gracefully as a dragonrider, guiding it across the city-wide labyrinth of temples toward the fallen, broken body of Morpheus Rex below. The full weight of the cross crashed into Morpheus Rex, splintering one leg, shattering a hip, dislodging vertebrae, and causing the rapidly spreading pool of blood on the floor around him to spread even faster. Debris rained down from everywhere. Dust clouds rose into the skies as every single one of the colossal snake statues in the entire temple complex, every statue except for the bust of Serpentikal himself, crashed to the ground. Pinned beneath the crucifix, Morpheus Rex tried unsuccessfully to crawl out from under it. Chariah loomed over him, crouching upon the ancient, bloodstained altar of sacrifice where he had silently landed. He caught Morpheus Rex with his crimson eye contact and growled, then looked to the west through a gap in the ruined temple. Tyterviax was sluggishly dropping, like an embolus sinking from Satan's brain and through his jugular vein, lodging itself in the horizon like a blood clot embedded itself in Satan's heart. The Necrodelic gazed meaningfully upon it, then back to the prone body of the Dreaming Predator.

With a gleaming snarl that contained the hint of a smile, Chariah raised his claws and began slashing himself apart, raking his own claws diagonally across his chest with savage glee, opening gaping wounds in his abdomen and torso. He growled in pain as he lay himself upon the altar of sacrifice and repeatedly dragged his claws over his own body, drenching the table with crimson rivulets that runneled like the blood of baptisms and sacrifices from the temple's past, completely incapacitating himself. Like Morpheus Rex just an hour before, the Necrodelic had become his own trap, his own bleeding flesh the bait. Lying in a dripping pile of self-mutilation, in a semi-conscious torpor upon the altar, the Necrodelic waited for Morpheus Rex to rise.

Morpheus Rex dragged his battered body from beneath the crucifix. He had watched the Necrodelic rip himself to shreds, wondering if the Death Addict had been driven mad by his flesh-smoking rituals, or perhaps by the serpent venom which had saturated his body the day before. Regardless, the Dreaming Predator did not question the methods by which he attained his prey, and raised the Darkprism in his hand to absorb the limp form of the Necrodelic just like any other victim. A flash of sable later, the Necrodelic was trapped inside the pendant. The Omnibeast watched all this stoically from above, but made no move to attack or defend its master. Perhaps, thought Morpheus Rex, it had no will of its own once its possessor had been defeated.

Morpheus Rex limped through the razed temples, stepping over debris and regathering his weapons. A premonition flashed through his brain and he walked back to the fallen cross. He pressed the Darkprism directly against it, for while the black hole pendant could absorb organic matter from afar, it could only vacuum up inanimate objects through direct physical contact. After capturing the crucifix, he turned and walked toward the setting sun. He did not notice the pair of large beady eyes inside the stone sockets of the bust of Serpentikal. The eyes were watching him intensely, and shifted to follow him as he exited the temple ruins and made his way across the badlands.

The Darkprism swung gently against Morpheus Rex's chest as he returned home, with the Necrodelic trapped inside, and inside the Necrodelic, the purple droplet containing the coded, hypnotic instructions of Mother Chaos, instructions which had just been carried out to perfection, a trap within a trap within a trap.

7

The Oneirophage slithered through Phantasmagorika on broken bones. His pulverized femur had translated into a half-shattered tail when he made the metamorphosis from the bipedal Morpheus Rex to the serpentine Oneirophage. His skeleton crackled as he dragged himself across the floor, sounding like a hundred small explosions with every movement. With several dislodged vertebrae, his spine felt and sounded like a saw, carving through the flesh of his back and torso with its serrated edge. Serpentine crepitus breaking the night air like glass, the Oneirophage made his way through the prism palace and into his bedchamber.

He closed the door behind him, then pulled the Darkprism from its obsidian chain around his neck. The dreams of his prey would heal his wounds and mend his broken bones. As always, the Oneirophage's memories of the day were hazy and surreal, just as Morpheus Rex's recollections of his were-serpent alter ego's nocturnal activities were often vague and incomplete. The concussion he had suffered made his memory even more murky than usual, an indecipherable kaleidoscopic whirlpool churning at the bottom of his brain.

The Oneirophage held the Darkprism over his head and hissed an incantation, commanding the pendant to release its prisoners. Sable beams of light reflected and refracted from the prism walls, floor, and ceiling for an instant. What followed was a virtual shower of mutilation. Instead of whole bodies, the Darkprism rained amputated limbs, extracted organs, and coils of entrails. Severed heads thudded upon the floor and rolled off in all directions. Hearts, stomachs, bladders, kidneys, livers, lungs, and brains landed with wet splattering noises, or were flung into the walls, which they adhered to with sucking sounds. Intestines fell in loosely tesserated piles. Dismembered, decapitated, vivisected torsos crashed down from all around. Gruesome barrages of castrated genitals spewed through the air. And then it began raining blood. The Darkprism sprayed a series of ruby droplets around the chamber like an intricate fountain, in mandalic patterns at rhythmic intervals, first in tiny sprinklings, then spouts and arches, then geysers and jetstreams, then finally bursting like a stormcloud, drenching the entire bedchamber in crimson.

The blood-soaked Oneirophage cast the Darkprism furiously across the ensanguined room, where it continued to spurt and vomit copious amounts of ichor and gore. His three forked tongues hissed angrily while his prismatic eyes gazed upon the carnage in mesmerized shock. After a few minutes the blood flowing from the Darkprism began to slow. The Darkprism lay half-submerged in the pool of blood, hemorrhaging like an artescerated heart.

The Oneirophage's bedchamber was completely covered in gore. Every last inch of the room had been painted crimson. Blood dripped from the ceiling and ran down the walls to join the flood of blood on the floor. His bed was soaked through like a thousand bandages. The Amputator had been painted red. Heads, limbs, and torsos littered the chamber. Mounds of viscera rose like landfills. All manner of internal organs were stuck to the walls and ceilings. Some of them were still pulsating.

The Darkprism had stopped bleeding and now lay in the corner like just another severed head, just another ripped-out organ, just another pile of severed genitalia. Slowly it began to glow black from beneath its coat of blood, creating a dark shade of crimson never before witnessed in the universe. The Darkprism pulsed, the Darkprism spasmed, and with a flash of scarlet-tinged sable, the Necrodelic emerged from its tenebrous depths. The Oneirophage's sentient chains reacted instinctively, lashing out at blinding speed from the wall to bind and shackle the Darkprism's prey. The Necrodelic was faster, raising his claws over his shoulders and slicing the chains into small pieces behind him without looking back. Chariah loomed over the Darkprism, which now lay beneath him like a discarded womb. The Death Addict appeared just as he had earlier in the day, his body ripped open with hundreds of lacerations that glowed like infrared light against his midnight-colored skin. Deep diagonal gashes had flayed his chest open from shoulder to hip. He had come dangerously close to eviscerating himself, small pieces of bleeding entrails peeking out from his open abdomen. Cuts spiraled up and down his arms and legs. The array of wounds covering his body looked at times like mandalic artwork, at times like the external circulatory system of Satan. His hair was soaked with blood, his claws maroon with coagulated scabs.

Blood dripped into his eyes and down his face from a wound in his head. He had slit his own throat and ripped chunks of flesh from his own back. He had mutilated himself for his own sinister purposes, and stood now before his arch-enemy, snarling, living death in black and red.

Memory assaulted the Oneirophage like another concussion. The diurnal battle of Morpheus Rex and the Necrodelic played itself over and over in his mind like a phantasmagoric reverie. The flesh-smoker had wounded himself so that Morpheus Rex would think him defeated and dying. He had been sucked into the Darkprism, and while inside its black hole realms had murdered and mutilated all of Morpheus Rex's prey. The Necrodelic had stolen his victims like a scavenger, ruining his feast of dreams, and for that, thought the Oneirophage, he would unleash Hell and a billion nightmares upon him.

Crimson eye contact met kaleidoscope eye contact from across the room, holding both of them as fast as if two double-pointed spears had been driven through their eyeballs, binding them together. The Oneirophage hissed vengeance and the Necrodelic growled victory.

"You'll not escape me at sunset any longer. At last, I have found your lair, and it is in your own lair that I shall slay thee. Now, we fight to the death, and I'll not leave this planet until you are boiling in my Bloodbong, or sucking the dreams from my corpse with your Umbilicus."

The Necrodelic loomed, the only darkness in the crimson bedchamber. Blood was another of his natural habitats. Blood was his environment, his territory, his den. Blood was his terrain, to be used to his advantage. Blood was his home.

Chariah flew across the chamber in one mighty leap, spinning once in mid-air and backslashing the Oneirophage as he landed. The edges of his claws opened four cuts on the Oneirophage's face, staggering him as Chariah splashed down. The Necrodelic slid on the wet floor, gliding towards the Oneirophage to deliver a second strike. Chariah pulled his right arm back, and then his claws flashed through the air, hurtling forward to impale the Oneirophage against the wall. The dream-serpent dodged the blow with one sinuous, sigmoid motion, slithering vertically, curving his chest and torso to one side. The Necrodelic's talons drove into the wall behind him, cutting through the prism as if it were flesh. As he struggled for a moment to pull them out, the Oneirophage rammed the Necrodelic's skull with a cobra strike, sinking his fangs into the side of his face and injecting a stream of venom. The blow sent the Necrodelic reeling, pulling him from the wall to slide backwards along the wake of blood he had left behind him just moments ago. The Oneirophage struck again, this time in the throat, shoving more toxins into the Necrodelic's jugular vein and carotid artery with his hypodermic fangs. He paused to wait for the poisons to take effect, but the demon only shook his black mane as if to clear his head.

"Your venoms no longer hurt me, slitherer," said Chariah. "You'll have to find another way to kill me."

The Oneirophage raised his right hand in the air and twirled it in an oneiromantic conjuring gesture. "If I cannot poison your blood," he hissed, his three forked tongues twitching, "then I shall drain it from your flesh."

The Umbilicus appeared suddenly in his hand like a weapon, twisted like a labyrinth, with tubes jutting out everywhere. The Oneirophage swung it like a whip at the Necrodelic. The Umbilicus unraveled and mutated in mid-air, instantly binding Chariah in its clutches and driving its tips into every one of his bodily orifices. Coils bound his arms and legs, wound themselves around his torso and throat. Straws jabbed themselves into his eyes, his nostrils, his mouth, his ears, and the tip of his penis, raising red rims upon the flesh around them and leaking blood from beneath their nearly hermetically sealed edges. The Oneirophage held the other end of the straw in his hands. He raised it to his rainbow lips like a calumet, then began to suck the Necrodelic's blood from every one of his bodily orifices at the same time.

Chariah felt as though he had been attacked by his own Bloodbong. The large mouthpiece and nasal tubes were suffocating him as the Oneirophage imbibed his blood, and then his dreams. As the Oneirophage replenished himself and began to heal, Chariah allowed himself to slip into a brief meditative state, slowing his breathing nearly to a stop, heightening both his awareness and his necromantic sorceries. A minute later he too was inhaling through the respiratory insertions, reclaiming the blood he had just lost, battling the Oneirophage through the conduit of the Umbilicus. With extreme pranayama and body control he began sucking with his eyes and ears, and with his knowledge of higher tantric powers his penis did the same. The Necrodelic reversed the momentum of the Umbilicus and now used it to his advantage. Likewise, the Oneirophage now found himself at the wrong end of the convoluted tubes, and it was his blood, his air, his flesh, and his soul that was simultaneously imbibed and inhaled from his every bodily orifice.

Through the twisted straw the Necrodelic sucked the cannibal vomit from the Oneirophage's stomach, the venom from his glands, the blood from his veins, and the dreams from his head. The Oneirophage thrashed in agony, then grasped the bulk of the straw's nexus, lifted it over his head, and used it to bodily hurl the Necrodelic across the room. Straws disconnected with wet sucking noises as Chariah flew through the air. He landed atop the rapidly rusting Amputator.

The Oneirophage tore the Umbilicus from his lips with a small spattering of crimson and cast it down into the pool of blood on the floor, where it lay half-submerged like some sort of giant tapeworm. As the Necrodelic gathered himself upon the slick roof of the Amputator, the Oneirophage joined him atop the limbing machine.

Clawed feet and serpent's tail alike skidded in the slippery blood. Chariah slashed and chopped with his claws while the Oneirophage bombarded him with tattooed fists. After several minutes, the Oneirophage captured the Necrodelic by wrapping his tail around his ankles and knocking him onto his back. A loud splash followed as blood and gelid rust exploded into the air. The Oneirophage's tail wrapped its way up Chariah's legs, until it held him in its spiraling boa constrictor grip from feet to waist. The broken bones in the Oneirophage's tail blazed with agony as they twisted under the pressure of their own flexing muscles, the sounds of crepitus abrading the air like grindstones. They lay this way for a long time, Chariah struggling to free himself, the Oneirophage squeezing with all his strength, trying to break the bones in the Necrodelic's legs. Some time later, the Oneirophage bent himself over double, so that he lay prostrated across the prone Necrodelic, his tail tying his legs up beneath them. Thus knotted together, they traded more blows, fists, claws, bites, and headbutts. With prism eyes locked into crimson eyes, eye contact drawing blood from both, both hands around each other's throats, the Oneirophage inched their entangled bodies to the edge of the Amputator, then dangled Chariah upside-down over it, bracing himself with his hands behind him while his curled tail held the Necrodelic fast, hanging him by the legs.

The Necrodelic raised himself on torn abdominal muscles to strike at the Oneirophage with his claws before his stomach collapsed and he fell back down. The next time he rose up, the Oneirophage caught him with a fist to the face, knocking him backwards with such force that he nearly carried the Oneirophage with him. The dream-eater braced himself again, then began lowering himself from the roof of the Amputator, twisting in mid-air as he did so to grasp its edge with his fingers. His lower body tensed as he picked the Necrodelic up with his tail and repeatedly slammed him onto the surgical table. Practically holding on to the edge of the Amputator by his long, painted fingernails, the Oneirophage gestured toward the Umbilicus. Lying like a burnt-out eel in the pool of blood, the Umbilicus twitched and came back to life. Resurrected, it launched into the air and flew to its master. The Oneirophage caught the end of it in his mouth, then used his prehensile forked tongues to spin it into a three-dimensional pentagram inside a circular frame. This configuration fit perfectly into the grinding wheel upon the side of the Amputator, which the Oneirophage then bade the Umbilicus attach itself to as he clasped the other end in his mouth. Moments later, the Oneirophage inhaled, and the wheel began to turn .

The surgical table lurched and began to move along its conveyor belt. The Necrodelic was splayed prone upon the device, still trapped in the Oneirophage's coils. The Oneirophage slowly lowered himself even further from the ledge of the Amputator's entrance. His arms were fully extended above his head, and the muscles of both demons were stretching as though on torture racks, dangerously close to the point of shredding. The first time the guillotines fell, Chariah reared up to avoid them, and remained in mid-air to further dodge them as they returned to their holders. The table continued to move along as the Necrodelic and the Oneirophage twisted and writhed,

Chariah trying to dodge the whistling guillotines, and the dream-eater trying to position him so that he could not. All the while the Oneirophage continued inhaling through the Umbilicus, grinding the wheel of the Amputator from afar.

They wrestled thusly until the dawn, which Chariah witnessed when the eastern window transformed from stained glass to pellucid crystal. The Necrodelic watched the red sun Tyterviax rear itself like a bleeding death's head over the horizon, and knew that he need only endure the Oneirophage's death-grip for a few moments longer.

At the exact instant of sunrise, the Oneirophage began his were-transformation. His tail thrashed itself in half, tearing apart into two legs. When the Oneirophage's lower half metamorphosed, Chariah was freed from the constriction of his tail. He dodged the guillotines one last time, then rose to his feet atop the moving surgical table.

The Oneirophage was transforming into Morpheus Rex while hanging from the edge of the Amputator. Chariah grabbed his dangling legs and ripped him from the ledge, then turned around upon the conveyor belt and, holding the Dreaming Predator's legs against his sides, began driving him backwards through the limbing machine, mere inches from the four guillotines. The Umbilicus remained in Morpheus Rex' mouth, and as the quartet of blades fell he blew a forceful, guided pneuma through it. The rush of air sought out the wheel which controlled the Amputator, bringing it to a halt and then, like a gale-force wind, blew it in the opposite direction.

The guillotines merely nicked his shoulders as they dropped. As the conveyor belt reversed and the surgical table lurched in the opposite direction, the Necrodelic's equilibrium was briefly disturbed, and Morpheus Rex took advantage of his vertigo by kicking the Necrodelic in the solar plexus with both feet. The blow was tremendous and sent the Death Addict flying through the air and into the eastern window. The window shattered with his impact, disintegrating into sparkling shards that opened thousands of cuts on the Necrodelic as he hurtled through it. Chariah flew backwards for a few more feet, then dropped and fell into the psychedelic moat below.

As shattered crystal tinkled upon the ground, their music was briefly joined by the loud slap of flesh striking gelid water.

Morpheus Rex made his way to the broken window and looked down. The ripples of the Necrodelic's splashdown were still fresh upon the surface of liquid drugs, but the Death Addict was nowhere to be seen.

The liquid gore flooding the room began draining from the demolished side of the chamber, running off the edge in a wide, shallow cataract, as though from a dam of blood. Some of the severed heads, amputated limbs, and extracted organs that lay strewn across the floor were caught up in the currents and washed over the edge, as well. Morpheus Rex scanned the moat one more time, and then the barren ground to the horizon and back again, before the urge to hunt overrode all else. The wastelands were beckoning, calling him to come and replenish the prey that had been destroyed the night before. It was the call of the hunted and the damned, and Morpheus Rex could do nought but obey its deadly command.

8

Chariah cursed as he struck the surface of the moat, not from disgust or anger at the Oneirophage's small victory, but because of his aversion to water. Such revulsions soon disappeared from his mind, however, for as he sank through the brightly colored waters of the psychedelic moat, the liquid drugs infiltrated his body from everywhere at once and immediately took effect. He inhaled them through his nostrils and swallowed them in gulping mouthfuls. They seeped into his cuts and open wounds. They crawled into his ears, creeped into his eyes, and slithered into his urethra. The Necrodelic floated in a liquid prism, a billion colors flashing and flowing around him. The red sun Tyterviax flickered like fire over the broken mirror of the surface. Both seemed to be within arm's reach and yet, at the same time, seemed parsecs away. Chariah felt like a grain of diamond in an hourglass filled with crushed jewels, its concave sides refracting and distorting the universe around him. Demonic contortionists danced around the timepiece and peered inside, where Chariah had grown from a fragment of diamond dust into a small fetus, a pet fetus kept in an hourglass, by whose development the demons kept time. He continued to grow until the hourglass shattered. The chronodemons dispersed in a swirl of broken colors.

The psychedelic drugs created unique sensations at every point of entry. One eye wept while the other hallucinated. One ear heard music, the other voices. One nostril smelled smoke, the other decay. He held an entire universe in his mouth, within which he could taste everything from the galaxies and supernovas and black holes to every single droplet of every single ocean, every grain of sand and dirt on every planet, every single organism from demon to beast to reptile to arachnid to insects and their eggs, and then all the living parasites and all the viruses in every single one of those organisms. His gashes, punctures, and abrasions filled with shamanic mercuries that were at once salve and salt, panacea and poison, analgesic and corrosive acid. His priapic phallus was in a constant state of orgasm, for minutes, hours, years, centuries, millennia, eons. Forever, the eternal orgasm would last, for as long as space and time existed, for infinity and beyond.

The moat-waters were a thick ambrosial swill. Chariah now felt as though he were trapped inside a crystal ball, floating inside its murky spectrum, swimming like a fish through reflections and refractions while eating and drinking colors. Mother Chaos appeared outside the curved glass, a pink and purple giantess, her features distorted by the concavity of the window through which she gazed. She peered into the transparent globe like a seeress and watched him floating inside it like an embryo in a womb, her child and her familiar. She placed her pink hands upon the scrying orb and hypnotized him with her purple eye contact.

"...you must find the dungeons..." she whispered, then kissed the glass with her purple lips. The crystal ball exploded into a million fractal pieces, and then Mother Chaos blew him along the rainbow currents, which then became the colored winds of space, carrying him further and further through the cosmos, until he washed up on a shore of crushed diamonds, the tides of the psychedelic ocean depositing him upon a glittering beach along with all the other bodies it had washed up before him.

Chariah walked across the diamond sands, the sea of liquid drugs sparkling before him. He approached the other bodies upon the beach and found them to be corpses, their flesh rotting murk, their decaying stench strong on the coastal winds. When he looked upon them a second time their flesh fell away, leaving behind skeletons made of jewels. Chariah glanced fearfully around himself. All the demons had turned into glittering, jeweled bones, their rictus grins smiling and laughing. The psychedelic sea washed another demoness ashore, who decayed when Chariah gazed upon her and left behind a diamond skeleton.

Then the waves of liquid drugs began to grow larger and stronger, until one massive psychedelic tsunami swept Chariah up in its grasp. The crystal waters pumped more liquid drugs into his body as he rode the crest of the giant wave, which continued to exponentially expand by the moment, until Chariah feared it was growing too large, and then it outgrew the entire universe, tumbling Chariah through the black void of the cosmos into the astral plane, where Mother Chaos caught him in her arms like a falling infant. Mother Chaos was still a giantess, and he was the still the size of an embryo. He suckled upon the purple nipples of her breasts and found her damson milk saturated with yet more mind-twisting drugs. Eventually, he transformed into the child of a shamaness, nursing itself upon hallucinogenic lactations. He drank from her gargantuan breasts until he had grown back to his normal size.

Chariah stepped outside his flesh to observe himself and found that he was made entirely of crystal, his brain a glass sculpture in his crystal ball head, his organs visible beneath the transparent panes of his flesh, as pellucid as the skin he pondered them through. He felt fragile, afraid that he would break if he moved; afraid that the winds and the tides, and the orbits of the planets and the gravitational pull of the stars, would shatter him if he did not.

Chariah floated in the liquid cosmos now, past planets that were giant eyeballs, stars that were flaming hearts, comets that were monstrous phalluses, and black holes that were bottomless vaginas. The universe was reflected in his fragile body, upon his suddenly mirror-like flesh and within his suddenly aquarium-like organs. Sparkling crystal spiderwebs began to fall around him, catching him in their diaphanous nets and becoming indistinguishable from his flesh. Soon, the humongous spiderwebs filled his vision, some with souls stuck in their viscid tangles. Onyx and obsidian spiders began to swim beside him, wrapping him up like prey in their crystallized tapestries. His limbs were bound in the restrictive fluids, his body wrapped in a sac of shimmering ectoplasm. The spiders escorted him to a gargantuan spaceship composed entirely of glittering spiderwebs, levels within levels with levels, a palace of ladders and hammocks, step pyramids and labyrinths. Mandala spiderwebs provided enlightenment and sorcery. Chariah gazed around in wonder as he was borne upon the back of an arachnid beast of burden. Within the spaceship were winged spiders, hybrid centaur-like spidaurs, and humongous arachnisauruses that were half-spider, half-dinosaur. The spiders bore him inward on a spiraling maze until they reached the chamber of the queen, a solid white hive of spiderweb, the only area in the entire spaceship with solid walls, floor, and ceiling. Chariah was carried inside a tunneling door that worked somewhat like a sphincter muscle and somewhat like a spinneret, and presented to Spidratha, the First Spider, from whom all spiderkind was descended and whom all spiders worshipped.

The gargantuan Spidratha was seated upon a throne of decaying corpses, in the center of which she laid her eggs. She had two legs, six arms, eight breasts, and a thousand eyes. Eight of those eyes glowed in red pairs upon her face. The rest were ommatidia, black window-panes adorning her entire head. All of them now gazed upon the Necrodelic at once. She gestured to some of her servants, who brought Chariah platters of flaming spiders, burning alive on steaming plates.

"Please accept our offerings of spiderflesh," the queen Spidratha spake.

Chariah inhaled the black smoke curling from the writhing spiders as they burned. The necrodelic drugs of flesh and death cleared his mind and calmed his soul.

"Necrodelic, I have a bargain to make with thee. Soon, we will be invading Grystiawa. In addition to the continued pursuit of the Jh'a'vyraa, we also have a blood debt to settle with the Oneirophage. We seek your alliance in the coming war against the dream-eater. In exchange, you shall be given one thousand spiders of your choosing, to smoke or do with as you please."

Chariah breathed the essence of the dying spiders. There were enlightenments to be gained from spiderflesh, and ten hecatombs of any organism was an offer he could not refuse in a universe which was becoming increasingly devoid of life.

"I accept," spake the Necrodelic.

"Excellent," Spidratha replied. "Together, we will annihilate the Oneirophage. Afterwards, perhaps you will join me, and rule the spider realm beside me. I might desire you for my king, Necrodelic..." Spidratha said in parting, her voice fading as Chariah found himself dropping straight down through the spiders' spaceship upon a single strand of webbing, descending through the arachnids' intergalactic lair and then through the cosmos, where he dangled amongst the galaxies on a single umbilical string.

Chariah hung from the strand of spiderweb for an indeterminate length of time, watching planets orbit stars, watching supernovas explode and black holes implode, all with massive synesthesias of every sensory organ, seeing, hearing, feeling, smelling, and tasting the cosmos he observed. Eventually, Mother Chaos flew to his hanging soul and detached him from the spiderweb. Together, they soared away in a new direction.

His pink and purple guardian angel swam alongside his diaphanous form, a creatrix and sorceress, his lover and soulmate, the Mistress of Entropy and Queen of Anarchy, his beloved Mother Chaos. The entire universe had been submerged in psychedelic liquids, so that he now had to swim from planet to planet, from star to star, through galaxies and wormholes. Mother Chaos led him by the hand to a ruby planet. Laughing severed heads occasionally floated by, as well as extracted organs that still pulsed, and amputated limbs that still reached out or tried to walk. Mother Chaos brought Chariah to the rim of the ruby planet, and they dove in together.

Chariah's glass soul felt as though it could break at any time. Narcissistic sirens came to admire their reflections in his glass body. They swam through the ruby water until the skies turned black, and then Chariah was suddenly plucked from the side of his protector.

The booming laughter of Satan made Chariah's body chime and start to crack. Satan held him by the nape of his neck like a cub, placing him down in the center of a black pentagram atop a flaming pedestal. Satan's phallic horns were bleeding. Chariah could see severed heads floating through the veins and arteries of his external circulatory system. Satan's aura was so hot it threatened to melt him where he stood, or make him spontaneously combust.

Satan spoke with a voice that reverberated a million times, so that every word echoed at once when he had finished speaking.

"Sweet larva, you are nothing but a maggot in the decay of my sperm... Such pleasures I shall know, once you have returned to Hell, my rapeling...The universe is my torture chamber, and I'll not have a sweetmeat like you, with so much blood to be spilled and so much sin to be consumed, transcending it..."

Satan lowered his horned head to fix his black hole eyes upon the Necrodelic, sucking at his very soul with his eye contact. Demons clambered about inside his mouth, some impaled on his fangs, some meditating upon his tongues, others copulating in sadomasochistic orgies. When Satan spoke again, his voice was full of fury, and every syllable he spoke caused a part of the crystallized Necrodelic to break off, shatter, or explode.

"This is my game. I created it. I possess it. I own everything in the entire universe. I own you. You are one of my favorite possessions, and my immortal soul will be destroyed before you ever become the Jh'a'vyraa."

Satan bent even closer.

"Listen to me. You will never become the Jh'a'vyraa. I am omnipotent, and I will use all of my powers to ensure that you never escape me. Cockroaches have a better chance of becoming the Jh'a'vyraa than you. You are my slave. You are my catamite. You are my bitch."

Chariah's crystal form fell apart as Satan laughed, leaving glass shards atop the pentagram and a spectral cloud of dust, as though an hourglass had exploded. When the cloud dissipated, Chariah had regained his black demon form, and stood with crimson eyes blazing, muscular chest slowly rising up and down, claws gleaming in the glow of Hellfire.

Satan continued to laugh, but stopped abruptly when he looked down again to find the Necrodelic before him in full demonic incarnation. His soul had not disintegrated into shards to be swept into Hell, and Chariah stood reborn before him, more evil and more powerful than ever.

"Who do you think you are?" Satan demanded.

"I am the Overdemon. I am the Messiah of Death. I am the Jh'a'vyraa."

"You are no Overdemon," Satan laughed.

"Fuck you," Chariah hissed.

"You are no Messiah of Death," Satan spat, expectorating souls as he chewed off each syllable.

"Fuck you," the Necrodelic repeated.

"You are no Jh'a'vyraa," Satan roared, as smoke began to billow from all around and the fires of Hell burned brighter and higher than ever before.

"FUCK YOU," Chariah screamed, in a voice loud enough to rival Satan's.

Satan smashed the pentagrammed pedestal beneath his fist, but the Necrodelic had already gone, faded away, floated elsewhere, drifting along the currents of the cosmos.

Mother Chaos rejoined him as they swam upwards towards a black hole at the top of the universe. She took his hand in hers and led him through space and time.

"...you must swim into that black hole, my love...labyrinths await...but remember that labyrinths are a form of chaos...and I will be able to aid you, should the need arise..."

With that, Mother Chaos let go Chariah's hand and fell as if from a great height, while the Necrodelic swam towards the black hole at the top of the universe. He flowed along its event horizon and then rode the waves of destruction inside, for one instant flying faster than he had ever imagined possible, as though he were being borne on a dark tsunami the entire length of the universe, billions upon billions of light years in a single second. His hair blew back, his lips curled away from his fangs. He couldn't move any of his muscles, his arms were fixed in place, spread out at his sides, his claws splayed and shredding the very fabric of space and time as he was borne through the universe in one infinite rush. Centrifugal and centripetal forces paralyzed him, paralyzed the very thoughts in his brain, paralyzed his very soul. For an instant, it was like Dark Orgasm, all emptiness and nothingness, voids and silences, and then an instant later he was deposited, dripping with liquid drugs, inside a dank hallway made entirely of prism. Behind him was a black pit, at whose bottom the rainbow waters of the psychedelic moat rose and fell in small waves. The Necrodelic had escaped into the dungeons of Phantasmagorika, somewhere beneath the Grystiawan surface, at the nadir of the prism palace.

Exhausted, Chariah laid down in a shallow, spreading pool of hallucinogens, their chemicals still pumping through his arteries and veins, their visions still replaying themselves over and over in his optic lobes. It was as though an oracle had been surgically implanted in his brain and then hermetically sealed within, never to be amputated or excised, forever to spin its dizzying sceneries around his throbbing mind's eye.

9

The Oneirophage reclined against the gore-stained pillows of his bed, a prism goblet full of blood in one hand, the Umbilicus in the other. As he sipped on blood and drank the dreams from the brain of a purple eunuch, he observed his bedchamber. He was surrounded by carnage. Twenty-seven limbless bodies lay upon the blankets, the remnants of a mass sacrifice earlier that evening. The Oneirophage had many wounds to heal after the previous night's battle with the Necrodelic, and had augmented the numbers of the day's prey with the remaining bodies from his flesh reservoirs. Everything in the room was stained with blood. Some of the blood was his own, and some the Necrodelic's. Most had belonged to the victims the Necrodelic had murdered in the Darkprism. Several internal organs were still stuck to the walls and ceiling, where they had adhered after the Darkprism had violently ejected them from its space-warping depths. The floor was still littered with body parts. Though much of the gruesome debris had washed over the edge of the broken window in a cataract of blood, a large amount of shrunken heads, swollen organs, piles of sodden entrails, and grotesquely eroded skeletons still decorated the bedchamber.

The eastern window, through which the Necrodelic had been defenestrated by a brutal kick from Morpheus Rex, was completely gone, which meant that one entire side of the Oneirophage's bedchamber was exposed to the night. A few winged spiders flew through the opening. The Oneirophage promptly murdered and devoured them, then turned his attention back the bodies on his bed. His sentient chains had healed themselves by the time he returned from the hunt, and shackled the day's prey after he emptied the Darkprism. The Amputator had been sluggish because of all the blood in its gears and the rust setting in from the drenchings of gore, but his nightly ritual had proceeded as normal.

The Oneirophage gazed through the window now and swallowed the dreams of a hermaphrodite, the bifurcated Umbilicus plunged symmetrically into both sets of genitalia. As he drifted into drugged slumber, the stolen dreams of the hermaphrodite unfolded in his head. The Oneirophage dreamt of double masturbation, of self-fertilization, of perverted narcissisms that led to infanticides, persecutions, and moments of solitude atop mountaintops and inside quarantined caverns, on forbidden planets and in bestial spaceships. He dreamt of worlds where hermaphrodites were worshipped as messiahs, and others where they were exiled as pariahs. He dreamt of double castration with a saw. He dreamt of hermaphrodite children, who raped and then killed him, or were raped and then killed by him. The Oneirophage dreamt he was a hermaphrodite, masturbating with a saw and giving birth to Morpheus Rex after Morpheus Rex, until he was buried in them. He dreamt of Siamese twins, one male and one female, making love to one another in a garden of drugs. He dreamt of himself and Morpheus Rex as Siamese twins, conquering Satan, slaying the universe, together becoming the Jh'a'vyraa. He dreamt of nirvanas where Morpheus Rex and the Oneirophage made love for all eternity.

As he slipped further into psychedelic enlightenment, his multicolored astrosome likewise slipped free of his corporeal form. The Oneirophage's astral body drifted to the blown-out window and watched the universe float by. He saw galaxies coasting, stars revolving, planets orbiting, moons tilting. He himself had no knowledge of where it was Phantasmagorika went at sunset. Gazing through the new window, he began to understand. Phantasmagorika was spinning through outer space. It didn't seem to be going anywhere in particular, just wandering and flowing in a transcendent fugue, somewhat like its master in his dream states at night, somewhat like a spacewalking somnambulist.

Later that night, the Oneirophage found himself back in bed. He had just awoken, but he wasn't sure if he was still dreaming or not. He gazed at the black square of cosmos which was now his bedroom wall. Starlight and nebulae, comets and black holes, samsaric cycles and apocalypses, the Oneirophage watched all with drugged fascination, the contrast of the light and the dark, the hypnotic movement of celestial objects, the mesmerizing, ephemeral patterns that were formed and then destroyed.

One of the black holes was coming closer now, flying toward his window. The Oneirophage wondered if he had fallen into its event horizon in his nocturnal journey, and if it was actually he and his palace which were flying towards it. The black hole grew larger and larger, like the shadow of Satan looming over the universe. As it got closer the Oneirophage could see that the black hole had wings. Hooked wings. And hooked horns, hooked shoulders, and a hooked phallus, as well.

It was not a black hole, but a soulmate: the fear-raping, nightmare-ingesting, phobiphiliac Democubus. The large, ebon, gargoyle cacodemon flew in through the blasted window, his sharp hooks silhouetted against the light of the distant galaxies behind him. He had hooks over his eyes, hooked fangs, and hooks on his elbows and knees. His fingers were miniature scythes, his thumbs and forefingers curved toward one another like pincers. His toes were hooked with gripping claws. He had hooks on his ankles, hooks on his genitals, hooks on his chest. Curved hooks arose from each shoulder like those found on certain types of battle armor, and two hooks adorned his skull like the horns of a helmet.

Democubus landed amidst the debris of body parts and began unscrewing the top of a severed head. He twisted the piece of scalp and skull off with his thumb and forefinger, then plunged his hooked phalanges into the brains inside. When he withdrew his fingers, they trailed long squirming organisms that looked like black tapeworms. With a grunt, Democubus devoured them, savoring the taste of fear and phobia as he swallowed, sighing as its dark ambrosia wriggled sensuously down his throat.

He floated across the room and crouched over the limbless

and gorily perforated body of a pink and blue succubus who had barely survived the tortures of the Oneirophage and now lay, breathing shallowly, upon the floor where the dream-eater had discarded her. Democubus crouched down upon her and began to satiate his sexual appetites with her wriggling husk. He drove his penis repeatedly into her vagina while she screamed, ejaculating Stygian sperm and fear toxins into her womb. When he finished and withdrew, his barbed phallus shredded her vaginal walls, spilling blood onto the floor. Another mass of parasitic strings, the same black tapeworms of fear he had scooped from the brain of the severed head, dangled from his genitals and pubic hooks

The succubus continued to scream, her limbless torso writhing and bouncing around the floor. Democubus subdued her, then unscrewed the top of her skull, tilted her head, and plunged his penis into her brain. He ran his glans along her corpus callosum, then thrust his phallus through her brain tissue, copulated with her cerebrum, and ejaculated nightmares into her mind until she perished with a shriek of terror. When he had finished raping her brain and pulled his phallus out of her skull, his crotch was completely immersed in the black tapeworms of fear. The mass of psychic parasites squirmed and crawled, and sometimes wrapped themselves around his thighs.

Democubus floated to the side of the Oneirophage, who had watched him ravish the succubus with mesmerized, dream-drugged fascination.

"Nightmares have a force all their own," spake the Democubus. "Tis their eros and thanatos which is both source and fuel of my psychomancy. You would be wise to include them in your indulgences, and incorporate them into your ritual dream-cycles."

The gargoyle cacodemon spoke articulately and eloquently. His voice was a raspy baritone and had to be dragged like a symbiote from his mouth, for he spoke with a hooked tongue, and his throat, larynx, and lungs were all adorned with hooks, as well. Despite its rasp, it was deep and booming. It often reverberated, but never echoed.

"My phagia doth often enough flow with phobia and philia," the Oneirophage replied.

"Only indirectly," said Democubus, "and diluted by the

dream spectrum."

Democubus floated to the severed head he had opened earlier and lifted it from the floor. He reached inside the brain once again, and with another display of psychomancy withdrew more of the black worming nightmares, as well as a writhing mass of white counterparts. "Tis these, Oneirophage" he said, "which are the stuff of death. Devour them raw, and thou shalt know the secrets of existence."

Democubus raised the worming fistful of black nightmares and white wet dreams to his lips. He thrust the writhing, undulating tapeworms of fear and sex into his mouth. Some dangled down his chin and he slurped them back up. He masticated with his hooked fangs with several minutes before swallowing.

"Tis dreams which are the stuff of death," the Oneirophage replied as Democubus chewed on his feast of eros and thanatos, "the raw materials of power which build one's tolerance for change, that make one immune to every possibility, potentiality, and eventuality. To conquer dreams is to conquer reality. Ultimately, reality and the universe are one and the same."

"In nightmares dwell both fear and lust, and tis these which inevitably lead a soul to its doom. To ingest phobias and philias is to strengthen oneself and obtain evolution. To expel philias and phobias is to cleanse oneself and attain enlightenment. Master this polarity, and you master your soul."

"In dreams I find pain and desire, and tis these which make a corpse of flesh and a ghost of even the most powerful demon."

"Pain is but a symptom of death, dream-eater, not its causality."

"I could say the same of fear."

Democubus ruminated for a moment.

"Do we fear death, or do we perish from our phobias?" Democubus pondered.

"Do we hurt because we are dying, or is it our own pain which murders us?" the Oneirophage responded with equal Zen.

"I think perhaps this dark trinity is symbiotic," spake Democubus.

"Fear, pain, and death," hissed the Oneirophage. "Three sides of a dark pyramid, whose base and foundation is Hell."

"And upon its zenith, the Jh'a'vyraa..." Democubus softly postulated.

"I will seek to devour nightmares, then, while I imbibe dreams," said the Oneirophage.

"And I shall seek to rape the wounded, the tortured, and the dying along with the paranoid, the fetishistic, and the oestral."

Democubus began to creep back towards the window.

"We shall speak of this again, Oneirophage," he promised, and then Democubus beat his large hooked wings and soared away into the cosmos, still trailing wet, black tapeworms of fear from his crotch.

The Oneirophage closed his eyes and began to suckle upon the Umbilicus again, this time drinking the nightmares from the hermaphrodite's skull. The tubes of the intricate straw bubbled with inky fluids and squirming, wormlike substances as the Oneirophage drifted once again into drugged slumber, dreaming the nightmares of his victim, the nightmares of rape by a hermaphroditic Satan, of giving oneself venereal diseases, and of committing suicide while masturbating with a saw and dripping meathook.

10

Jackal-headed and hyena-headed harpies gathered around the unconscious Necrodelic, their small breasts dangling and waving back and forth as they lapped up the shimmering, viscous synthesis of blood, drugs, and filth pooling around his limp body. The long, brown hair of the thirsty bird demonesses became matted with the thick melange as they dragged their tresses through the rancid oasis, their pointed lupine ears twitching, their sabretooth fangs gleaming in the shadows, their forked serpents' tongues flicking in and out while they drank.

Vampire bats and giant, sable leeches poured into the corridor, attracted by the scent of blood. Various gnarled, stunted mutants converged upon the pool, tempted by the sight and smell of drugs. Giant larvae and black, anaconda-sized maggots squirmed from crumbling corners and deep cracks in the walls, drawn by the stench of offal and decay. The jackal-headed and hyena-headed harpies, who were a rare breed of carnivore, vampire, and necrophage, had come for all three substances. The fiendish bitches were soon biting the heads off of bats, swallowing large, wriggling larvae, tearing chunks of meat from the flanks of giant leeches and maggots, and drinking the blood of mutants.

As the various bloodsuckers and scavengers gathered around the septic watering hole, the virulent brown lake being fed by the crimson rivers seeping from Chariah's hemorrhaging wounds and the shimmering, multi-colored streamlets of psychedelic liquid dripping from his body, the Necrodelic stirred from slumber, awakening from the unconsciousness that had befallen him after escaping the mind-bending moat and the depths of his own twisted brain.

Chariah's first perception was of a void in his sentience: he could not discern or comprehend time whatsoever, knew not if he'd been lying there for seconds or millennia after fainting. It was as though time had ceased to be, and, just as it was in the deepest stages of dreaming, there was neither future nor past, prophecy nor history, and no end or beginning to anything, including the universe and his own existence. The present was a black hole womb, trapping him in a dimension where time did not pass and keeping him blind and numb to its very concept, a helpless embryo never to be born, to be imprisoned eternally in the same infinite instant.

It was the magic of Mother Chaos that rescued Chariah again. His soul trapped in the fetal position in a womb of nullity beyond time and space, her powers of entropy countered the inertia of his prison. Her spells of anarchy destroyed its oneness, its singularity. Mother Chaos brought change to the black hole womb, and thus time. Slowly, surgically, as though performing a womb transplant, the purple womb of Mother Chaos replaced the cold black hole womb of nullity. Inside her damson sanctuary, the senseless Necrodelic found metamorphosis, evolution, and enlightenment. Time flowed again, and change had been reintroduced to the universe. The blindness lifted as Chariah observed the giant walls of Mother Chaos' purple vagina from the inside. Maternally, the Mistress of Entropy delivered her demonic devotee beyond the event horizon of her labia, and back into his corporeal body.

He slowly reoriented himself, regaining awareness in small

doses, piecing together the fractal memories in his mind like an interdimensional puzzle box. His nerves came to life one by one, like braziers being lit by torches aflame with the fires of Hell. The Necrodelic's eyelids parted. He looked directly into the eyes of one of the jackal harpies and abacinated her with his incandescent eye contact. The harpy collapsed with a shriek, her empty eye sockets smoking in her skull. Four more harpies circled around the Necrodelic. He abacinated them one by one, burning their eyes out with his crimson gaze. A swarm of mutants charged. The Necrodelic transfixed them with his glowing stare and enoculated them, ripping their eyeballs out of their heads with his lethal eye contact, to bounce and roll and spin in the muck. As the blinded creatures writhed around him, Chariah made eye contact with their third eyes and mind's eyes. Hellfire roiled in the infernal sockets of his skull and he cremated every one of them simultaneously. Their immolated corpses briefly held their shapes in the air, ephemeral sculptures of ash and smoke, then collapsed and disintegrated and scattered through the corridor.

The remaining scavengers swarmed, and Chariah slashed every one of them to pieces with his claws. Slabs of mutilated flesh splashed into the brown puddles. Severed jackal, hyena, and demon heads hissed and growled as they died. Chariah skewered and spitted bats in mid-air, impaling them on his talons, then flicking them to the floor as they squealed their ultrasonic death-screams. The giant maggots, leeches, and larvae he hacked to pieces, leaving them in quivering segments.

Empowered by murder, the Necrodelic healed his flesh and battered mind through the slayings. With every blow dealt he grew a little stronger; with every drop of blood he awakened a little further; with every death he became more powerful, until he had stolen all the life energy from the scavengers and bloodsuckers and left their ashes and mutilated corpses behind in the polluted crimson-brown pool of gore and offal that had been their watering hole and was now their grave.

Able to walk once again, Chariah made his way from the carnage through the dungeons of Phantasmagorika. They were part of the same giant prism from which the rest of the palace had been carved, and were more like sewers than dungeons. The cells were inhabited by skeletons, if at all. He suspected the gnarled mutants were the descendents of ancient prisoners, now so in-bred and devolved that they couldn't find their way to the surface.

Cockroaches cast enormous shadows on the walls as they scuttled past, while the muck and filth along the floor created unhealthy looking rainbows in shades of umber throughout the passages. Chariah removed grilles and gridwork from the ceilings, tearing them from hinges or slashing them asunder, and climbed from level to level through the portals he created. Cisterns of old blood stank like ancient, used armor that had been worn by thousands of different demons, each dying during battle while wearing the rotten iron and bequeathing it, uncleansed and unwashed, to the next generation of warriors. Chariah circumnavigated a myriad of such cisterns as he wandered, some the size of small lakes, some filled with blood so senescent it was the color of rust. However, though much of the blood in the cisterns had been spilled several millennia ago, none of it had ever scabbed, coagulated, or evaporated. In fact, as Chariah made his way through the bowels of Phantasmagorika, it seemed that nothing within the sewers ever dried.

Puddles of gore were ubiquitous, and just as ancient as some of the blood cisterns, in the labyrinths of sewage. Some of them were waist-deep, forcing Chariah to wade through their depths as he crept through the maze. When he came to another blood cistern, he discovered a ladder constructed from the bodies of dead snakes. As he climbed the rungs of serpent corpses, nailed together at heads and tails, along the concave wall of the cistern, he observed the condensation of blood, bodily fluids, and waste materials mere inches from his face. The droplets and drippings upon the cylindrical walls cast blood rainbows across the chamber, rainbows that encompassed the entire spectrum of red, a sevenfold arch of maroon, crimson, scarlet, vermillion, cerise, incarnadine, and carmine. As he reached the top, Chariah gazed down upon a dizzying array of kaleidoscopic reds, spurting through the air, criss-crossing one another and casting a ruby glow throughout the blood cistern.

Chariah climbed into a narrow passage, making his way once more through twisting corridors and ancient puddles. Sanguinary condensation continued to pour from the walls like hemathidrosis. Weaving his way around corners for an hour, the

Necrodelic found yet another shaft to deliver him unto a higher level of the palace's dungeons. The opening was a square in the prism of the ceiling, and just below it was a large puddle of blood with several eyeballs floating on its surface. The Necrodelic waded into the pool of blood, sending the eyeballs afloat on concentric ripples of crimson. He paused to look at the eyeballs.

They were staring back at him.

As Chariah started to dig his talons into the sheer walls of the shaft, the blood he was half-submerged in began to churn, forming itself into clawed arms that rose like waves from the surface to clutch at his flesh, dragging him back down the shaft with the piercing sounds of razors scraping diamond. Mouths began to form upon the crimson surface, complete with fangs that tore at the Necrodelic's flesh.

The puddle of blood was alive.

The living puddle tried to drown and dismember the Necrodelic simultaneously. Liquid tsunami claws raked his back. A tentacle wrapped itself around his throat and began to strangle him. An underwater fist seized his testicles and attempted to crush them to a pulp. Mouths gibbered and gnashed. Eyeballs dilated and observed as they floated on the red tides of combat. Chariah slashed at the living pool of blood. Liquid limbs dissipated and fell like rain across the surface. Faces began to emerge from the depths as the elemental entity gained power, eyes and mouths aligning, complete with horned heads and scarlet hair.

Chariah sliced off the tentacles around his throat, then used his freed larynx and vocal cords to recite a spell of exorcism. The words came like a horde of bats from his mouth. A moment later, the ghosts which possessed the puddle were fished out like flukes by the Necrodelic's claws. The spirits writhed like maggots between his fingers. Chariah raised his hands to his face and, with one necromantic breath, blew the ghosts down the corridor at light speed on the black winds of his lungs. The spirits dispersed like spores in a storm, the living puddle fell silent and still, faces and limbs melting with gentle splashes, mouths closing, eyeballs sinking to the bottom as though suddenly weighted down with iron. Chariah's sable breath blew the ghosts to Hell, where Satan received them with his sadomasochistic embrace.

The living puddle died around the body of its exorcist. Chariah climbed through the blood-speckled shaft in the ceiling and continued his journey. He made his way up a few more levels, fighting off more possessed pools of blood as he did so. There were several more cisterns to negotiate as well. Cisterns of opium residue filled one level, along with the requisite opium-eaters that swam within it and populated their shores, whom Chariah promptly murdered. There were cisterns of ancient sperm and spent venom as well, to be crossed on catwalks above or tunnels below, or circumnavigated in the surrounding labyrinths. Finally, he came to the upper levels, where solid wastes and garbage were accumulated. The main chamber was a vast, open repository filled with towering heaps of garbage and landfills full of body parts and internal organs. Mounds of severed limbs filled the room like mountain ranges. The gleaming white femurs and humeruses of those who had recently been picked clean intermingled with the brown and brittle bones of eons past. Still-enfleshed arms and legs abounded, in various stages of decay. From the fossilized to the shriveled to the ivory to the gangrenous to the maggot-infested to the still-warm, the chamber was like a vision of drug-induced thanatopsis, like performing ashubha after eating peyote and ergot.

The gruesome heaps of body parts buzzed with millions of flies, crawled with maggots and nightworms, and were frequently partaken of by the hungry denizens of Phantasmagorika's sewers, which were present upon this level in abundance, including the jackal-headed and hyena-headed harpies, the starving mutant demons with translucent skin and their bloated, bony, sickly children. Four mycomorphs, fungus demons sculpted into hideous shapes, shuffled slowly through the refuse.

Chariah made his way through and around the piles and pits of waste. The jackal-headed and hyena-faced harpies growled and barked as he passed, but did not attack, for the intruder showed no interest in their rotten food and precious carrion. Still, the Necrodelic's mission was genocide, and every death was a step toward the ascendancy of the Jh'a'vyraa, so he gestured toward the jackal-headed and hyena-faced harpies with his right hand and the scavenger demons spontaneously combusted, adding their steaming shrapnel to the piles of offal and midden, becoming part of the refuse they had dwelled in and feasted on just moments before. The gnarled, genetically twisted demons melted into translucent puddles of liquid flesh with another pyromantic gesture. Maggots, nightworms, and cockroaches were likewise roasted, or crushed underfoot. Swarms of flies were set afire as a single entity, glowing like will-o-the-wisps for a few moments before dropping one by one to the ground. Finally, nought survived but Chariah and the fungus demons. As the oily smoke of burning bodies, the incense of immolated flesh, and the stench of charred garbage billowed in the air, the Necrodelic prepared to battle the gigantic, shuffling, fungoid monstrosities.

The mycomorphs were as tall as twenty feet and perpetually quivered, even when standing still. Their bodies of amorphous mold could be shaped in any manner they chose while they matured, and thus no two were even remotely similar. Their evil spirits sculpted their malleable physical incarnations with psychotic whim and wicked purpose until they reached adulthood, growing body parts as they saw fit, molding their flesh like clay. Mycomorphs were autosurgeons, experimenting on themselves while they developed from spore to monster, performing their own amputations, augmentations, grafts, transplants, and sex changes. They were sculptors of their own flesh, artists whose very bodies were their masterpieces. Because of their adaptability, they were common throughout the universe, and extremely dangerous.

The largest mycomorph was a sickly shade of green, waving hundreds of tentacles around the fanged mouth in the middle of its body. Its gullet formed a spiked tunnel all the way to its other side, where a duplicate mouth opened and masticated. Another mycomorph was brown with black splotches, a giant horned slug of tremendous girth with scales down its back and a manticore's tail. A smaller mycomorph resembling a gorgon had mushrooms for hair and dripped electric blue psilocybin from her breasts and vagina. Upon the wall was a gray-black mildew that stretched for several feet, with hundreds of eyestalks that stood phallically erect as it became sexually excited, its myriad eyeballs watching voyeuristically from where it clung.

The fungus demon with green tentacles and the spotted, sluglike behemoth attacked first. Chariah's claws flashed like ten poignards in the air, leaving dozens of severed tentacles writhing on the floor in a matter of seconds. As the giant slug charged, Chariah breathed fire from his lungs, driving it back with a high-pitched shriek, mold sizzling and crackling upon its body. As Chariah fended off the slug, the tentacled mycomorph crept up behind him, grabbed him in its tendrils, and began dragging him toward its gaping mouth. The Necrodelic could see the other side of the chamber through its second mouth as it drew him closer.

Chariah braced his clawed feet against the mycomorph's fangs, preventing it from chewing or swallowing him. The rings of teeth clashed all the way up and down its throat like a meat grinder. Calling upon his necromancy, Chariah unleashed the power of Satan into his muscles and veins, causing the tentacles which gripped him to explode and rain down in showers of pyrotechnic shrapnel as he powered from their clutches with Hellborn strength. The Necrodelic alighted with pantherish dexterity upon the creature's lips. As the tentacles sought him out again like heat-seeking missiles, he deftly caught them in his clawed fists and shoved them into the fungus demon's maw. A second later, as the Necrodelic jumped from the creature's mouth to the floor below, the mycomorph chewed off its own tentacles with a muffled scream of anguish.

As Chariah alighted upon the ground, the horned slug charged again. When it was within mere inches of him, the Necrodelic jumped straight up, flipped over, twisted in midair, and landed atop the creature's back, all the while severing the flailing tentacles shooting towards him.

Chariah rode the horned slug like a bestial steed, using his palms to take over its brain and driving it headfirst into the tentacled mycomorph's iron maiden gullet, which reflexively closed and decapitated its brother. The headless body fell heavily to the ground, knocking over heaps of severed limbs and waste as it did so, then several more as it thrashed about with violent death throes.

The mushroom gorgon approached the Necrodelic, her tits and vagina leaking electric blue psilocybin, flowing in streamlets down her torso and thighs. As she drew closer, her eyes wept shimmering psilocybin, and she began drooling and sweating the psychedelic substance as well. Just the fumes were enough to disorient the Necrodelic. She shot more psilocybin from her erect nipples in two long, fountaining arches, dousing the Necrodelic with blue hallucinogens. The drug seeped through his skin by osmosis, and the room began to breathe and sway and shift.

An instant later, he found himself suckling from the mushroom gorgon's teat. She sang to him like a siren and caressed him like a mother as she nursed him with psilocybin, then gripped his hair and buried his face in her genitals. Her siren's song coaxed his tongue between her labia, her temptress' sorceries hypnotizing him to perform cunnilingus upon her fungoid body, drinking the blue psilocybin dripping from her vagina as he did so.

Fighting his own consciousness, Chariah struggled against the psychedelic fluids and called forth Hellfire from his throat. He breathed the Hellfire into the mushroom gorgon's vagina. Her labia blackened and peeled back like skin from a wound. Her vaginal walls melted into black lava.

The Hellfire blew through her womb and up into her body, scorching everything in its path. She burned from the inside out, her vital organs reduced to little bits of charcoal before the flames even reached her brain. When they did, they burst from the crown of her head like a raging inferno. The mushroom gorgon dissolved into ashes as the smell of cooked psilocybin filled the air.

The smoke of her burning flesh turned the psychedelia in Chariah's consciousness into necrodelia, making him even more deadly. Halfway submerged in the astral plane, his senses razor-sharp, the Necrodelic burned the psilocybin from his brain. He was enlightened from the drug of her immolated flesh, and power raged through his body like black electricity. He caught the tentacled fungus with his claws as it descended upon him, lifting it into the air with the strength of a thousand demons and hurling it at the mildewy mycomorph on the wall, who had been merely observing the combat with its voyeuristic eyestalks. Those same eyestalks which had been so erect with sexual arousal now shriveled in terror. The tentacled mycomorph splattered against the wall with an ear-splitting, wet, smashing sound, instantly killing it and its mildewy brother beneath it. The two fungus demons dripped down the wall as one, sliding to the floor with sucking noises like those of copulation, their blood and liquefied flesh intermingling and pooling on the floor. While their pulped corpses continued to runnel and seep through the chamber, Chariah found a stairway in the back corner and ascended to the upper levels of the sewers.

As Chariah came closer to ground level, the piles of severed limbs grew progressively fresher, so whereas he had seen mostly mummified remnants before, he now saw several still-bleeding appendages. Finally, Chariah climbed one last ladder of dead serpents, this one stretching for over one hundred feet along a curved wall that overlooked one last cistern of gore. This cistern served as the main depository of the castle, where all of the waste initially accumulated. The foul lake bubbled and foamed, churning with loud machinery grinding and scraping at its bottom, unseen beneath the murky depths, which filtered the blood and other substances before sending them further downwards. Hundreds of pipes jutting from the walls were pouring blood, sperm, venom, opium residue, and used dreams into the cylindrical chamber. Several others lay dormant.

As Chariah ascended the ladder of ophidian cadavers, the light of Phantasmagorika's ground level a shining beacon high above, he reflected upon his quest through the sewers of the prism palace. He began to notice the correlations between the architecture, functionality, and quiddity of Phantasmagorika with the inner workings of the body, mind, and soul of the Oneirophage. Recalling pipes that bore spilled blood like aqueducts throughout the palace, garbage chutes jammed with body parts, and overflowing landfills and trash compactors, Chariah realized that, like the Oneirophage's brain, the workings of Phantasmagorika's sewage system were as intricate as those of a city, though not as efficiently maintained. Chariah did not believe that they were they were maintained at all, much like the Oneirophage's subconscious. It also seemed as though everything the Oneirophage had ever used was obsessively retained in his palace sewers and cisterns, like precious, rotten, festering memories accrued in the dark corners of his brain. Chariah also observed that nothing within the sewers of Phantasmagorika ever dried. Drug residue, snake venom, vomit, sweat, spilled blood, sperm ejaculated in both masturbation and rape, and the remnants of everyone he had ever slain, all seemed to be preserved in the subterranean labyrinth, along with all the accumulated waste and garbage of the Oneirophage's millennia of existence within the opulent palace.

Upon reaching the top of the dead snake ladder he gazed down one last time upon the sewers, using his necromantic powers to observe with sorcerous and X-ray vision the path of psychic residue he had left behind, the black trail of his own soul through the maze of glittering gutters and cisterns. Casting a spell of memory, Chariah etched a map of Phantasmagorika's sewers and dungeons in his mind, carved in crimson with a psychic dagger upon the innards of his brain. Then, with the freshly incised map still bleeding deep within the labyrinths of his mind, amongst a myriad of other such cartographic lacerations and scars, the Necrodelic emerged into the light of Phantasmagorika's rotunda.

II

Serpentikal was a labyrinth, a living ophidian maze whose infinite coils were the walls and edifices of the twisted and spiraling streets of his realm, whose bodily orifices were snakepits, and whose very body formed Serpentopolis, a city for his kin to dwell in. Floating in the cosmos like a bestial spaceship, Serpentikal's neck stood more than a thousand feet tall, culminating in the head and hood of a gargantuan king cobra. He carried his queen, his soulmate, the Constrictress, in his mouth, her tail and arms wrapped around his right fang like giant serpents unto themselves. Twisted and contorted into a hanging sexual knot that closely resembled the yab-yum position, the Constrictress copulated with Serpentikal's pike-sized tooth, its hypodermic tip ejaculating venom into her womb as she dangled and writhed.

The Oneirophage spied upon Serpentikal from his bloodstained bed, one hand languidly holding the Umbilicus to his lips while he sucked dreams from the exposed brains of his writhing bedmates. Voyeuristically stargazing, he watched the universe flow by, enjoying for another night the scenery of the cosmos. As the orbits of Serpentikal and Phantasmagorika slowly pulled the two together, their gravities attracting one another at the same time, the Oneirophage made eye contact with the ophidian titan, drawing the gigantic floating fortresses even closer. The colossal cobra head soon filled the entire window. When Serpentikal spoke, his forked tongue flickered in and out of the room, lashing the cool air of the open bedchamber.

"Oneirophage," Serpentikal hissed, "my dream-swallowing scion. It has been many skins since last we met."

The Oneirophage nodded towards his ancestor, speaking the serpent tongue with the same susurrating tone.

"Welcome," he said, stretching out his tattooed arms, his three forked tongues dangling from his lips, "to Phantasmagorika."

Serpentikal spoke again, his voice a whisper as loud as a scream.

"I see you have evolved into a powerful entity, a demon worthy of becoming the Jh'a'vyraa. I have come to you this night with both a warning and an offering. Soon, Spidratha and her minions will attack Grystiawa. She has allied herself with the Necrodelic, and together they seek to destroy you. You will be outnumbered when her arachnid armies land, and shall be forced to flee your homeworld or die with it. Though your blood is not pure and your genes have been contaminated, still you are one of my descendants, and so, half-breed, for the opportunity to gain vengeance upon my former lover and end the ancient Spider-Serpent Wars once and for all, and in our mutual pursuit of the Jh'a'vyraa, I offer you my protection and alliance. Speak the word, and I shall direct my course to Grystiawa. The serpents and spiders shall wage one final, apocalyptic battle before the universe comes to an end. Consider this, my mutant grandson, while you enjoy the gift of two hundred gorgon heads."

As Serpentikal spoke of the gorgons, the Constrictress gestured toward the back of her lover's throat. Shortly thereafter, a long anaconda slithered up Serpentikal's gullet, over his tongue, between his fangs, and into the bedchamber. Upon its back, in one solid row, were the severed heads of the gorgons. The anaconda poured into the room for several minutes, folding back upon itself to fit within the confines of the bedchamber, until its tail emerged with the skull of the two hundredth sacrificial victim impaled upon its tip. The gorgon heads were still alive, and arrayed like chalices of wine on a table, their dreams ready to be imbibed.

The Oneirophage reached out with the umbilicus and began partaking of the gifts, first sipping bubbling green dreams through a gorgon's eyeball, then driving the Umbilicus into her brain, sucking out her optic nerve, swallowing it, and then thirstily drinking more and more dreams from her brain with increasingly greater swallows.

"Thank you, First Serpent," the Oneirophage said in gratitude as he drove the Umbilicus through the forehead, third eye, and pineal gland of the next gorgon head, who screamed a bloodcurdling cry as he did so. The Oneirophage began sucking the dreams from her brain and swallowed her pineal gland whole.

"I will indeed accept your offer," said the Oneirophage. "Come to Grystiawa, and together we shall annihilate Spidratha and Necrodelic alike."

Serpentikal hissed his approval. "Tis done. Constrictress, prepare Serpentopolis for war. We leave for the Tyterviax system immediately."

"Yes, my lord," the boa queen replied, spiraling from his fang like an unraveling vine, then disappearing down his vast, hollow throat.

Serpentikal began pulling away from the open window, speaking one final time as he retreated.

"Prepare yourself, Oneirophage. Your red planet is about to become much redder."

With a final flick of his tongue, Serpentikal soared back into the cosmos, leaving the Oneirophage to contemplate his wake. After spending several minutes in rumination, the Oneirophage made his way over to the gorgon heads. The large anaconda had been left behind to serve him as a table, submissive living furniture for him to dine from. With the Umbilicus in hand, the Oneirophage began to suck the dreams from another gorgon's brain. He dreamed of Serpentikal, and of making love to the Constrictress. He then dreamt prophecies of the impending combat. Plunging the straw through the skull of another gorgon and imbibing green dreams, the Oneirophage dreamt that his own head was the head of a gorgon, and that all of his body parts were snakes. His hair was a nest of rattlesnakes, his lips an ouroboros, his tongue a dipsas, his eyes and testicles mating balls of garter snakes, his twin penises a cobra and an asp with hoods for prepuces, his arms anacondas, his fingers coral snakes, his intestines an amphisbaena, his esophagus a sidewinder, his lungs a black mamba and a green mamba, his ribcage a symbiobaena, his spine the Constrictress, his heart the severed head of Morpheus Rex, his circulatory system the coiled labyrinth of Serpentopolis, and his entire lower half the neck and head of Serpentikal, with great beady eyes reflecting the Oneirophage's own hypnotic gaze.

Gathering up four more gorgon heads and carrying them by their ophidian tresses to the bed with him, the Oneirophage lay himself down once again and drank gorgon dreams until he was in a soporific stupor. As he closed his eyes, he saw green darkness instead of black. The last thing he dreamt before falling into a deep slumber was a simultaneous pair of parallel nightmares, one about a spider caught in its own web, and the other of a serpent caught in its own coils, each struggling, contorting, screaming, bleeding, retching, thrashing, twitching, and ultimately dying within their own traps.

12

Chariah spent an entire day exploring Phantasmagorika and analyzing his enemy. As twilight began to fall, Chariah ascended a long stairway. At the top of the steps was a window facing the descending red sun. Tyterviax glowed like Satan's third eye. Chariah watched it drop. At the exact moment of sunset, the stairway transformed into a ramp, throwing Chariah off his feet. He tumbled violently down the sheer and slippery length and struck the back of his head upon the floor below. After a few moments, he slowly rose to one knee and shook the pain from his skull. Then the voices came.

Soft and solemn, the voices gradually grew louder and louder, and were soonafter accompanied by the plodding tread of footsteps. Chariah began to follow the voices through the palace. The heavy footsteps, likewise, began to follow him.

"The universe is its own torture chamber...

Step...

Echo...

"It lashes itself with nebulae..."

Step...

"And infects itself with demons..."

Step...echo...step...echo...step...

Chariah froze in the alcoved hall, gazing back and forth. His eyes flared red with night-vision as he illuminated corners and sifted through shadows. The voices beckoned him like the song of a siren, even as the footsteps of the unseen stalker slowly hunted him from behind. The Necrodelic chased the ephemeral speaker while simultaneously fleeing the plodding pursuer.

Caught somewhere between the realms of predator and prey, the Necrodelic followed the voices up a spiral rampway. He had traveled this way earlier in the day, and recalled that the spiral rampway had been a spiral staircase then. He paused at the top, peering down another corridor. There was silence before him and darkness behind him. He turned into a hall filled with stained glass windows. He remembered this corridor from the day's sojourn as well. The stained glass windows had been transparent when last he viewed them.

The footsteps began again. Chariah used his powers of echolocation to try and locate their creator, but found only vertigo in doing so. He peered down the ramp. The alcoves had gone pitch black. Chariah refocused his night-vision, but saw no one. He cast blood-red laser beams from his eyes like crimson searchlights all around. Again, he found nothing.

The voices began again, from far down the hall. This time, the speaker recited an entire dialogue.

"The Somniloquist calls you to die. The Somnambulist hungers for flesh. The Somniloquist will sing you a lullaby dirge while the Somnambulist digs your grave. Come to the Somniloquist. Come to the matriarch of death. I will give you the suicide you desire. Succumb to the Somnambulist. You know you wish to be eaten. You remember when you were dead. You want to be dead again."

There was silence for many moments, and then the Somniloquist began speaking in fragments once more.

"Satan is a voyeur..."

Chariah followed the echoing words down the hallway

"Satan is ylem..."

The whispers came now from around the corner at the end of the corridor.

"Satan is a chronophiliac..."

Chariah burst into the foyer. There were five open doorways and a pentagram drawn in blood upon the ground. When the voice came again, it seemed as though it came from all five openings, and did not stop, but continued chanting in concentric unison, asking the same question repeatedly as it moved from doorway to doorway in a disorienting, spinning echo.

"Who..."

"Is..."

"Jh'..."

"A'..."

"Vyraa???"

The Necrodelic froze as the voices circled him and every doorway chanted each of the five words simultaneously, like a mantra.

"Who is Jh'a'vyraa?" "Who is Jh'a'vyraa?" "Who is Jh'a'vyraa?" Who is Jh'a'vyraa?" "Who is Jh'a'vyraa?"

And then the steps began again, from the corridor behind him, at the base of the spiral rampway. Chariah turned around. The creature was ascending to the second story.

The words began to blur into strange rhythms and sounds around him.

"Jh'a'vyraa is who?" "Are you Jh'a'vyraa?" "Who are you?" "You are Jh'a'vyraa..." "...but you are no Jh'a'vyraa."

Chariah gazed down the hallway he had just traversed. Another step rang like a gong in the darkness. As he started to head back the way he had come, he felt blood drip onto his face and gazed upwards.

Dangling from the ceiling was a jungle of severed limbs. Arms and legs were arranged like plants in a topiary, a blossom of death, wreathed in blood that dripped like sap, like pollen, like crimson nectar. The Necrodelic wiped the blood from his face and trod back down the hall.

The steps echoed from all around, but when he reached the rampway, there was nothing there. The voices, too, had stopped. Chariah descended once more into the main hall, then took a different rampway, all the way to the top story of the prism palace, where he found himself inside the Oneirophage's drug gardens. He walked through fields of black lotus and green lotus, hedge-mazes of peyote bushes, and forests of towering opium poppies. The greenhouse was filled with every mind-altering plant imaginable; ganja, jimson weed, morning glory, and more; plus orchards blooming and blossoming with aphrodisiac and soporific fruits the size of his skull, and fountains and brooks bubbling with soma and ayahuasca. As Chariah made his way through the drug gardens, he saw that the greenhouse walls, built for absorbing sunlight, were shadowy and cold. The skylights overhead revealed the stelliferous firmament, but it was one filled with constellations and zodiacs alien to the Tyterviax system. More than the night skies of Grystiawa, Chariah suspected, were passing before his crimson eyes. The Necrodelic gazed out for a moment more, then exited the drug gardens into another five-way foyer.

Another mass of severed limbs dripped blood from above, spattering the pentagram below with ruby dewdrops. Chariah stood in the center of the pentagram, the ornate gates of the drug gardens swinging shut behind him, and peered down each of the four hallways in turn. The voices began again, followed by the footsteps.

"Hell is a place inside you..."

Step...

"The end of time is a razor's edge..."

Echo...step...echo...

Chariah chose a hallway and ran down it at full speed. He could hear the voices growing closer now, and the footsteps moving faster behind him.

"The planes of existence copulate..."

The footsteps were loud heartbeats behind him now, the voices a mesmeric siren's song.

"Love is a slow death..."

Chariah could hear the voices, mere inches away. He charged through the darkness and into a sudden dream state, and then he was plummeting through space, the primordial fear of falling gripping him from within, the dizzying, terrifying sensation of one's astrosome snapping back into the physical body like whiplash, over and over again, and then blackness, blindness, nothing.

*

Chariah awoke upon the floor of the Oneirophage's living art gallery. His senses spun in a few last centrifugal revolutions around the rim of his inner skull, then settled back into their resting places. The Necrodelic found himself amongst hundreds of paintings composed entirely of bodily fluids. The artwork was drawn and colored, on canvases of skin and flesh, with blood, tears, sperm, venom, sweat, bile, leprosy, necrosis, and liquified organs. The paintings were amalgamations of pornography, sadomasochism, war, and demonography. There was a room filled with abstract mandalas. There was another devoted entirely to sexual torture. Just like everything in the sewers, the paintings were still wet. The gruesome art gallery was a labyrinth unto itself, one which took the Necrodelic several minutes to escape, observing every damp, glistening masterpiece as he did so. He exited into yet another pentagrammed foyer with five doors and hanging limbs.

The Necrodelic crept through hallways and rotundas, up rampways and living serpent ladders, and through a myriad of the grisly foyers. The voices and footsteps were still audible, but they seemed to be far in the distance, the spoken words indecipherable babbling. He made his way through serpentariums where menageries of snakes were kept in glass tanks, crossed a bridge over a large reservoir filled with thousands of still-living brains, and walked past a row of sleeping chambers, one with a bed of nails, one a bed of broken glass, one a bed of hot coals, one a boiling waterbed, one a Procrustean bed, one a horizontal crucifix, one an iron maiden for two, one an oven, one a funeral pyre, one a coffin, and one a cocoon. In one room he discovered a cage of prism marked with ancient runes that read "The Lunatic". Inside dwelled a feral, scarlet beast, menstruating from all of its numerous genitalia, both male and female, slavering blood, its bulging eyeballs psychotic, its limbs and tentacles thrashing. It had an external circulatory system like Satan himself, and several hearts hanging like scrotums and breasts all over its body.

Chariah experienced the sudden falls a few more times. Each of the mysterious, steep precipices were disguised by mirages and shadows, and every fall delivered him unconscious to a random part of the prism palace. He had no idea what part of Phantasmagorika he now inhabited, for the falls included many directions other than down. Chariah had no way of mapping the dream-eater's castle. Phantasmagorika very much resembled the drugs of its master.

The voices and footsteps continued to bait and beckon him, to chase and flee, to stalk and seduce. They had grown closer again, and Chariah found himself once more on the precarious edge of a predator/prey continuum. He decided to stalk the predator, and make the prey hunt him.

"The night is a womb..."

Step.

Chariah crept towards the oncoming footfalls.

"We are all damned..."

The footsteps grew closer, louder, faster.

"Suicide, homicide, genocide..."

The voices grew farther, softer, droning.

"Matricide, patricide, prolicide..."

Chariah stopped. The footsteps were coming from behind now.

"Chronocide, necrocide, Diablocide..."

He was chasing the voices again.

"Death is a drug for Satan to dine on, the dark ambrosia of souls. A spirit menagerie in Hell did Satan decree, for Satan is the omniphage and the omniphiliac."

The footfalls grew louder behind Chariah, heartbeats, then drumbeats, then hoofbeats, then small explosions. The voices were descending upon him, first death-screams, then battle-cries, then dirgelike hymns, then whispered mantras.

The floor disappeared and Chariah fell through it, the primal fear welling up inside him once again, the hallways and chambers of Phantasmagorika swirling past in centrifugal orbits, his body striking the floor heavily and knocking him unconscious, his astrosome hurtling through time, then striking his flesh once, twice, thrice, each blow a psychic whip, flogging him mind, body, and soul.

*

The Necrodelic awoke on the floor of an empty rotunda.

As consciousness slowly crept through his flesh, he listened to the darkness. He could hear the voice of the Somniloquist around him, as if in a dream, and the footsteps of the Somnambulist walking towards him, in perfect synchronicity with the slow gong of his heart.

"In the genesis of the universe we were blessed with Satan's sins. Through time, we nurtured that evil and continued to grow, spreading death throughout the cosmos and spilling enough blood to fill entire galaxies. For decillions of years we have battled, died, and reincarnated on the torture wheel of the samsaric cycle. As the apocalypse approaches, the holocaust is within our grasp. Our demon hands deal genocide as the astral and physical planes copulate and time burns to its end. Now, as damnation claims everything that has ever lived, the true Messiah of Death must arise, to torture Satan in his very Hell."

Chariah opened his eyes and gazed upon the two tormented beings looming over him. The Somniloquist's eyes were nailed shut, two long nails driven through her eyelids, from the tops of her eye sockets to the skin at their bottoms. Her lips and cheeks had been ripped back from around her mouth in one circular flap and nailed to her temples, the sides of her neck, and her breastbone. Her crimson jaws were exposed as she spoke, moving up and down, her tongue thrashing like an animal on a leash. The connecting tissues of her upper and lower lips were completely torn. Her cheeks had been slit so that they could be pulled farther back and pinned to her skull behind her ears, which she had torn from her head long ago so that she wouldn't have to listen to her own somniloquies. Her nipples had been severed, and her vagina was nailed shut, six nails hammered horizontally through her labia from right to left.

Conversely, the Somnambulist's mouth had been nailed shut, the tips of the nails jutting like a spiked collar from his lower jaw, and his eyes had been nailed open, a ring of eight small nails pinning lower and upper eyelids to the surrounding flesh. A long nail had been driven into each ear, their spikes hidden deep in his brain, their large grey heads filled his earholes. His testicles had been nailed together left to right with a single blow. The opening on the tip of his penis had been enlarged by what looked to be the work of a nail and hammer as well, and gaped redly, like the mouth of a nightworm.

Both of them had metal zippers from their groins to their throats, and both had been shaved completely bald, bodies, pubes, and heads alike. The Somnambulist had been given metal claws, driven beneath his fingernails, while the Somniloquist's fingers were permanently splayed by metal wires passed through her fingertips. She had been given one long metal fang, which stretched scythelike to the point of her chin. They were the victims of the Oneirophage's sadistic surgeries, existing in a state of perpetual torment.

And they were fast asleep.

The Necrodelic rose to his feet as they circled him. The male Somnambulist was more aggressive, and attempted to strike first with his prosthetic claws. Chariah guarded himself with his own talons, which were so sharp that they cut those of the Somnambulist in half when they closed, scissorlike, around them. The Somnambulist unleashed a powerful headbutt next, which staggered the Necrodelic into the waiting clutches of the Somniloquist. Chariah spun as she attempted to bury her prosthetic fang in his cervix, held her at arm's length when she tried to bury it in his larynx, then caught the fang between two of his claws when she stabbed it towards his eye, severing it as cleanly as he had the talons of her mate. The Somnambulist attacked from behind at a diagonal angle while Chariah was engaged with the Somniloquist. Chariah spun quickly with both of his arms extended, simultaneously catching both the Somnambulist and the Somniloquist in the face with slashing blows, backhanding the Somnambulist while striking the Somniloquist in the side of her neck with a ridge-hand chop. The Somniloquist fell to the floor. Chariah continued spinning and backslashed the Somnambulist, this time cutting his head and torso into four pieces. He completed the revolving assault by kneeling as he spun back again, leaving eight quivering leg pieces amongst the rest of the gory wreckage.

The Somniloquist rose up, lost in another one of her deranged somniloquies. She stood passively, arms at her sides, and spoke. "We are all exhibitionists for Satan. Our souls are fertilizer for Hell. We are all Satan's whores."

Chariah reached out and grabbed the dangling zipperhead at her throat. Sensing the danger, she began frantically attempting to use sorcery, speaking runes and mantras in her soliloquies, but none of them were coherent, or even resembled actual spells. The Necrodelic yanked the zipper all the way down to her nailed labia. All of her organs spilled out at once, hearts, livers, kidneys, intestines, stomachs, lungs, spleens, pancreases, bladders, ovaries, all fell onto the floor with accumulative wet noises. They had been tightly packed into her torso, and most of them were not her own.

The Necrodelic stood briefly over the fallen body of the vivisected Somniloquist, then turned to leave the room, only to find himself being clawed at by the amputated arms of the Somnambulist. The Somnambulist's severed head rolled across the ground and began biting his legs. The other pieces of the Somnambulist's mutilated flesh began flinging themselves at him as if thrown by unseen hands. Chariah snarled and began slashing at the shrapnel, cutting the Somnambulist into hundreds of pieces.

Breathing hard from the combat, the Necrodelic stood over the tiny bits of flesh, only to hear the voice of the Somniloquist again, this time a hundredfold. He turned to find that each of her spilled organs had formed a rudimentary mouth with valves and sphincters and other openings, and each was now speaking a somniloquy while her battered head lolled, singing, upon the ground. Chariah went into another rage, dissecting each of her organs into slivers, carving up her entire body, decapitating her and beating her severed head repeatedly against the wall until her skull disintegrated. Her brains liquified and spread in a pool on the floor, leaving her face a gory dead skin mask in his hand.

The tiny pieces of the Somnambulist were stirring again, jumping around like fleas and launching themselves at him. They stung like hail, raising welts on his body. Some of them tried to burrow into his flesh. Enraged, Chariah called forth Hellfire, scorching himself in the process but immolating all the tiny pieces of the Somnambulist. The bloody remnants of the Somniloquist were starting to gibber behind him. Chariah turned and unleashed the Hellfire upon them, too. The flames filled the rotunda, then faded, leaving the Necrodelic ankle-deep in ashes and surrounded by smoke, with burn wounds covering his body.

Chariah exited the searing heat of the rotunda. The skin was burned from his left forearm, his right bicep, and part of his chest. Exposed beneath it was crimson blood scorched to blackness, wickedly complementing his naturally black tissue and black muscle, the black wounds of a black soul, already beginning to ooze with black pus. They would heal within an hour. The Necrodelic was practically immune to burns and it was impossible to kill him with heat, flames, or smoke because of his advanced levels of pyromancy, pyromania, and necrodelia. The only fire that could affect him was Hellfire, even when brought forth from his own lungs.

He wandered through the prism palace a while longer. Finally, he reached the top floor, where the Oneirophage lurked. Chariah could smell the exposed brains and dreams along with the scent of his nemesis in the bedchamber at the end of the hall.

The cosmos faded in the skylights above as Phantasmagorika spun down through the atmosphere of Grystiawa, to land in some random, dawnlit location upon the planet. The prism palace hit with a jolt, driving its moat and dungeons forcefully, as if by rape, into the ground below. Chariah paused on the way to the Oneirophage's quarters, gazing upwards through the skylights and whistling once, sharply and loudly. He looked out into the morning for a moment longer, and then, satisfied, walked on down the hall. Outside the Oneirophage's bedchamber, he carved a small alcove in the ceiling, then climbed inside it and curled up like a scorpion to await his prey.

13

The mammoth, atramentous, bestial spaceship hovered in the crimson skies of Grystiawa, sucking up the red rays of Tyterviax like a black hole, reflecting not a single piece of daylight, radiating nothing but midnight darkness and an aura of evil. Unto itself a partial eclipse of the sun, the immense spaceship lurked in the bleeding stratosphere, waiting to ambush the prone fortress below. Slowly, like a spider upon a single strand of web, the Omnibeast began to lower itself, the eight legs of the Arachniotics, which served as its landing gear, unfolding segment by segment to dangle in the dawn. Shadows fell like bodies across the crimson wastelands, the blood-red plains, the scab-colored moors and dunes and plateaus. Directly below the deathly intergalactic monstrosity lay its target, its victim, the prism palace of the Oneirophage, Phantasmagorika.

The rainbow spectrums of the shimmering castle were unaffected by the bestial spaceship's shadows, and remained glittering and glowing while the areas around it were plunged into darkness. The tentacles of the Omnibeast waved and slithered as it descended upon the fortress, wrapping themselves around parapets and adhering themselves to the palace walls. The eight curved legs of the Arachniotics spread to enfold Phantasmagorika in their grasp, and then the Omnibeast unleashed its innards upon the fortress. A mass of black entrails, tongues, veins, arteries, phalluses, umbilical cords, and tentacles spilled wetly across the roof of the prism palace, shattering its skylights and penetrating its inner chambers. Gigantic mouths and vaginas closed around parapets and minarets, suckling and thrusting upon their gleaming phallic forms. Hundreds of lips and labia snarled, growled, dilated, suckled, and salivated.

The bestial spaceship nestled atop the Oneirophage's prism palace like a symbiote. The Arachniotics held Phantasmagorika fast with its spider legs, as though it were ravishing the entire palace. The body of the Omnibeast was mounted atop the helpless fortress like a giant hermaphrodite rapist. Its four figureheads stretched out to the north, south, east, and west like sentinels, intently studying the planet. The Hydratowers thrashed on the roof as though trying to devour the rising Tyterviax. After a few minutes, several streams of blood and sperm began oozing down the palace walls.

Morpheus Rex awoke to the sight of black tentacles and a long, prehensile penis bursting through his open window and squirming into his bedchamber. The tendrils were lifting gorgon heads with their tips, groping the floor and walls, and thrashing on the bed beside him. One of the tendrils wrapped itself around his waist, while another encircled his throat. Morpheus Rex stabbed the tentacles with the Umbilicus, lining them with wounds that looked like crimson suckers. The tendril around his neck strangled him, lifting and hanging him like a living noose. His freshly transformed legs kicked in mid-air as he struggled to free himself. He clawed at the tentacle and tried to pry it loose. He stabbed it with the Umbilicus, over and over, and then, with a twirl of his fingers, transformed the Umbilicus from a single straw into one with ten tips, increasing its potential for damage tenfold. Blood began to drip down the length of the tentacle as the circular puncture wounds grew exponentially in number.

The tendril's grip began to loosen in the slick ichor, allowing Morpheus Rex to slip down several inches and sink his fangs into the moist spongy flesh of the tentacular gallows. The long tendril fell instantly in a dead coiled mass to the bed, the body of Morpheus Rex dropping down right beside it. Morpheus Rex bit and stabbed his way through the tentacles, catching them in his mouth and saturating them with serpent venom, or impaling them on the tips of the Umbilicus. The sentient chains on the southern wall shot out and captured the gigantic, probing, anaconda-like penis in their shackles.

Two of the tentacles were tactilely exploring the Amputator with nerve-sensitive suckers and nerve-clustered tips. The Oneirophage stepped to the side of the machine and turned its giant wheel. Guillotine blades began to fall, over and over, slicing the inquisitive appendages apart.

The bedchamber fell silent as the battle ended. The poisoned tendrils and amputated tentacle stumps withdrew through the window. Only the shackled phallus remained.

Morpheus Rex surveyed the carnage. The sliced remnants of tentacles were everywhere. He twirled the Umbilicus back to a single straw, then stuck it into its skin-sheath in his forearm. He looked upon the mass of living tissue breathing in his window, recognizing it as that of the Omnibeast, then flicked his gaze to the bound phallus. A premonition came unbidden to his mind, and the Oneirophage immediately acted upon it.

He redrew the Umbilicus and bifurcated its tip. With a surgical thrust, Morpheus Rex jabbed both prongs into the urethras of his penises, like a double catheter, and shoved the Umbilicus deep into his body. The twin tubes narrowed, slithered through his gonads, and inserted themselves in his testicles. A third tube grew from the first and branched into his lower abdomen, then used Morpheus Rex's urogenital labyrinth as a path to his digestive system. It emerged into his stomach, then shot up his esophagus and tunneled into his brain.

Morpheus Rex commanded the opposite end of the Umbilicus to lodge itself in the urethra of the captured phallus. The device elongated itself and plunged into the tip of the black mamba-like penis, then mazed through the Omnibeast's urogenital systems to its innards in the same manner with which it had snaked through those of Morpheus Rex. After reaching one of the bestial spaceships wombs, the tube divided, branching off in more than a hundred directions, impaling a myriad of organs and power points deep within the vessel's flesh.

Hissing concatenations of oneiromantic and ophidimantic incantations, and chanting ancient spells of sex magick, Morpheus Rex raped the Omnibeast through the conduit of the Umbilicus, ejaculating a continuous stream of sperm, venom, hormones, pheromones, engrams, wet dreams, and hypnotic suggestions into the bestial spaceship. Several minutes later, his testicles and mind spent, he recalled the Umbilicus. The Umbilicus retracted itself from the Omnibeast, and the chains released the spaceship's penis from their grip. The gigantic phallus snapped back into the Omnibeast like a pizzle and disappeared. Morpheus Rex pulled the Umbilicus from his own urethras, changed it back into a single, tiny straw, and reinserted it in the skin of his wrist.

The sex magick ritual complete, Morpheus Rex departed the bedchamber and headed for the weapons gallery. As he walked down the hall, he could see the tentacles, entrails, organs, genitals, and eyeballs of the Omnibeast pressed grotesquely against the skylights above, smashed up against the ceiling beneath the immense weight of the spaceship. All the way down the hall he could see nothing but flesh enwombing his palace, mixing its shadows with the rainbows of his walls in an unholy union of color and darkness.

With the hallway bathed in tenebrous gloom, Morpheus Rex failed to notice the one part of the ceiling that was even blacker than the rest. He passed underneath it, oblivious to the presence over his head. As he continued down the hall, Morpheus Rex failed to hear the silent feet of the Necrodelic as the Death Addict dropped down behind him. Not even the highly sensitive snake glands of the Dreaming Predator detected the approach of his stalker.

Chariah crept up behind Morpheus Rex and pulled him backwards into his lethal embrace, one arm around his throat, the other hooked under his armpit. The tattooed skin of Morpheus Rex's back stuck to the Necrodelic's burn wounds. He raked the Dreaming Predator's chest with his claws, then buried his talons in the bloody furrows left behind. With a single claw, Chariah slit Morpheus Rex's throat like an assassin. He drove his talons deeper into Morpheus Rex's chest, cutting through ribs and cartilage. Like a vampire, the Necrodelic jabbed his fangs into Morpheus Rex's neck and began drinking his dream-laden blood.

One razor talon grazed Morpheus Rex's heart and a second nicked his aorta. The other three pricked his sternum, solar plexus, and entrails. Morpheus Rex twisted against the fangs of the Necrodelic. The Necrodelic's claw sunk into the crevice between Morpheus Rex's atria and ventricles. Morpheus Rex was impaled by the circulatory system. His hands, however, were free. He pulled the Umbilicus from the skin of his forearm, raised it to his frothing rainbow lips, and blew. The straw immediately shot out in all directions, arching backwards over his head and embedding itself in the Necrodelic's face, skull, neck, and back, and then Morpheus Rex began to suck, imbibing dreams, spinal fluid, and blood. Some of the blood was his own, having already begun circulating through the flesh-smoker's veins and arteries. As Morpheus Rex suckled upon the Necrodelic's bodily fluids, the straws drove even deeper into the Death Addict's body, loosening his grip upon the Dreaming Predator. Morpheus Rex was able to disengage himself from the Necrodelic's clutches and, with the straws still stuck in the Necrodelic, used the Umbilicus to lift his nemesis into the air and bash him against the walls, floor, and ceiling. He continued to drink the Necrodelic's blood and dreams as he swung him around with the sorcerous straw apparatus. As he attempted to smash the Necrodelic into the ceiling yet again, the Necrodelic flipped over in mid-air and blocked the blow with his clawed feet. Using the ceiling for leverage, he launched himself at Morpheus Rex like a battering ram. He landed atop the Dreaming Predator and knocked him to the floor.

With a myriad of straws still sticking out of his flesh, the Necrodelic pummeled Morpheus Rex with ridgehand chops like neutronium hammers, breaking the bones in his face and opening cracks in his skull like those wrought by earthquakes on solid ground, branching out in all directions from the main faultline of his suture.

After beating Morpheus Rex into near-unconsciousness, the Necrodelic stood and loomed over the Dreaming Predator's prone body. He lodged the claws on his feet in Morpheus Rex's armpits. Taking a deep breath, Chariah placed his palms together and turned his hands down, all ten claws joined together to form a single black broadsword. Holding his hands at heart-level, as though in upside-down prayer, the Necrodelic prepared to deliver the deathblow, to drive the points of all ten claws through Morpheus Rex's throat at once and decapitate the Dreaming Predator.

Morpheus Rex watched the tips of the ten claws gleaming above him. They seemed to have welded together. The tips of the claws suddenly flashed and seemed to elongate, then fell like a two-fisted sword being driven into the ground. The Dreaming Predator bit down upon the mouthpiece of the Umbilicus and blew as hard as he could, emptying his lungs into the twisted straws. The air rushed through the tubes and struck the Necrodelic in the chest like a gale force wind, blasting him into the air. As Chariah careened down the corridor his flesh jerked free of the Umbilicus. After he landed, he continued to roll and bounce for several feet before coming to a stop in a pool of his own blood and a bed of his own broken bones, lying in the center of a pentagrammed foyer, a hanging jungle of severed limbs dangling above, seeming to reach for him as he lay there in semi-consciousness.

Morpheus Rex got back to his feet and ran the short distance down the hall to his weapons gallery. He flung open the door and grabbed his Prismsword, Spectrumhammer, and Rainbowspear from their racks. He turned and reentered the hallway, but the Necrodelic was gone.

Morpheus Rex raced to the foyer where the Necrodelic had lain in a broken heap. A crimson chiaroscuro etched the shape of the Necrodelic's body in blood upon the pentagram, but of the blood's master there was no sign. The hanging limbs overhead were rustling, as if they had just been shaken, or blown by a strong wind. As Morpheus Rex looked upwards, a torrent of blood fell over his face. He licked his lips and tasted it. It was the blood of the Omnibeast.

As Morpheus Rex continued to puzzle over the disappearance of the Necrodelic, a huge noise, like a meteorite striking the ground, rumbled and thundered and exploded, unleashing earthquakes and skyquakes alike, shaking and rattling the walls around Morpheus Rex and jolting Phantasmagorika all the way from its foundations to its highest parapets. Holding his Prismsword aloft, Morpheus Rex raced down the stairways, forgetting about the Necrodelic, wishing only to reach the first floor of his palace. The echoes of the earth-shaking sound were sonic booms, and the prism palace continued to vibrate and tremble as Morpheus Rex strode swiftly but cautiously through its entrance hall.

The Dreaming Predator emerged onto the drawbridge of his palace and turned his head to the south. There, in the distance, Morpheus Rex beheld the gargantuan source of the thunderous noise. As he did so, he instinctively raised the Prismsword a few inches higher and tightened his grip on the Spectrumhammer, for what he observed upon the Grystiawan plains could mean only one thing.

The war had begun.

14

The Constrictress soared through space atop a winged serpent. She held the large flying snake within her vast coils in much the same way she held prey or a lover, her emerald scales wrapped around its triple-arched body in continuous loops. She controlled the flight of her steed by applying different levels of pressure, constricting it more tightly to increase its speed and loosening her grip to slow it down, and steered it by means of an iron choke-collar, leashed to her forked tongue by a single length of chain. The Constrictress reared up over the creature's head like a striking cobra, her massive, elongated arms, which were like boa constrictors unto themselves, coiled at her sides, ready to unleash death in an instant.

Serpentikal flew at a slower speed behind his mistress and her fleet. The size of a palace, Serpentikal achieved the power of flight through his own psychic force. His elongated neck and gargantuan, hooded head protruded from the front of Serpentopolis, dragging his labyrinthine city/body him.

The front walls of Serpentopolis brimmed with cannons and crossbows. Parapets and living snakehead turrets encircled the perimeter of the city. Some were manned by spitting viper sentinels whose aim and range was such that they could expectorate a stream of venom into the eye of a creature a thousand miles away.

The fleet of winged serpents and their riders, led by the Constrictress, scouted ahead while Serpentikal slithered through the cosmos, darting in and out and all around the voids of space while protecting the walls and wake of Serpentopolis. Thousands of flying serpents soared and whirred around the battle fortress as the ophidian society traveled across the galaxy. As they reached the orbit of Tyterviax's seventh, outermost planet, a small, frozen ball of ice called Vrisstinoma, the Constrictress sent some of her fleet ahead and circled back to inform Serpentikal that they had entered the Tyterviax system. The great cobra hissed in acknowledgement, his tongue flickering like a bolt of lightning, and shifted the labyrinthine girth of his body towards the red planet. The Constrictress sped off again into the distance, swerving and hurtling at light-speed towards the crimson star of bleeding light, the suppurating sore upon the cosmos that was Tyterviax.

A few hours later, Serpentikal and his army appeared in the Grystiawan skies like a new moon. As preparations were made to land, the Constrictress came firing from unseen space to hover on her winged serpent, eye to eye with her colossal lover.

"My lord," she said, with jaws that hinged and unhinged as she spoke, "Spidratha is descending towards Grystiawa as we speak. My scouts estimate the spider armies will arrive within the next few hours."

"Excellent," hissed Serpentikal. "We shall wait for her here, in Grystiawa's orbit. When Spidropolis drops into the system, report to me again. We shall strike first, here, in space."

"Yes, my lord," the Constrictress said, then soared away again upon her winged snake.

Behind her, the large, hooded head of Serpentikal was relaxed and content, enjoying the calm moments before battle the way a cobra enjoys the silent time before its deadly strike, or a boa constrictor enjoys a slow, weeks-long digestion in the tranquil period following a worthy combat.

*

The white, shimmering hive of Spidropolis descended through the cosmos on a single, endless strand of cobweb, stretching into infinity above. Deep inside the spiderwebbed lair, Spidratha sat upon her throne of cadavers, surrounded by three giant tarantulas from her harem and a room full of arachnid strategists and overlords. The queen spoke to her entourage with a voice that scuttled through the air, a long series of the scrapings and rustlings which comprised the spider language.

"I have positioned the nest directly above Grystiawa. We are descending as we speak, and shall fall into the Tyterviax system within the hour. Once we drop through Grystiawa's atmosphere, we will be landing Spidropolis in whichever mountain range is nearest to Phantasmagorika at that time. I want the mountains immediately covered with webbing, and the spider army ready to march upon the prism palace at my command. And now," Spidratha said, waving three of her arms towards her attendant mates, "I wish to be alone with my husbands. I must prepare myself for the battle to come."

Upon these words, every spider except the three tarantulas departed the queen's chamber. Her two eight-legged sentinels spun a mass of solid webbing in the entrance tunnel, to give their mistress the solitude she required. Spidratha reached forward and grabbed the first tarantula with one hand. She placed him between her knees, whereupon he slowly crawled up her thighs and nestled in her crotch, looking as though he had become a prosthetic vagina for his queen. He pumped his seed into Spidratha's cloaca, his eight legs stiffening like those of a corpse. Spidratha screeched with orgasm, and as she reached her climax. she brought one of her arms down like a spear upon her lover, impaling him through the back. Her appendage bore straight through his body and tore through his abdomen, then traveled between her own thighs and into her vagina, crowding his turgid phallus. Moaning, Spidratha moved her arm up and down, masturbating with her appendage even as it impaled her mate. She dragged her spider arm through her lover and her own genitalia simultaneously, squealing as she reached a second climax. When she stopped, the spider in her lap had died, perished at the exact same moment when he, too, had reached a second mutual orgasm. Spidratha raised her bloody arm to her fanged mouth with her dead lover still skewered upon it, then began chewing his flesh off, rotating his dead body slowly, crunching each of his legs in her mandibles one by one, devouring him entirely, leaving her with blood dripping from her face and an arm tipped with vivid crimson.

Spidratha took another tarantula upon her lap. As the male furiously copulated with his queen, she pounded his back with her six arms, raining blows repeatedly until he lay torn and dripping, eventually hammering his entire body past her labia and into her vagina as she achieved orgasm. She reached an arm down and pushed him further through her cloaca, through her spinnerets, through her egg sac, through her intestines, and into her stomach, where he would be digested alive with the remnants of the first tarantula, which were just now beginning to rain down into the steaming acid lake from the long gullet above.

Spidratha's arm was sunk to the hilt in her vagina, thrust all the way up into her digestive system. When she removed it, it was coated in blood and wreathed with spiderwebs. With this appendage, she grabbed her final tarantula lover by his thin tufts of brown hair and held him up to her lips. She kissed him, and when she did so, he could taste the other two spiders who had copulated and perished before him in her hot breath.

Releasing her lips from her mate, Spidratha dragged him down her torso, between all eight of her breasts, running his body along the erogenous zone that was her red hourglass marking. She rubbed him up and down upon the crimson hourglass until she was in an orgasmic frenzy, then dropped the tarantula into her wet and waiting lap, where he spent his seed immediately into her vagina as she shivered with yet another orgasm.

After a few moments of heavy breathing, Spidratha lifted her final lover by the fur once again. This time, she did not devour her mate raw, but placed him in a boiling cauldron beside her throne. As the tarantula was cooked alive, Spidratha added several drugs to the concoction, drugs that would heighten her senses and make her more formidable and bellipotent during the imminent warfare. She brewed the drugs together with the tarantula, his moist, softened flesh absorbing the stimulants and analgesics into his body. She withdrew the limp, wet spider meat from the cauldron and sprinkled a powdered psychedelic seasoning upon it. The drug, known as spiderdust, was made from mosquitoes that had siphoned the blood of manticores, tapeworms that had infested the entrails of basilisks, maggots that had eaten from the corpse of a dragon, and those rarest of all flies that carried malaria, bubonic plague, gonorrhea, and psychosis simultaneously.

The powder was only effective upon arachnids, and was deadly to anything else. For Spidratha, it was an enlightening psychedelic which she ingested before every battle. With one gulp, she devoured the pulpish remnants of the tarantula, now pliant as mushrooms in her mouth. The drugs went to work instantaneously, and Spidratha was ready for genocide.

*

The Constrictress had caught two of the first winged spider scouts in her arms and was sadistically squeezing the life from their bodies, their blood dripping into the cold void of space while she laughed. She called to members of her fleet to report back to Serpentikal, then released the pulped arachnid corpses and flew off upon her winged serpent. Soon after, she had two more of the flying tarantulas in her grasp, their wings beating frantically as she crushed them with her rippling muscles. Others of the serpent fleet had engaged the flying spiders as well, and the sights and sounds of battle soon filled the Tyterviax system.

Winged tarantulas were being struck by cobra warriors, bitten by rattlesnake gladiators, and crushed by anaconda warlords. Serpents, likewise, were being strangled and hung by nooses of spiderweb, bitten by venomous fangs which paralyzed them or wracked them with intense burning agony, and spun in cocoons of cobwebs that incapacitated them and left them vulnerable to murder.

Spidropolis descended into sight, and Serpentopolis traveled toward it on a perpendicular path of destruction. Crossbows and cannons fired suicide serpents into the hive, where they impaled spiders with their very bodies, or latched onto them with their fangs as they collided, releasing their deadly venom. Others exploded upon contact, tearing rifts in the gossamer spun hull of Spidropolis and blowing huge holes in its webbing. Spidratha shot from an opening at the top of the hive and floated into battle. Empowered by spiderdust, she had the psychic capabilities of flight within the vacuum of outer space. She shot spiderwebs from all eight limbs, striking serpents and their steeds in the head, shattering their skulls and breaking their necks, leaving the riders to die with their brains dripping over their flying serpents, or career out of control on the corpses of their beasts until striking other objects in deadly collisions. Spidratha used spiderwebs like whips, lashing serpents in the face, clotheslining them off their steeds to fall into the atmosphere of Grystiawa and die upon striking the ground. The arachnid queen flailed away with all eight spiderlegs, her webbing so strong and fast that it could impale or decapitate her victims. The tide of battle quickly turned, and Spidratha made her way toward a confrontation with Serpentikal.

The Constrictress intercepted her on her winged serpent. Giant coils and spiderwebs met in the void of space. They pulled at one another in a deadly contest of strength, Spidratha trying to reel in the Constrictress and her steed. The Constrictress battled back, straining with the effort. She squeezed her winged serpent around the ribcage, spurring him to charge towards the giant spider demoness. The winged serpent bashed Spidratha with his head and gnawed at her eight breasts. The Constrictress tried to free her arms from the grip of the spiderweb, but the powerful unguents prevented her from doing so. She constricted her coils around her steed again, trying desperately to incite it to speeds and strengths capable of bursting Spidratha's web. Instead, she snapped the winged serpent's spine and crushed its heart, and it died in her grip.

Spidratha released another strand of spiderweb, this one wrapping itself around the throat of the Constrictress like a sticky noose. The titanic arachnid jerked the boa combatrix back and forth, trying to break her neck, then trying to strangle her to death. Finally, she unleashed yet another strand of spiderweb, ensnaring the Constrictress by the tail. With each spiderleg gathering up the slack webbing and stretching the Constrictress like a torture rack, Spidratha attempted to pull the Constrictress apart. The Constrictress' arms pulled out of their sockets with two loud pops, and her spine slowly bent until it was on the verge of snapping.

Just before Spidratha broke the Constrictress' back, Serpentikal flew in at light speed with a cobra strike, knocking Spidratha backwards, her eight legs thrashing as she spun out of control. He bit through his lover's bonds with his giant fangs, then took her inside his mouth for protection. Her dead steed plummeted to Grystiawa below.

Spidratha recovered, and this time she released a strand of spiderweb not only from all eight appendages, but from all eight breasts, her eight red eyes, her mouth, her vagina, and her cloaca. Each wrapped around Serpentikal's mighty neck, but Spidratha knew better than to try to strangle him. Instead, she chose to use his weight against him, and, using the twenty-seven strands of spiderweb like a giant harness, began dragging Serpentikal and his labyrinthine coils into the Grystiawa's atmosphere.

The mighty Serpentikal strained against the strength of Spidratha, but his forward momentum betrayed him. Once the Spidropolis dropped into view, Spidratha attached herself to her hive and pulled the giant cobra and his entire Serpentopolis down with her. They fell into the morning skies, ripping through crimson clouds, hurtling towards the maroon surface. Mountain ranges pricked into view, followed by the shimmer of Phantasmagorika. Soon, they could make out the little creatures in the badlands beneath, running to escape the fortress falling from the vermillion firmament.

Spidratha disengaged all twenty-seven ropes of spiderweb at the last possible moment, riding the exterior of her hive as it drifted towards the nearby mountain range. Behind her Serpentikal and his labyrinthine coils struck the ground with titanic force, setting off sonic booms and shaking the planet like a cataclysm.

She looked back to see Serpentikal spitting up blood, huge gobbets of plasma that formed scarlet oases wherever they fell upon the maroon wastelands. He was alive, but injured, with no doubt many a broken bone and bruised organ. More importantly, though, was the damage undoubtedly unleashed inside Serpentopolis, like that of a city beset with earthquakes, tornadoes, hurricanes, tsunamis, volcanoes, or any other number of natural disasters. Many of the warriors had assuredly been killed or injured during the impact with Grystiawa, their weapons broken, their supplies depleted by the fall, their snakepits caved-in and their homes demolished, burying corpses in debris and rubble.

As Spidropolis settled into the mountain range, Spidratha scuttled across the woven ziggurats, smiling to herself as she retreated into her lair. Already she and all spiderkind had the advantage in the battle against the Oneirophage and Serpentikal. Spidratha crawled into her hive with a satisfied look upon her grotesque visage. It was the exact same facial expression she had displayed in the postcoital moments following orgasm with her sacrificial mates, the malevolent duality of a demoness simultaneously satiated and starving.

15

Morpheus Rex stood side by side with the Constrictress in Serpentikal's mouth, watching Spidratha and her arachnid army approach. Arachnisauruses, giant hybrids of spider and dinosaur (the progeny of Serpentikal and Spidratha, spawned in a bygone age), standing fifty feet tall and measuring twice as long, came on hairy, pillared legs like those of wooly mammoths. Their mouths were filled with fangs the size of broadswords, and their tails ended in deadly morning stars the size of wrecking balls. They bore hundreds of sapient spiders upon their broad, saddled backs, arachnids that walked on two legs like Spidratha, carrying all sorts of weapons in their six arms, from swords and axes to maces and warhammers. Tarantulas the size of hellhounds ran like wolves alongside, their mandibles slavering with battle-lust. Six-legged spidaurs, arachnid centaurs, galloped across the plains with them, their right arms brandishing the same weapons as their kindred, their left hands holding either spears or quarterstaffs. Underfoot and often getting crushed were smaller spiders of every species in the universe. Behind them marched the long-legged Sentinel Spiders, Spidratha's personal guard, whose elongated appendages made them the swiftest of the arachnids. Their long, slender legs culminated in a central torso, from which arose the chest, arms, and head of a male spider warlord bearing either a two-handed broadsword, a crossbow, or a morning star and shield. In their midst, surrounded on all sides, were the elite Black Widow Amazons, which resembled lesser versions of Spidratha, with only two breasts. They bore weapons dipped in their own personal venom, from which one blow was usually fatal.

Above the Black Widow Amazons loomed Spidratha herself, looking like the mother of death. Her eight breasts were battle-swollen upon her chest, her hourglass so crimson it throbbed. She walked on her two lower limbs with a bow-legged gait, dripping acid and spiderwebs from her vagina. Her lower left arm held a net made of spiderweb; her central left arm wielded a whip made of spiderweb; and her upper left arm carried a large broadsword wrapped in barbed wire made from spiderweb. All three of her right arms grasped the long handle of an enormous pike, whose staff touched the ground when she walked. Its enlarged adamantium tip was a nightmare of spikes, eight evenly ringed rows protruding in all eight directions. A total of sixty-four spikes Spidratha held aloft on the war-pike, whose iron head was almost as big as her own.

As the forces of Spidratha poured from the mountains and swarmed across the badlands, Serpentikal's warriors charged forth to meet them. Erectly slithering cobra, adder, black mamba, cerastes, rattlesnake, boa constrictor, and anaconda demons comprised the front lines of the serpent army. Their chests were criss-crossed with bandoliers full of projectiles, their belts arrayed with daggers and swords in snakeskin sheaths and scabbards, and their hands gripped longswords, lances, hatchets, double swords, or morning stars. Gorgon and lamia gladiatrixes followed behind them, each carrying a shield in one hand and a weapon in the other. Nagas and naginis hurled spears and javelins. Entire artilleries mounted in rows on the backs of immense sidewinders were fired by snakemen and snakewomen. Suicide serpents were launched from the parapets of Serpentopolis and the wheeled battle turrets that rolled from the gateway in Serpentikal's abdomen. Above all, discussing strategy with Morpheus Rex and the Constrictress. He had assured the Dreaming Predator that his injuries from the fall were not severe, and would not factor in the outcome of the battle.

Tyterviax transformed into the head of Satan as the war began, looking on with eyes like glowing thromboses and a smile like a bloodless laceration. The serpents and spiders converged upon Phantasmagorika, which became the initial line of attack.

The snake warriors threw ouroboroses, living serpents biting their own tails, at the species of spider demons which possessed protruding heads. The serpents landed like lassoes around their necks, then proceeded to devour their own tails even further, thus strangling their victims. Several of the Sentinel Spiders were felled this way, as well as a few of the Black Widow Amazons. Serpentikal spat larger versions of these weapons, ouroboroses of anacondas, boa constrictors, and bushmasters, over the heads of arachnisauruses. The heads of the arachnid dinosaurs were so large that the anacondas and boa constrictors served as garrotes rather than nooses, squeezing their skulls tighter and tighter until their heads burst and their brains exploded all over the battlefield. Many warriors from both armies were killed and injured whenever the colossal, headless beasts toppled to the ground.

The arachnid forces cast nets of spiderweb, capturing serpent warriors and dragging them into their midst, where they gathered around them in circles and mauled them like enraged mobs, beating and slashing them to death. As the serpents infiltrated Spidratha's ranks, many of them sank into the desert as if quagmired in quicksand, thrashing and flailing as they tried to escape before being pulled down into hidden dens, where they were killed and eaten by trap-door spider demons. The well-concealed pits had been laid out all over the desert like land mines, and claimed the lives of many a serpent gladiator.

Morpheus Rex and the Constrictress joined the fray. The Constrictress broke bones in her twin coils, her elongated arms shooting out and wrapping around everything in sight. She even snapped the legs of arachnisauruses in her powerful appendages. Her muscles rippled beneath her shimmering snakeskin as she cracked spines, broke necks, and strangled victims in her coils. She used her boa constrictor arms like garrotes as well, exploding heads with even more force and velocity than the ouroboroses launched from Serpentikal's mouth.

The razor-sharp laser beams cast by the Prismsword and the Spectrumhammer cut the legs out from under the giant tarantulas and spidaurs, and cut the heads off of Sentinel Spiders and Black Widow Amazons. Morpheus Rex swung the two weapons masterfully, and every remaining arachnisaurus was dismembered before the spider forces even realized they were under assault from the lethal rays of colored light. Huge heads and entire flanks fell to either side as the arachnisauruses were dissected and sliced apart, left laying in the sands like gargantuan pieces of meat, raw and red and precisely carved.

Spidratha was trapping warriors by the hundreds in her battle net, like a titanic retiarius, dragging them back toward her body in a tangle of struggling arms, legs, and tails, then laying into them with her giant pike. Her whip lashed out at flying serpents that attempted to attack from the skies, killing them all with one blow. She made her way rapidly through the carnage to Phantasmagorika, cutting a path of death through the desert.

Serpentikal started forth immediately after Morpheus Rex and the Constrictress leapt from his mouth, dragging his immense body across the battlefield, rolling over the wounded, the crippled, and the dead, serpents and spiders alike, grinding their bones to dust beneath his girth. His powerful lungs blew sandstorms at the enemy, leaving many blinded and vulnerable, to die moments later. At times he would vomit cataracts of acidic venom onto the battlefield, disintegrating the enemy forces and many of his own soldiers as well. He dragged himself across the desert to Phantasmagorika, reaching the prism palace at the same time Spidratha did.

Atop Phantasmagorika, the Omnibeast lay in wait for anything foolish enough to fly near it. It defended itself from stray projectiles when necessary, but mostly seemed content to just observe the warfare below. The Overdragon, War Mantis, Scythetooth, and Darkworm were all spectators to the carnage, poised high above the action. As the remaining survivors of both parties regrouped, however, the Omnibeast became the center of attention. Chariah, the Death Addict, the Necrodelic, had emerged from the Omnibeast, riding high atop the head of a Hydratower, looming over the battlefield. He stood silently, his silhouette an imposing figure, his dark aura a palpable force. Everything stopped around him, the entire war came to a halt, as everyone gazed upwards upon the alpha demon.

Chariah's eyes were focused directly upon Serpentikal. The Hydratower bore him upwards until he was eye level with the First Serpent. Serpentikal attempted to hypnotize Chariah. Chariah, in turn, tried to abacinate Serpentikal with his lethal gaze. Serpentikal's eyes began to ooze. Cursing, he looked away from the Necrodelic, shaking blood from his eyes. He blinked away the ichor, then sought the eyes of the Necrodelic once again. Chariah held his hands out at his sides, palms up, claws splayed. Serpentikal tried to hypnotize him again. The Necrodelic was unreadable, his face expressionless, a mask of black patience. Serpentikal's eyes began to burn in their sockets. Wisps of smoke trailed from the corners of his eyelids.

The First Serpent became enraged. In less than a nanosecond, he unleashed his cobra strike. His neck extended, his humongous head reared up, and his face hurtled towards the Necrodelic at the speed of light, his fangs bared to impale the little demon where he stood. Even faster than Serpentikal, the Necrodelic leaped into the air, out from the Omnibeast in a deadly arch across the desert skies, flying at the speed of thought, the incomprehensible, supraluminal speed of necrodelic thought, the speed of pure, enlightened evil. He joined all ten of his claws to form one giant black Hellsword. As he soared through the air, he brought the Hellsword back over his shoulders, then swung it full strength at Serpentikal's throat. For one brief moment his claws sorcerously elongated until each extended well over a hundred feet in length, soldered together as surely as if they were one colossal adamantium blade tempered in the forges of Gehenna. While amplified, the conjoined claws passed through Serpentikal's colossal neck, leaving behind a wound so straight and thin, so precise and surgical, that for several seconds it barely even bled. As Chariah leapt over Serpentopolis, blood trailing from his whistling claws as they returned to their normal size, the head of Serpentikal began to slip and slide. For one eternal instant his head hovered on a razor's edge of blood, precariously balanced on a narrow laceration that seemed no wider than a vein or artery, and then, as if in a dream, slowly began to fall. The blood-stopping screams of the Constrictress tore the air. The severed head of Serpentikal toppled over and crashed into Serpentopolis, slaying hundreds of snake demons and crushing pieces of his own labyrinthine body.

Behind Serpentikal's death-spasming coils, his broken labyrinth, his ruined civilization, his fallen society, Chariah dropped as silently as an assassin. For now, the Necrodelic had disappeared, but only in the eyes of the onlookers, for his image had been indelibly burned into their brains and their souls, and no matter where he was, or what they were doing, they still saw him, and would continue to see him, eternally, mercilessly, a living nightmare, even after they had died and their spirits were being tortured in Hell.

The Constrictress lay sobbing by Serpentikal's head, bent over with grief, her coils slack with despair. Around her, all of the serpent demons were retreating back into Serpentopolis. Morpheus Rex continued the fight on his own, beating giant tarantulas into the ground, carving up spidaurs, and decimating everything else until only he and Spidratha remained on the battlefield.

Spidratha cast her net at Morpheus Rex. It fell heavily around him, as solid as adamantium even though it was made from spiderweb. She assaulted him with her giant whip, opening gaping wounds where she could catch exposed flesh in the mesh of the battle-net. She drew Morpheus Rex to her, dragging him across the corpse-strewn ground.

The Dreaming Predator fought his way free of the battle-net, only to be struck forcefully in the side by the full brunt of the spiked war-pike. Spidratha aimed her barbed wire-wrapped broadsword at his head. He blocked it with his Prismsword, then swung his Spectrumhammer in an uppercut towards her crotch, bludgeoning her vagina and thorax. She jabbed her pike at him as he ran between her legs, then caught him with a double-jointed backhanded blow of her blade while he simultaneously thrust the Prismsword into her back. The barbed wire caught at Morpheus Rex's flesh even as the blade tore into his skull. When Spidratha swung the blade back, the barbed wire ripped out pieces of Morpheus Rex's skin and hair. Spidratha turned, and swung her pike in a high overhanded arc. Morpheus Rex again darted between her legs, but this time her cloaca released a mass of sticky spiderweb, catching him completely within its viscous clutches. He writhed on the sand like an invertebrate, unable to get to his feet with the web clinging to every part of his body, wrapping him in a cocoon of bondage.

Spidratha poked her pike into the net, lifting the spiderweb and her prey by the crossed mesh of her secretions. Morpheus Rex was forced into a fetal position by the tight clutches of webbing, as though being compressed in a scavenger's daughter. Spidratha raised him to her crotch and masturbated with her captured prey, shoving his entire body between her labia and in and out of her womb. Morpheus Rex fought the entire time, sinking fangs full of venom into her vaginal walls, severing one of her clitorises with an awkward swipe of his Prismsword, clawing at her insides with his long fingernails and then driving the Umbilicus into her organs as well. The pain only seemed to heighten her sexual enjoyment, and Spidratha began to tremble with mighty, bloody orgasms, shuddering with sexual explosions.

She dragged the netted Morpheus Rex dripping from her womb and raised him, spiderwebs, weapons, and all, to her mandibles. Her mouth opened to devour him, the same way she devoured all her lovers, but something caught her eyes and glassy ommatidia, and she hesitated. In the distance, Chariah emerged from the Serpentopolis, walking slowly from the open gateway in the abdomen of the decapitated snake lord, holding the Constrictress over his head. As Spidratha watched, the Necrodelic began to bend and twist the ophidian virago in his hands, breaking her arms and snapping her spine.

"You have served me well, demon," spake Spidratha. "Together we have conquered the serpents."

Chariah did not respond, but continued folding the still-living Constrictress, her bones breaking loudly, her vertebrae exploding.

"I will take you for my lover, Necrodelic."

Violently wrenching the body of the Constrictress into sharply pointed angles, splintering her skeleton into several pieces, the Necrodelic replied, "And devour me, like all the rest."

"Thee I shall spare. We will rule the universe together. As soulmates, we will become the Jh'a'vyraa. I will sacrifice anything to possess you. I will give you sexual pleasures undreamt of. I will give you anything you desire, anything in the entire universe. Tell me, sweet demonling, what it is that you desire?"

Chariah manipulated the decimated body of the Constrictress like an invertebrate in his fists, grasping her by the head and twisting her one last time. He slowly held the Constrictress up to his face with both hands. He had sculpted her into a living pentagram. Her eyes were wild with agony and necrophobia, knowing her demise was imminent.

"Fire," Chariah finally replied, blowing a jetstream of flames through the living pentagram of the Constrictress, unleashing a tsunami of fire the likes of which had never been seen beyond Hell. Amplified by the sorcery of the living pentagram, the inferno reached thousands of feet into the skies and miles into the distance. It tore through Spidratha, blowing her eight legs asunder, disintegrating her abdomen and thorax, lifting her head high into the air on a giant crest of flames where it all at once blackened, shriveled, and exploded. Her dying shriek pierced the entire planet, was heard in distant solar systems, and would continue to echo until the end of the universe in certain black holes.

Chariah cast the deformed, scorched corpse of the Constrictress to the ground. For a moment he reveled in the familiar euphoria of pyromania and the newfound ecstasy of betrayal. He then ran back toward Phantasmagorika and his spaceship perched thereon, yelling "Drakhus" as he did so, for there was little time before the Hell he had unleashed would incinerate and then detonate the entire planet. Already the mountain ranges in the near distance had been leveled. The long tongue of the Overdragon reached down and bore its master up.

As the Omnibeast squirmed and prepared to launch itself into space, Morpheus Rex slowly crawled out of the Darkprism. The sable pendant had fallen to the ground as Spidratha was blown apart, and the Dreaming Predator had hidden himself within its depths a mere instant before. The flames of Hellfire were still raging, a gargantuan tsunami that would circumnavigate the entire planet within minutes. He drenched himself in his own venom to protect himself from the roiling fire and its blistering heat, then did his best to extinguish the flames around him by blowing through the Umbilicus, cutting himself a safe path to Phantasmagorika. He ran across the drawbridge and through the heliotropic gates, hoping the breeding spells he had cast upon both Phantasmagorika and the Omnibeast had worked.

Morpheus Rex tore through the palace, making his way towards its nexus. If the central chamber of Phantasmagorika had metamorphosed into a cockpit, he would survive. If it had not, he would perish in Hellfire. Throwing open the door, Morpheus Rex stepped into the room. There was an oracle on the ceiling. There was a bed upon the floor. And there were living serpents reaching from the ceiling, walls, and floor. His sorcery had been successful. The Omnibeast had impregnated and fertilized the prism palace. Phantasmagorika was pupating, and would soon evolve into a living, saurian spaceship.

He gazed into the oracle on the ceiling and watched the tsunamis of fire overwhelm the twilit Grystiawan horizons, cresting and falling and rising again, sending billowing cumulus smoke all the way into outer space. As he watched Tyterviax set for the final time, he transformed once again into the Oneirophage. The serpents in the cockpit latched onto his eyes, mouth, ear slits, phalluses, solar plexus, and third eye, as well as the horned devil head tattoos on his shoulders and the hourglass tattoo on his left palm. The umbilical serpents stretched through the entire palace, and through them the Oneirophage controlled the rudimentary space vessel. Green tentacles emerged from the palace rooftops and wriggled into the underbelly of the Omnibeast like gargantuan larvae, inextricably tangling with the spaceship's Arachniotics, entrails, and genitalia in serpentine knots, forcing the vessel to carry Phantasmagorika into space along with it. After a brief hesitation, during which the Necrodelic had, undoubtedly, assessed the situation and realized he had no alternative, the Omnibeast launched into the atmosphere, lifting Phantasmagorika from its chasm and into the air. Gargantuan, newborn butterfly wings emerged from the four corners of the prism palace, helping carry the castle into the sky.

Peering down the gullets of the serpents attached to his eyes, his dream-vision allowing him to see around curves and corners and through the kaleidoscopic eyes, mouths, and vaginas forming in the outer walls of the palace, the Oneirophage gazed upon the blazing battlefield and the ravages of the final spider-serpent war. Below the rising palace lay the dead bodies of Serpentikal and the Constrictress. Though the maze city needed some reparation, the labyrinthine coils of Serpentikal were largely intact, while Serpentikal's head had been cleanly severed and could easily be reattached and reanimated as a figurehead for the new spaceship.

He held the Darkprism to the mouth of one of the umbilical snakes. The black hole pendant sent its magic through the serpent and formed a wormhole just beyond Phantasmagorika's walls. Through this wormhole it sucked Serpentikal-labyrinth, city, snake demons and all-into its infinite depths. Morpheus Rex directed the spacetime portal to absorb the singed, broken, pentagram-twisted corpse of the fallen Constrictress as well. She had appeared in several of his wet dreams in the past, sexual fantasies he would like to transform into realities, and he was not averse to necrophilia.

As Phantasmagorika lifted into space, the Oneirophage watched the Hellfire consume Grystiawa below. The flaming planet now resembled a small star. An instant later it exploded. As the blazing debris blasted through space, the red lights of Tyterviax turned inwards, and the sun he had watched rise and set his entire life collapsed into a black hole. The Oneirophage lay still for several minutes, in silent meditation, and then a premonition began forming in his mind. As it unfolded, the Oneirophage observed its every detail, then slipped into the astral plane to pursue already-dead prey.

16

The freshly murdered spider queen crawled towards Hell along her silver cord, and the dreaming slayer serpent followed. Spidratha had abandoned her upright, bow-legged gate to crawl through the astral plane on all eight legs like a common spider, humiliated, defeated, and beaten into submission. The Oneirophage, seeking one last domination, one final degradation of the spider queen before her soul descended to Hell, launched his astral body at her spirit, intercepting her with such force that it sent them both ricocheting across entire galaxies. The violent collision broke three of Spidratha's legs and left them dangling at grotesque angles, whipping about as they sped through the voids, but never breaking off. A fourth leg impaled the Oneirophage through the palm, and its lower half twitched where it emerged in a crimson spray on the back of his hand. At the moment the Oneirophage had made contact, Spidratha had sunk her pincers into his guts, where one had broken off and lay entrenched in a coil of entrails. The Oneirophage, meanwhile, grabbed Spidratha by the head with one hand, driving his thumb through several of her ommatidia and shattering them like fragile obsidian, to fall in ebony shards through the cosmos below. He hooked his thumb into the pulp of her brain, digging out a fingerhold in the bleeding tissue. Gripping Spidratha thusly from the inside, and by the dark fur of her neck and shoulders on the outside, the Oneirophage rode beneath her, dominating her as though she were his submissive demonsteed. With her breasts striking him in the face as they swung pendulously back and forth, and her red hourglass filling his kaleidoscopic vision, the Oneirophage rode Spidratha through the cosmos like some mutant offspring or giant parasite, hanging onto her underbelly as she scuttled through the astral plane, trailing free-floating ribbons of blood in her wake.

Struggling for position, the Oneirophage mounted Spidratha in a grotesque upside-down parody of bestial rape, even as the spider demoness released her venom into his carotid artery. The poison only served to heighten the Oneirophage's dream-drugged state, to further enhance his consciousness and his oneiromantic powers. With the crimson of blood and the clear runnels of venom dripping from their entangled, flying bondage, the Oneirophage and Spidratha hurtled through the universe. They passed through an entire solar system as the Oneirophage swung his Prismsword, leaving behind it a rainbow millions of miles long. Its edge passed through Spidratha's silver cord of spiderweb, severing their connection to the fabric of space and time and sending them spinning in chaotic revolutions through the atmosphere of a planet's astral body.

They struggled for position as they fell, each gaining the upper position three times as they hurtled downwards. Spidratha's legs snapped off where they had been fractured, and fell alongside them in the streaming cloud of blood and gore which accompanied their plummeting combat. As they neared the planet's surface, gravity pulling them in like some greedy, titanic necrophage, Spidratha assumed the dominant position for the fourth time, seeking now to trap the Oneirophage against her hairy, eight-breasted, red-hourglassed underbelly. Her remaining pincer had the Oneirophage impaled through the roof of his mouth, and did not relent even as his three forked tongues shattered her remaining eyes. The Oneirophage thrashed in

Spidratha's grip as the ground drew ever closer. Spidratha used her remaining legs to impale him through his lower back, two of them simultaneously skewering his kidneys as well, her legs passing through his body and then into her own, holding him fast as they plummeted. As the Oneirophage writhed against his captor, he managed to free his sword hand. He swung the Prismsword at the giant spider, slashing her entire left flank apart, but was unable to loosen her grasp or reverse his position. With his prismatic eyes, he looked down. They were within seconds of striking the planet. With one last muscle-tearing wrench of his arm, he brought the Prismsword around his back and plunged it beneath his own ribs. A second later, the Oneirophage and the spider hit the pulverizing ground of the planet.

The Prismsword impaled the Oneirophage through the back. It had been positioned along his right side to miss his spine, and more importantly, his heart. The Prismsword did not, however, miss the heart of Spidratha. As chitinous body armor shattered and fell like breaking glass around them, the Prismsword clove directly through the center of the demoness's heart. Blood exploded. Spidratha slid down the razor edges of the blade at light speed, severing the breast over her heart and further lengthening her own wound as the sword widened toward its hilt. As her three severed legs fell to the ground with musical tinkling sounds beside them, Spidratha heaved, vomiting blood and venom into the Oneirophage's face, and discharged her remaining coils of spiderweb in one gigantic, bloodstained, gore-strewn, astral labyrinth, the Path of Spiderwebs Never Spun.

The Oneirophage's battered body was trapped beneath the tonnage of Spidratha, but more importantly, she was impaled upon his Prismsword, paralyzed, trapped, as helpless as her myriad victims had been within her webs over the eons, as subjugated as all the former lovers she had raped and then devoured. The Oneirophage squirmed painfully beneath his defeated prey. His right arm, still clutching the hilt of the Prismsword, was pinned behind his back. His elbow was shattered, and jagged bones were ripping through his flesh and into the dirt below. His ribs were broken, his skull split, his pelvis pulverized. He still had a spider leg stuck through his left hand like a spear, and a pincer buried somewhere in his chaotically disarranged guts. The other pincer had severed his carotid artery upon impact, which now spurted blood in crimson arches up to ten feet into the distance. The vomited venom was eating his face like acid, and he was blinded with eye sockets full of spider blood.

Empowered by this world of astral agony, for pain was another one of his lairs, the Oneirophage spoke a single, mellifluous word of sorcery. At his call, the Umbilicus came alive in his hands, forming labyrinths of tubes that stuck out in all directions around his body, cauterizing his lacerations and mending his bones. The Oneirophage then used it like a straw to drink the dreams from Spidratha's ruined head and gaping, dripping wounds, renewing his strength and repairing his broken body with the sorcery of the psychedelic dreams on which he depended. Like a vampire, he imbibed life for himself from the death of his victim. Within minutes, the Oneirophage was once again at full power. Then, the ritual began.

The Oneirophage bade the Umbilicus to metamorphose again. It changed to a giant needle in his hand. Their bodies still impaled together by the Prismsword, the Oneirophage plunged the Umbilicus into Spidratha's red hourglass marking, sucking it from her flesh as though removing it with a scalpel. The Oneirophage then plunged the red-tipped needle into his left, spider-tattooed hand. The large needle hummed and vibrated, and when he removed it the Oneirophage had another crimson hourglass tattooed upon his palm, this one simultaneously brighter and darker than the first, more vibrant and more real.

He penetrated the remains of Spidratha's astral body again, loading the needle with her blood, brains, venom, hormones, webbing, and dreams, and then imbuing his left hand with her bodily fluids and substances. Partaking of Spidratha until his entire left hand was midnight black, until his left hand bore pincers and urticated fur, venomous fangs and a spider-web producing abdomen, the Oneirophage transformed his left hand into a living black widow. Where before he had borne a lifeless tattoo, he now adorned a wriggling, venomous, conscious familiar, a sentient spider gauntlet. The Oneirophage used the Umbilicus to gather up what remained of Spidratha's eyes, and tattooed them upon his knuckles. The black widow writhed and wriggled at the end of his arm as the power of sight was bestowed upon it. The Dreaming Predator gathered up the trio of severed legs that had fallen around them, severing and then inserting their tips into the flesh upon the sides of his hand like thin daggers. Within seconds, they twitched with renewed vigor, renewed life. Now, with his new eight-fingered hand, he broke the tips off of Spidratha's remaining five appendages, and one by one, plunged his fingers into their wet, dripping, scarlet ends, adorning them like a gruesome glove.

Once joined to his flesh and having absorbed his fingers within them, the spider legs came to life again, and one by one, the five fingers of his left hand became giant, hairy, living, creeping appendages, with barbed hairs like those of a tarantula. Along with the other three, they formed the eight legs of the spider, completing the possession ritual.

Simultaneously, on the physical plane, while the Oneirophage slumbered, his left hand grew three extra fingers, which then blackened and transformed into spider legs. His other fingers parted in the middle of his hand, to form the exact replica of a black widow. Upon his palm, a red hourglass of blood slowly seeped through the black flesh, usurping the hourglass tattoo which had previously adorned it. While the Oneirophage slumbered, his left hand metamorphosed into a living spider and began crawling up and down his side, along his chest, across his face and over his genitals, its mandibles clicking, dripping venom upon its somnolent master.

Back in the astral dimension, as he lay back against the bloodstained rocks of the sacrificial grounds, the Oneirophage pulled the Prismsword loose from Spidratha, at long last releasing her from her final incarnation. Her organs spilled from her wound as the Oneirophage withdrew the blade. No more than a blind, legless, bloody piece of meat, she wriggled and squirmed her way to Hell like a grub, denigrated and mutilated, to take her place in the eternal netherlife.

*

The Oneirophage awoke in his bedchamber several hours later, his physical body having somnambulated through Phantasmagorika during his astral projection.. Flexing his new spider hand, the Oneirophage sat up. He released a pile of mutilated, dead, and half-dead arachnids from the Darkprism, then feasted upon a breakfast of spiderflesh, spider organs, and spider dreams. The organs still stuck to the walls and ceiling were pulsating, coming back to life as Phantasmagorika continued to evolve. He watched them glisten and beat and quiver as he drugged himself.

An hour later, he sipped upon a concoction of blood and venom from a goblet made out of prism and walked through the changing corridors of Phantasmagorika. The prism palace continued transforming into a living spaceship around him, larvating, pupating, and incubating; adapting, evolving, and mutating; rainbow cells reproducing by mitosis and spreading like cancer. Still attached to the Omnibeast like a gargantuan, intergalactic remora, Phantasmagorika rode the bestial spaceship through the cosmos, a leviathan parasite in a behemoth host.

Outside the metamorphosing castle, the stars and planets glittered like runes and hieroglyphics that had been etched upon the cosmos, and galaxies stretched like entire necronomicons written on palimpsests of spacetime. Mandalic nebulae gleamed in hypnotic, enlightening patterns. The Oneirophage gazed upon all this through the stained-glass windows of Phantasmagorika, which were now simultaneously opaque and diaphanous, and as he slowly toured his living palace, he realized that he would always travel the cosmos as the nocturnal Oneirophage, and never as the diurnal Morpheus Rex, for space was a form of night, and night was a form of space.

He made his way into his entrance hall and bade his drawbridge lower itself. Stepping out into the chill of space, he lifted the Darkprism and whispered a spell. Serpentikal and the entire Serpentopolis shot out of the black hole pendant and immediately bonded to the prism palace. Leaving his new figurehead behind, the Oneirophage returned to his bedchamber and refilled his prism goblet. Lounging on his bed, he sipped the intoxicating melange of blood and spider venom, and stargazed through the regrown, stained glass, diaphanous/opaque window on the wall to his right. He was so close to becoming the Jh'a'vyraa that he could feel it in his blood, coursing through his veins like the sweet, poisonous wine he imbibed. With every dream and every death the Jh'a'vyraa grew nearer, so near that the Oneirophage felt he could reach out and tattoo his body with moksha, drink nirvana through the Umbilicus, and make love to the end of time itself.

17

Chariah meditated while smoking a thousand spiders at once. True to her word, Spidratha had bestowed ten hecatombs of her devotees upon the Necrodelic, leaving them inside the Omnibeast in a giant net of spiderweb. Chariah had emptied the entire chiliad into the dungeon above his meditation chamber, then descended to the level below, entered his private lair, and released the spiders into the Bloodbong. The frantic arachnids thrashed around, climbing over one another, trying to scale the walls inside and leaving pieces of their flesh stuck to the heated glass. The spider millitomb was a menagerie of the arachnid warrior species Chariah had witnessed in the spider-serpent war. Tarantulas, black widows, violin spiders, recluse spiders, trap-door spiders, funnel-web spiders, Spidaurs, Sentinels, and Black Widow Amazons all floated within the giant heart of the Bloodbong.

Chariah assumed the black lotus position and parted his lips. The mouthpiece of his pipe obediently inserted itself between his fangs, and the Necrodelic began smoking spiderflesh. He watched with slowly increasing levels of hypnosis as the arachnids treaded blood with their eightfold, desperately scurrying legs. Many drowned in the depths of boiling plasma, trapped beneath their brethren. Spider legs were being amputated by the hundreds, ripped from their sockets by the powerful inhalations of the Necrodelic. Many of them floated into the labyrinthine tubes of the Bloodbong, making their way into smaller bubbling chambers or towering demonic totem poles and getting stuck in narrow corridors and shafts, where they slowly disintegrated. Hourglasses were scorched black between the breasts of the Black Widow Amazons, stripping the elite spiders of their rank and battle-prowess.

For over an hour, the Necrodelic smoked the ten hecatombs of spiderflesh, drifting deeper and deeper into a psychedelic trance. He meditated upon the nature of spiders, gaining several of their powers as he ingested their very essence. He reveled in the euphoric effects of betrayal, the intoxicating new evil which he had discovered that day, whose effects now saturated his floating heart with a surge of black adrenaline, until it felt as though his heart had flown free of his chest and immersed itself within the inky waters of the river Styx, to be further demonized by the inherent evils within those cursed currents. His soul had been stained with newfound sins, and had grown darker and heavier than ever before, collapsing in upon itself like a black hole. Rushes of pure power shot through his shuddering flesh as he grew more and more drugged by the psychedelic stimulants of betrayal. Blood-soaked reveries of the Grystiawan aceldama played themselves over and over in his mind, like the music of a never-ending song. Vivid flashbacks of the apocalyptic battle assailed all five of his physical senses at once, as well as wreaking hallucinatory havoc upon his powers of echolocation and other psychic and esoteric modes of perception, then weaving them all together in strange and mind-blowing synesthesias. As the final burnt pieces and organs of the sacrificial arachnids swirled in crimson whirlpools, sinking and rising on exploding bubbles, Chariah detached from his own flesh and descended into the astral plane on his silver cord, like a spider lowering itself on a strand of webbing.

Mother Chaos embraced her dangling demon lover, kissing him while the souls of dead spiders fell around them like snowflakes.

"The Oneirophage lives, my mistress," said the Necrodelic. "I have seen it in my visions; sensed it as I smoked the spiderflesh."

"...yes, my love...it was always destined to be so...you two shall meet again...in proximal futures...adjacent destinies...he is your soulmate, my child...a dark soulmate...but a soulmate nonetheless...your fates are intertwined...your paths run parallel and form many helices...but for now, you must focus on something else...come with me, my child...I have much to show you..."

Mother Chaos' vagina tightened like an iris around the pupil of her womb, allowing Chariah to look upon her inner oracles and gaze upon the universe. A crimson eyeball grew in the tip of his penis. He saw the Oneirophage, stalking the soul of Spidratha far below them, near the bottom of the universe. He watched as the Oneirophage severed her legs and defeated her astrosome, then watched her organs spill from the wound in her chest. He watched Spidratha fall to Hell in pieces, each amputated limb and dislodged organ descending upon its own silver strand, like a mobile of severed body parts, followed by her wriggling torso and blinded head.

Chariah looked on stoically, his phallic eyeball blinking as it absorbed strange realities with its sorcerous gaze. As he thrust into Mother Chaos' oracle, opening several new worlds to his sexual vision, he asked, "Who is to be my next victim?"

Mother Chaos' oracular womb tightened around the Necrodelic's third eye phallus, revealing to him a green planet in a distant galaxy.

" ...you will seek out the Tantradox...upon the garden planet of Elasvai...the mission of genocide continues...megadeaths grow as fast and as furious as Hellfire...go now, my dark disciple...my incarnate prophecy...go, and show the Tantradox that you are the Messiah of Death..."

Chariah's eyeballed phallus came to orgasm in Mother Chaos' oracle, its single eyelid, like the eyelids of his face, fluttering with light speed rapid eye movements that revealed several psychic visions every nanosecond, flashing through his brain while he wept sperm, and then Mother Chaos' eye sockets became vaginas, and the Necrodelic's eyes became penises, making love to her skull and ejaculating black sperm and teardrops of darkest ink into her brain. The Dark Orgasm came and obliterated all else. The crimson eyeball on the Necrodelic's phallus slowly closed with sleep, and then Chariah was ascending the long strand of his silver cord like a spider, climbing upwards toward the physical plane, climbing upwards into his body, to set the Omnibeast on a direct course with the garden planet of Elasvai.

18

The Omnibeast's living dungeons crept through the prism palace of Phantasmagorika like sentient abysses, dripping from the ceilings like drops of liquid nothingness, absorbing entire chambers like black holes, forcing themselves like serpents of nullity through the tunnels and corridors. Like the giant segmented tentacle of some chthonic beast, the dungeons wound and flowed and crawled and grew throughout the glimmering castle, haunting its hallways like a parasite, dragging its shadows behind it, a slow rapist, an expanding womb, a proactive prison seeking out its own captive. The pulsating dungeons conquered passage after passage, doorway after doorway, filling the labyrinths like the river Styx, as if the Stygian floodgates in Hell had been opened to drown Phantasmagorika in atramentous deathwater. The dungeons quivered, the dungeons slithered, the dungeons stalked in utter silence until they surrounded the cockpit of the Oneirophage's pupating spaceship, where the dream-eater lay in a hypnogogic state. Adamantium bars lowered like a hexagonal portcullis and the iron clang of gateways shutting resonated through the chamber, trapping the Oneirophage like an animal in a cage. With the Oneirophage sleeping in the six-sided prison cell, the living dungeons withdrew to the belly of the Omnibeast with their prey in tow, slipping back through the mazes as though on a tether of intestine or umbilical cord, pulled and tugged by unseen forces to some higher surface beyond.

*

The Oneirophage lay imprisoned in the Necrodelic's dungeons, having been captured by the Death Addict's sorceries and the strange machinations of the Omnibeast, the dual powers of necromancer and bestial spaceship combined. At first believing himself in the throes of nightmare, the Oneirophage gradually awakened from his slumber. He quickly realized he no longer lay in the cockpit of Phantasmagorika, nor his bedchamber, nor any part of his prism palace/spaceship whatsoever.

Consciousness slowly crept back into his flesh like maggots, then came alive with flies of pain. His wounds were still fresh and bleeding; he could smell them in the fetid air as he awoke. The living black widow of his left hand was crawling back and forth in a panic, nearly dislocating his shoulder as it dragged his limp arm behind it. Surrounded by pitch-black, absolute darkness, the Oneirophage relied upon his sense of touch and his viper's pits to synthesize reality. He explored the hot, pulpy, living walls of the cell and the unforgiving adamantium bars that criss-crossed them. The cell felt like a behemoth sex slave in armored lingerie, flesh bulging from beneath its iron restraints and bondage devices. It was as though he had been locked in a cage which had then been swallowed by a gargantuan black monstrosity with a sensory deprivation chamber for a stomach, or a prison cell that a gargantuan black dominatrix with a sensory deprivation chamber for a womb had masturbated with until it was lodged deep inside her and she found that she could not pull it back out. There seemed to be no entrance or exit in the fleshy walls, just a continuous hexagonal portcullis that also covered the ceiling and floor. He would have to make his own door.

The Oneirophage drew the Umbilicus from his forearm. Fumbling through the darkness, the Oneirophage pressed the Umbilicus against a pulsing slab of wall and sucked at the visceral substance. The wall shivered and dripped blood onto the iron bars below. The Oneirophage suckled and drank and chewed and devoured an entire square of flesh from iron boundary to iron boundary, opening a bleeding window into the spaceship's interior and peering down the crimson and black hallways of the Omnibeast's dungeons. The adamantium remained undaunted by the straw, nor was it affected by the physical blows of the Oneirophage, forcing the serpent to direct his attention upon the living organic tissue of the walls behind the iron mesh, cannibalizing the bestial spaceship from within, drinking its blood, feasting upon its flesh, and drugging himself with its dreams.

The taste of the Necrodelic's spaceship was like candy death, candy made from corpses' organs, freshly excised and coated with sugar and drugs, or embalmed with wine-soaked bandages and fermented for centuries in perfumed canopic jars. The gustatory sensations invigorated the Oneirophage. As he sucked his escape route through the visceral walls, he also sucked forth the dreams of the bestial spaceship's bowels, dreams of Satanic sodomy and erotic evisceration. The spaceship itself responded to the strange visions with a gentle shudder.

His blood began to coagulate as he invigorated himself with raw meat and stolen dreams, his wounds knitting themselves back together, his strength returning to his muscles and mind. When he had regained his power, he hissed and sprayed a thick mist of green, acidic venom which dissolved the adamantium bars. The cage melted and warped until it was malleable enough to resculpt and climb through. The flesh around it dissolved wherever the serpent venom dripped, recoiling into nothingness with only a wisp of oily steam to mark its passing. The Oneirophage slithered through the escape route and into a corridor that led him through the dungeons and guts of the spaceship. Below his crawling belly, as his ridged scales wriggled along the organic floor, his engorged consciousness sensed the cosmos passing beneath him, passing at the speed of thought. He could feel the flight of the Omnibeast in his glands as well, the interstellar winds of space travel throbbing in the pits above his fangs.

Tapping into the nervous system of the Omnibeast with the Umbilicus and overriding its reflexes, the Oneirophage commanded several of the dungeon cells to open themselves. As the valvelike passages irised and gaped, the Oneirophage abducted the Necrodelic's prisoners. He greedily drank their dreams, leaving their lifeless husks and hollow skulls behind in the womblike cages, then absorbed several others with his Darkprism, to devour and ravish later. The rest he bound in shackles torn from the dungeon walls. The excised shackles left bloody holes behind, like those left by amputated limbs or castrated genitalia. The Oneirophage forced the chained prisoners along in a single line, driving them through the maze of the bestial spaceship.

With revenge on his forked tongue, Hell in his dilated eyes, and dreams of becoming the Jh'a'vyraa spinning in his head, the Oneirophage hunted for the Necrodelic. He cared not where the pathways led. He slithered through round corridors and explored the Necrodelic's lair, observing the flesh-smoker's demonium and possessions so that he might better know how to annihilate him.

The living walls radiated a natural black phosphorescence, a raven bioluminescence which provided light inside the spaceship. Umbilical cords were ubiquitous and served a myriad of purposes. Several levels of dungeons and oubliettes, sometimes bi-level and sometimes tri-level, took up much of the lower spaceship, many of them uninhabited, containing chains and shackles and nothing else. He could sense sentient sewage systems, with both mechanical and living organs, in the levels beneath him. Beyond the dungeons were empty, high-ceilinged chambers with black ribcages supporting their lofty domes.

Gothic architecture adorned doorways, gates, and portcullises that led to unfurnished, unused, and uninhabited womb-chambers. Stairways of black bone, sometimes with entire skeletons built into a single step, with skulls for finials and ribcage balustrades, led to hundreds of different destinations. There were locked doors leading only to balconies, and labyrinths that seemed to exist merely for their own sake. Empty alcoves. A single weapons gallery. No windows, no bedchambers, no food, and no other inhabitants besides the prisoners confined in the dungeons. The Necrodelic was an ascetic, an anchorite, a minimalist, a demon concerned only with the smoking of flesh, the destruction of the universe, and his own evil enlightenment. He required neither food, drink, air, nor sleep. He cared not for possessions. His was an existence of black austerities and lethal meditations, of necromancy, genocide, and raw malevolence, his every energy focused upon becoming the Messiah of Death.

*

Chariah followed a trail of dreams through his vessel, a path of rainbow bits writhing on the floor like tapeworms freshly exposed to light, the spoor of the escaped Oneirophage. Through dungeons where captives were shackled and imprisoned, through oubliettes where they writhed on torture racks and crucifixes, and through abattoirs where they were stored like food, the Necrodelic stormed like an enraged reaper. Down blackboned stairways and lifts made of giant, horned skulls, through circular corridors like veins and arteries and vertical shafts like throats and vaginas, Chariah trailed the dream-eater.

A puddle of blood and rainbow dreams marked one of the Oneirophage's communions. Chariah traveled on in the direction it led. Ahead, he heard drippings and smelled fresh death. Looking upwards, he discovered the four limbs of a victim, suspended from the ceiling like a hanging jungle, leaking crimson onto the floor beneath.

Chariah tore down the severed limbs, gathered them up, and inserted them into a mouth farther down the hallway, which swallowed them whole and sent them on their way through the ship's inner digestive labyrinths, to be deposited in the flesh reservoir above the Bloodbong. Several more hanging jungles of arms and legs awaited him as he quested along. Occasionally a dream-dried husk littered the floor beneath the drizzling limbs.

The Necrodelic tore a womb from the ceiling and began filling the sac with the organic detritus, dragging it through the corridors by an umbilical cord. Chariah emptied the bulging womb and fed the severed body parts to the various mouths and vaginas of the ship whenever possible.

At the centerpoint of the dungeons was a foyer, with corridors leading off in eight different directions, and two large, twin staircases. Limbs dangled in every archway and from every lip-like and labia-like balcony. Like windchimes of flesh they swayed in the air, making soft death-music as they collided and bled. The Oneirophage had deliberately left trails in all directions to confuse the Necrodelic. Cursing, Chariah bashed the womb he was holding by the umbilical cord into the wall, scattering arms, legs, limbed bodies, blood, and organs all throughout the foyer in an explosion of gore, and leaving behind a purple bruise upon the stricken flesh of the spaceship.

Sniffing the air, Chariah snarled. Not only had the Oneirophage left trails of blood, dreams, and severed limbs in ten directions, but he had spread his scent and sprayed his venom down all eight corridors and along both staircases as well. Closing his eyes, Chariah psychically probed the nearby halls and chambers. The Oneirophage was gone, or, more likely, had cast a cloaking spell to disguise his presence. Chariah knew with the black wisdom of the most enlightened demons that to proceed would be to trigger a laid trap. But the Omnibeast belonged to him, and contained several traps of its own.

Chariah retreated down the hallway from whence he came, back through the dungeons and upwards through the ship until he reached the oracle chamber. Therein could be viewed entire maps of the Omnibeast, and he could look through any and all of the living spaceship's internal eyeballs as well. Stepping into his oracle chamber, Chariah connected the tubes to his body. The umbilical cords held him aloft in the grip of their vacuum-like suction, and he dangled, hovered, spun, and somersaulted gently in the middle of the zero-gravity chamber, floating weightlessly in mid-air as he tracked the Oneirophage through the various oracles, studying the glowing, three-dimensional, cartographic projections of the Omnibeast and its every tunnel and chamber.

Chariah tapped into the nervous system of the Omnibeast, temporarily overriding its every function. He closed doorways and sealed off levels, then began sending pyropathic thoughts through the umbilical cords, setting controlled fires within the Omnibeast to flush out the Oneirophage. He would trap the dream-eater with flames and use the conflagrations to herd him into the Bloodbong.

Watching the fires burn through the oracles, Chariah observed the Oneirophage fleeing through the Omnibeast's innards, speeding through the labyrinths as flames roared and smoke billowed around him, as passages flashed open and slammed shut and entire rooms and corridors rotated and writhed and crawled within the spaceship, bearing the frantic Oneirophage in their clutches. Satisfied, Chariah disengaged himself from the umbilical cords and exited the oracle chamber. He made his way to his meditation sanctum, where the Oneirophage would momentarily be dropped through the ceiling into the waiting doom of the Bloodbong.

The Necrodelic waited with black patience. Morbidly, time passed.

*

A shot of flame raced down the corridor like a hungry phallus, ejaculating smoke, a piece of sexual Hell eager to rape the Oneirophage to a crisp. The fire caught the Oneirophage as he imbibed dreams from the nipple of one of the Necrodelic's prisoners. With a violent start, the Oneirophage withdrew the Umbilicus, severing the nipple of the demoness with a wet popping noise and leaving it twitching on the floor below. Prodding the caravan of prisoners he had abducted from the Necrodelic's dungeons, the Oneirophage fled the conflagration, leading his chained captives down the corridor to an intersection where more flames waited. The assaulting heat drove him left, the two gouts of fire coalescing into one and chasing him through the spaceship.

The fires herded the Oneirophage through the maze, springing up from the floors beneath him, blocking off passageways, driving him deep into the Necrodelic's vessel and trapping him in small pockets of safety against the fleshlike walls. The Oneirophage wondered if the Necrodelic somehow planned to smoke his flesh from a distance, if there was some intricate framework of piping that even now stretched through the ship to his jet lips, or if the entire Omnibeast was, in actuality, a behemoth hookah. Smoke swirled and heat beckoned as the Oneirophage attempted to ascertain his adversary's intentions. Impaling his hostages through the skull with his sorcerous straw and drinking their dreams, the Oneirophage enhanced his psychic abilities and formulated a counter-plan. Slipping into a lucid dream state, he called upon the serpentine soothsaying powers of his subconscious to witness the Necrodelic in his meditation chamber, waiting for the Oneirophage to fall into the boiling plasma of the Bloodbong. The Oneirophage visualized every aspect of his counterattack, virtually living the experience in his lucid dream state, so that when he carried it out in reality it was during a psychedelic trance of deja vu.

The Oneirophage ducked into a rising blister on the sizzling wall and dragged his remaining hostages in with him. Once inside, he cast defensive wards to insulate the small chamber from the firestorm, hissed several cloaking and camouflage spells, and then shook the Umbilicus once, like a switchblade. A small, saw-toothed dagger shot out from its tip. The Oneirophage placed the serrated blade under his chin and dragged the miniature saw down his throat, over his chest, and past his sternum to his lower belly. The large slit caused loose flaps of snakeskin to open over his breast like the folds of a robe, and like a robe, the Oneirophage slithered out of his snakeskin to stand beside it with a new, shimmering, wetly glistening set of tattoos and reptilian integument unveiled to the universe. He held the limp snakeskin in his right hand, then chose one of the male hostages, one of his approximate size and hair color, to hypnotize with his kaleidoscopic, ophidian gaze. The mesmerized victim adorned the shed skin limb by limb, like a suit of armor. Like ophidian leather, the snakeskin clung tightly to the sacrificial victim, his legs pressed together in the tight cocoon of the serpent tail, his left hand brandishing a spider glove, his penis ensheathed in a snakeskin condom, and a dead skin mask complete with shed fangs about his face and head. The Oneirophage hermetically sealed the serpent leather with the Umbilicus, spoke a series of hypnotic commands into both of the doppelganger's ears, one for each hemisphere of the brain, then thrust him into the inferno of the spaceship's corridors.

The Omnibeast immediately detected the imposter Oneirophage in its labyrinth, its senses perceiving the shape, size, tattoos, and male energy of the Oneirophage and being fooled by the ruse. The ship continued to set the controlled fires as it had been commanded, herding the false dream-eater deep into its labyrinths and far from the real Oneirophage. The fires continued to burn around the Oneirophage's sorcerously cloaked sanctuary, so there was nought for the serpent demon to do but wait with predator's patience and imbibe the dreams of the captives he had dragged inside the giant blister chamber along with him. With a swirl of his hand, as though by legerdemain, the Umbilicus transmogrified, and the Oneirophage was soon slumbering in a psychedelic dream trance upon a bed of perforated, bleeding corpses. Oblivious to the conflagration without, the Oneirophage slept as peacefully as a parasite hibernating in a deathmonk's brain.

19

Severed limbs floated at the surface of the Bloodbong's heart-chamber like detritus from a shipwreck, like vestiges of genocides left behind for carrion-eaters and carrion-smokers. Whirlpools and tides created a danse macabre of arms, legs, and torsos, body parts rearranging themselves as if trying to find their proper partners and rebuild their mutilated bodies. The psychoactive ingredients of the flesh, bones, and organs hit Chariah like a white-hot warhammer. He breathed in, the slow systole of the succubus. He breathed out, the slow diastole of the incubus. Instantaneously drugged, he stared enraptured at the expressions of death on the floating faces, as if animated in their moments of realized mortality, and saw arms reaching for him through the transparent chamber, like those of zombies. The Necrodelic, rocketing with the phantasmagoria of higher consciousness, saw his death-oven boil the corpse-pieces to nothingness, dislodging fingers and toes, severing heads, extracting organs, peeling skin and muscle from arms and legs. In psychedelic tranquility, Chariah awaited the presence of the Oneirophage.

The fires that burned through the spaceship would chase

the dream-eater directly into the Bloodbong. Chariah closed his bloodshot eyes and listened, his evil clairaudient powers at their peak. The crackle of flames and the soft susurrus of smoke were soon joined by the scrape of reptilian scales dragging across mammalian hide, a moist song of abrasion, like the sound of a dragon raping a sphinx. Chariah could hear the Oneirophage's sibilant breathing as he slithered through the corridors, could feel his heartbeat like sonic booms in his soul. As Chariah inhaled more flesh from the severed limbs and torsos floating in the boiling blood of the necromantic pipe, he heard the rush of firestorms above, the silence of the Oneirophage halting as he was cornered, the sharp clicking of iron gears, the groaning of trapdoor hinges springing open, the rush of air as the Oneirophage fell hundreds of feet to the adamantium floors of the flesh reservoir, the scrabbling of his long fingernails as he struggled to climb the sheer, sloping sides, the sound of snakeskin sliding down metal inclines, the loud clap of another trapdoor opening in four pieces, and then the satisfactory splash of the Oneirophage falling into the boiling lake of ichor in the heart chamber of the Bloodbong.

The drugged, semi-conscious Chariah opened his dilated eyes to watch the Oneirophage dissolve. The Necrodelic breathed in, and snakeskin sloughed from the undulating serpent and disintegrated. Tattoos melted together and embued the plasma with bizarre colors. Jaws unhinged, fangs fell out, venom hissed and spat on the surface of the churning pool. Chariah began to leave his physical perceptions behind, diving through the astral plane, downward and outward, before being caught in the soulmate's gravity of Mother Chaos. She embraced him with lithe pink arms, kissed him with purple lips, and spoke with the voice of a disembodied siren.

"...your enemy, the Oneirophage, lives yet...open your eyes, my darkling...return briefly to your flesh...and partake of sooth..."

Chariah's eyelids fluttered open as though from hypnotic suggestion. He fixed his gaze upon the Bloodbong and then, with a single inhalation, smoked the entire snakeskin from the Oneirophage's body. Tattoos split and exploded, large chunks of scales fell sizzling to the bottom of the pipe, and the serpentine face of the Oneirophage loosened and then detached, revealing the face of another beneath it as the dead skin mask floated to the bubbling surface. Chariah recognized the features of one of his prisoners, a demon he had cast into his dungeons in some distant past. An impostor, wearing the Oneirophage's scales and posing as the dream-eater. Chariah had the snakeskin, but not the snake. He had not captured the dream-eater. He had captured only a dream.

Chariah smoked the flesh of the doppelganger with one breath, simultaneously resigned and vengeful. His spirit drifted back into the astral plane. Mother Chaos regathered him in her arms and whispered, "...come with me...I will show you where the Oneirophage has made his sanctuary...you shall haunt while I shall heal... "

Chariah knew psychically that both the Oneirophage's astral and physical bodies were embedded somewhere in the Omnibeast. He followed Mother Chaos through parts of the spaceship that had been consumed by fire on the physical plane. On the astral plane, salamanders and fire elementals lingered about the burnt wreckage, hovering in the heat alongside the ghosts of pyromaniacs, hungry for karmic smoke and ash, craving the feel of the flame through the dimensional fabric.

The wraiths and revenants scattered and watched from a distance as Mother Chaos and Chariah floated through the scorched corridors to the charred antechamber which had been forged by sorcery, fire, and agony during the inferno. The Oneirophage's astral body was semi-conscious inside, lost in dream and unresponsive to the physical and spectral worlds surrounding him. He lay curled like an embryo in one of the numerous blisters that had formed in the burned corridors, a hybrid of broken bathysphere and suppurating sore, filled with pus on the physical plane and ectoplasm on the astral plane. Mother Chaos burst the pustule with one purple fingernail, and Chariah reached in and dragged forth the Oneirophage. The procedure closely resembled an abortion.

The Oneirophage's eyes flickered open but shone with disorientation, projecting razor-bladed rainbows from his dreaming mind across Chariah's flesh. Chariah was startled as the sharp beams of color lashed criss-crossing wounds over his astrosome, having not expected the Oneirophage to awaken into astral consciousness. He quickly realized, however, that the

Oneirophage's astral consciousness was extremely minimal, as the dream-eater once again closed his eyes and slept, seemingly oblivious to the imminent jeopardy inherent in the Necrodelic's sable presence. Snarling, Chariah attacked the astral body of the Oneirophage, raking his face with his claws. The Necrodelic, however, had unwittingly lavished the Oneirophage with the pain he enjoyed, the masochistic ecstasies which stimulated his dreams, and these dreams now played themselves out in kaleidoscopic oracles floating in the air, coalescing into images of fire, rape, and Satan. The Oneirophage began to instinctively devour the dreams orbiting his brain, licking them up with his tongues and sucking them out of the air with his third eye, all the while gaining strength, and ultimately awakening into complete astral projection. Jerked suddenly into his astral body, the Oneirophage's vibrations were sometimes severe, like that of a maggot being electrocuted. Drooling rainbows, he arose and turned weightlessly to engage the Necrodelic in battle.

Mother Chaos saw this as she healed the Omnibeast and uttered a spell of sleep. Just as suddenly as his astrosome had awakened, the Oneirophage fell once more into dreaming slumber. Alighting at the Necrodelic's side, Mother Chaos took Chariah by the hand. With one caressing, healing fingertip she erased the scarlet wounds criss-crossing his face and chest.

"...your wrath betrays you, my prince...I asked for haunting, not violence...come now, beautiful Chariah...we shall haunt the Oneirophage together...our subtle specters shall visit him while he dreams...come, and I will teach you the ways of haunting ...just like I showed you the ways of love...my devotee...my black messiah..."

Chariah and Mother Chaos whispered subliminal messages, hypnotic suggestions, and self-destruct mantras into the Oneirophage's slitted ears. Mother Chaos breathed cold air across his body while the Necrodelic blew hot gases in his face. They summoned forth devices of agony from various parts of the universe, then tortured both his third eye and his mind's eye with branding irons, flaming drills, red-hot jackhammers, white-hot miniature scavenger's daughters, and a form of excruciating water torture utilizing the boiling saltwater of the lower Phlegethonic deltas of Hell.

The dreaming Oneirophage perceived them as an incubus

and succubus come to copulate with him while he slept, interpreting their hauntings as a tantric assault upon his mind, a combination of rape and menage a trois, and it was of this he dreamt, his physical body trembling with the paroxysms of wet dreams and erotic nightmares, sweating venom and ejaculating adrenaline. The haunting had been executed to perfection, and a barrage of nightmares and suffering awaited the Oneirophage.

Mother Chaos guided Chariah back to his meditation chamber, back to his body. She kissed the length of his returning silver cord and whispered, "...your ship is well and cleansed of its wounds, save one...within this one, the Oneirophage lies...remember, a dream is a double-edged blade, but higher consciousness is a barbed lightning bolt...battle well, my soulmate...my love..."

Mother Chaos faded and Chariah returned to the world of flesh. Her mystical words and hypnotic suggestions were like spiders laying eggs in his brain and spinning relationship-webs of vengeance. He detached himself from the Bloodbong, exited the meditation chamber, and made his way into the depths of the Omnibeast. In his drugged mind, Chariah vowed to inhale the Oneirophage's flesh, vowed to smoke the dream-eater alive, and vowed to do so as the most powerful yogi who had ever existed, with the highest and darkest levels of pranayama in the history of the universe, for as many hours as was physically possible, and then a little longer.

20

Dreams spread like venom, venom like dreams, through the hallucinating brain of the Oneirophage, rising up like a tyrannical virus and poisoning his mind. His sleep was disturbed, and it was his own torturous slumber he dreamt of. Night sweats became hemathidrosis. Wet dreams resulted in chancres and priapism. The necrotic dripping vaginas of succubi infected him with gonorrhea and syphilis. He slept on a bed of nails, with a garrote for a pillow. His blanket was a straitjacket, cutting off his blood flow and causing cramps in his arms, legs, and genitals. He cast it aside and was numbed by frostbite, the chancres on his phallus turning to chilblains. He wrapped his body in a blanket of tarantula fur and became feverish. The urticated spider hairs pierced his skin like a form of acupuncture that utilized asbestos fibers. Rapid eye movement was like violent surgery. His mind's eyes were painfully squeezed in iron maidens of dream, turning even the beloved source of his addictions into methods of torture.

He attempted to perform oneirocritics upon his own dreams while he dreamt them, with disastrous consequences. A universe of horror and void where his head was its own sensory deprivation chamber was the horrific karma invoked by such autodivinatory experiments. His skull grew over his eye sockets, ear slits, nostrils, mouth, throat, third eye, and crown chakra, forming one solid fusion of bone that rendered him blind, deaf, and mute, nullifying every one his senses except the sense of touch, sealing the nightmares in and trapping him in his own dreams. The nightmares were so intense that his body eventually rejected its own mind, and his brains slowly dripped from his penises until his skull was completely empty.

Excruciating nightmares of his head turning inside-out and exploding followed, and then an eternity of vertigo and ennui as his decapitated corpse blindly wandered the universe, recollecting the shrapnel of his face, the shards of his skull, and the droplets of his brains, and reconstructing them piece by piece with an incandescent forceps and a soldering iron.

The nightmare of his head's reattachment was as agonizing as its explosion. A barbed, red-hot, floating, sentient needle ascended from the infernos of Hell and threaded itself with a thin string of flesh from his first penis, then used the bloody ribbon to sew his head back to his torso. His upper phallus slowly unraveled during the surgery, followed by his lower phallus, scrotum, and testicles. Over a period of several hours he stitched his head back onto his neck, completely castrating himself in the process.

He chased down a passing succubus and raped her with an act of forced cunnilingus. With his mouth buried in her vagina, his jaws unhinged like a boa constrictor's and he sucked, turning her womb inside-out and then swallowing it. The womb settled in his abdomen and he used it to regenerate his phalluses and testicles, incubating them and finally birthing them like demonic quadruplets, twin serpentlings and twin leeches that tore through his groin, ripping a prosthetic vagina in his crotch and wracking his flesh with excruciating birthing contractions. When his penises had regrown, he raped the succubus again, this time with his reincarnated genitals, and when he withdrew them they were wrapped, like mummified snakes, in black tapeworms of fear.

The Oneirophage moaned in the semi-consciousness which separated dreams like synapses, then fell silent as another tortuous nightmare began.

The Oneirophage dreamt a threefold dream of himself as the Beast. First, he was the steed of Satan, forced through an endless cycle of death and reincarnation at the prodding of his omnipotent tamer's red-hot whip, recycling himself through space and time while Satan rode atop him on a flaming saddle. Secondly, he dreamt that he was Satan's pet, his leash lit like the wick of a candle, continually burning down to his flesh but never extinguishing, his mouth frothing with rabies and his guts churning with white-hot tapeworms, forced to sleep in an ensorcelled cage which prevented dreams. Last, he dreamt he was Satan's livestock, forced to eat and drink dreams from a trough, his nipples and penises milked daily for the blood Satan drank with his meals, and then one day finding himself laid out, while still alive, upon a banquet table as Satan casually devoured him, plucking his out organs one by one with a fork, scooping his brains out with a spoon, and carving the flesh from his bones with a meat cleaver. His blood dribbled down Satan's beard while his body was eaten piece by piece, and then his bones were picked clean while he watched helplessly, and he could feel every mutilated body part and every morsel of meat being masticated in Satan's mouth, could feel every bolus of flesh swallowed to free fall through the abysses of his esophagi, and then burned and dissolved in the boiling digestive acids of Satan's infernal stomachs. He could still feel his own flesh as it was broken down into nutrients, and then he could feel each individual cell that had once comprised his body being put to use in the various parts of Satan's anatomy. After the Oneirophage's body had been completely absorbed into Satan's, Satan sugared and salted the dream-eater's soul, covered it in spices and saturated it in wine, and then swallowed his entire spirit into a bottomless digestive system of purgatories and Tartaruses.

*

The Oneirophage awoke with salt in his eyes and wounds, and realized that he was not awake. The dream salt regenerated itself like a virus and soon suffused his entire body, inside and out, and began dissolving parts of his soul. The iron maidens of dream constricted tighter around his mind's eyes. Winged instincts flew around frantically in his head until their pinions were broken, then jumped out his ears, committing suicide. Memories then did the same, making their death plunges from his eyes. Archetypes lined up in single file on his tongues and one by one, like lemmings, leapt to their deaths from his mouth to the abyss below. Serpents and spiders, succubi with phalluses for noses and fanged mouths for vaginas, self-castrated incubi with severed penises in hand, nightworms eternally devouring their own tails, a leprous king with his young virgin princess impaled on his penis, the fanged fetus of a prince raping a terminally ill queen upon her wheeled deathbed, a bloody maggot pushing a sarcophagus occupied by the corpse of a fly, a bloody caterpillar pushing a coffin filled with the cadaver of a butterfly, a demon holding the ashes of his brother in the cup of his hands, a soliloquizing philosopher on a torture rack, a winged harpy singing siren songs on a crucifix, a hydra in a multiple guillotine and his demon executioner, a thousand-armed demon being drawn and thousandthed by a thousand and two dragons, and then finally Satan himself marched in a cortege across his tongues to the rim of his lips, then committed suicide by jumping to the hard darkness below, their blood and brains painting the ground with mandalas, yantras, sigils, symbols, labyrinths, and optical illusions. The Oneirophage then himself committed suicide, gnawing at the silver cord of his astral body like a wolf, chewing his own soul free from the trap of his flesh like a desperate animal would gnaw off its own leg to escape from a snare. He bit through the silver cord and plummeted to the hard black bottom of the bottomless abyss, splattering his blood and soul upon the stains of those who had gone before. Overhead, in the sable skies, loomed the ethereal busts of the Necrodelic and Mother Chaos, their top halves visible amongst the stars as they smiled with mysterious pride before disappearing.

When he awoke, he was The Labyrinth, the seducer of

sanity, luring demons into its twisted body with promises that the first to solve the maze would become the Jh'a'vyraa. He spied the Necrodelic and Morpheus Rex amongst the hundreds who entered his flesh, saw his dark soulmates wandering its depths and writhings. The lost demons were red-hot, as painful as lava, searing the circulatory system of The Labyrinth. The Labyrinth saw the Necrodelic and Morpheus Rex simultaneously arrive at the end of time and awaiting their destinies. First Mother Chaos appeared and carried the Necrodelic off in her winged embrace like a child. Then Morpheus Rex turned into the Oneirophage, trapped in his own labyrinth. As the Oneirophage gazed over the edge of time, Satan reared up with red-hot surgical instruments in his hands, scalpels and bonesaws and tongs, and performed a diabolical and excruciating sex change upon the Oneirophage with the Hell-forged tools. When he had completed the surgery, Satan raped the universe's newest female, impregnating the castrated and wombed Oneirophage with crimson nagas and lamias that would be born tail-first and would forever wander The Labyrinth in search of salvation, each bearing a fragment of the Oneirophage's consciousness and torturing him from afar.

The Labyrinth wept to death...

...and he became The Ocean, a cesspool of every tear ever wept, coagulating at the bottom of the universe. The Necrodelic and Mother Chaos made love in the firmament far above, at the prodding of Satan the Breeder and his flaming spears, tridents, and branding irons. The melancholy of orgasm caused the Necrodelic's penis to weep sperm, which fell through the cosmos to land in The Ocean with tortured sighs. The whole universe warred above The Ocean, spilling all the blood it possessed until The Ocean turned red and crimson, and mermaids and sirens emerged from its depths. Somewhere in The Ocean, a giant heart beat, creating rhythmic, sanguine tides. The mermaids and sirens sang dirges and threnodies in the vermillion waters.

Suddenly there was a large thunderbolt, followed by a tiny splash. The Ocean beheld the Oneirophage, who had been betrayed by his own dreams and sent hurtling to the bloodsea at the bottom of the universe. The dream-eater immediately swam off in search of someone's heart, someone whose identity he did not know. In the distance, amid the scarlet surf, the crimson mermaids seductively called. A bright thunderbolt was followed by a black splash, raising tsunamis of blood in The Ocean. The Omnibeast had been shot down from the starlit skies of outer space by the flaming arrow of Satan in his Sagittary incarnation.

The Oneirophage swam back from the horizon and climbed atop the Omnibeast as though it were an island, floating in the middle of The Ocean, The Ocean whose shores had never been glimpsed and probably did not exist, unless they were, perhaps, the very edges of time and space, or cataracts pouring into the caldariums of Hell. The Oneirophage lay down atop the Omnibeast while the bestial spaceship drifted, half-submerged in The Ocean, and then all three went to sleep simultaneously.

The Oneirophage could telesthetically perceive the Omnibeast's sensations as he slumbered. The stains of the bestial spaceship's black and crimson ichor were on his rainbow lips and the rim of the Umbilicus, as well. Clutching the Umbilicus to his chest with his right hand, the Oneirophage began sensing the gentle caresses of Mother Chaos and the Necrodelic through the conduit of the dreaming spaceship, as the flesh-smoker and his omnisentient soulmate healed the Omnibeast's burns and lured it back to health from the fires that had been blown through its insides. He felt the touch of Mother Chaos on the astral plane, trying to assuage the spaceship's fears and massage its nightmares away. The Oneirophage trembled as he telepathically felt the touch of Mother Chaos upon the Omnibeast. The Oneirophage desired the Mistress of Entropy for his own, and vowed to one day claim her as his bride while standing over the corpse of the Necrodelic.

Just the very thought of the Necrodelic was enough to summon his presence, and now the two stood face to face on the astral plane, sharing a spiritual crossroads with Mother Chaos and the Omnibeast. Their eye contact lasted for several moments before each returned to their bodies, and in that eye contact was the raw stuff of vendetta. The battlefield shifted then to the physical dimension, to the labyrinths of the Omnibeast, where demons played. The psychic wars were over for the moment, but there would come a reckoning day in the future where the astral plane would once again be their battlefield, in a spiritual combat where dreams were both blood and weapons, and consciousness itself was the trophy.

*

The phantom of the Oneirophage floated through the crumbling corridors, floors turning to ash in his wake and old smoke dissipating with his passage. While he slept, his dreams were like werewolves, stalking him and cornering him in the recesses of his own brain before transforming back into intelligent life forms beneath the dawn's light of reason. He cowered at the fringes of his consciousness, hung by loose visceral strings over the abyss of his own mortality, as if swinging over Hell by his own exposed guts. When he was disturbed, his specter traveled the fire-blasted corridors of the spaceship like a senescent lunatic, muttering to itself, and he longed for the very dreams which haunted him in slumber. But, when he made his way towards the dungeons to gather new dreams, he found every way sealed, not just physically, but with astral barricades and spells of warding as well, no doubt by the touch of the Necrodelic at the ship's control center. The Oneirophage resorted to licking the black flesh of the spaceship and plunging the Umbilicus into the cracked and immolated walls, sucking up soot and ashes. The cells of the tunnel had yet to repair themselves from the Necrodelic's controlled fire, and their fibers had yet to recollect their genetic knowledge and intelligence. Thus, the wandering shade of the Oneirophage found itself without dreams to devour and returned to its slumbering flesh, settling itself back into its embryonically curled body.

Some of his older dreams began slowly overtaking the nightmares. Buried too deep in his consciousness, they did not provide him with the sustenance he craved, and thus he succumbed once more to nightmares, preferring them to dreamlessness, his addiction such that even their malefic assuagings were preferable to not dreaming at all.

The Oneirophage trembled during his hypnogogic ordeals, his flesh jumping in little spots as if it sought to commit suicide by plunging from its own self into the afterlife of bodilessness. His muscles quivered like a liquid musical instrument, carrying notes of pain and nausea. He wept in his sleep, yet, paradoxically, continually ejaculated from both penises, aroused by the sadomasochistic tangle of pain, sex, and dream that defined his very essence.

The Oneirophage became euphoric with nightmare. The raw surges of paranoia made a toy of his nauseated guts, as if to play a game of evisceration with Satan. Lifted out of his body and jerked into a state of higher consciousness, the Oneirophage could feel Satan ready to play that game of evisceration, ready to play with his every organ as though each one were a piece in that twisted game.

Satan laughed, his voice reverberating through the spaceship halls and sending the specter of the Oneirophage scurrying back once more to its physical body. The Oneirophage broke through the membranes leading to his sanctuary and climbed once more into the pustule that sheltered his slumbering form. Curled up in white viscous fluid to his chest, the Oneirophage shuddered and sweated.

The Oneirophage lay in the fetal position, and his surroundings slowly took on the air of a womb, a pus-filled womb. The Oneirophage regressed, and prepared to meet his death as the child he had once been, the fetus who had sucked sludge through an umbilical cord, the fanged serpentling who had sucked milk and blood from a nipple, the demonling whose first kill had been the slaying of his own mother, after which he had sucked the dreams from her every orifice and wound. He fingered his straw as cramps overtook him, combining with nausea to abrade him from the inside out. The heat was unbearable. The pus was like a boiling fountain of youth, a pool of innocence regained at the moment of doom. Satan's image filled his mind. The master of the universe reached for the Oneirophage's soul with one externally veined and arteried hand, his hot fingernail puncturing his consciousness, sending thoughts flying like debris in excruciating rainbows through his brain.

"Come, my child..." spoke Satan. "This incarnation has proven futile. ..You are the underdemon... You are dead... You are mine..."

A crimson eye filled the air in the womb as the burning claw stroked his consciousness, and then the face of Satan coalesced around it.

The Oneirophage clung to his last dream, his final dream, his ultimate dream, the dream of becoming the Jh'a'vyraa.

"You are no Jh'a'vyraa...," Satan said in response.

"Behold...You have never even escaped your mother's womb..."

The Oneirophage held the Umbilicus with twitching fingers and tried to suckle upon Satan's eye, but found it ephemeral as mist. The Umbilicus extended itself through the floating death's head of Satan and lodged itself in the living flesh of the wall behind it. Instinctively, the Oneirophage began to drink. The Omnibeast had been healed by the thaumaturgies of Mother Chaos, its fires extinguished, its wounds cleaned, its flesh regenerated. After hours of tortured sleep in the incandescent blister, drenched in night sweats from the boiling temperatures, suffering from massive smoke inhalation and dreaming in heat shimmers and mirages, the Oneirophage was finally able to drink pure dreams rather than ashes, memories, and agony. Strength poured back into him, filling his muscles, suffusing his scales and skin like armor, balancing and synchronizing his brainwaves, and assuaging his soul. Satan laughed once again and then faded.

The Oneirophage drank his fill of the Omnibeast's dreams and then splashed back against the side of the pus-filled womb. He gazed through the transparent membranes of the giant blister and observed the healthy pulp of the healed corridors and passageways. The scenery was beautiful to his dream-drugged mind. He knew, however, that there was no time to enjoy it, for the Necrodelic had discovered his ruse and tracked his exact location. This he had divined by unremembered methods while he slept, half-dead from the smoke inhalation and the scorching heat, in the tenebrous sanctuary of the blister-womb, while infernos raged all around.

The Oneirophage arose on his serpent's tail and slithered over the grey and black corpses littering the small alcove that had been burned into the wall. Their limbed, dried husks were ashen and crumbled to dust as he passed over them. He burst through the membrane of the blister, which was the only part of the spaceship that had been left unhealed, to serve as a suppurating landmark for the Necrodelic to determine the Oneirophage's whereabouts. Pus dripped from the ceiling as the Oneirophage tore through the veil of skin, and then the Oneirophage was free of the accursed antechamber, though still a prisoner within the Omnibeast. Snaking through the corridors, the Oneirophage plotted his next attack

"Sweet evil-ling, you are nothing but a maggot...A maggot in the feces of my sperm...Your doom draweth nigh...I will collect your soul..."

Satan haunted Chariah like a telepathic, telekinetic, brain-eating vampire pederast, planting words in his vulnerable consciousness and irrigating his brain with his razor-fangs and barbed phallus. Chariah forced his laughing overlord away with a singular push of consciousness, like a sexual thrust, aided from beyond by Mother Chaos.

Clad in onyx armor, armed with an onyx broadsword and an onyx shield, and wearing a horned onyx helmet on his head, the Necrodelic hunted the Oneirophage. His crimson eyes glowed through the shadowy visor, and his long ebon claws protruded from fingerholes in the wickedly studded gauntlets that covered his fists. A black dragonskin scabbard hung from his waist. A necro-compass was bolted around his left forearm, pointing him towards his prey. He followed its throbbing dial now and came upon the remnants of the Oneirophage's brief sanctuary, a giant burst blister in the wall of a corridor, still leaking pus into the hall. Inside, the temporary shelter was filled with psychic residue, demon ashes, and half-cremated corpses riddled with grotesque perforations.

The Oneirophage had fled, leaving the gargantuan blister behind him like shed snakeskin. The Necrodelic glanced down at the necro-compass bolted to his gauntlet, and its flesh-magnets pointed him toward potential death. Brandishing his onyx broadsword, Chariah stalked the Oneirophage through the labyrinth, cutting off escape routes and hounding the dream-eater. Confused and lost, the Oneirophage soon found himself cornered, trapped in a dead end, with the Necrodelic fast approaching. He opened a trapdoor and dropped onto a catwalk fifty feet below. He landed on his resilient, coiling serpent's tail and looked to either side. The narrow bridge led to two different portcullises. One of them was opening.

The sound of chains unraveling and clanging to the floor reverberated along the catwalk. The adamantium grille of the portcullis raised and stuck itself in the spaceship's pulpish flesh with a splattering of blood. A moment later, the Necrodelic stepped forth from the darkness, resplendent in onyx, large spikes on the shoulderplates of his armor complementing his horned helmet, the edge of his sword gleaming even though its blade was more caliginous than midnight. The portcullis dropped behind him.

The Oneirophage drank in his surroundings. He stood amongst a labyrinth of bridges, suspended over a reservoir of blood, in a gigantic, cylindrical chamber. The lake of plasma lay hundreds of feet below, its surface a vermillion gloom, its depth indeterminate. The reservoir was thousands of feet in circumference, an enormous storehouse of precious blood, the largest amount of blood owned by an individual demon in the entire universe. It was the result of millions of sacrificial victims, and easily the largest room in the spaceship, a stark contrast to the asceticism found throughout the rest of the vessel. The intricate network of bridges, catwalks, balconies, platforms, and stairways stretched like spiderwebs throughout the reservoir. The Oneirophage was unable to perceive the entire intricacy of the complicated architecture in the pervading tenebrosity of the chamber. Levers and cranks were sparsely interspersed upon the walls and amongst the platforms. There were hidden machines and engines at work within the reservoir; they could be heard pumping and churning the blood far below, purifying it and directing it through the circulatory system of the Omnibeast. There were several hearts beating in the chamber as well, and some of them did not sound mechanical.

The Oneirophage had mere moments to absorb these perceptions as the ominous, intimidating, horned silhouette of the armor-clad Necrodelic approached. The flesh-smoker's footsteps were like death-knells. The combination of labyrinthine bridges and the confusion at seeing the Necrodelic armed and in battle garb sowed confusion, vertigo, and trepidation in the mind of the dream-eater. For the first time in all his billions of incarnations, the Oneirophage backed up. Serpents were not constructed to slither in reverse, however, and the Oneirophage found himself off balance as the Necrodelic seized the very moment of hesitation for which he had adorned the suit of armor, the very moment for which he had plotted and planned, the raison d'etre of the psychological warfare which the onyx armor was. Upon this bridge the two demons would do battle above the pool of ichor, trapped blood over freed blood.

The Necrodelic launched himself through the air. His onyx sword slashed, lacerating the Oneirophage across the chest and knocking him further back. The center of the bridge gradually narrowed, becoming thinner and thinner, its nexus mere inches in diameter. The Oneirophage slipped and fell, bracing his fall with his left elbow, scrambling to hold on to the edge of the bridge with his right hand while raising his black widow hand for protection. The Necrodelic alighted in the heavy armor with his characteristic feline dexterity, but this time the silence was accompanied by a loud, tolling clang. That he could even maintain his balance in a suit of armor on a catwalk less than a foot wide was a testament to his highly evolved levels of demonica.

The Oneirophage vomited a spray of venom onto the catwalk in an attempt to make the Necrodelic slip and fall. Instead, the armor-clad demon trod defiantly through the slick green coat of poison, walking across the slippery bridge as though he were walking on solid, level ground in the middle of a desert. He swung his onyx broadsword overhand, driving the stumbling Oneirophage further back. The dream-eater barely avoided the gleaming blade as the Necrodelic continued swinging for his chest. The sword repeatedly struck the iron catwalk and sent black sparks raining through the gloom.

From his supine position, the Oneirophage lashed out at the Necrodelic's legs with his tail. The Necrodelic effortlessly jumped straight up into the air, his demonic strength completely unaffected by the heavy armor. As he landed, he drove the point of his sword into the tip of the Oneirophage's tail. The dream-eater thrashed like a harpooned triton, trying to rip himself free. Chariah held the sword fast, pinning the serpentine warrior to the adamantium catwalk, impaled by the tail, then tossed his shield on top of the Oneirophage. The unforgiving onyx smashed the Oneirophage's face and cracked three of his ribs. Chariah, using his sword for leverage, vaulted into mid-air, turned upside-down, and catapulted himself through the darkness. He somersaulted as he fell and landed back-first on the shield, crushing the Oneirophage beneath it with a loud, reverberating crash and the sound of more ribs splintering. Blood began to drip from the catwalk to the bridgeworks and reservoir below.

The Necrodelic slid from the shield feet-first and twisted so that he faced the Oneirophage. The Oneirophage pushed at the onyx shield, trying to rid himself of its stifling weight. The Necrodelic pounded the shield with his gauntletted hands, scoring its surface and pulverizing the Oneirophage. The Oneirophage attempted to push the shield off his chest to no avail, as the Necrodelic's blows rained down too fast, too hard, and too heavy. The Oneirophage twitched his punctured tail as the Necrodelic continued his bonecrushing onslaught. Using his tail prehensilely, like a third limb, the serpent demon withdrew the broadsword and used the sudden momentum to push the Necrodelic away. The Necrodelic slid backwards across the catwalk, then sprang to his feet. The Oneirophage used his tail to throw the broadsword at the Necrodelic. The whistling blade tore through the air, spinning end over end like a gigantic shuriken. Chariah twisted sideways as it flew past, deftly grabbing it by the hilt with his right hand, then pirouetting and leaping across the catwalk to deliver a mighty, spinning, two-fisted, overhead blow to the Oneirophage's chest. The broadsword dented its companion shield down the middle, causing it to slide across the Oneirophage's slick sternum, headed directly for the side of the bridge to Chariah's left. The limp body of the Oneirophage was simultaneously slipping over the edge to Chariah's right. The Necrodelic flung the onyx sword into the distance with a flick of his wrist. It sheathed itself in the crimson wall a thousand feet away, quivering and resonating. Chariah reached down with his right hand and grabbed the Oneirophage by the hair, preventing him from falling. His left hand retrieved the shield before it toppled into the lake of blood below. Standing atop the catwalk with his ophidian nemesis in one hand and his onyx shield in the other, the Necrodelic repeatedly bashed the face of the Oneirophage into the shield, then tossed both Oneirophage and shield high into the air. As they came down, Chariah leapt up to meet them, spinning and delivering a flying roundhouse kick to the shield, which then ricocheted into the face of the Oneirophage with an explosion of blood and the loud snap of a septum breaking.

Not only had Chariah timed the deadly maneuver

perfectly, he had controlled the force of his kick to knock the Oneirophage precisely twenty feet into the distance, no more, no less, so that he would land on a platform beneath the catwalk more than one hundred feet below. The Oneirophage was accompanied on his descent by the shield, which landed once more upon his chest with a clatter before the thud of his flesh had even begun to reverberate in the vast hollows of the chamber.

Chariah stood atop the catwalk, a hulking silhouette in his onyx armor. He watched the battered body of the Oneirophage strike the platform below and the heavy shield land immediately on top of him. For one eternal instant the Necrodelic loomed, a bird of prey, a reaper on a zenith, and then the Necrodelic leapt from the catwalk. With his arms spread-eagled he plummeted through the darkness, the air whistling through his helmet as he fell cruciform, gaining more and more speed as he made his descent, and then landing chest first on top of shield, Oneirophage, and platform alike, with an impact so great that pieces and shards of flesh, onyx, and adamantium became inextricably intertwined, embedded in and dangling from one another.

The force of Chariah's kamikaze dive drove both he and the Oneirophage through the platform, leaving behind a jagged hole of twisted, bloody metal, then through another platform immediately below, and then two more below that. By the time their fall was finally broken, they had plunged an additional four stories through the reservoir. The sound of onyx armor striking onyx shield was deafening, a thunderbolt that echoed for several minutes. Blood rained down from the spiky pits and mangled iron above, soaking the platform on which the Necrodelic and the Oneirophage lay in an ever-expanding pool, creeping out in all directions and then dripping over the sides.

Chariah extricated himself from the pile and staggered to the edge of the platform. He had broken a few ribs himself, and was dizzy from the blow, his horned helmet resonating around his skull, its vibrations ringing in his ears. Meanwhile, the Oneirophage had shrugged off the shield and was rolling to the opposite edge of the platform. Chariah came to his senses in time to make one desperate lunge, but the Oneirophage was too far ahead and rolled away, plunging into the open air.

The Oneirophage landed on a balustraded bridge below and recollected himself. Overhead, he could hear the gong of the Necrodelic's footsteps as the flesh-smoker descended an adamantium stairway. Blood oozed from the Oneirophage's broken nose and dripped from a deep gash in his forehead, and internal injuries caused blood to drool from both corners of his mouth as well. One of his splintered ribs had torn through his flesh and protruded from the bruised skin of his breast. Another part of his chest was caved-in, and a deep diagonal laceration from left shoulder to right hip etched a scarlet furrow across his tattooed flesh. While he waited, the Oneirophage tore loose a jagged piece of adamantium railing to use as a weapon, the spider legs of his black widow hand wrapping around it like eight fingers. His right hand produced the Umbilicus from his wrist. With a click he unlocked its saw-edged switchblade, then assumed his battle posture, a coiled cobra waiting to strike.

The Necrodelic made his way down the stairway, onyx shield once more in hand, his every step a black bell tolling death, his gauntleted fists drenched in crimson, his armor splattered with drops of blood. He stepped onto the bridge and turned to face the Oneirophage. With dark synchronicity, they simultaneously attacked.

The Oneirophage caught the Necrodelic on the side of the face with the railpiece as the Necrodelic slashed a red smile on the Oneirophage's torso. They drove each other back and forth along the narrow walkway. Ultimately, neither gained an inch of ground. The Oneirophage beat the Necrodelic about the head with the piece of adamantium balustrade in a berserker frenzy, knocking dents in his helmet until the Death Addict stumbled with vertigo. The piece of bridge rail eventually cracked, and the Oneirophage broke the weakened piece of adamantium in half over the Necrodelic's skull. The Necrodelic swooned and took an unsteady step backwards. Tossing the busted pieces of balustrade over the side of the bridge and into the blood far below, the Oneirophage reared back, hissed, and unleashed a cobra strike that caught the Necrodelic in the face.

The Oneirophage tossed the Umbilicus in his hand, caught it, and spat two jetstreams of venom through the tube. The poison flew directly into Chariah's eyes, blinding him. The Oneirophage flipped the Umbilicus into the air again, then plunged the switchblade at the opposite end between the eye slits of the Necrodelic's horned helmet and tried to carve the Necrodelic's eyes from their sockets. The Necrodelic was too powerful for that, but the steady stream of blood pouring from the eyeholes of his helmet augured deep and serious wounds that would continue to blind him. The Oneirophage ripped the onyx shield from the Necrodelic's grasp and bludgeoned him with it. The Necrodelic shook his head like a wolf between blows, flinging blood from his eyes before the shield bashed him in the skull once more. The Oneirophage drove the Necrodelic along the bridge to the far side of the chamber, repeatedly smashing his face with the shield. Chariah crumpled in a heap against the wall. The Oneirophage laid the onyx shield over the Necrodelic's fallen body and then clubbed it with his tail. The dry slap of scales striking gemstone were followed by the sound of fracturing bones. The Oneirophage whipped the Necrodelic with his tail until it was raw and bleeding.

The Oneirophage paused, espying the onyx sword above, still sheathed in the bleeding wound of the wall where the Necrodelic had thrown it. The black blade jutted out like the shadow of a crucifix, hundreds of feet overhead. The Oneirophage spun the Umbilicus in his hands, over and under and through his fingers, until he had created a lasso long enough to retrieve the weapon. He cast the Umbilicus upwards to draw the sword from the wall, but the blade would not budge. The sentient spaceship was holding it tight to protect its master. Cursing, the Oneirophage climbed the Umbilicus like a vine to the stuck sword. Once atop the straw's zenith, he pulled and tugged at the hilt of the sword, but to no avail. The flesh of the wall constricted and tightened around the blade. He twisted the sword inside the wound and began ripping at the flesh around it with his bare hands. Preoccupied, he failed to notice that the Necrodelic had arisen on the bridge far below.

Chariah grabbed the base of the Umbilicus and shook it, hoping to dislodge the Oneirophage from his precarious perch. The dream-eater held fast to the hilt of the sword with both hands.

"Drakhus," spoke Chariah, and the wall relinquished its grip on the sword. The Oneirophage still held the hilt of the blade in his right hand and began to fall. Gripping the Umbilicus with his spider fingers, he wrapped his tail around the lengths of tubing. Chariah lifted the entire contraption in his mailed fists and began swinging it like an enormous rattan cane, smashing the Oneirophage into the sides of the adamantium bridges above. He then swung the Umbilicus overhand like a club, bouncing the Oneirophage's bloody body off of platforms, and up and down stairways. The Necrodelic's berserker fury was such that the Umbilicus was a blur as he swung it around in a wicked frenzy, so fast and with such force that the Oneirophage could neither react nor retaliate for several moments, until finally he managed to swing the onyx broadsword at a downward angle and bisect the elongated Umbilicus.

The Umbilicus was a resilient instrument, and the Oneirophage was able to transform even the truncated piece remaining in his hand, spinning it into a hammock-like web that knotted itself around the balustrade of a bridge and dangled like a gibbet. The Oneirophage landed in the mesh. Moments later, the impromptu net delivered the Umbilicus to the railed bridge, spinning the Umbilicus in his hand. He held it to his rainbow lips and inhaled, calling its sundered portions back to it. Those cloven pieces happened to be in the fists of the Necrodelic, and dragged him through the air as they flew back to their master.

The Oneirophage lay in wait, and swung the onyx sword when the Necrodelic came within range. The blade cracked its kindred armor open and tore a deep gash in the Necrodelic's chest and stomach. The Umbilicus then shrank back into itself, leaving the Necrodelic suspended in mid-air with nothing to hold onto. The straw slipped from between his gauntleted fists, and the Necrodelic plummeted a thousand feet into the blood reservoir below.

The Oneirophage immediately followed, leaping from the bridge with his arms outstretched like pinions and his head reared back to deliver a kamikaze cobra strike. He held the onyx sword in his right hand and the Umbilicus in his left, prepared to attack with both. His prism-plaited hair streamed in the air behind him, as did the Darkprism, blown over his shoulder by the winds of his descent, straining against the chain that held it around his neck. The Oneirophage focused on the concentric ripples and bubbles that marked the spot where the Necrodelic had landed in the blood reservoir. As the crimson plasma grew closer and closer, he could make out the dark form of the Necrodelic beneath the currents. He raised the onyx sword over his head and began to bring it down in a deathblow, with the force of a one thousand foot free fall behind it.

The Necrodelic lay waiting, submerged in the lake of blood. His hatred of water did not extend to bodily fluids, and blood was another one of his natural environments, another one of his territories, another one of his lairs. Blood was his home. When the Oneirophage burst through the surface, brandishing the onyx broadsword in an arcing quietus, Chariah swam to the side as gracefully as the shade of a shark, grabbing the Oneirophage's left arm and restraining him from behind. The force of the Oneirophage's momentum plunged them both to the bottom of the reservoir. Chariah struck pressure points in the Oneirophage's right wrist to make him release the sword, then trapped his forearm and elbow in an unbreakable, paralyzing armbar. The Oneirophage's hand and fingers were splayed forward as he descended into the crimson depths. Chariah's suit of armor was like an anchor, sinking both of them more rapidly. Scarlet bubbles whirled upwards from the bottom of the reservoir. The Necrodelic's plasmoptic vision allowed to him see through the blood as clearly as though it were water, but the Oneirophage found himself half-blinded and unable to penetrate the ichor with his serpent-sight.

The Oneirophage could hear and sense that the reservoir's bottom was alive with machinery, mechanical hearts beating, engines burning, fans whirring, filters spinning, vacuums sucking, incubators bubbling, submersibles skimming, and large ominous purification devices gurgling, churning, boiling, homogenizing, and amalgamating. Suddenly the adamantium floor of the giant cylindrical chamber came into view. The Oneirophage struggled and desperately squirmed as he glimpsed the sinister machines. The entire collection of intricate devices resembled a torture chamber, a submerged torture chamber, a torture chamber at the bottom of some Stygian, Acheronic, or Phlegethonic ocean, where mermaid dominatrixes dwelled.

Chariah tightened his grip on the Oneirophage, pinning his right arm and elbow even further back. As they crashed into the adamantium floor, Chariah maneuvered the Oneirophage so that his hand plunged directly into the irising blades of a meat grinder. The flat razors opened and shut, opened and shut, and as they opened, Chariah thrust the Oneirophage's forearm into their midst. When the blades closed again they severed the Oneirophage's hand at the wrist, to be borne away upon the crimson currents to the innards of the ship.

The Oneirophage clutched his fresh bleeding stump with his spider fingers, then cradled it to his chest and swam away from his enemy with one clawing arm. The Necrodelic followed, unsheathing the onyx sword from the bottom of the reservoir where it had stuck fast and hacking at his nemesis with the black blade, lacerating the Oneirophage along the length of his spine. Finally, defeated, the Oneirophage sought to escape into the blood sewers and excretory systems he could hear running through the bottommost levels of the Omnibeast. He located a small iron grille and ripped it from its hinges. He submitted to the violent suction that immediately roared from the shaft and allowed it to carry him into the hazardous tunnels below. The Oneirophage rode the rivers of blood down and away, into a gauntlet of narrow labyrinths and treacherous traps.

Chariah treaded blood for a moment before swimming back to the surface and climbing onto a nearby platform. He exited the reservoir through another portcullised doorway, already making plans to eradicate the Oneirophage. He would raise the temperature of the blood in the sewers to a degree far beyond boiling point and flush the Oneirophage from the living pipes with a series of controlled floods. Hopefully, he would be able to collect the corpse of the Oneirophage to smoke. However, he realized there was a strong possibility that the dream-eating demon would be dissolved, disintegrated, mutilated, or shot into space by the deadly organic processes below. Either way, he did not expect to ever see the Oneirophage alive again.

22

His bleeding arm-stump forming a crimson confluence with the rivers of blood, the Oneirophage drifted along the sanguine surf of the Omnibeast's sentient sewers, enduring the sharp turns and declines of the narrow pipes as the blood flowed with the speed of whitewater rapids. Some of the tunnels were barely wide enough for him to squeeze through, bruising his body and abrading his skin and scales. It was a claustrophobic labyrinth, a cramped and unforgiving maze. The sewers were giant veins and arteries interspersed with natural and mechanical valves, and pipes composed of iron that had been ripped from blood cells. These pipes often contained jagged edges around their entrances, exits, and corners, tearing his flesh as he sailed past their saw-toothed spikes. He maintained his strength by sucking dreams from the ship's blood with the Umbilicus, tearing fantasies from iron like baby leeches with his straw as he floated, imbibing the very currents that bore him through the liquid labyrinth.

As the dreams burrowed like tiny predators into his consciousness, he was overcome with the sensation of swimming to someone's heart, until he could not, at certain moments, distinguish the dream from reality. He was borne through the maze, and he sometimes saw crimson mermaids around the corners ahead, but they had always disappeared by the time he reached them.

Gradually the blood began to heat, slowly turning lethal at the influence of the Necrodelic, who lurked somewhere in the upper realms of the Omnibeast and was no doubt hooked into the spaceship's nervous system again in an attempt to destroy him. As the already naturally warm blood grew hotter, the Oneirophage was occupied by the ever-changing labyrinth. He frequently had to decide between up to ten different passages in a split second, for that was all the time the rushing currents of blood allowed. To choose erroneously could mean injury or fatality. There were no dead ends in this labyrinth, but there were plenty of pitfalls, traps, and killing machines.

There were no patterns either, no order to the tunnels whatsoever, nothing to help one comprehend the intricate twistings and windings. It was a labyrinth of chaos. Dodging giant meat grinders was a matter of timing, slowing down or speeding up to dive through the holes that opened briefly before the blades irised shut again. A giant liquifier loomed ahead, a hideous machine that looked like it would turn the Oneirophage's flesh into colored water. He took a detour through some septic tanks, acquiring malaria and syphilis as he did so. He sucked the sudden chancres from his penis with the Umbilicus and blew them into the crimson wake behind him.

The malaria he forced out with one powerful pneuma, the winds of which caused whirlpools and waterspouts in the rivers of blood.

The sound of trash compactors crashing shut echoed in the distance. Farther on, the Oneirophage observed the garbage spilling from those trash compactors into liquifying machines. As he watched the giant iron contraptions do their work, he realized that he had been correct in his earlier theory that the liquifiers would turn him to water. Not viscous sludge. Not dripping slime. Not even cannibal's wine. Water. Pure, monochromatic, odorless, soulless, crystal-clear water.

The streams and lakes of plasma had heated to the point where they bubbled as the Oneirophage drifted onwards. Floodgates were opening to increase the blood flow, and the currents bore the Oneirophage on their crimson waves at even faster speeds than before. He washed through some of the floodgates, being sprayed into the air like cataract foam and landing in the blood far below, where he was whisked away again. He traveled sideways in a curving tube against the bulge of the Omnibeast's underbelly. He could hear and taste the cosmos just outside, could feel the passage of solar systems in his serpent glands. Chutes into outer space began opening along the rim, shafts both short and long spewing wreckage and organic detritus into the interstellar voids. The Oneirophage exhaled continuously through the Umbilicus to maintain equal pressurization with the vacuums and avoid a similar fate.

Finally, the now-steaming blood deposited him into the lower digestive, reproductive, urogenital, and excretory systems of the Omnibeast. The giant, living, pulsing organs of the Omnibeast were multitudinous and resembled fungus demons. The veins and arteries of the spaceship ran directly through their throbbing masses. They were unavoidable and carnivorous, and he would have to go directly through them.

Each one tried to devour him. A black liver reached out with spongy hands as he sailed its dank caverns, stealing scales and trying to dig its fingers into his flesh to get at the chemicals within. The Oneirophage fought them off as he traveled through. One hand stole a fang while another stole a spider leg from his arachnid hand, then a third ripped off one of his eyelids. Others seemed intent on milking the fluids from his body, their hands masturbating him for sperm, sticking their fingers in his mouth for venom, and dabbing up blood from his wounds, then absconding back into their pulpy depths with the precious chemicals. The Oneirophage left many of the soft hands floating in their own veins and arteries before the currents of blood finally bore him onward.

Kidneys tried to liquify his flesh, passing him through valve after valve, filter after filter, collecting his sweat and blood but unable to turn him into fluids with their weak tissues. They poured salt on him as he exited, corrosive salt that burned his eyes and open wounds, and like some form of acid stinging the parts of his body that weren't injured or exposed.

The intestines were mazes unto themselves, from which many would never escape, would wander through eternally from dead end to dead end, or in circle after circle, until death or the end of time. They were pitch black inside, as well as completely devoid of sound. The Oneirophage cursed and could not hear his voice. He splashed the rivers of blood around him, and listened to silence. Blind, deaf, and mute, he would have to solve the labyrinth with only his senses of touch, smell, taste, and psychic abilities, and those esoteric perceptions known only to serpents through their specialized glands and pits. He waded through blood, felt his way around ribbony corridors with his black widow hand and his bleeding right stump, using venom to mark where he'd been and attempting to use the holes over his fangs to determine a basic outline or map of the visceral maze. After several hours of wandering, as senseless as a newborn grub, he finally emerged, blinking, from their coiled catacombs.

He wove his way now through giant wombs, chamber after chamber, each trying to mutate him. They used their umbilical cords like nooses around his throat to strangle him, or like shackles to bind him hand and foot like a dominatrix's lover, then held him captive in their wombs and tried to manipulate his genetics and evolution with psychedelic amniotic fluid and hypnotic suggestions. The Oneirophage feared he would exit the wombs with some chaotic mixture of new physical features, unwanted attributes such as horns, wings, fur, gills, flagellae, teats, a vagina, a second head, an exoskeleton, or worse. He was relieved to make his departure from the dominatrix wombs without any evolutionary enhancements to his body.

The cloacas that would shoot him into outer space opened at random on the walls and floor, and the Oneirophage had to avoid them like land mines. Finally, he came to a concentric circle of rivers, a downward spiral of blood within the bottommost realms of the spaceship, beneath which he could see the glimmering spires and parapets of his beloved Phantasmagorika. As the blood began to bubble and boil and toss like flames around him, scalding his flesh and raising red blisters on his skin, the Oneirophage used the Umbilicus to blow a hole in the wall of the Omnibeast's underbelly. Phantasmagorika lay directly beneath, still interlocked with the Omnibeast but partially detached, its rooftops a forest of minarets and tendrils.

The Oneirophage dropped down into his prism palace, the black mass of the Omnibeast pulsating overhead. The underbelly of the bestial spaceship was dripping incandescent blood, blood as hot as a burning star. The Oneirophage couldn't return to the circulatory labyrinth because of the boiling blood, which would soon be as hot as the flames of Hell and rip the flesh from his bones before incinerating his skeleton and immolating his soul. The Oneirophage watched as the scrotal sacs and wombs dangling from the Omnibeast's belly began to bulge, steam, and hiss as they filled with boiling blood, the ropes of black intestine lurching and sometimes bursting open like hoses to spray igneous blood like lava across the palace roof. The eight legs of the Arachniotics, folded together against the Omnibeast's underside, seemed impervious to the heat and magma, but they were also solid and impenetrable. There was no escape in any direction, no ascending back into the Omnibeast. He would have to return to his prism palace and hope that his spaceship had evolved enough to fly free of its host and progenitor.

The Oneirophage returned to Phantasmagorika by spiral rampway and evaluated its growth. The walls breathed and pulsated, and the myriad eyeballs, mouths, phalluses, vaginas, and umbilical serpents that had grown throughout the castle indicated that the spaceship was evolving as he had planned. Serpentikal had been surgically grafted on as a figurehead and revived as a zombie. The Oneirophage observed that the serpent lord breathed and was coherent. Outside, the palace's four giant butterfly wings had grown considerably, and were beating with the synchronized rhythm of flight.

The Oneirophage explored his larvating spaceship until he was assured that it had grown strong enough to soar through the cosmos on its own, with the undead corpse of Serpentikal to drag it through the interstellar voids and butterfly pinions to control its speed and direction. He regretted his defeat at the hands of the Necrodelic, but knew that it was best to continue the vendetta at some point in the future, with more dreams and memories accrued within his brain, more black karma dripping like leprosy from his soul, and even greater levels of oneiromancy and bellipotence attained. For now, he needed to heal. regenerate his hand, and raise his newborn spaceship like brood. He could not risk another battle with the powerful Necrodelic at present. It lacerated his pride to flee, to wait, but the stakes were too high in this eschatological war for salvation.

23

Chariah felt his wounds cauterize with the indrawn heat of the bong, felt his wounds heal as he smoked the Oneirophage's hand. The severed appendage floated at the top of the bong's heart chamber, ripping apart finger by finger with each breath of the Necrodelic, long painted nails transforming into wet ash. Within the smoke from the hand Chariah could taste the Oneirophage, taste the dream-eater's very soul, taste that he still lived, taste that he soared away even now in his pupating spaceship.

With psychic vision, the Necrodelic watched the Oneirophage depart, then smoked the rest of the hand he'd left behind. The lines of divination in the Oneirophage's palm burned down like the wicks of black candles, turning into ashen nothingness and altering his destiny. Chariah swallowed their one-dimensional ghosts like superstring serpents. He ripped the skin from the palm and then the rest of the hand, then smoked the flesh, blood, and bones underneath. He smoked the Oneirophage's fingerprints, and the entire chamber filled with kaleidoscopic, synesthetic yantras. Each finger dissolved with a hiss, as if they were serpents unto themselves. The phalanges looked briefly like fossils in tar pits before they, too, disintegrated.

157

Slowly, ever so peacefully, Chariah's awareness flowed in rivulets to the astral plane. Mother Chaos gathered the threads of those rivulets, wove them into an altered state of consciousness, and welcomed him into her womb and mouth.

"My Mother, I have failed."

Myriad tongues slithered their way through Chariah's lips, born forth from Mother Chaos, then detached and swam down his throat, through his guts, and into his sinuses. They cleared the way for words, astral words, the dream-language of Mother Chaos which could be heard with all six senses.

"...no, you have only begun...there will be other wars between you and your dream-devouring soulmate...this mission is not yet complete, my messiahling...but now, a new mission awaits...peer with me through the veils of time...gaze into this purple oracle...and observe the akashic records chronicled therein...look upon the origin of the Tantradox...the revolutions of the garden planet of Elasvai...and lo, even now your ship approaches the Dzandra system... where another piece of your destiny will be revealed..."

After observing the perverted rituals of the Tantradox for several hours within the oracle of Mother Chaos' purple eyes, Chariah blinked and found himself enfolded within the purple wings of his soulmate, riding beneath Mother Chaos like a possum child who had already learned to play dead. Together, Mother Chaos and Chariah traveled through the astral plane. Undead souls drifted by. Elementals played. Stars twinkled. Chariah's long black hair floated behind him, entangling with Mother Chaos' even longer purple hair, stardust shimmering in their silken tresses.

Chariah could see all the chaos in the universe from his perch, the chaos of the physical plane, which was born here, in the astral plane, the very chaos which Mother Chaos adulated forth, in part to aid him, in part because it was her essence, and in part to defy the order of Satan, the laws of physics, science, nature, and reality which Satan had created to govern the universe. Mother Chaos was every motion of the universe, but Satan was its every catalyst. Mother Chaos, omnisentient, was the apotheosis of all pleasure and pain, and a slave to their domineering continuum.

Chariah gathered a shred of that omnisentience through her

spine, up through his penis which grazed her back as he embraced her from behind. A taste of reincarnation, a tingle of immortality, and then all the suffering of decillions of souls, each one incarnating billion of times, living billions of lives filled with sorrow and pain, dying billions of deaths and returning to Hell to suffer billions of damnations. Chariah shuddered, knowing he must break this cycle to know peace, and take Mother Chaos with him, to the waiting beyond, to shatter her omnisentience.

Mother Chaos then turned around to face Chariah, drew his black phallus into her vagina, and loved him with an iron maiden womb, which punctured his astral sex and caused his physical penis to bleed on the plane above. The spikes were sharp and vibratory, and the pain stimulated the Dark Orgasm, stretching Chariah at once to Hell and the physical plane, from genesis to nirvana, before depositing him in the dripping meditation chamber of his spaceship.

Chariah left the smoky room and followed the maze to his cockpit. Once inside, he seated himself in the black lotus position. As he crossed his legs, his punctured penis touched his thigh with blood and Satan smiled. Chariah attached himself to the chamber's umbilical cords and psychically steered the Omnibeast through the Dzandra system. As the bestial spaceship drifted unto the garden planet Elasvai and the demonic Tantradox, the Necrodelic meditated in the zero-gravity cockpit, floating in mid-air in the black lotus position for several hours, readying himself for the battle to come.

24

Deep within the gardens of the planet Elasvai, in the sanctuary of the shadows of the megachariot Fiendfarms, amid sprawling amaranthine fields of medicinal and psychedelic flora, beneath the seclusion of giant belladonna leaves, hidden behind the privacies of poisonous forests and mandalic topiaries, on a bed of diverse flowers, surrounded by piles of exsiccitae ranging from the pungent to the fragrant, and wreathed in the smoke of lotus and opium, the tantric demons began their ritual. Two soulmates seeking the salvation of the Jh'a'vyraa, the crimson-fleshed, black-horned incubus and succubus arranged their surgical instruments on the flowerbeds and lush grasses like their very destinies. Cloven, six-fingered hands aligned rows of gleaming weapons and sharp tools. Gently, the two lovers smoked opium from a conjugal pipe, whose bowl was a vagina ringed in blossoming labia and whose twin mouthpieces were the tapering thighs of a spread-eagled sex slave, an incarnadine marble statuette which was a sinister transposition of the busts often found amongst the sculpture gardens of Elasvai, with hips and thighs instead of shoulders and arms, cut off at the knee rather than the elbow, female genitalia chiseled betwixt and atop them in place of a cold, staring head. Inhaling opium from the pornographic pipe, the incubus and succubus began numbing their bodies from the pain to come, and imbuing their minds with the higher states of consciousness required for the tantric sorceries and surgeries they planned to perform.

When the meadows, flowerbeds, plants, and trees surrounding them had taken on their true mystical properties, when their bodies had grown paler and their dark green eyes had shrunken into their skulls, the incubus Drelrei began the ritual, the sacrifice which was rebirth. Humongous scissors gleamed in his six-fingered hand as he positioned the blades, one over his succubus lover Junisia's right shoulder, the other grazing her armpit. Slowly, he brought the scissors together. Wetly, flesh tore, muscles recoiled and sprang back, and bones popped. The severed arm fell to the grasses and blossoms beneath, pouring blood into the gardens. Paradise had been stained.

Drelrei placed the scissors in the six fingers of Junisia's remaining hand. She opened the scissors around Drelrei's left shoulder, the opposite of her own, and yet also the mate of her bleeding socket. Junisia squeezed, and Drelrei's arm dropped to land beside that of his lover's, the two severed extremities sharing fluids like copulating worms.

Drelrei continued the ritual with a scalpel, slicing downward from the gaping wound of Junisia's armpit, opening up the entire right side of her body, all the way to the delicate, cloven hoof on the ensanguined grass below. Semen started to drip from the large crimson caldera in the tip of Drelrei's phallus. His erect, opium-engorged penis perceived Junisia's long wound as a giant virgin's vagina whose freshly-burst hymen was leaking crimson nepenthe down her thighs.

Junisia applied the same dripping scalpel to her soulmate, opening a mirror-image of her own elongated laceration on Drelrei's left side, her lover's surgery revealing his blood, tissues, and inner organs as if they were private parts, raw genitalia awaiting her touch. She dropped the scalpel, caressed the length of the wound, and looked lovingly into Drelrei's eyes.

Drelrei was already preparing for the next stage of their surgery. He held two glistening black needles in his hand, one of which he gave to Junisia. They then began to sew their veins and arteries together, severing their blood vessels and then tying them together in intricate knots, or fusing them at their sundered, dripping tips. Arteries, veins, arterioles, venules, and capillaries were threaded through the eyes of the black needles and sutured to one another, then stitched into exposed muscle tissues in elaborate red tapestries. Arterioles were inserted into arteries and venules were inserted into veins, and sometimes capillaries were inserted into those same arterioles and venules, and then all was hermetically sealed. Their circulatory systems now interwoven into one continuous network of conjugal blood vessels, Drelrei and Junisia shared each other's blood and could feel one another's heartbeat. The bleeding of one was the bleeding of both, their bodies bonded and bound by a tantric symbiosis.

Gathering a fistful of ropes made from hemp, Drelrei beckoned his lover to rise. Slowly, lovingly, as one, they sewed their bodies together with the hempen ties, flesh to flesh, bone to bone, consummating their devotion to one another by becoming Siamese twins. The needle flashed in and out of their scarlet, exposed muscle as they performed the surgery, drawing them closer with every stitch until their anatomies were inextricably enmeshed.

They folded the two halves of their conjoined bodies together, like the wings of a butterfly, and made love, satyriasis and nymphomania merging into one tantric continuum. Their suture was infinitely flexible, allowing them to twist and contort and copulate without tearing apart. As Siamese twins the incubus and succubus shared one symmetrical, synchronous, synergistic, synesthetic orgasm, finalizing the ritual and transforming into a single entity. They christened themselves the Tantradox.

Drelrei caressed the black nipples upon Junisia's swollen breasts with his clawed and cloven hand, while she in turn fondled his large genitals with her tapered fingers and curled fingernails. Massaging the two small horns on Junisia's forehead, Drelrei wrapped himself in his Siamese twin's ankylosaurus tail. Junisia brushed her palm and sable scalplock against the row of large, pointed, black dragonscales that rose like a mountain range along Drelrei's skull and down his spine, and twined his stegosaurus tail around her waist. Kisses laden with opium breath drugged them even further. They bit each other with black fangs and probed one another with barbed alien tongues. Their mouths within mouths within mouths continually opened and shut. Junisia's ten clitorises resonated in perfect synchronicity with Drelrei's ten testicles.

As they lay together some time later in postcoital serenity, Drelrei whispered to Junisia, "Soon, my love, we shall become the Jh'a'vyraa. Everyone, the entire universe, will be dead, and then, at last, we can be alone."

Junisia sighed and kissed her Siamese twin lover as he ran his cloven hand along her hundredfold labia. She caught the tip of his monstrous phallus and its cavernous crimson opening in her thin fingertips as he did so. For the rest of the day the Tantradox lay entwined with itself upon the gradually flattening flowerbed, trampling the fragrant petals beneath their enlightened intercourse. The most powerful tantric demons in the universe, they could delay an orgasm for several days, or have several orgasms in the course of a minute. During periods of postcoital ananda and enlightenment they philosophized together, imbibing wine and nectar from golden chalices that had caryatids and telamones for handles and were arabesqued with baberies and erotica, or ingesting various torrefied herbs, petals, and leaves from pornographically sculpted hookahs, calumets, and syringes.

From time to time they were visited by Pestilentia, Empress of Insects, who had followed the scent of opium and opium trances alike, the sickly sweet sugars of sperm and milk, and the stench of freshly severed limbs to the garden planet. A titaness the size of a small spaceship, Pestilentia was a living death-trap whose flesh was composed of ambrium, a sentient golden-brown melange of honey, opium, amber, and ectoplasm, within which could be seen the trapped and perfectly preserved corpses of thousands of insects, beasts, and demons. Her body was jointed and segmented like machinery. Her hindlegs were the powerful jumping catapults of the flea, her forelegs the incessantly cleaning, prehensile appendages of the fly, and her pincers the lethal forceps of the praying mantis. A giant scorpion's tail had been bestowed upon her by her sister Spidratha, a stinger the size of a lance that dripped several kinds of deadly venom. Her massive wings were the wings of the wasp, her plastron and carapace the impenetrable shell of the cockroach, her mouth the mandibled reaper of the locust, her nose the proboscine siphon of the mosquito, and her eyes the multiple, window-paned ommatidia of the spider. She had long, brown, semiliquid hair which flowed like syrup over her spiky back, towering and teeming termite mounds for breasts, and a bee hive for a vagina. Her entire body was honeycombed and served as a hive for millions of living insects, those that managed to avoid the sticky trap of her flesh, flying and crawling through the shadowy spaces between her joints and segments, and in and out of her eyes, proboscis, mouth, nipples, vagina, dorsal spikes, stinger, and other various orifices and tunnels, both natural and unnatural. She hovered on loudly whirring wings above the conjoined lovers, watching them with a myriad of voyeuristic eyes.

Pestilentia flitted in and out of their circle throughout the day, visiting them during each postcoital meditation, sometimes bringing them offerings of opium which all three smoked together. As the sun set, the Empress of Insects offered Drelrei and Junisia one million sacrificial victims for usage in their mutations and genetic experiments. Pestilentia, however, was a destruction addict, and desired in return the devourment of several crops and the infestation of several gardens.

"Begone, virulent one," Drelrei commanded, and Pestilentia flew back into the cosmos amidst a cacophonous buzzing of wings and a high-pitched chirping of curses, heading back towards whatever planet she'd been ravaging before being distracted by the scent of their ceremony, or perhaps retreating to her mysterious Darkhive, or the clandestine, cabalistic, fabled lair of her reclusive lover, Lord Panzebub, the location of which was known to none save the insect kingdom and omniscient Satan in Hell below.

Later that evening, Drelrei and Junisia began the three-day copulation that would complete their metamorphosis. Inside a greenhouse pagoda of the Fiendfarms, their wheeled, white marble, megachariot citadel, the Tantradox made love to itself. Heliotropic plants grew and bloomed in the burning light of their souls, bending toward their copulating bodies. The smell of recently-smoked opium and jasmine-scented aphrodisiacs perfumed the night air as the Tantradox seduced itself in a shower of moonbeams. Throughout and around the Fiendfarms they continuously made love, rolling through the gardens, courtyards, greenhouses, pagodas, menageries, laboratories, abattoirs, and Stormtower of their megachariot, beneath the jungle of meathooks dangling from the white marble underbelly of the citadel's bottom level, and through the acres of towering psychedelic crops and multi-colored flowerbeds surrounding it. Their tantric sex nursed them both back to health, healing, cauterizing, closing, and hermetically sealing their wounds. Even their scars dissipated, leaving behind healthy, continual bridges of flesh. The Tantradox committed sexual suicide and sexual homicide, one Siamese twin at a time, with hara-kiri thrusts of Drelrei's penis and hara-kiri impalings of Junisia's womb, the torture rack stretchings of Drelrei's lingham by Junisia's yoni wringing the sperm from Drelrei's turgid member. One Siamese twin at a time, the Tantradox's two souls traveled in and out of their respective body-halves, joining their astrosomes so that they would now astrally project as a single entity, and, if ever they were damned to Hell, they would be eternally tortured as a single spirit. Gradually, throughout this sexual ritual, their heartbeats, their breathing, and all their inner processes and bodily functions synchronized. Their biorhythms and astrologies aligned. They soon discovered, in their newly transmogrified form, that they could feel each other's orgasms. They were a single demon now, twice as powerful as before, ready to battle the universe with their sexual sorceries and become the Jh'a'vyraa.

On the fourth day the Tantradox emerged from the Fiendfarms onto a balcony ringed with caryatid and telamone balusters. The balcony projected from the citadel's front and overlooked a pair of Siamese twin brontosauruses below. The gargantuan dinosaurs had been naturally conjoined inside their shared egg and thusly hatched and raised, an extremely rare phenomenon of genetics and evolution which, like other rare freakish geminis throughout Elasvai's beast and demon populations, had been worshipped by Drelrei and Junisia for centuries.

The brontosauruses were restrained by a spiked leather harness that girdled their immense torsos and yoked their scaly girth to the Fiendfarms with a multitude of reins and leashes. With a whip in each hand, the Tantradox urged the dinosaurs forward, and the brontosauruses dragged the entire stone-wheeled palace behind them.

The effects of the opium, lotus, and psychedelic aphrodisiacs faded as Drelrei and Junisia gazed upon the passing landscapes of Elasvai. The ritual was complete. Where there had been pain, there was now only pleasure. Where there had been superfluous limbs, there was now only union. Where there had been two, there was now one. Drelrei and Junisia had been permanently fused into the Tantradox, and, together, as a single entity, they shared a single dream, a single destiny, and a single raison'd'etre: to slay the universe so they could be alone, in Siamese twin sadomasochistic ecstasy, for all of eternity, the way true incubus and succubus lovers should be.

25

The Omnibeast swooped down like a bird of prey from outer space, its behemoth shadow creating artificial nights in the jungles, forests, and fields over which it soared, awakening nocturnal animals in its tenebrous and mammoth wake. The bestial spaceship's four figureheads preyed upon the creatures of Elasvai. The Overdragon breathed flames across the gardens, incinerating the various demons, beasts, and lotophagi in its path, and igniting forest fires that dotted the landscape with bright orange conflagrations that glowed like the calderas of lit pipes, or the tips of hemp-filled cigarettes. Scythetooth caught bats and black eagles in mid-air, impaling them on his titanic fangs or engulfing them with one bite, chewing them up in the iron maiden of his teeth or swallowing them whole. War

Mantis, likewise, grabbed pterodactyls as they flew past, gripping them tight in his pincers and biting their heads off with one swift motion, then casting their decapitated bodies to the ground below. The Darkworm vacuumed harpies into its gullet like a black hole.

Chariah flew the Omnibeast from the womblike cockpit at the spaceship's nexus, using oracles to navigate and telepathic umbilical cords to steer and command his bestial vessel. As he gazed through the window-like oracles in the chamber, he noticed that War Mantis was decapitating his prey not once, but twice or thrice, and sometimes even more. The Necrodelic looked through the optic umbilical cords of Scythetooth and watched as the fanged beast snatched bats from the skies with his towering incisors and masticated their broken-winged bodies. Each of the bats had two or three heads. One had eight. Every manner of animal consumed by the sabre-toothed figurehead, from dragonflies to hawks to harpies, had multiple heads. He observed the pterodactyls struggling in the deadly embrace of War Mantis, and discovered the same phenomenon. The insect figurehead was decapitating each winged dinosaur more than once, but each head shared a single body. The harpies sucked out of the skies by the Darkworm were geryons. All of the prey were conjoined beasts. Siamese twins.

The surreal revelation elicited a nameless response in the Necrodelic, a strange twist of angst, dread, and nausea. There was something disturbing, something unnatural about the mutants that he couldn't quite identify, a vague sense of perverted nature and alien philosophies at work. The flight of some was unbalanced and erratic, often seeming drunken or epileptic. It was as if they flew with a limp or a damaged nervous system, lurching, staggering, flailing. Their sense of balance and equilibrium had been upset, and the distribution of their body weight was uneven. Many of them were visibly suffering. Sometimes tragic, sometimes repulsive, and always hypnotically surreal, they were among the strangest abominations the Necrodelic had ever witnessed.

Preoccupied with his observation of the soaring menagerie of conjoined animals, Chariah flew the Omnibeast into a trap. The spaceship skimmed along the treetops of a massive forest, whose trees were several miles tall and whose canopy camouflaged all beneath it. Upon closer examination, the Necrodelic found that the green leaves which formed the treetops were not leaves at all, but fingers and phalluses. Their green was the green of reptile scales. The scales did not form one continuous integument, however, but were each a separate entity, phalanges and genitals rustling in the wind like hair or fields of grass, parting and rearranging. Entire hands, with anywhere from three to a hundred fingers, were folded together as though in prayer, or clasped one another as if in greeting. Some of the hands had ophidian fingers, rising like cobras and erections. Fingers reached out or balled themselves into fists. Penises twined between both fingers and each other. Hands masturbated phalluses like snake handlers. Curved fingers performed fellatio on penises. The treetops were a writhing, seething mass of life.

Through this scaly, sentient, living integument, the branches of the forest burst. The branches were made not of wood, but of flesh, with fingers and phalluses for twigs, and mouths and vaginas for knotholes. They grabbed at the Omnibeast with their million writhing limbs, grappling and clawing, pulling the bestial spaceship down from the sky. Chariah channeled all his dark energy into the Omnibeast, and it struggled like a fly in a spiderweb, rising against the living tethers, trying desperately to escape the tangled trappings of the Forest of Flesh. The murderous maws of Scythetooth and War Mantis amputated branches left and right, ripping them from their trunks and tossing their dismembered remnants high into the air. The mutilated trees dripped not sap, but blood, as crimson and viscous as that of an animal. The Overdragon breathed fire and the reaching limbs blackened, their burned skin blistering, cracking, and crumbling. Still, the Forest of Flesh dragged the Omnibeast inexorably downward. The Omnibeast's Arachniotics were kicking frantically. Its multitude of mouths were screaming, and its myriad eyes were agape in horror.

Every time its living branches were severed or destroyed, the Forest of Flesh, like a hydra, immediately regenerated longer, more powerful limbs, and in greater numbers. Every time one of its soldiers were wounded or killed, its army grew. The battle was a downward spiral. The Forest of Flesh paradoxically multiplied via reduction, and was fortified by its own destruction. The more Chariah and the Omnibeast fought, the stronger their enemy became, like a gargantuan virus mutating and evolving over time, responding to every cure by becoming even more powerful.

The Darkworm was subdued and used like a rope by the trees to rein the Omnibeast in. The Omnibeast roared and fought madly, but was finally swallowed up by the Forest of Flesh and bound tightly by countless prehensile branches. The roots of the trees were intestines, and rose from the ground like hatching serpents to help bind the spaceship. After mere minutes, the Omnibeast hung like a corpse from a gallows in the viselike branches, suspended in mid-air over the visceral forest floor. The canopy of the Forest of Flesh had closed its scaly, hairlike integument over its captor, camouflaging it in their midst from any who soared above. The Omnibeast had been captured in a natural cage, a prisoner of the garden planet.

The Forest of Flesh not only resembled an organism, but it possessed and utilized tools like one as well. The mouth of the Overdragon was bound shut with lengths of black barbed wire. The pincers of War Mantis were immobilized in adamantium handcuffs. A giant iron wrecking ball served as a ball gag for Scythetooth. The Darkworm had been choke-collared from base to tip. The eight heads of the Hydratowers were each restrained by garrotes. The eight legs of the Arachniotics were broken and placed in sadomasochistic bondage-slings and spiked casts, the type that dominatrixes with fetishes for broken bones used upon their lovers and victims. The tips of the spider appendages were inserted into gargantuan thumbscrews. The Omnibeast was thoroughly and utterly imprisoned in the Forest of Flesh.

As the trees twitched and their wounds healed, a dark red stain spread across the underbelly of the Omnibeast. Internal injuries were leaking blood to the nadir of the spaceship. As the blood pooled, pieces of plastron became soaked with plasma and fell away. The stain grew more and more crimson and took on the form of an hourglass. Blood pushed through the Omnibeast's skin as if by osmosis and fell in tear-shaped droplets. The underbelly of the Omnibeast swelled up like an impregnated womb, gravid with internal hemorrhaging, distended with a gargantuan thrombosis. The blood began to fall more freely. Shadowy forms stretched against the tissue of the spaceship's abdomen. The wet sound of placentas ripping and tearing filled the air. A shower of blood poured from a new orifice in the Omnibeast's underbelly, dousing the ground below. With a burst of darkness and amniotic fluid, the Necrodelic tore through the ventral flesh of the Omnibeast with his bladelike claws, ripping himself out of his spaceship to dangle from a grappling hook embedded in the Omnibeast's guts, riding a black length of coil and a waterfall of blood to freedom. The sanguinary cataract splashed into the swamp of the forest floor. Chariah landed gently in the marsh, aided by the grapnel lodged in the innards of the Omnibeast.

The Necrodelic tugged upon the coil, and a pentagram-shaped grappling hook fell quickly from above. The lengthy cord retreated into a thin scabbard carved in the skin of the Necrodelic's wrist and forearm as he reeled the grapnel in. He caught the spinning pentagram with his right hand, where it lodged in five small sheaths of flesh in his palm, ready to be whipped out again in a nanosecond, if necessary.

Chariah looked around and began to walk through the Forest of Flesh. The marshlike surface was rotten, composed of the fluids, regurgitations, excrements, and diseases of the trees. A brackish, mephitic, knee-deep melange of blood, pus, vomit, bile, amnion, sperm, fungus, leprosy, decay, and half-submerged body parts formed a swamp of gore. The Necrodelic shuddered as he waded through the sludge, his aversion to water, even in such a semi-liquid state, briefly overwhelming him.

Branches swung at the Necrodelic with fists and slashed at him with claws. The mighty demon severed limbs with dark efficiency, leaving them to writhe in the murky swamps like feeding crocodiles. They were replaced almost immediately, in multitude. The intestines which formed the Forest of Flesh's roots reared up like cobras as Chariah passed. Those that attacked were sundered. The entrails pumped nourishment to the trees from the soil in a sort of perverted digestive system, a reverse digestive system whose strange purpose was unknown. Their strange black foodstuff poured into the swampy waters as they were sliced in half.

As the trees grew more aggressive, Chariah threw fireballs and breathed flame with equal force, setting parts of the Forest of Flesh ablaze. Some of the trees began quivering in fear, their skinlike bark growing sweaty and runneling with perspiration, their branches submissively pulling away from the Necrodelic as he trod in their direction. Some of the trees remained aggressive, while others seemingly ignored him, neither attacking or withdrawing, neither enraged or frightened. It was as though each tree had its own personality. The Necrodelic slashed his way through an army of striking, coiling, and constricting visceral roots to the base of one of the massive tree trunks. Examining it more closely, he could see the veins and arteries pumping beneath the soft skin that took the place of bark. Chariah hissed. Looking around, he noticed that the trees had faces as well, sunken into the trunks at varying heights, dispersed seemingly at random throughout the forest, murmuring to themselves or conversing amongst each other in alien languages. The undersides of living branches often bore breasts and testicles like fruit, and vaginas which served as lairs for two-headed arboreal creatures.

Chariah touched the skin of the peach-colored tree. It was as soft as flesh. Other trees varied in color and feel. Some were albino, some dark brown. Others bore the scales and snakeskins of reptiles, or the red and black flesh of various demons. Chariah ran a single claw along the trunk of the tree, opening a small surgical incision in its skin. The cut welled up with blood, dripped for a while, slowed, and then coagulated, leaving behind a dark scab. The Necrodelic struck a sudden blow to the tree with the side of his hand. The skin purpled and bruised, and the sentient tree whimpered.

The Necrodelic had abandoned his captured spaceship with only two items on his person. One of them was the pentagram-shaped grappling hook which he had used in his descent from the Omnibeast. He utilized this device now, turning his right palm upward and sliding the grapnel from its five tiny sheaths of skin. He swung the grapnel over his head and lodged it in one of the branches miles above. Droplets of blood flowed down the taut wire as Chariah ascended into the air.

The adamantium coil bore him swiftly upwards, his long black hair streaming behind him. As the cord used itself up, it recoiled itself beneath the Necrodelic's skin, sheathing itself in its scabbard of flesh until needed again. Alighting silently upon the large branch, Chariah slid the grappling hook back into the open sections of skin on his palm. He then brought forth the second item with a half-swallowing, half-fire breathing motion. A compact, obsidian pipe unfolded from beneath his tongue, growing and expanding until it emerged from his mouth. The pipe clicked and turned and rearranged itself with tiny gears, transforming into a miniature sculpture of a winged dragon, whose mouth opened on hinges so that it could be filled with drugs. Far less effective than the Bloodbong, it would nonetheless provide the Necrodelic with the sustenance he needed while exiled from his lair.

Chariah filled the sable dragon pipe with the skin, flesh, and blood of the sentient trees, ripping chunks of muscle right out of the trunks and branches around him, and opening gaping wounds overhead so that he could catch the dripping blood with the pipe. He caught and crushed a two-headed hawk in his fist as it flew by. Chariah squeezed and pulped the blood, organs, and entrails of the conjoined bird over the dragon's mouth bowl of the pipe, then stuffed the limp corpse inside after them. The Necrodelic seated himself in the black lotus position upon the base of the branch, his spine against the tree trunk. He placed the mouthpiece of the pipe, the tip of the spiked tail of the dragon, between his charred lips. Using his pyromantic powers, he breathed forth the fires of Hell, to light the flesh and blood within the pipe. For a moment, an interplanal portal opened in his lungs, through which he could feel the heat of Hell and synesthetically glimpse the damned souls being tortured in the underworld. He briefly saw, heard, felt, smelled, and tasted the voyeuristic red eye contact of Satan, as well.

The flesh in the dragon pipe's fanged mouth ignited, and as Chariah inhaled, its mechanical wings began to flutter. When he exhaled, the dragon's mouth spat fire, and its wings beat as though it were soaring through the skies. Chariah drifted into a deeper state of consciousness, a higher state of awareness, a darker version of evil. He observed the Forest of Flesh with bloodshot eyes. All the trees were connected like Siamese twins, joined at the arm, the hip, the head, or the groin, in every conceivable variation. Some bore the stitchlike scars of surgery. Others looked as though they had been fused or grafted together. There were faces everywhere, on every type of body part.

Sometimes the fingers, arms, and phalluses grew their own fingers, arms, and phalluses, which then repeated this process themselves, sometimes to infinity. The Forest of Flesh was one continuous conjoined entity, a million souls sharing one piece of flesh, the apotheosis of the Tantradox's sorcery.

His astral body began to tremble, then wriggled free into the air. Chariah projected through the Forest of Flesh. Everywhere there were two-headed animals, Siamese twins, from flies and mosquitoes to hawks and owls, from tree sloths and fauns to wolves to lions, surgically and genetically welded together at hundreds of different points. The Tantradox was more than a tantric demon, more than a conjoined incubus and succubus with the powers of a high-ranking occult sex-wizard. The Tantradox was also a practitioner of sorcerous breeding programs and selective mutation, a genetimancer, creating and altering life in its own twisted image. It was an ancient order of tantra they practiced, one which encompassed not only orgies and sexual ceremonies and sacrifices, but the births and offspring which those rituals begat, as well.

Flying high above Elasvai in his astral body, Chariah observed as much as possible about the garden planet, etching maps of blood in his brain with psychic blades for his memory to absorb, noting various features of the landscape, climate, foliage, and indigenous life forms. The planet had an extremely high population, and was home to thousands of wild animals.

Throughout his astral projection, the Necrodelic hunted the Tantradox with his sorcerous powers of demonsight and echolocation. The Siamese twin demons had highly developed powers of camouflage, both physical and spiritual, an aspect inherent to and derived from their garden planet and its flora and fauna, which hunted and were hunted amongst the foliage-laden paradise in an eternal predator/prey continuum. This camouflage forced Chariah to employ a third method, a spell of temporary prescience, which finally enabled him to locate the whereabouts of the Tantradox.

Gazing through time, the clairvoyant vision of the Necrodelic revealed the form of his Siamese twin adversaries approaching from the northeast in the very near future. Observing this, it became clear to Chariah that their first encounter would be inside the Forest of Flesh.

Returning to his corporeal form, Chariah found that midnight had descended upon Elasvai. Midnight was one of the Necrodelic's natural habitats, and it was to his advantage to battle at night, when his nocturnal powers and sorceries were at their peak. The nights on Elasvai were brief, though, because of the demand for sunlight by the gardens that ruled it and the extremely eccentric and frequent tiltings and rotations of the planet, which often changed the speed at which it revolved and sometimes stopped spinning entirely. With this in mind, Chariah touched the phallus of the dragon pipe with the tip of his tongue, triggering the mechanism that made the pipe refold itself and retreat to its lair inside his mouth. He slid the pentagrammed grapnel from beneath the skin of his palm and measured a small length of coil in his hand, and then, with burned flesh on his breath, murder on his mind, and Hell in his eyes, took to the trees to wait for the coming Tantradox.

26

As the towering citadel of the Fiendfarms shrank beneath the verdant horizons, dwindling from sight in the distance behind them upon the veranda where they had left it, the Tantradox rode a pair of Siamese twin chimeras to an ancient temple. The chimeras were bound in a spiked leather harness, and shared a single bridle and saddle, a bestial bondage device signifying its submission to the Tantradox. Its saddle was ten feet tall and Drelrei and Junisia sat atop it like monarchs, the conjoined king and queen of Elasvai. Drelrei held the chimeras' reins and Junisia held a long whip, like a dominatrix. Together, as one, they steered and directed their congenitally joined chimera steed, rearing it in and lashing it as necessary.

The paws of the six-legged mutation padded softly upon the stone steps as it bore the Tantradox to the temple entrance. The edifice had no roof, and thus the topaz sun Dzandra lit its chambers like a giant brazier. The Tantradox rode the chimeras to an altar of sacrifice that had been engraved with a sexual yin-yang symbol and dismounted. Their cloven hooves clattered upon the stone altar and echoed throughout the empty temple. Drelrei continued to hold the chimeras in check while Junisia lowered a gallows that was hanging overhead. Together, they tied the reins of the chimeras and the straps of their spiked leather harness through several of the small holes in the gallows, knotting them tightly into a series of body nooses. After removing the saddle and casting it to the floor ten feet below, the gallows was raised back up so that the Siamese twin chimeras dangled helplessly, its six legs clawing at the air, its weight causing the gallows pole to creak and make sharp cracking noises.

The Tantradox spent the next few hours smoking opium and psilocybin from pornographic pipes, their mouths within mouths within mouths chanting spells and mantras in ancient Elasvaian languages. They made love upon the bloodstained altar, imitating the sounds of various beasts as they fornicated. When midnight came like a saviour, the Tantradox was deep in a psychic and tantric trance. Together, with their hands mirroring one another, Drelrei and Junisia drew a ceremonial dagger from a sheath built into the gallows pole. Moving slowly, as if in a dream, the Siamese twin lovers raised the blade over their heads and inserted the knife just below the hanging chimeras' ribcage, in the hollow between its middle foreleg, where its conjoined bone socket formed a fontanel-like soft spot.

The Tantradox began to surgically drag the dagger along the creature's abdomen with one long motion. The chimeras roared and thrashed, but still the Tantradox maintained the same slow cutting motion, oblivious to the temple-rattling screams of agony and the slashing claws of the beast as it swayed in mid-air on its leather body-nooses, fighting desperately to free itself from its harnessed bondage to the gallows. Deliberately, in dream-motion, the Tantradox sliced the Siamese twin chimera open from breast to genitals. Fur and flesh parted, and blood began to drip upon the altar, collecting and runneling along the carven circle and wavy meridian etched into the stone. The Tantradox spent nearly an hour cutting the beast open with one continuous meditative motion, their hands moving the ceremonial dagger so smoothly and slowly that its movement was barely perceptible, like when watching stars moving through the skies, blood coagulating into a scab, or a corpse decaying over a period of days. Once the incision was complete, the Tantradox leaned back against the gallows pole, still gripping the ceremonial dagger between its hands, and waited with tantric patience for their handiwork to take effect. The long gash upon the conjoined chimeras' underbelly had been performed as cleanly and as straightly as if by surgery, as if done with a thin scalpel on a bloodless cadaver. Its rims were crimson and smooth, its opening but a slit. The wound barely bled at first, but this was not to last. After a few minutes, the belly of the Siamese twin chimeras began to bulge and swell, as though it were about to give birth. Then blood began to rain. The slit became a laceration and then a gaping deathblow, dilating like a vagina and then opening wide like the jaws of an Acheronic shark. Loops and coils of entrails suddenly began to emerge, dangle, and drop, and then two entire sets of intestines burst from the vivisected beast and fell in a hot pile across the altar of sacrifice, labyrinthine mounds of gore landing with wet slapping noises and splattering sounds, obscuring the engraved yin-yang symbol beneath.

Overhead, the death throes of the Siamese twin chimeras rocked the entire gallows. Its tormented roars shook the walls of the temple. The Tantradox paid the dying beast no heed, however, chanting tantric spells and drawing runes of blood in the thin tissues of the excavated innards with sharp black claws and curling fingernails. As the conjoined chimeras slowly perished above, the Tantradox began to copulate amongst the eviscerated intestines, laying down atop the altar of sacrifice and folding themselves together to fornicate in the gore, making love upon a bed of entrails. Drelrei and Junisia rolled and writhed amongst the warm intestines. The coiled lengths of viscera twined around their arms and legs and encircled their body. Junisia's scalplock was repeatedly dipped in the pool of blood as they made love, until her jet hair was sopping wet and seemed more crimson than black. Drelrei's ten testicles resonated harmoniously with Junisia's ten clitorises. Their bodies drenched in blood and wrapped in intestines, their souls alight with tantric sex, Drelrei and Junisia came to simultaneous orgasm amongst the offal at the exact moment the Siamese twin chimeras shuddered and died on the gallows above.

The ritual was half complete. The Tantradox carefully stood up amongst the loops of intestines. Junisia pulled a pipe from her dripping scalplock. The Tantradox smoked yet more opium and psilocybin. Once the proper state of consciousness had been achieved, the Tantradox began to study the patterns of the entrails they had made love in. They observed the way the entrails had fallen, the distances, the shapes, the labyrinths, and the impressions of their own bodies upon them. They noted the way the blood had flowed, the hieroglyphics it had written. They could read the future in the spilled intestines of the conjoined chimeras, their demonic skills of tantric haruspication feeding their eyes with revelation after revelation until their brains felt as though they would burst.

One thing, more important than all else, was foretold not only in the patterns of intestines and blood, but in the signs left by the Siamese twins' tantric sex. Where Drelrei and Junisia had made love upon the altar of sacrifice, they had unwittingly created a bloody chiaroscuro of the Necrodelic, and their indentations and sexual sculptings of the intestines had raised an abstract relief of the flesh-smoking demon within his own crimson outline. The future was clearly etched before them in a work of sacrificial art. Similar rituals, which were performed routinely by the Tantradox, had hinted at this potential future in the past, and would continue to confirm these divinations over the next several weeks. The higher levels of evil now possessed by Drelrei and Junisia, having been unleashed when incubus and succubus had been reborn into the archetypal form of the Tantradox, had strengthened and darkened the gravity of their shared soul, thus pulling adversaries and soulmates into their orbit like planets and stars. Their newfound powers had not gone unnoticed amongst demonkind, and the Tantradox was beginning to attract vendettas like erotomaniac and nymphomaniac necrophiliacs to mass graves of fresh bleeding corpses.

27

Drelrei and Junisia were nomads, continually wandering the gardens of Elasvai together. Whether in the enormous wheeled citadel of the Fiendfarms, on the backs of Siamese twin beasts of burden, or on their own hooved and cloven feet, Drelrei and Junisia maintained a perpetual state of peregrination. The very planet itself was their lair, their sanctuary, and their palace, and Drelrei and Junisia perpetually explored and circumnavigated their paradise, experimenting with its ambrosias, discovering its strange secrets, and communicating or battling with its plants and wildlife. The lovers never remained in any one territory for long, rarely making love, partaking of food and drugs, or performing their tantric ceremonies in the same place for more than a day. Drelrei and Junisia were simultaneously feral and enlightened, their wanderings equal parts hunting and gathering, musk and bloodlust, warmongering and spirit quest. The Tantradox was an eternal gypsy, a beast migrating to the end of time, a demon on a pilgrimage to the edge of the universe.

This day, however, was different. It was a day foretold by haruspicy and predestined in Hell. The Tantradox spent this day observing the heavens from the Cliffs of Caine, awaiting the arrival of the demon augured in the entrails of the chimeras. The Cliffs of Caine were the highest point on all of Elasvai, the zenith of the garden planet. They served as the Tantradox's observatory, for they were the best location for stargazing and astrological divination on the verdant world.

Coca plants more than one hundred feet tall surrounded the Tantradox, saturated with pure, photosynthesized, fully alkalized cocaine. Amongst the plants they could hear the rustlings of cocanaeds, the albino cocaine demons that inhabited the cliffs, foraging, fornicating, and satiating their addictions. Chewing on coca leaves, Drelrei and Junisia studied the sapphire skies. With their senses heightened and their consciousness quickened, not a detail of the landscape nor the heavens escaped their dilated eyes. Herds of animals roaming the plains below could be seen individually, their features clear enough to study, their vast numbers exactly counted within a nanosecond. Clouds grew like tumors in the endless firmament, and the Tantradox knew the various forms they would sculpt themselves into hours before they began to do so. The sun Dzandra shone luminously, and they watched the plants in the fields absorb its topaz light.

The Tantradox watched carefully throughout the day as Dzandra rose to its peak, plateaued, and then began to sink. They watched as the herds of animals grazed, played, settled, and then rested; watched as the clouds rearranged themselves, drifted past, and then dissipated. For hours, the Tantradox waited, eating the leaves of the giant coca plants to improve its vision and its powers of discernment and observation, The coca leaves also served as an aphrodisiac, and the Tantradox made love several times as they spent the day in the Cliffs of Caine, kissing with benumbed lips and tongues, their hearts beating pulpishly, adrenaline rushing like whitewater rapids in their veins, their orgasms like seizures accompanied by booming thunderclaps.

The copious amounts of cocaine they ingested inspired philosophical conversation between the two soulmates as well, interspersed throughout the day between lovemakings.

"I wonder," whispered Junisia, during one of these post-coital interludes, "if love can make two souls one...can hate make one soul two?"

"That seems a wise stratagem for battle," Drelrei responded. "Or the inspiration for a pair of weapons. A handheld iron maiden and a spirit-splitting sword, perhaps...," he mused. "The Soul Cleaver and the Flesh Compactor," he titled the imaginary weapons a moment later.

"How many souls, do you suppose, could be joined as one?" Junisia asked her twin. "Do you think it would be possible to sew and weld every living creature in the universe together, every single soul in existence from here to Hell, and then collectively achieve the Jh'a'vyraa?"

Drelrei pondered this idea for a moment. "A Siamese Infinity," he entitled the concept. "Would you add Satan to this amalgamation of souls as well?" Drelrei asked his conjoined lover.

"Perhaps, but without Satan, I believe there can be no Jh'a'vyraa. They are polar opposites, and like light and dark, or love and death, they cannot exist without one another. So, by becoming Siamese twins with Satan, be it as an individual or as a universe, you can never become the Jh'a'vyraa, and since the ultimate goal of every sentient entity is to become the Jh'a'vyraa, this union is either impossible or one that would nullify your very existence. Satan is the antithesis of everything else, of everything which is not Satan. He is the antithesis of all creation, and of the universe entire. Therefore, I do not believe it would be possible to add Satan to this all-encompassing entity."

Drelrei plucked another coca leaf from a nearby tree and began to chew. "The Siamese Infinity is physically possible, but

I personally would not want to spend the eternity of the Jh'a'vyraa with every other soul who has ever existed, my archenemies, my subservients, my former lovers, and my former slayers. Nor, I believe, would any of them like to spend eternity with us. It is this natural enmity between souls which is, in part, why the apocalypse rages and we all seek to kill one another, rather than sewing ourselves together or uniting ourselves into a massive army to battle or escape Satan. Besides, if every soul in existence were to join in a Siamese Infinity, and who's to say that it never has, then this universe in which we live in right now would be the Jh'a'vyraa or an exact replica of it, and I can proclaim without doubt that this universe is no Jh'a'vyraa. The Siamese Infinity would inherently create a karmic warp, a samsaric loop from which there would be no escape without individualization. Therefore, the Siamese Infinity, though physically possible, is spiritually impossible. And a war against the omnipotent cannot, by definition of the term, concept, and properties of omnipotence, be won, no matter how great or numerous the soldiers. Googolplexes upon googolplexes upon googolplexes of the most powerful demons possible would still be unable to overthrow Satan."

Junisia ruminated for a moment upon these mind-twisting enlightenments before speaking once more. "What is the maximum number of souls that can exist in the universe?"

"There is no maximum. Satan can create as many souls as he wants, googolplexes upon googolplexes upon googolplexes, and, with all eternity and infinity in his grasp, can add further googolplexes to their number as he pleases. No matter how many souls populate the universe, Satan can always add another, and then another, and then another. Conversely, I ask you this: how many pieces is it possible to cut a soul into?"

"Either an infinite amount, I would speculate, or none at all," spoke Junisia, as she, too, partook of another coca leaf.

"Would each severed piece of soul live on, like a dissected worm? Would each possess its own personality and identity? Would each have its own consciousness? Or would they merely be clones, fragments, even aspects of the original, and therefore remain under his or her control, and never beyond his or her realms of perception?"

"Perhaps the soul is ylem, an inexhaustible supply of energy that can be infinitely combined or divided as needed. Perhaps everything in the universe really shares one communal spirit, or are each small pieces of one greater oversoul."

"Satan," Drelrei replied laconically.

"Perhaps the oversoul represents the finite energy of the universe, and as the souls are cloven again and again, that energy is exhausted until only the singularity of the Jh'a'vyraa is left, and nothing else."

"Nothing except Hell and Satan," Drelrei said cynically, then added, "whom I fear, in his omniscience, is the only one who knows the answers to these philosophical riddles."

The Siamese twin lovers then sat in silence for a time, twice filling their pornographic pipes with crushed coca leaves and immersing their minds and bodies in yet more of the chemical stimulants. As twilight began, the Tantradox counted every star in the sapphire skies and committed their locations to memory. The rush of cocaine in their heads helped them draw numerous starcharts in their brains, starcharts that would remain accurate for millennia. With pounding hearts and tingling extremities, Drelrei and Junisia waited for the prophesied shooting star to fall.

The omen came just before sunset, the black and yet radiant celestial body that was much more than a meteor. The Tantradox watched it arc through the skies and bombard the planet with fireballs and gouts of flame.

Standing on the very edge of the cliffs, the Tantradox loomed like a giant effigy, and when it spoke, it was with a heavy and commanding voice, like that of an ancient and powerful idol that had just been resurrected.

"To the Forest of Flesh," Drelrei decreed. "The end of time has begun."

28

On the backs of Siamese twin griffins the Tantradox soared, seated atop a thronelike howdah. The conjoined griffins glided beneath the orange moon, the metal spikes of its leather bridle, harness, and saddle glinting in the starlight. Drelrei held its reins, Junisia its whip, guiding it through the night. Every few minutes the griffins beat their wings simultaneously, then coasted on currents of air for another several miles. Behind them the Cliffs of Caine, to which the griffins had been summoned by the call of the Tantradox, loomed like frozen tsunamis, hundred-foot tall coca plants forming pentagram-shaped silhouettes against the nocturnal horizons.

A giant battle axe rested on the lap of the Tantradox. Its curved edges gleamed sharply in the blackness from time to time, the quick smile of death. Above the shimmering battle axe the glow of small fires flickered as Drelrei and Junisia smoked coca leaves from a conjugal pipe, each holding a phallic mouthpiece between their lips and drugging themselves with the bounty of the pornographic sculpture. The breeze of their passage and the soft, cold winds of the night served to further numb their flesh, creating intense tingling sensations like orgasms throughout their entire body.

The Siamese twin griffins turned slowly to the southeast, their flight gradually arcing downward, gliding on a curving path. A glimpse of the Forest of Flesh quickened its wings, its destination finally in sight. A few minutes later, the Tantradox and its conjoined flying steed approached the wriggling green shell of the biodome, the leaves which were not leaves. The Forest of Flesh obediently opened a portal in its impenetrable wall for its master, hands unclasping and releasing their brethren from their grip, phalanges slithering out of the way, genitals squirming, twisting, and withdrawing from one another in order to create an entrance. The griffins soared through the irising gateway and into the Forest of Flesh. The portal closed behind them, hands folding in prayer, fists closing like locks, fingers resettling, phalluses thrusting and raping themselves back into place, all reassuming their positions in the outer defenses of the living forest.

Over, under, and around the thick limbs the Siamese twin griffins flew, deftly navigating the gauntlet of flesh-colored branches and tree trunks. The Tantradox urged its steed onwards with a lash of the whip, raising yet another welt upon its golden hide. Deeper and deeper into the Forest of Flesh the Tantradox flew, Siamese twin soulmates on a quest, Siamese twin demons on the hunt.

*

Black patience. One of the most difficult powers of evil to

attain. The ability to wait in a state of dark meditation for years at a time while maintaining and even increasing one's intensity, savagery, and propensity for violence. The ability to fuel one's anger throughout that period without being consumed by it, to plot vengeance for centuries without a single quickening of the heartbeat. A state of pure evil known by only the most enlightened of demons. In its trance, Chariah perched invisibly upon a tree branch, his grapnel ready, his crimson eyes glowing, his dark flesh completely camouflaged by the consuming nocturnal pitch, a shadow lying in wait, a predator hungry for prey, a sniper zeroing in on the raw stuff of murder itself.

Chariah first sensed the presence of the Tantradox with his echolocation. A few seconds later he could smell the Tantradox coming. Within moments, his Siamese twin adversaries would be in range. The time for black patience had ended.

The Necrodelic dropped silently through the branches until he was level with the approaching griffins. From a hidden perch, he watched as the Siamese twin beasts bore the Tantradox through the trees, closer and closer, until he could make out the features of Drelrei and Junisia's faces, see the protuberances of their black nipples and swollen genitals, and smell the cocaine on their breath. At the last possible second, with a sudden flick of his wrist, he sent the pentagram-shaped grapnel whistling through the air. It embedded itself in an incarnadine tree trunk, its coil stretched tautly across the forest, invisible in the shadowy night. The griffins flew under the wire an instant later, their wings and saddle passing beneath it. Drelrei and Junisia, however, were Chariah's intended targets. Their heads snapped back with whiplash as the stalwart coil clotheslined them. The force of the blow knocked the Tantradox from its howdah. The griffins flew onward with an empty saddle as the Tantradox flipped over in mid-air and plummeted to the ground, bouncing and tumbling off tree branches all the way to the swampy forest floor.

All of this happened before even a droplet of blood had welled from the flesh of the tree that had been punctured by the points of the grapnel. As quickly as it had struck, the star-shaped projectile was withdrawn, leaving behind it a sudden rush of blood and three screaming faces in the bark of the tree. Chariah caught the spinning grapnel in the flesh of his palm with a small spattering of scarlet, crouched, and then jumped from branch to branch as the Tantradox fell. The Siamese twin demons landed on their backs in the grotesque marsh of ordure and bodily fluids, splashing brackish water onto the tree trunks around them.

Chariah perched upon a branch several hundred feet above them, looming over his fallen prey. The Necrodelic looked down upon the Tantradox with incandescent eyes, a reaper of fallen souls. With feline grace he sprang into the air, his right hand held just over his head, his claws lacerating the sable forest gloom as he pounced. As he plummeted, he readied his gleaming talons for the deathblow, his black biceps bulging, his black triceps rippling with lethal tension, his musculature like three-dimensional shadows in the night. Chariah swung his claws in an arching strike just before he landed, aiming to impale the Tantradox through both of its hearts upon the swampy ground.

The quietus never connected. As the Necrodelic brought his claws over and past his head at the speed of thought, the Siamese twin griffins barreled into the side of his prone and falling form like a flying battering ram. The griffins knocked Chariah from his path of descent and sent him twisting uncontrollably through the air until he crashed painfully into the wide trunk of a tree some hundreds of feet in the distance. The Necrodelic fell limply into the viscid swampwater, but retained consciousness. He rose to one knee in the dark green, semi-fluid marsh, just in time to see the Siamese twin griffins soaring towards him again, skimming the surface of the bog with their claws outstretched, each leonine head snarling and baring its fangs. Chariah kneeled directly in its path, shaking swampwater from his long hair and beckoning the kamikaze monster forward. He then rose to stand before the hurtling beast, motioning it towards him with his claws, baiting the soaring brute. Just before the Siamese twin griffins connected with another bone-shattering blow, the Necrodelic slipped liquidly onto his back to lay supinely on the forest floor, completely submerged in the shallow marsh. The only part of the demon still visible were his long claws, stabbing upwards from the water like the spikes of a pit-trap, glistening wetly and sharply in the darkness. The low trajectory of the enraged Siamese twin griffins bore them directly through

Chariah's claws. Each half of the conjoined beast was sliced open from gullet to anus as it flew past. Its guts and all its organs immediately poured into the swamp. The momentum of its flight carried its lifeless husk onwards for several feet before it crashed into a tree, just like the Necrodelic had a few moments before.

The griffins were already dead by the time they collided with the trunk and fell to the ground. Their conjoined corpses lay half-submerged in the rapidly crimsoning swill. Chariah continued to lay beneath the surface of the foul pool, bringing his claws down to his sides so that he was completely underwater, resting as though he was enclosed in a coffin. His evil was such that he had long ago replaced the need for oxygen with death-addiction, and was thus incapable of drowning. Once again, he waited with black patience. Only a few minutes passed before the Tantradox blundered into him. He could hear the Tantradox splashing towards him, feel the vibrations of its grotesque gait in the currents of the swamp. The Siamese twins were not only searching for him, but they had also come to check on their stricken pet, the fallen beasts of burden that they had made in their own image.

Drelrei and Junisia were wounded and coughing up blood, their throats purple from the vicious clothesline, their bodies scraped and bruised from the fall through the trees, but the Siamese twins were so full of cocaine that neither of them felt even a twinge of pain. They reached the hulking corpse of the eviscerated griffins, observed its dead form, then retrieved their battle axe from its mangled howdah. Searching around and screaming animalistic battle-cries, Drelrei swung the battle axe wildly around his head, and then down into the swamp, over and over, suspecting that the Necrodelic was hiding nearby.

The Necrodelic remained still, waiting for his prey to come closer. He could feel the reverberations of the axe parting the waters and digging into the earth in his black spine, growing stronger, louder, until each blow was a thunderclap. Chariah calmly waited an instant longer, then summoned Hellfire into his lungs and breathed into the very swamp. The greenish waters immediately heated beyond the point of boiling, slime and detritus flaming along its surface, intestinal roots blackening and shriveling. The entire forest cried out at once. The

Tantradox, brimming with the painkilling effects of the cocaine, could not feel the heat through its tingling numbness, and was thus burned all the worse. When it realized what was happening, it screamed and stumbled through the boiling water, eventually dropping the battle axe into the bubbling currents and climbing out of the steaming swamp to take refuge in the branches above, where the Necrodelic was already lurking, having escaped the scalding marsh with his grappling hook.

The entire forest floor bubbled and churned like lava. The corpse of the Siamese twin griffins burst into flame and was cremated. The living trees of the Forest of Flesh were melting and burning, as though an entire race of demons had spontaneously combusted. Their faces became disfigured and scarred. Their visceral roots were burning out like the wicks of candles. The conflagration spread rapidly, and the Necrodelic swung through the trees on his grapnel to escape it. The faces in the trees began to cough and gag from the billowing smoke, their red eyes tearing, or closing in death. As the smoke wafted into and inside the trees through their myriad mouths and vaginas, the conjoined creatures which dwelled within their inner tunnels began pouring out through the faces and genitals at the top of the forest. Gaping mouths, flaring nostrils, and dilated vaginas vomited swarms of wasps and hornets, hordes of bats, and two-headed harpies from their depths. Amphisbenic nightworms burst through living eyeballs. All manner of winged creatures flew to the forest canopy and escaped, or perished in the attempt.

The Tantradox stood upon a thick branch and examined its wounds. The skin around their cloven hooves was burned, leaving behind a sticky, magma-colored residue. Drelrei and Junisia still couldn't feel any of the pain from their wounds. As the flames of Hell once more approached, the Tantradox ascended to a higher branch. Chariah was watching them from above all the while, and as they climbed through the trees, he once again threw his grapnel, this time high into the air, where it lodged in the scrotums lining the underbelly of a large tree limb. He swung through the air in the direction of the Tantradox, landing a side kick to the back of Drelrei's skull. The Tantradox struggled to keep its balance, at one point leaning face-down over the edge of the branch.

Chariah swung back into view and drove the claws of his

right foot into Junisia's face with a vicious front kick, knocking the Tantradox into the air. The Tantradox flailed and plummeted toward the cauldrons below. This time, the Forest of Flesh reached out with clutching hands to catch its master in a protective, netlike cradle.

By now, the Forest of Flesh was an inferno. It tried desperately to regenerate its lost limbs, but the Hellfire burned too fast and too strong. Arms and legs fell like bodies to the broiling waters below, leaving behind bloody stumps and sticky, cauterized wounds. As whole sections of the Forest of Flesh toppled in flames, Chariah and the Tantradox began scrambling in opposite directions, seeking the writhing green barriers of fingers and phalluses.

The Necrodelic opened a dripping exit in the living walls with his claws, slashing and castrating and dismembering his way to freedom. As he escaped, he noticed that the Tantradox had retreated deeper into the Forest of Flesh, and the Forest of Flesh itself was fleeing the fire on burning legs, transforming and rearranging itself so that it could run along its own living trunks and branches to a safe haven. It bore the bloody and battered Tantradox in its limbs, carrying their master off into the distance. Chariah observed that the sentient forest still held his spaceship as the trees disappeared over the horizon.

Somewhere on Elasvai, the Forest of Flesh would take root again, with the Omnibeast as its prisoner. Somewhere on Elasvai, as well, the Tantradox would survive. Chariah stood serenely amongst the flames and the ashes, tranquilly pondering the wet bloody remnants of the death and destruction he had wrought. His demonsight then zeroed in on his adversaries and he began to walk slowly through the smoking ruins in pursuit. With the burning taste of Hellfire still in his mouth and throat, the Necrodelic stalked his prey with a calm, even stride, hunting his victim step by step, by blackest step.

29

The flaming Forest of Flesh fled with an odd, tangled, effeminate gait as it frantically attempted to outrun its own conflagration, its thousands of steps falling in a broken rhythm across the grassy steppes and plains, leaving an uneven spoor of ashes and brushfires in its wake. The Necrodelic pursued his massive, wounded prey with the unwavering red gaze of his demonsight, tracking it along the burning horizons where smoke rose like spirits and ashes fell like bodies. Chariah hunted with deliberate strides, a black lion stalking, ashes filling his pumping lungs as he began to breathe faster, inhaling the raw heat of Hell and the sweet scent of immolated flesh, deeper and deeper with each quickening breath, delivering him into a trancelike state of tranquil necrodelia as he accelerated to greater and greater speeds across the plains. Like a wormhole, the powerful and heavy black aura of the Necrodelic warped and folded space, allowing him to traverse several miles with a single step, bending reality to his indomitable will. The Necrodelic was a caliginous blur, a spark of sable electricity, the brief shimmer of obsidian illuminated by a bolt of lightning, the final shadow of light before being sucked into a black hole, an event horizon unto himself, the entire darkness of all outer space concentrated into the size and shape of a single demon. The midnight that only lasts a second, the death which only takes an instant, Chariah flashed across the garden planet like one of Satan's neurons, the ultimate predator, invigorated and empowered from breathing in the charred and burning flesh of the injured monstrosity he chased, sucking the wet, ensanguined smoke into his expanding and quickening lungs as he ran, growing more and more evil at an exponential rate.

For one brief nocturnal moment the Necrodelic ran blindingly through the gardens of Elasvai, leaving tall grass rippling and giant leaves and flower petals stirring in the black breezes of his darkling passage. A shadow on the edge of a blade, cutting a swath through the night, visible only as an ephemeral silhouette to the eyes of the unenlightened, Chariah covered entire miles in mere seconds, gaining ground on the frenetic Forest of Flesh and then launching the pentagram-shaped grapnel from the palm of his right hand into the midst of the panicked trees, where it lodged itself with a loud sucking noise in the flesh of a sentient trunk.

The Necrodelic traveled the last few miles on the adamantium thread of his grappling hook, a light-speed spider in the night. As the iron rope recoiled into the sheath of flesh beneath his wrist, Chariah was borne upwards through the dark skies to the treetops of the stampeding forest. This time, it was the Tantradox who awaited the Necrodelic. Lurking high amongst the branches, hidden in the shadows, smoking a concoction of cocaine and opium from a hookah as they leaned against the sanctuary of a thick tree trunk and contemplated the karmic implications of their role reversals, Drelrei and Junisia watched with drug-heightened vision and fascination as the Necrodelic hunted with demonspeed, covering the miles of distance between them in moments. They heard the whirring, slashing sound of his adamantium grapnel as it flew past their heads, and the slapping sound of spikes landing gorily in muscle and tissue a moment later.

As the Necrodelic hurtled at supersonic speeds through the Forest of Flesh, the Tantradox peered around the side of the whimpering tree trunk they were hiding behind. Drelrei and Junisia waited with tantric patience, letting time accumulate like sexual energy before being released in one powerful sorcerous orgasm. As the ebon demon neared, the Tantradox leapt straight up and caught an overhanging branch in its clawed and cloven hands, from which it then hung with arms outstretched, as still as Siamese twin vampire bats. When Chariah passed into their boundaries, their circle, their orbit, the Tantradox twisted its conjoined bodies violently in the air, one swift, savage, spinning attack that shook the entire branch. Both of its armored tails lashed out like whips, a pair of deadly, weapon-tipped flails tearing the night.

The mace of Drelrei's stegosaurus tail struck first, catching the Necrodelic in the guts with its spikes amidst an explosion of blood and a crashing, ripping noise. The Necrodelic doubled over in mid-flight with the force of the blow, the spikes of Drelrei's tail shredding his abdomen and half-eviscerating him in the process. The ankylosaurus tail of Junisia trailed just inches behind its mate, and struck almost within the same instant. As Chariah's body bent over, the living mace burying itself in his guts, his head was automatically whiplashed forward and downward at a speed which superseded even the blazing fastness of his predatory flight. It was into his whiplashing skull that the club of Junisia's ankylosaurus tail struck, connecting with tremendous impact as it swung full-force into Chariah's face at the exact same moment his head was being jerked violently forward by the blow to his stomach. A second explosion of blood combined with the first to form a bursting red supernova of ichor. Chariah's black skull shattered like broken glass, with a sound to match as the solid bone splintered and cracked. The resultant concussion was instantaneous, and it was an unconscious Necrodelic that concluded his flight through the Forest of Flesh, black entrails reaching like tentacles from his torn abdomen, his hemorrhaging head lolling limply from side to side, up and down, back and forth as he swung directionlessly from the cable of his grapnel.

Chariah ricocheted from branches and tree trunks, raising indigo bruises on his sable flesh and scraping his skin with arabesque scratches. Finally, the adamantium coils became tangled and knotted, and the dazed and wounded demon was left dangling loosely from a tree branch like a corpse from a noose, twisting in the breeze.

The Tantradox climbed through the trees until they came to the protruding grapnel. There the Tantradox loomed victoriously. Portions of the Necrodelic's entrails were impaled upon the spikes of Drelrei's stegosaurus tail. Blood was splashed all the way up the back of the Tantradox, in mandalic drip-drop patterns not dissimilar to the starburst-like explosion of vermillion that had briefly filled the air like constellations of scarlet stars a moment ago.

The Siamese twin demons smiled wickedly. Together, Drelrei and Junisia dislodged the grapnel from the tree. A severed artery in the branch began spurting blood in bright red arches across the forest. Slowly, they dragged the limp form of the Necrodelic back through the trees, jerking the line when necessary, bouncing his body from branch to branch. When the Necrodelic had been retrieved, the Tantradox used the Death Addict's own rappelling wire to string him up, binding his wrists and ankles together with the coils and, thusly bound, to a pair of parallel branches, stretching his prostrate body tautly between the two, doubly hanging him upon a Siamese twin gallows. There, the unconscious and bloodied Necrodelic hung, suspended prostrate in mid-air.

The Tantradox beckoned for one of its servile creatures in the ancient, goat-like language of Elasvai. Several minutes later, one of the Tantradox's conjoined monstrosities, a vampire bat and a nighthawk sewn together, flew into the still-creeping Forest of Flesh with a ceremonial dagger betwixt its hooked claws. The beast alighted upon the outstretched arm of Junisia, where it remained perched as Drelrei gently took the bloodstained blade from its clutches. An instant later the conjoined winged mutation fluttered away into the distance. The Tantradox began sharpening the large knife upon the horns of its own head. The glint of scraping steel flickered in the night, small sparks showering the Tantradox as they used their horns, and then their cloven hooves, as whetstones. Finally, Junisia sharpened the ceremonial dagger upon the tip of Drelrei's phallus, grown rigid for the purpose, as hard as any grindstone in existence, creating an edge so fine that it could sunder atoms. The knife was so sharp it glowed. The Tantradox raised it over their horned heads together and slowly, meditatively stabbed the Necrodelic in the sternum. A series of liquid rubies ran in succession along the arete of the blade. The Tantradox gently inserted the ceremonial dagger in the Necrodelic's chest, then began gradually drawing it toward his half-exposed guts in a perfectly straight line.

*

The astral plane was an avalanche, crashing down around Chariah like the thousand fists of Satan, each gripping a neutron star in its palm to multiply the concussive force of the blows. Shards of reality fell in broken pieces around his battered soul. Fragmented perceptions bombarded him like boulders. The Necrodelic fell violently into his astrosome in much the same way one was often jerked back into their physical flesh from the spectral dimension. Shocked and disoriented, he felt the astral plane forming in fusillades around him. The sensation was that of rapid water torture from every possible angle, where the drops of water were successively replaced by morning stars, wrecking balls, and asteroids hurtling at the speed of light.

The Necrodelic awoke into the open grave of the astral plane, but it would be his physical corpse in a similar tomb if he did not act quickly. His mortal flesh was in extreme peril, and his very soul was at stake. Hell and Satan beckoned below, and the open grave of the astral plane was rapidly closing. Chariah flew in astral form to the garden planet of Elasvai, to the shimmering, silver Forest of Flesh, to the side of his incarnate self. Mother Chaos was already there, sexually joined to his suspended underside and blowing healing energies from her purple lips into the open rim of his phallus with interdimensional fellacio. Chariah focused on the Tantradox, the conjoined incubus and succubus simultaneously raising a ceremonial dagger to the breastbone of his physical body. The blade passed through the scintillant back of Mother Chaos like the wraith she was, just below her beating wings.

Purple drops of blood spattered the currents of the astral plane. Chariah hovered above his Siamese twin adversaries, haunting them with his vague black presence. Floating upon the vibrations of the spectral plane, Chariah aligned his astral body with that of the Tantradox. His ebony spirit was a shadow pouring itself into their flesh, settling like nightfall between their bones and organs, filling their inner chambers and orifices like ink. The heat of his soul dissolved the cocaine in their brains, blood, and nervous system, disintegrating its painkilling effects and awakening the Tantradox to the pain of its myriad wounds. Chariah slipped his right arm into Drelrei's, his left arm into Junisia's, immersing his own arms in theirs, all the way to the fingertips. Their hands became his living gloves. His legs he placed in theirs as though into a suit of armor. He draped their torso, chest, and back over his own like a sentient robe. The Necrodelic adorned the Tantradox like a dead skin costume. Their faces became his mask, their flesh his cowl. His fangs dropped like a portcullis into their teeth. His scorched mouth swallowed their six smaller mouths in a grotesque pantomime of a food chain. His eyeballs incubated within theirs, like larvae in egg sacs. His black heart beat painfully inside both of their red hearts. Their animal lungs filled to bursting, choking on his own. Their abdomen grew swollen with his entrails. His black penis he inserted into Drelrei's own and wore it like a condom of incubus leather. Slowly, like a crown or helmet, the Necrodelic pulled their brains down over his own. With the sorcerous benedictions of Mother Chaos and his own evil powers, the Necrodelic infiltrated the flesh of the Tantradox, invading his enemy like a disease, wearing their bodies like living garments. The possession was complete.

*

The Tantradox caught drops of blood on their tongues as

they began the ritual evisceration of the Necrodelic. Deliberately, they slit the demon open and dragged the ceremonial dagger down his chest. The pure, meditative slowness was a vital aspect of the ritual. Their hands barely moved as they slashed the Necrodelic asunder with a single motion that could not be detected by the eyes of the unenlightened, so slow that the Tantradox itself did not even notice when the dagger came to a complete halt. After several moments, the Siamese twins sensed the cessation of the blade. Disturbed, the conjoined lovers tried in vain to restart the gradual gashing of their sacrifice's underbelly. Disturbance turned to panic as the Tantradox then attempted by turns to slice, stab, twist, wrench, and withdraw the blade. The ceremonial dagger was stuck fast in the Necrodelic's chest, as though the demon were made of stone.

When the blade did move again, it was not by the Tantradox' volition. Suddenly, the dagger removed itself from the flesh of its intended victim, seemingly with a sentience all its own. The Siamese twin incubus and succubus could only watch in horror, helpless observers of their own bodies, as their arms pulled the dripping weapon down. Their limbs were not their own, but had been turned into broken doll parts, prosthetics controlled by an external force. The Tantradox couldn't even use its own throats to scream as their hands turned the ceremonial dagger inwards and plunged it into their conjoined chest.

The knife buried itself in their right breast, then slowly drew a complete circle from ribs to abdomen and back again. When it reached its point of origin, it slashed quickly downward toward their conjoined navel at a sharp angle, then upwards once more, diagonal, horizontal, and diagonal a second time. As the knife tumbled from between their fingers, the blood welled forth from the continuous wound, revealing in bright crimson the perfectly drawn form of an upside-down pentagram in a circle of containment.

The Tantradox could not control its body, but it could feel the pain that had been wrought upon its flesh. The pentagram of blood unleashed an unnatural form of agony, a suffering beyond imagining, a burning, throbbing mass of excruciating torment, as if they had been forced to bear the pain of every surgery ever conducted since the origin of the universe, as if they had suddenly grown a billion more nerves in rapid succession, each one twice as sensitive as the one before, until they could literally feel the wrath of Hell inside their very bodies.

By the time the black soul of the Necrodelic had discarded the flesh of the Tantradox, the pain in the Tantradox' chest was so great that it could do nought to reclaim control of its nervous system. The pentagram of blood hemorrhaged profusely, in strong surges that soon superimposed their own crimson designs over the ancient sigil, then cascading over the Tantradox' genitals, runnelling down its thighs and legs, and raining upon the forest below.

The Tantradox stumbled drunkenly along the branch, hoping desperately to cling to the bloodsoaked skin of the tree with cloven hooves ill fit for such feats of balance and dexterity. Somehow, the Siamese twins managed to keep from falling and finally regained enough control over their own muscles to reach out and grab hold of the Necrodelic, who hung unconsciously between the branches above. Using his body for support, they clung to his flesh with scrabbling claws and battled the collective vertigo of their shared consciousness. They grabbed at his long, thick hair, drove talons and fingernails under his skin for leverage, seized his genitals like a lifeline and held on with every last piece of strength they could muster.

The Necrodelic opened his eyes.

The Tantradox stumbled backwards beneath the palpable force of his eye contact, their grips loosening on his hair, his flesh, and his sex. Chariah's crimson gaze refocused immediately upon the bloody pentagram carved into their dripping chest. His eyes blazed with an igneous red. An instant later, the portals of Hell were opened and the pentagram of blood burst into flames. This time, the Tantradox lost all control over its clutching fingers and tightly fisted hands, releasing their grip on the Necrodelic and falling backwards from the tree branch, a burning pentagram blazing in their flesh. As they fell, they left behind a trail of oily smoke which perfectly replicated the shape of the pentagram branded on their chest.

The sigils of smoke rose high amongst the treetops and wafted into the Necrodelic's charred lungs, giving him the power to rip free of his bonds and drop silently to the ensanguined branch below. Blood poured in sheets over his head and face, from lacerations in his skull, from his broken nose, from between his split lips and broken jaws. His hair was drenched with viscous crimson, sopping with blood, plastered to his back. The entire right side of his skull had been shattered by Junisia's ankylosaurus tail. His abdomen was torn open and parts of his entrails dangled from the ragged wound left by Drelrei's stegosaurus tail.

Chariah stood bleeding upon his vertiginous perch, too weak to fully heal himself from the injuries he had suffered. He cast aside his grapnel and its shredded adamantium coils with a curse, throwing them far into the depths of the Forest of Flesh and rededicating himself to the forces of black patience, dark serenity, eternal evil, and immortality of the soul, and simultaneously shunning the forces of demonspeed, berserker rage, battle fever, and kamikaze tactics.

Several moments later, the Necrodelic spread his arms out like the wings of a dragon and floated gently to the forest floor below. He landed astride the Tantradox, its chest still afire with the flames of Hell. His taloned feet dug themselves into the parched ground, now dry and full of fissures and cracks like the sides of a volcano, the swamp that had previously coated the forest floor having completely evaporated in the massive Hellfire. Chariah formed two loose fists with his clawed hands and raised them to his lips, one before the other, forming a narrow tunnel with his palms. He inhaled, and for a moment the flames flickering on the Tantradox' chest drew together as one and were sucked into his hands. Chariah breathed in for several minutes, then exhaled, blowing thousands of tiny flaming pentagrams through the shaft of his palms. The flaming pentagrams soared and gusted to all parts of the Forest of Flesh, in every direction and at every possible angle, as Chariah slowly turned around. They flew from his hands like small creatures that had been set on fire, like burning moths, butterflies, doves, and bats on a mission from Hell. The living forest, which had only recently ceased its flight and begun to regenerate its dead parts, once again burst into flames, much worse than before, and this time took off running like a pack of pinioned screaming banshees.

Chariah dropped his soot-covered hands to his sides and admired his pyromancy. He breathed the incense of burning flesh as the forest blazed, rekindling his inner energies. As the smoke of the forest fire billowed around him and sparks flew through the air while the trees burned, Chariah inhaled again, this time to heal the massive, bleeding wounds in his skull, chest, and abdomen with the necrodelia. His chest expanded as he attempted to smoke the entire forest like a gargantuan drug, like a shaman attempting to smoke an entire forest of cannabis with a single breath. His eyes fluttered shut as he drew in the healing smoke and regenerative heat, sucking the pyromancy and the necrodelia into his lungs. His flesh began to tingle as the first wave of healing energy flowed through his wounds, but then, just as suddenly, all the breath was driven out of the Necrodelic's body with one enormous blast. Cumulus clouds of black smoke billowed from his mouth, combining with the torrentially hailing cinders and ashes to completely obscure the form of the Necrodelic and everything around him for several seconds.

When the smoke dissipated, Chariah was on his knees, and the enormous, deformed, combined middle leg of the Tantradox was buried in his groin. The Siamese twin demons had regained enough strength to unleash one mighty blow, and with the force of a feral destrier had driven the large, iron-shod, cloven hoof of their third leg into the Necrodelic's testicles.

Chariah knelt in a crumpled heap, coughing and then vomiting blood along with the smoke and ashes still issuing from his lips. Exhausted, the Necrodelic momentarily fainted, falling face-first to the ground beside his screaming adversary, who was too immersed in its own universe of pain to even notice.

Meanwhile, the Forest of Flesh continued to burn, and fled frantically across Elasvai like an insane behemoth, bouncing and rolling the unconscious forms of the Necrodelic and the Tantradox along with it, ricocheting their limp bodies from its knotted roots and thick tree trunks as it ran. The Forest of Flesh trampled entire gardens, temples, and herds of Siamese twin dinosaurs in its path, its thousands of legs churning as its trees screamed in pain, desperately seeking sanctuary from the conflagration that would condemn its multiple conjoined souls to Hell. One hour and several miles later, the living forest finally found its haven in the form of a lake, in which it gratefully immersed itself, doused its fires in the crystal waters, and began the slow process of healing and regeneration.

30

Mandalas of bubbles swirled like strange amorphous haloes around the heads of the Necrodelic and the Tantradox. The demons awakened simultaneously, all six sets of eyes blinking open in perfect synchronicity. Below them a garden of anemones blossomed in the pure waters of the lake bottom. Around them was the Forest of Flesh, its skin pink and irritated with various degrees of burns, oozing black pus into the water. Its intestinal roots were laid out in clear view before them, many severed during its flight. Many miles above lay the surface of the lake, obscured by tons of floating ash.

Chariah's first reaction upon regaining consciousness was to slash the Tantradox with his razored claws. His blows were not slowed at all by the waters and their currents, his muscles so powerful that he attacked with all the speed and strength he possessed in any other environment, from planets of the densest gravity to moons with virtually none at all, from the deepest vacuums of space to complete submersion beneath an ocean. His claws raked the Tantradox across both of its faces, releasing little red pearls of blood to float in the water and accumulate like coral. The Tantradox flew backwards through the water as if caught in a strong undertow, eventually slamming gently into the trunk of a sunken tree. The Necrodelic moved to attack, but his wounded head spun beneath the pressure of the water and darkness descended over his open eyes. The jagged, bloody clefts in his face and skull still hemorrhaged, burning now with salt and pounding with the heavy water pressure and the lake's underwater currents. His torso was still torn open, as well, the black tips of his entrails waving in the water like jellyfish.

Chariah's healing sorceries, reliant upon pyromancy and necromancy, did not work underwater. He began to swim for the surface, his claws cutting the water like swords. The Forest of Flesh attacked him as he did so, seeking vengeance for the fires he had unleashed upon them. Mouths bit and tore at him as he swam by. Hands grabbed at him by the hundreds, trying to drag him down further, to capture him in their grasp and hold him underwater until the end of time. Branches pummeled him about the head and back. Severing limbs, Chariah ascended in circles around the living trunks and branches, swimming a violent gauntlet to the surface. As he rose higher, the ashes grew thicker, invigorating him and restoring his strength.

Upon reaching the odd canopy which served as the exterior of the Forest of Flesh, Chariah cut a large hole in the writhing mass, using his long talons like scythes and sickles. The integument reformed itself immediately, however, keeping him trapped beneath the surface of the lake. Worse yet, he had angered the many entities which comprised the treetops, and found himself assaulted by striking cobras and bludgeoning fists, knocking him further below the surface. Chariah flew upwards through the soot-filled waters once more, placing all ten claws together to form the giant Hellsword. He opened a large gash in the green hordes, large enough to swim through. Chariah kicked out with his rippling thighs and tried to shoot through the hole, but the fingers and phalluses caught him before he was halfway through, biting and flogging him and pummeling him back down below the surface again.

The Necrodelic cursed, for it was his own attacks that had strengthened the strange living integument of the Forest of Flesh, had forced it to evolve and now, like a mutated virus, it was immune to him. Chariah tried one more time to rend the violent mass asunder. This time the coils of a boa constrictor-like phallus grabbed him around the throat and began to strangle him.

The Tantradox began ascending toward the surface of the lake, wielding once again the ceremonial dagger with which it had attempted to sacrifice the Necrodelic. Chariah watched the Siamese twins, swimming upwards like conjoined mermen, the black mark of the pentagram still burned into their chest. He kicked Junisia just beneath the chin as she drew near, and her head jerked back in a jetstream of blood. Chariah freed himself from the serpentine noose, only to be stabbed in the side by the curved dagger of the Tantradox. He lashed out with his claws, but the Tantradox ducked by simply floating downwards through the water, then rapidly countered with its dinosaur tails. Drelrei's stegosaurus tail came flying from one side like a morning star, catching Chariah in the left cheek and twisting him sideways in the water. The Tantradox reversed its battle spin and Junisia's ankylosaurus tail bashed his right cheek like a club. Chariah contorted sideways and floated backwards, his head lolling limply upon his chest. Like a piece of living detritus the currents dragged him through the water in long, slow, circular patterns.

The Tantradox dragged Chariah to the bottom of the lake, where the garden of anemones beckoned hungrily for his flesh, their tentacles writhing, their mouths dilated and rimmed with poisonous fangs or barbed tongues. Drelrei and Junisia inserted the right hand of the Necrodelic into one of the irising maws. The carnivorous polyp immediately clamped down and tried to chew Chariah's hand off. Its sharp, hooklike teeth severed the veins in his wrist, and then, instantaneously, the feeding frenzy began. Anemones of every color, shape, and size clashed their fangs together and lurched through the water to bite off pieces of the Necrodelic's flesh. Hideous round gullets dilated to partake of his blood. It was like a thousand set traps had been triggered simultaneously, a thousand animal snares snapping shut at once.

Semi-consciously, Chariah fought back, hacking the anemones from their seabeds and slicing them to ribbons. The Tantradox was poised over him now, smiling sadistically. It had retrieved its battle axe, and was already bringing it around in a whistling arch that would decapitate the Necrodelic. Chariah called upon the one spell of fire which did work underwater. He closed his eyes and pyrokinetically heated the entire lake to a temperature beyond the point of boiling. The sea anemones wilted and died. Some of them exploded. Drelrei and Junisia cried out in agony, bloody bubbles streaming from their mouths as they swallowed the incandescent water and it scalded their digestive system. The pentagram carved upon their chest blazed anew with the fires of Hell, which were capable of burning underwater. The Siamese twins flailed about in the roiling lake, looking upwards as if to escape through the Forest of Flesh. The sentient trees, however, did not react in any desperate manner to the boiling water. The heat painfully seared their skins, but it was fire, not heat, which was capable of destroying the Forest of Flesh, and the sapient trees, still traumatized by their burnings, were not about to leave their oasis.

The Tantradox whistled for one of its subservient beasts.

Moments later, Siamese twin sharks appeared at their sides, already saddled. The Tantradox climbed onto the conjoined selachian steed and headed east.

Meanwhile, the hot water helped cauterize Chariah's wounds, stopping the incessant bleeding and restoring some of his strength. He still had no conceivable means of departure from the lake and its deceased anemone garden, and was too weak to battle the Forest of Flesh underwater, where his powers were severely diminished. Chariah determined that the Tantradox knew of an alternative escape route as it rode off upon the back of the Siamese twin sharks, and swam after them, trailing in their wake like a slipstreamer. Chariah's theory proved correct, as the Tantradox rode the sharks into a hidden underwater tunnel in the eastern side of the lake.

The Necrodelic continued to swim behind his nemesis and their slaves, following them through several twists and turns until they finally emerged into a dank grotto. Chariah climbed from the water into a cavern of moldy rocks, where he immediately began to heal. He gathered some moss into a pile and blew on it, lighting it on fire and drugging himself with the deaths of the tiny souls trapped inside. Meanwhile, the Tantradox realized their adversary had been trailing them and pulled upon the leather reins of their steeds, jerking the heads of the sharks to the left and circling back into the grotto. Chariah greeted them with a fireball, lobbed like a slow comet into the water around them. The Tantradox deftly steered the conjoined sharks around the flames and sailed for the moldy bank where the Necrodelic stood. The rocky shore was narrow, and the sharks leapt out of the water and snapped their jaws at the Necrodelic. Chariah brought an elbow down upon the top of one of the shark's skulls, caving it in and dislodging one of its eyes. The Tantradox swung its battle axe at the Necrodelic's side, but he twisted and caught the weapon's handle under his arm. The Tantradox tugged with both hands, but could not pull the weapon free. An instant later the battle axe was snapped in half by Chariah's powerful biceps and triceps muscles, its metal head clanging to the mossy shore, its broken staff still clutched tightly in the cloven hands of the Tantradox.

They battled for several minutes, causing small avalanches in the grotto and its surrounding caverns and opening minor wounds on one another. After a sustained period of the sounds and vibrations of combat, something beyond the grotto had been disturbed, awakened by the irregular rhythms and loud battle cries. A pervading rumble echoed through the subterranean caverns, shaking the ground like an earthquake and causing the underground river to ripple with unseen tides. Both Chariah and the Tantradox halted as the fanged head of a giant worm burst through the walls of the cavern.

The blind, segmented beast wriggled forward, devouring whole chunks of rock, splashing through the murky water and then drinking the entire underwater spring with its circular, tooth-ringed gullet, swallowing the Siamese twin sharks whole. The Tantradox jumped free of the conjoined sharks as the helpless creatures succumbed to the undertow of the worm's enormous maw, leaping to the shore as their steeds were sucked into oblivion behind them.

The Necrodelic, however, was waiting. As soon as the cloven hooves of the Tantradox clattered upon the mossy promontory, the Necrodelic spun out of the shadows with a devastating roundhouse kick, his foot-talons raking Drelrei and Junisia's faces as his heel knocked them into the air and sent them flying into the far distance, directly into the waiting mouth of the vermian behemoth. The fated demons would do battle again, but for now, the fight was over.

Chariah escaped into a small network of caves beyond the grotto, leaving the worm to thrash about, searching blindly for its escaped prey and causing avalanches as it did so, until finally it retreated back into the rocks and whatever subterranean lair it had come from, taking the Tantradox and its pet sharks with it. Its vibrations grew fainter and fainter as Chariah climbed, squeezed, wriggled, and slid his way through the caves. Hours later, the Necrodelic found a large patch of psilocybin in a lightless cavern. He lay his weary, battered body down upon the soft, dream-inducing mushrooms, and at last allowed himself to slip into the unconsciousness he had been fighting for so long.

31

When Chariah awoke, he found the cavern filled with a strange, gemlike illumination. Psilocybin bloomed all along the floor, a garden of mushrooms, some taller than he. They grew in alcoves along the curving walls and dangled from the ceiling like stalactites, dripping their psychedelic syrup onto the small forest below. It was from the mushrooms that the ethereal glow emanated, tinting everything it touched the color of lapis lazuli, jade, and amethyst. Chariah arose from his bed in the soft mushroom meadows, psilocybic dreams playing in his brain. He walked slowly through the curved heads of the giant fungi, which seemed to bow down and worship him as he passed.

There was another light in the far corner of the cavern, the flicker of fire flashing against the wall. It drew the Necrodelic pyrotropically in its direction. Amongst the mushrooms Chariah found an ancient demon with a blazing hookah. The elder creature was seated in the black lotus position. He was bald, and for that matter, completely hairless, his wrinkled skin pitch black, as dark as Chariah's. His eyes were open but he was blind, seeing nought but the same deep milky blackness which colored his eyeballs. In one hand he held a totem staff of shriveled heads. The other held the hookah, filled with piles of mushrooms, its water chamber bubbling with hot, liquefied brains extracted from the heads on his staff. He gestured toward the Necrodelic with the water pipe as he approached, offering to share his feast of psilocybin.

Chariah sat next to the demon yogi and inhaled from the hookah, falling deep into a psychedelic trance. The elder spoke, and in his mouth were fangs, and his voice was the whisper of spiders crawling through shadows.

"You have suffered many wounds. Come, partake of the healing mushrooms. They have kept the Cacoshaman alive for many eons."

Chariah smoked the psilocybin from the hookah. When it was gone, the Cacoshaman offered him a syringe full of mashed mushrooms, which Chariah injected into his arm. His pain began to fade, his wounds to slowly heal. The Cacoshaman offered him a skull full of blue mushroom wine, which Chariah imbibed. Meanwhile, the Cacoshaman had replenished his hookah, and was smoking from it once more.

"Elasvai is a beautiful planet," said the Cacoshaman.

"I don't believe in beauty," Chariah replied, accepting the hookah once again and inhaling more of the burning psilocybin.

"Still, it shall be a shame to see it die."

"Tis a matter of perception, ancient one. Your sentimentality will serve you ill in this universe." Chariah handed the long pipe back to its owner.

"What brings you here...Chariah?" the Cacoshaman asked.

Chariah sat in silence for several moments before hissing threateningly at the elder, "How do you know my true name, Cacoshaman?"

"The Cacoshaman knows much, my child. He knows where the black holes lead. He knows where Satan's weaknesses lie. He knows, perhaps, who will become the Jh'a'vyraa..."

"Who?" Chariah demanded, his interest suddenly aroused, but the Cacoshaman had passed into a state of incoherence and semi-consciousness. The demon yogi was delusional.

The Necrodelic cursed and grabbed the hookah from the Cacoshaman's limp fingers. As Chariah smoked more of the sorcerous fungi, the Cacoshaman came back to awareness and felt around blindly for his missing hookah. Chariah placed it back in his withered hand.

"Thank you, demonling," the Cacoshaman spoke, as Chariah raised his gleaming claws into the air.

"Drelrei and Junisia, I warned their mothers of such abomination when their souls began copulating in the astral plane, even as their embryonic bodies had yet to develop within their wombs."

Chariah's claws whistled to a sudden stop.

"Are you their father?" he asked the Cacoshaman.

"Their father I am not," the ancient one replied, "although their mothers were once concubines in my intergalactic harem. I'd have ripped their fetuses stillborn from the womb had I the chance. Now, they have perverted this paradise planet with their genetic sorceries, their twisted religions and their tantric abominations," the Cacoshaman rambled.

"Where are their mothers now?" Chariah asked the Cacoshaman.

The old yogi raised his totemic staff and pointed in succession to two shriveled, black, horned devil heads upon it.

"Come now, partake of more mushrooms. You've not fully healed yet," the Cacoshaman said.

"It will take more than mushrooms to heal these wounds,

old one," Chariah replied.

"Well," said the ancient demon, resignedly, "do what thou wilt."

Chariah looked puzzlingly upon the elder, although his crimson eyes did not betray any hint of his perplexity. Chariah raised his claws into the air once more, this time bringing them down in a wide arc and slashing clean through the old demon's throat, decapitating him with a single blow. His withered head rolled through the mushrooms before coming to rest amongst the psilocybin he had so enjoyed.

The body of the decapitated yogi did not crumple or fall over, however, but maintained itself in the black lotus position, its spine as straight and its muscles as rigid as if he were still alive. Blood fountained from his severed jugular veins and carotid arteries in waterspouts and arching streams. Chariah caught the sacred crimson greedily on his tongue and imbibed it like elixir. Once the jetstreams of blood had been reduced to mere rivulets dribbling down the corpse's chest, Chariah retrieved the severed head of the Cacoshaman.

With one flash of his claws he removed the top of the demon's bald, ebony head, then emptied the brains from his sable skull. He set the brains aside for later, then began to carve and vivisect the decapitated corpse. The headless Cacoshaman continued to sit upright in the black lotus position even in death, even as Chariah excised large chunks of muscle from his skeleton and spitted his inner organs on his claws. He filled the Cacoshaman's skull with his own mutilated flesh, hot blood, and still-beating organs, then replaced the brain and scalp, bore a small hole in the back of the skull with one claw, and used the severed head as a pipe. Cobalt smoke tinged with veins of electric blue billowed from the eye sockets, nostrils, mouth, and ears of the Cacoshaman's head as Chariah inhaled its grisly contents. Finally, Chariah's wounds completely closed and healed, his body melting back together like shadows. The pain of his injuries was abolished as broken bones knitted and lacerations closed seamlessly into jet black skin without even the faintest of scars.

Several hours later, the regalvanized Necrodelic arose and departed the psilocybin gardens through an opening in the far wall of the cavern. His victim had been picked clean, as though by carrion eaters and scavengers. Not a trace of meat, flesh, organ, or blood remained. The Necrodelic left behind nothing of the Cacoshaman but a scorched skull and an ebony skeleton, still seated upright in the meditative black lotus position, his totem staff of shrunken heads in one hand, his still-lit hookah in the other. The Cacoshaman's black phalanges remained joined around each fetish, forefinger to thumb upon black patellas, with black femurs, tibias, and fibulas crossed, black spine straight, black ribcage intact. As Chariah made his exit, the Cacoshaman's charred, sooty skull rolled slowly across the chamber, levitated into the air, and balanced itself precariously upon the tip of the Cacoshaman's spine. Still weeping smoke from its empty eye sockets and drooling liquid ashes from its rictus, the skeleton of the Cacoshaman meditated in its tomb of psilocybin, smoldering like a gruesome thurible.

32

The Psilocybin Labyrinth shimmered and crawled like a thing alive, the floor, walls, and ceiling continually melting into one another as Chariah made his way through the spinning tunnels. Surrounding him were the dripping colors of the maze: magenta, indigo, aquamarine, cerulean, carnelian, carmine, rose, olive, saffron, and silver, flowing over and into one another with slow, hypnotic waves. There were colors the Necrodelic had never seen before, or which he had not previously perceived as colors, joined with the others in what seemed the Psilocybin Labyrinth's private, secret spectrum. Diaphanous was a color here, as was effulgence and mirror. The gelid drops of mirror reflected distorted images of the Necrodelic as he passed, perpetually stretching, bulging, and rearranging parts of his body while drenching them with the ephemeral hues of the amorphous labyrinth, creating various combinations that were sometimes disturbing, sometimes tragic, sometimes frightening, sometimes absurd, sometimes disgusting, and sometimes religious.

Arabesque rainbows criss-crossed the air. The corridors spun faster and faster the further Chariah travelled, colors racing in mad orbits around the ceilings, walls, and floors. In the distance, like a vortex, a small opening in the tunnel continually changed color and shape, but never size, even after Chariah had been walking towards it for hours. He often lost sight of it in his twistings and turnings, but always seemed to locate it again later, though it remained perpetually unattainable.

The colors were simultaneously bleeding, raining, and melting around the Necrodelic. Chariah watched with hypnotized eyes as time slowed down, sped up, and sometimes stopped entirely. Observing the colors was sometimes like watching a year's worth of clouds in one minute, seeing them race across the sky in all their permutations and transmogrifications without having to wait for hundreds or thousands of days, or like watching the process of erosion over several millennia in mere moments, or the entire existence of the universe, from genesis to armageddon, in one second, as one singular, gigantic, simultaneous, infinite, amorphous mass.

The Psilocybin Labyrinth played with his tunnel vision, entire corridors shrinking around him to the point where he couldn't move and was trapped for several minutes, then expanding into the size of rotundas or colosseums until they were so vast that Chariah was constantly lost and wandered their changeling floors for hours. The tunnels often spun in place, leaving Chariah walking on the walls or ceiling. Sometimes he would sink into the ground, as though a pool had opened beneath him, immersing him in the tides of floating colors up to his neck, then raising him back to the original floor. Faces appeared in the dripping colors, moaning and chanting, before melting back into oblivion. Oracles opened in the ceiling and floor, revealing evanescent glimpses of distant futures and ancient histories.

Mycomorphs made entirely of psilocybin attacked. Many took on the appearances of Chariah's enemies: the Oneirophage, Morpheus Rex, the Tantradox, Democubus, Serpentikal, Spidratha, Pestilentia, Panzebub, the Plaguepossessor, Sadimancer, the Horned Ones, and even Satan himself, as well as numerous other beasts and demons he remembered from his billions of past incarnations, and others he had yet to battle.

Chariah struck down the fungoid homunculi with his claws, in brief parodies of his previous battles that were somewhat similar to past life regression, reliving wars both won and lost throughout the eons. Streams of blue blood spread from the mutilated fungus demons and joined the other fluid colors of the maze. The Necrodelic continued his journey, leaving in his wake piles of quivering corpses in the shapes of demons he had known.

A rich viridescence joined the changeling colors of the labyrinth, adding its hue to the rest. As Chariah continued on, the viridescent colors became more dominant, until they were half of the maze, interspersed like camouflage amongst the other shades. Chariah touched a patch of the emerald color on the wall. It felt thick, dry, and smooth, and was ridged with miniscule hooks. The entire labyrinth began to change shape as he felt his hand turn green. Further ahead, the colors ceased melting and began forming bright patterns of stripes, diamonds, and camouflage. The maze sometimes led the Necrodelic in circles now, sometimes elevating slightly, sometimes forming bridges over the corridors he had previously traversed, sometimes taking him in concentric rings or downward spirals in a labyrinth that seemed to have been inspired by a pile of entrails and then constructed in their image.

Chariah halted, realizing that the labyrinth was not only reminiscent of spilled viscera. It was also similar to the coils of a snake in repose. The Necrodelic stopped and smelled the air. Venom. He examined another piece of viridescence on the wall, ran his palms over it, breathed the chemicals in it. Snakeskin. Chariah turned, hissing aloud as he bared his black fangs.

"Serpentopolis."

Cautiously, the Necrodelic trod the spiral corridors. The walls continued transforming into patterns of snakeskin. Ahead, he saw sunlight and the silhouette of two thin fangs. He walked along the passageway to the snakehead and looked beyond its open mouth. The first thing that caught his crimson gaze was the reanimated body of Serpentikal. The snake lord's head had been reattached and loomed once more over its civilization, which had been thoroughly repaired and augmented with additional levels. Chariah stood on the high balcony of one of the snakehead turrets, gazing at the back of Serpentikal's skull. The labyrinth below him was a mass of tangled coils, forming the writhing streets, alleyways, and bridges of the city. The Necrodelic swept his gaze around in a semi-circle. There were more snakehead turrets and parapets across from him, some revolving upon their own necks. Balconies and eyries were built into the upper levels as well. To the far right, its extracted dungeon levels obscured in a thick wrapping of serpent coils, was the prism palace of Phantasmagorika, towering over all. Its foundation was level with the parapets of Serpentopolis, now that its dungeons had been torn from the ground like a behemoth's tooth and accompanying nerve. Its heavily guarded drawbridge, currently raised, formed the lone passageway between Phantasmagorika and Serpentopolis, leading into the largest of the snakehead towers. The entire castle had been transplanted, psychedelic moat and all, onto this living monstrosity. The revelation was an instant one for the Necrodelic, for he had known the manner in which the dream-eater had survived and escaped Grystiawa, and similarly slipped from his clutches in the Omnibeast and fled into outer space. Chariah was gazing at this moment upon the living, saurian spaceship of the Oneirophage.

Chariah refocused upon Serpentikal. The crown of the First Serpent's head was the spaceship's secondmost zenith, rising as high as the middle levels of the prism palace. Serpentikal was engaged in combat with a foe beyond Chariah's sight. With his hood flared and fangs snapping, Serpentikal unleashed a cobra strike, and Chariah caught a glimpse of the green cords that bound him to the ship. The tethers looked to have been made with living anacondas and boa constrictors, flexible enough that Serpentikal could fight but strong enough that he could never escape.

An arrow whistled past the Necrodelic's head. Serpentman archers had taken up positions in the snakehead turrets directly across from him, which had rotated to face the intruder. The serpentmen were firing upon him with crossbows and bow and arrows. Their missiles were coral snakes, black mambas, and asps. Chariah sliced the venomous vipers in half with his claws before they could strike him fang-first and inject their poisons into his flesh. With his right palm he launched a volley of fireballs over the coils of the Serpentopolis and into the towers, destroying the serpent archers one by one, knocking them backwards into the open mouths where they perched or toppling them in flames to burn in the streets of the city.

The jaws of the living snakehead turret which Chariah

stood within began to unhinge. Chariah climbed out of the aroused snakehead just as its jaws crashed down in an attempt to impale him, its throat spasming in anticipation of swallowing its wounded prey whole, to capture and deliver him through its esophagi to the unknown depths of Serpentopolis. The Necrodelic emerged from its mouth and alighted upon the crown of its head, then began running across the ophidian turrets, leaping from snakehead to snakehead until he reached the front wall of the city. He turned and ran across the towers of the front wall in the same manner, then jumped high into the air and landed upon the hood of Serpentikal.

The ancient First Serpent had been reanimated through voodoo and served as the figurehead of the Oneirophage's saurian spaceship. The scar of its decapitation was still fresh, and the pungent smell of embalming fluids radiated like pheromones from the suture. The gargantuan, ophidian zombie hissed and swayed as Chariah knelt atop its skull, but could do nought to harm the Necrodelic in its current position. It refocused, instead, upon the struggle at hand, and Chariah watched from above.

The giant worm which had devoured the Tantradox and its conjoined sharks had burst from a mountainside cave and was trading headbutts with Serpentikal. Its blind head was bloodied, and several of the fangs which ringed its circular mouth had been knocked out or blasted down its gullet. Still, it continued to thrash and lower its head like a battering ram, striking Serpentikal about the face and chest, its tail hidden inside the cave.

Serpentikal's mouth was dripping with blood, but he had clearly asserted himself as the dominant warrior in the brutal combat. His cobra strikes bashed the worm against the rocks of the mountain, his fangs tearing into its segments, sometimes catching between them and peeling them off like a rind, leaving exposed and bloody tissue behind. The worm was already filled with gallons of venom. Its defeat was imminent.

Serpentikal unleashed a fury of headbutts upon the vermian behemoth, in rapid succession, nearly driving it back into the cave. The serpent lord then caught the great worm in his mouth and began shaking it from side to side, gradually pulling it from its lair. He retracted his cobra head and dragged the entire length of the worm from the mountain, throttling it like a rabid hellhound.

Chariah watched the battle unfold, noting with some astonishment that when the worm was pulled wriggling from the mountainside, it possessed not a tail, but another head, identical to the first, like an amphisbaena. Yet another Siamese twin mutation. The battered worm vomited crimson ichor from both of its spiked mouths, drenching the mountainside like a volcano that erupted blood instead of lava. Serpentikal continued to shake it between his fangs, his paralyzing agents finally taking effect in its large, amphisbenic body.

As the worm was being thrashed about, it vomited the still living Siamese twin sharks amidst a cataract of blood. The conjoined selachian monstrosity fell to the rocks below, bouncing down the mountainside before landing on a stone promontory far below, where it twitched about violently, shuddering and spasming from the lack of water it required to survive, flopping around in the deadly air for several minutes before finally lying still.

Serpentikal had bitten clear through the giant worm, and thrown it into mid-air only to catch it by one of its heads. He engulfed it with his entire maw and sank his fangs into its segments, then began sucking on the worm's head, vacuuming its muculent and sanguinary insides and its fourteen beating hearts into his mouth and down his throat. When he had succeeded in exterminating the beast, and had imbibed its insides to his satisfaction, Serpentikal spat its corpse contemptuously onto the rocky terrain several thousand feet below.

Chariah watched all this with drugged fascination, still feeling the effects of psilocybin as well as the smoked flesh of the Cacoshaman. Once the melee had ended, Chariah surveyed the gore from above, searching for augurs in the patterns of bloodstains.

A familiar voice broke his concentration as he enjoyed the ensanguined mountain vista from the observation tower of Serpentikal.

"A dream, Necrodelic. Nothing more. Nothing less."

Chariah turned to see Morpheus Rex seated upon a throne carved from a single prism, high atop a dais in the shape of a pillar that had arisen from the roof of Phantasmagorika. The Dreaming Predator reclined as though in thoughtful meditation, a Satanic serpentine stylite. He was positioned directly in front of the sun, forming a partial eclipse in his image, like an idol or an omen, or both.

Morpheus Rex stood up and spread his arms wide. Sunlight flickered off the prisms in his hair, shimmered on the prisms inlaid upon the white gossamer robe he wore, gleamed from the three-foot tall prism-inlaid crown upon his head, and flashed from the Prismscepter in his right hand.

Pondering the Dreaming Predator's statement, Chariah found it laden with multiple meanings. Did Morpheus Rex refer to his new spaceship, his relationship with the Necrodelic, or reality itself? Was he commenting upon the Necrodelic's experiences in the Psilocybin Labyrinth, or perhaps his commune with the Cacoshaman? Had he proclaimed his own solipsism, or that he no longer believed in Chariah's existence? Was he telling the Necrodelic what he desired from him, either freely given, sacrificed, or taken by force? Or was he just pretending to be the king of some strange realm in his perverted imagination (which would explain the royal raiment and regal accompaniments surrounding him)? All this and probably more, Chariah determined, for forked tongues always spoke in double meanings, and dreams were a language filled with symbols and archetypes.

The susurrus of Morpheus Rex's voice fluttered through the air again. "Welcome," he hissed, gesturing to Serpentopolis and Phantasmagorika with one sweeping motion, "to the Metasaur."

The Necrodelic snarled in response, looked directly into the eyes of the Dreaming Predator, and burned him with crimson eye contact. Morpheus Rex returned his gaze and mesmerized the Necrodelic. The heat of Chariah's stare disintegrated Morpheus Rex's robe and melted his crown. Morpheus Rex hypnotized the Necrodelic, and the chemicals still pumping through Chariah's body intensified beneath the Dreaming Predator's glare. They stood thusly joined by dueling eye contact for several moment, beams of Hellfire red and kaleidoscopic rainbow merging in the vastnesses of air, labyrinths, height, and distance separating the two of them.

Both demons launched themselves into mid-air

simultaneously, leaping over the hundreds of feet which separated them. Like magnets, they drew each other into combat. The Necrodelic leapt upwards in a straight diagonal angle. Morpheus Rex stepped from his precipitous dais to free fall downwards at the exact same angle. They converged in mid-air at a point equidistant from Serpentikal's skull and the Dreaming Predator's zenithal throne.

Morpheus Rex swung his Prismscepter at the Necrodelic's skull, leaving a bloody dent in his temple. The Necrodelic simultaneously swiped at Morpheus Rex's exposed ribs, opening five red gashes in his tattooed snakeskin. For a brief second, the two adversaries were joined in evanescent contact, and then they passed by one another in mid-air. Chariah landed atop the towering dais as Morpheus Rex alighted upon the head of Serpentikal.

The wounded warriors turned and locked themselves together with bellicose eye contact once again. Chariah placed his right hand upon the prism throne and emitted an electrical charge from his palm, which filled the refracting chair with white heat and crackling energy. He lifted the prism throne over his head with both hands and hurled it at Morpheus Rex. It spun end over end in a perfect arch and exploded when it reached its target, sending shards of blasted prism everywhere, some of which lodged themselves in Morpheus Rex's flesh.

With the dark synchronicity of demon soulmates destined to do battle since the beginning of time, the two fighters jumped once more through the air, meeting at the same equidistant point, halfway between Serpentikal and dais. Chariah plummeted with both hands over his head, bringing his ten claws down in the form of the Hellsword and opening a deep gash on the crown of Morpheus Rex's head. As he did so, Morpheus Rex raised his right knee and slammed it into the Necrodelic's testicles. The two ricocheted off one another with the force of the savage blows, back along the same paths they had just traveled. Chariah backflipped onto the high dais as Morpheus Rex backflipped onto Serpentikal.

Again the demons leapt, flashing through the sky. Chariah twisted and delivered a side kick to Morpheus Rex's face while simultaneously catching a spinning blow from the Prismscepter in the base of his spine. They landed and then jumped once more. Chariah arched through mid-air in one long, inverted backwards somersault, kicking Morpheus Rex under the chin and knocking blood and venom from his mouth. Morpheus Rex did a sudden backflip at the same time, and caught Chariah with the exact same blow after the Necrodelic had revolved again in mid-air. Chariah somersaulted backwards again, this time in the opposite direction, landing once more upon the head of Serpentikal. Morpheus Rex was sent careening upwards in a series of rapid backflips until he crashed onto the dais upon his stomach.

Morpheus Rex lay prostrated atop the prismatic pillar, slithering on his belly like a snake, his forked tongues flickering, his fingers clasping the shimmering edge of the tower. Chariah stood defiant over the Serpentopolis below, his eye contact drilling the prone Morpheus Rex with burning heat. The dream-eater smiled and licked his rainbow lips. Undulating like a komodo dragon, he gripped the edge of the dais and propelled himself from the pillar, diving head-first at the ascending Necrodelic. His cobra strike landed in Chariah's throat, but he received five vertical gashes on his chest and torso for his effort.

The duel continued. Chariah dove from the dais with arms cruciform. After completing a full front somersault, he brought his skull down upon Morpheus Rex with a brutal headbutt, right into the wound he had previously opened. Blood exploded, and the Dreaming Predator was driven forcefully back. Morpheus Rex reached out and drove his fingers into Chariah's chest as he suffered the concussive jolt of the headbutt. When he landed once more atop Serpentikal, this time heavily enough to nearly break his legs, he held a dripping black rib in his bloody hand.

The Necrodelic's footprints and talon marks formed two purple bruises and ten red scratches on Morpheus Rex's chest, for the Death Addict had used him as a springboard to propel himself back through the air. Chariah stood once more atop the dais, the pale orange sun Dzandra directly behind him. His shadow was an imposing figure for all Elasvai to see, a hieroglyphic epitaph, the shadow of Satan. He breathed heavily, leaking blood from the hole in his chest where his rib had been torn out. He had two puncture marks in his neck where Morpheus Rex had bitten him. He gazed down at the ophidian demon. Their eye contact assaulted one another once more.

They jumped.

Chariah held his ten claws together and to the right of his head, his palms flat, his talons whistling through the air. Morpheus Rex held his Prismscepter to the right of his own head with both hands. Each connected with each other's temple as they converged, but this time, there would no next leap of combat, no more stages in their demonic duel, for a large lasso of hemp had encircled their battered bodies, pinning their arms to their sides. As the giant noose squeezed tightly into their flesh and swiftly dragged the bound demons through the air, the Necrodelic and Morpheus Rex made one last scorching, mesmeric, painful eye contact. As the battle came to an abrupt end and the two battered combatants were pulled by the enormous lasso toward mutual captivity, Morpheus Rex smiled at his nemesis, licking the blood from his rainbow lips with masochistic ecstasy.

"Next time...," he hissingly promised the Necrodelic between breaths, his sibilant voice bursting in anticipation, "with weapons galleries."

33

After being swallowed by the gargantuan worm, the Tantradox set about at once to mutate and domesticate the vermian behemoth from inside its own body. On the backs of their conjoined shark steeds, Drelrei and Junisia sailed through rapids of freshly swallowed cave water and across pools of digestive juices, deftly maneuvering their selachian mounts around whirlpools of stomach acid and steaming bile, and weaving back and forth as they dodged its beating hearts. Once the creature had settled back into its rocky bed, the Tantradox set to work metamorphosing the primarily sedentary beast into a vessel of escape.

Drelrei and Junisia climbed down from the dorsal saddle of the Siamese twin sharks, leaving them free to swim around the pools of water, blood, mucus, and enzymes which filled the worm's interior. They waded through the phlegmatic river of bodily fluids to the worm's head, then crawled inside its ovaries and began copulating like earthworms to establish telepathic contact, sexual arousal, and dominance with the behemoth.

Being a hermaphrodite, just like the worm, the Tantradox was able to form an instant psychic bond with the creature. The Siamese twin lovers fondled each other's genitals as Junisia began inserting the black hairs of her scalplock, one by one, into Drelrei's pores, like the tiny, hooked spines that earthworms fornicated with and exchanged sperm through. She drove one hair into each of Drelrei's pupils, one into each ear, one into each testicle, and one into the red urethra of his penis. He similarly stuck his pubic hair like quills into her nipples, abdomen, naval, thighs, urethra, labia, and clitorises.

They used the advanced tantras which gave them full control over their bodies to stimulate the production of mucus and lymph from their glands. Mucus leaked from their nostrils and genitals, and their mouths coughed up gobbets of phlegm. The Tantradox slowly surrounded itself with a gelid, yellow puddle. In a pool of their own mucus, Drelrei and Junisia made love, Drelrei's ten testicles resonating in perfect harmony with Junisia's ten clitorises. Junisia's nipples leaked mucus. Drelrei's phallus ejaculated mucus and lymph. As they attained orgasm, so too did the giant worm. At that moment, with their tantric powers, the Tantradox telepathically commanded the worm to crawl through the caves and tunnels to the mountain range in the east. The segmented monster immediately obeyed, bearing its interior passengers to freedom with its second head now in the lead, burrowing through dirt where there were no established passages, emerging into the underground caverns below the mountains and finally peeking its round head out from between the rocks and into the light of Dzandra.

As the giant worm became visible, it attracted the attention of a passing predator. The worm became frightened and began to retreat, no longer responsive to the commands of the Tantradox. A moment later there was a humongous crash, as if a moon had fallen into the mountains. Large avalanches blocked the worm's retreat and the creature froze, paralyzed with fright. It would remain this way until the head of a giant serpent dragged it out of the mountain and engaged it in combat.

The Tantradox struggled to regain control of the behemoth, repeating the tantric ritual in the worm's two sets of testes and inside the ovaries near its second head, all to no avail. The concussive impact of the worm's battle jarred them from their bed inside the ovaries, and they bounced around for several moments in the worm's swirling innards. Acrid cataracts of venom poured down the worm's gullet and dripped from the multitudinous fang holes in its skin. Their shark steed was lost, vomited in a river of blood, and then the giant serpent dragged its vermiform prey out, tossed it into the air, and clamped its fangs around its head.

The Tantradox tried to escape through the amphisbenic worm's other mouth, but the ophidian giant began sucking out the innards of its prey, and the Tantradox was unable to escape the strong, tornado-like force of its mouth and lungs. The serpent swallowed all fourteen of the amphisbenic worm's hearts, all of its organs, blood, mucus, and half-digested soil, and then the squirming Tantradox itself. Drelrei and Junisia fell through a giant green throat, along with the worm's fourteen hearts and all its other organs, and landed in a tangled pile of gore.

The fourteen hearts slapped against the ground around them, followed by the ovaries and testes they had copulated within, the impressions of their bodies still indented in the tissues. The reins and torn saddle of the Siamese twin sharks fell on top of them a moment later. Drelrei dragged it from their backs and held it in one hand, knowing it might be the only weapon they would find. There was a growing pool of blood and half-digested liquid spreading through the foyer. The Tantradox arose from the puddle of ichor and observed its surroundings.

The walls, floor, and ceiling were lined with snakeskin. The corridors ran off in nine different directions, with long curves instead of corners. Five similarly wavy spiral stairways led to the upper levels. Two snakeman guards in armor and helmets were approaching them from either direction, with tridents and spears in their hands. Another was descending one of the curved staircases directly in front of them.

"Serpentopolis," Drelrei whispered. "The serpents have returned."

"They've disavowed their banishment," Junisia replied. "We must destroy them this time."

As the ophidian sentinels approached, forked tongues flickering, beady eyes gleaming below the pyramidal frontpieces of their helmets, the Tantradox attacked. Helmets, scales, flesh, skull, and brains became one beneath their cloven hooves, each sticking out of one another like shards of broken glass. They kicked the first two sentinels in the head, killing each instantly. The other they trampled as he ran down the round corridor in search of assistance.

The Tantradox reversed its direction and fled through the labyrinth, still holding the saddle. They accidentally burst into the courtyard, where fountains of venom sprayed high in the air, in mandalic shapes, amongst marble statues of multi-headed nagas and large-breasted gorgons and lamias. There were several of the serpentmen here, guards, sentinels, soldiers, and archers. The Tantradox turned and fled. They wandered throughout the corridors of Serpentopolis, avoided the snake demons whenever possible, as well as the doors with names and hieroglyphs in ancient ophidian languages etched above them. Finally, they emerged into one of the snakehead turrets, just in time to watch the demonic duel between the Necrodelic and Morpheus Rex from a fanged balcony.

Drelrei began to smooth the reins of the saddle in his cloven hand. It was made from strong hemp, and thus he was able to make it grow longer within his very fingers as he watched the two demons bludgeon and bloody themselves. He waited until they had inflicted more damage upon one another, then swung the elongated rope from the tower in a large lasso, catching the two combatants as they collided in mid-air. He pulled the body-noose tight, capturing the demons in its unforgiving grasp.

Laughing, the Tantradox began swinging the demons around by the hempen noose, bashing their bodies against the walls and towers and down upon the coils of Serpentopolis, where they bounced in a bloody bundle like a sadist's plaything, or a necrobestialist's pet. Their sinister game alarmed the guards to their presence, and every fanged balcony across from them soon filled with serpentman archers.

Using the tangled, bound bodies of the Necrodelic and Morpheus Rex as a grapnel, the Tantradox hurled the elongated lasso into the mountain peaks in the distance and swung to freedom, soaring over a barrage of ophidian arrows. After safely escaping to the opposite side of the mountain range, holding the captured demons down with the heavy cloven hoof of its giant middle leg, the Tantradox whistled for one of its beasts.

"We will break them apart," Drelrei said as they awaited their steed.

"And then sacrifice them in the Temples of Tantra," Junisia replied. "They will be offerings to the demiurge of our love."

From the gardens below a pair of Siamese twin sphinxes came rumbling from the east, each bound by a complex leather yoke. Behind them the hybrid beasts dragged a chariot covered in ornate, pornographic wood-carvings. The sphinxes were harnessed in succession, bridles and reins slipped over their heads. The sphinxes galloped up the mountainside, pulling the chariot behind them, their paws kicking up small avalanches. The creatures came obediently to the Tantradox's side. As the Tantradox had commanded by the pitch of its whistle, the chariot contained a weapon's rack, a hookah, and a treasure chest full of drugs. It also contained two spiked ball gags, which were like tiny morning stars with a pair of chains that clasped together like a necklace. These were fitted over the heads of both the Necrodelic and Morpheus Rex, to keep them from breathing fire and spitting venom, respectively, and to prevent them from casting spells or summoning their living spaceships.

Drelrei and Junisia bound the Necrodelic and Morpheus Rex separately now, weaving their magic on the hemp to make it grow around their arms, wrists, and ankles, then tying it in two long ropes to the yoni-shaped rings of the chariot. Once bound and immobilized, the demons were laid supinely on the ground.

The Tantradox climbed inside the chariot. They closed the wooden doors of the chariot and bolted them with an iron lingham-and-yoni configuration. Drelrei pulled upon the reins of the sphinxes, and the trained Siamese twin beasts began running at full speed down the mountain, dragging the bound and gagged Necrodelic and Morpheus Rex behind them. The Tantradox gazed from the back of the chariot upon its helpless victims, bouncing down the mountainside, the skin on their backs being torn off by friction and abrasion. Sometimes their flesh hit jutting rocks, which the laughing Tantradox found sadistically amusing.

Drelrei pulled on the sphinxes' reins, shouting, "To the rose gardens."

The sphinxes stampeded across the planet obediently,

dragging the Necrodelic and Morpheus Rex behind.

For an hour the Death Addict and the Dreaming Predator were pulled through fields of roses, their skin catching and tearing on thorns, leaving large dewdrops of blood behind, and then, for another hour, they were dragged through fields of poison ivy. The Tantradox smoked opium from its hookah and began making selections from its weapons rack. Drelrei grabbed a long spear, which he jabbed at Morpheus Rex like a phallic symbol of dominance. Junisia wielded a whip like a dominatrix, flaying the Necrodelic as he was jostled through the poison ivy, opening red wounds on his irritated skin.

They traded weapons when they came to the meadows of poison sumac, and the Necrodelic was punctured while Morpheus Rex was flogged. An hour later, as they entered the Venus flytrap gardens, the two bound victims were covered in welts, cuts, bruises, and rashes. The Venus flytraps snapped at the intruders being dragged through their midst, clamping down hard on their flesh. Some of them had teeth and fangs, while others had sticky tongues which ripped the skin right off their prey.

Morpheus Rex flipped over onto his stomach, and a Venus flytrap grabbed ahold of both of his penises. The Dreaming Predator ejaculated with masochistic delight as the plant tried to devour his members, then ejaculated again when its viscous tongue ripped all the skin from the underside of his upper phallus. Chariah, conversely, was seething with wrath, more from the bondage than the pain, plotting thousands of different forms of revenge.

Drelrei and Junisia unwound two morning stars with extremely long chains from the weapons rack and beat their victims as they traveled through the cactus garden. Another hour in the apiary and a forest full of hives provided thousands of stings from Siamese twin bees, wasps, and hornets. An hour in the jungle of tree frogs added painful venom and curare to their open wounds. An hour of fire ants added burning, swollen bites all over their bodies. As evening fell, the Tantradox spurred the sphinxes to their fastest possible speed. The chariot careened toward the topaz sunset, through an open plain of razorgrass whose edges were as sharp as blades. The sphinxes were further inspired by repeated lashings from the whip, as well as words uttered in the primal goat-like languages of Elasvai, to a bludgeoning gait that resulted in broken bones and concussions for the Necrodelic and Morpheus Rex.

When night fell, Morpheus Rex transformed into the Oneirophage. The hemp around his tail reflexively tightened. Chariah watched the entire metamorphosis with stinging, bloodshot eyes, eyes filled with dust, dirt, sand, pollen, and debris. The Necrodelic wondered to himself if he could use the Oneirophage's were-nature against him somehow, in future battles, after they were freed from the infernal chariot and he had slowly dismembered the Tantradox.

The evening began with a trip to the belladonna gardens. After being submerged in nightshade, the demons were dragged through patches of psilocybic mushrooms, ergot, jimson weed, and morning glory. They continued with a journey through an ancient, tick-infested forest, which consisted of bouncing off trees, being lacerated on jagged tree stumps, and being infested and masticated by thousands of ticks and termites. A gauntlet of termite mounds was next, the large insect edifices exploding as Chariah and the Oneirophage rolled into them while the chariot careened around them in the distance, navigating the teeming hills like a minefield while making sure their victims crashed into every single one.

The ancient hunting grounds had been abolished by the Tantradox long ago, but had been left intact through the centuries and preserved as a piece of history. The sphinxes broke through its gates and stampeded through the anachronistic forest. All the old animal snares and traps were still in place, and were now triggered by the passing forms of the Necrodelic and the Oneirophage. Steel teeth closed around their ankles, their genitals, their arms, their hair, and their faces. Old, leaf-covered pits were disturbed, and the Necrodelic and the Oneirophage fell inside them, to be briefly impaled upon the wooden stakes before ricocheting off the dirt walls and bouncing back to the surface. Nooses closed around any part of their bodies, leaving them momentarily suspended in mid-air between trees and chariot, stretching them like torture racks until the branches broke, then releasing them to tumble awkwardly to the ground.

The Oneirophage was ejaculating again. Golgothas pummeled them with the skeletons of extinct animals, breaking their bones with the bones of others. The short night came to an end. Dzandra rose in the sky. The Tantradox celebrated the dawn by beating the Necrodelic and the freshly transformed Morpheus Rex with fifty-foot quarterstaffs.

The only time the sphinxes ceased their incessant running was at the behest of the Tantradox, which called out a command and begun to rein them in as they came upon a flowerbed of hyacinth. A slow rumble was building along the horizon, as a herd of Siamese twin triceratops were thundering closer and closer. Minutes later, the stampeding dinosaurs trampled the Necrodelic and Morpheus Rex to a bloody pulp beneath their thousand hooves. Once the herd of triceratops had passed, leaving the Necrodelic and Morpheus Rex broken and moaning in their wake, the sphinxes were spurred once more into action.

The morning hours were passed with a trip down a piranha-infested river. The sphinxes and their chariot ran alongside the shore, while the Necrodelic and Morpheus Rex were dragged through the waters, where the frenzied piranhas attempted to devour them. The demons were then dragged through whitewater rapids filled with jagged rocks, in which they were often turned completely around and knocked into strange positions, spinning in mid-air and then twisting underwater.

The sphinxes ran down a hill which corresponded with the river and its eventual waterfall. The Necrodelic and Morpheus Rex descended via the raging and towering cataract, landing in broken, bleeding masses on the rocks below, then resurfacing in the catfish-infested pools of Candiru Falls. The thin catfish embedded themselves immediately in the Necrodelic's black phallus and both of Morpheus Rex's penises. They swam like living needles straight into their urethras and entrenched themselves within. Morpheus Rex's penises hardened into twin erections and trembled with multiple orgasms. The masochistic dream-eater had begun to enjoy the prolonged torture, and as they were dragged through various fields and gardens until the afternoon, often masturbated by turning over on his stomach and rubbing his phalluses on plants, flowers, grasses, and the abrasive, decorticating ground.

Finally the chariot came to the Temples of Tantra. The Necrodelic and Morpheus Rex were dragged over paved pathways and bridges and through stone pagodas, leaving long smears of blood in their wake. Entire temples were razed by the force of their bouncing bodies as the Tantradox deliberately steered them into the stone edifices, dragging them through the walls with explosions of dust and bringing the ceilings and rooftops down around them like a rainfall of monoliths and obelisks. The sphinxes dragged them to the largest temple, up its steps, through its gothically arched entrance, and down a pathway between several rows of ornately carven wooden pews, all the way to the altar of sacrifice at its end, where the Tantradox dismounted. At long last, the forced tour of the garden planet had ended.

The Tantradox began sharpening a ceremonial dagger on its horns. Chariah looked into the eyes of the Siamese twins with his burning crimson gaze. The Tantradox thought he and Morpheus Rex would be weak sacrificial victims after the long hours of torment. It was a severe miscalculation. Chariah was so enraged that he no longer felt the alarums of pain shooting through his nervous system. The only thing the Tantradox had done was arouse his Hellish wrath.

He glanced at Morpheus Rex beside him. The Dreaming Predator seemed to have enjoyed the ordeal. Pain and pleasure were often the same to the masochistic dream-eater, and the Tantradox's torture had heightened his oneiromantic powers in much the same way it had raised Chariah's fury. The Tantradox would have been better served to let them finish their duel, in which one or both of them could very well have met their demise.

The Necrodelic snarled and growled beneath his spiked ball gag. The Siamese twins were as foolish as they were perverted. When they released him from his bonds, he was going to fuck them up worse than Satan himself could possibly imagine. Fuck them up all the way to Hell.

34

The Tantradox had summoned every creature on Elasvai to witness the sacrifice of the Necrodelic and the Oneirophage. As the topaz sun Dzandra set behind the Temples of Tantra, a cortege of the wicked and the damned made their way across the garden planet. The main temple, where the two demons were to be sacrificed, quickly filled with centaurs, satyrs, minotaurs, maenads, cocanaeds, lotophagi, shamans, birdmen, and beastmen. Hydraman entered behind them and seated himself in the last row of pews. A towering, green-scaled, hominid reptile with two legs and nine heads, Hydraman stood over fifteen feet tall, each one of his necks longer than his entire lower body. His necks were arrayed on a candelabra-like arch of flesh that curved upwards to both right and left on a single, base neck which was shorter, thicker, and stouter than its brethren above. Hydraman's nine necks were perfectly symmetrical, and each bore an identical dragon head atop it.

Hydraman was followed into the temple by the Triskadekaminotaur, a thirteen-headed minotaur from the Tantradox's genetic farms. Behind him came the Multiworm, another of the Tantradox's mutations, a wriggling mass of worms joined by heads, tails, segments, and spiny hairs, shaped like a giant homunculus and walking upright with a hideous gait, stepping, wriggling, and shuffling all at once, its extremities waving in the air. Cerberus, the black, blood-slavering, five-headed hellhound, was chained to the vermian abomination, and walked beside it like a pet and a familiar both.

All around the temple the Siamese twin creatures of Elasvai gathered, to watch through the open, diamond-shaped windows of the stone edifice. Manticores, basilisks, chimeras, sphinxes, and leucrotas, herds of conjoined dinosaurs and packs of conjoined beasts, and all manner of hybrids, cross-breeds, mutations, and geryons from the Tantradox' genetic farms, including demons with animal heads, animals with demon heads, and every species of fauna indigenous to Elasvai sewn, grafted, and welded to members of different species in infinite combinations, as well as an entire pack of crocattas that had been surgically combined into one massive, multiple entity, and an entire pride of ligers to which had been done the same. Many of the animals had yin-yang symbols branded on their hides.

From the griffin, cockatrice, harpy, bat, and raptor clouded skies Pestilentia descended, to observe the ceremony through the large cleft in the temple roof. She brought with her a retinue of insectoid royalty, stuck to her ambrium flesh and riding her like a spaceship. Upon her back she carried one of the ten leaders of her army, the gigantic Warlord Centipedicus IV, who carried a different weapon in each of his hundred hands and was a master of them all. Sheltered in Pestilentia's honey-dripping womb were Madam Mantis, Mistress Mantis, and Mater Mantis, the three matriarchs of her drones, her slaves, and her young. The wasp demon Stingmeister, slavedriver of her worker hordes, and her young nephew, Prince Scorpio, lay entrenched in her inner thighs. As usual, Pestilentia's mysterious and reclusive mate, Panzebub, did not accompany her.

As the moons rose and starlight fell over the Temples of Tantra and the surrounding fields, the face of Satan appeared in the skies like aurora borealis, his crimson head the size of a planet on a collision course with Elasvai, filling the stratosphere with his smiling fangs, his smoking eyes, and his external veins and arteries. The sadistic creator of the universe had come to watch as well, the ultimate voyeur.

The temple had been filled. The throngs of animals were gathered around in a circle stretching beyond every horizon. Pestilentia and her insects hovered and perched around the opening in the roof. The winged creatures fluttered in mid-air. The gargantuan death's head of Satan glowed in the night sky. The moment of sacrifice had arrived.

The Tantradox emerged from the temple's antechambers wearing a black, hooded robe of animal fur. The mark of the pentagram was still burned into its chest, visible between the open folds of its robe. The Siamese twin demons slowly walked to the altar of sacrifice with their peculiar, three-legged gait, a lit brazier in their hands releasing a psychotropic incense of opium, lotus, myrrh, and sandalwood. They used the brazier to light the candles in the sconces ringing the chamber and the altar. The flames illuminated the temple, flickering over the faces of the audience and illuminating the temple's myriad bloodstains, which had previously been draped in shadows. A large gallows loomed over the altar, and from it the bodies of the Necrodelic and the Oneirophage were suspended cruciform, side by side, on one continuous, complicated harness of inflexible hempen rope. Their necks were constricted in nooses, their arms outstretched and tethered by the wrists to the poles of the gallows on either side, and to the yoni rings in the gallows above. The spiked ball gags were still in their mouths, and their bodies were covered in scrapes, scratches, cuts, punctures, bruises, abrasions, and rashes. Stretched tautly in mid-air on the binding mesh of the harness, the legs, arms, and head of the Necrodelic formed the five points of a star, the ancient, sacrificial pentagram position.

The Tantradox laid its sacrificial tools upon the altar. Along with a double-bladed ceremonial dagger was a giant pair of scissors, a long saw, a scalpel, a lit torch, and a giant, threaded needle. Drelrei and Junisia removed their hood and climbed atop the altar. Each grabbed one handle of the broadsword-sized scissors. They placed the blades over the Necrodelic's shoulder and attempted to sever his arm. The scissors bit into the Necrodelic's flesh. Blood spattered the altar. The Tantradox tried to close the blades, but could not slice through the Necrodelic's muscles. They tugged and pulled, shoved and yanked, cursed and chanted, all to no avail. His muscles had become like an adamantium fiber, impenetrable and resistant to steel.

The Tantradox turned their attention to the Oneirophage. Chariah began sifting through stratagems and battle plans as he relaxed the muscles in his shoulder, letting the dark energy he had concentrated into that area flow back through the rest of his body. He shuddered with wrath as he realized what the "sacrifice" planned by the Tantradox entailed: the joining of his flesh with the Oneirophage's, transforming them into Siamese twins. Whether the Tantradox intended to murder, torture, enslave, breed, or rape them, or simply cast them back into the universe in this mutated and execrable form, was irrelevant to the Necrodelic, for he would never allow the gruesome and perverted ceremony to be completed.

Astral projection and possession of the Tantradox, as he had done in the Forest of Flesh, seemed his best option. He quickly discerned that the Siamese twins had cast a spell of warding to prevent that very thing, however, before the commencement of the ritual. He turned his gaze to the audience. Perhaps he could possess one of them. He began to evaluate the creatures with black logic and dark psychic probings.

The Tantradox had positioned the scissors over the right shoulder of the Oneirophage. They closed the blades, and this time, unlike their attempts to amputate the Necrodelic's arm, the dream-eater's tattooed limb easily detached. The severed arm dangled from the hempen fetters until the Tantradox bisected it at the wrist, and it fell from its remaining bond to the altar below. The Tantradox turned, kneeled, and picked up the lit torch to cauterize the wound. When the Tantradox rose again, however, the Oneirophage's arm had regenerated itself.

With four wide eyes and two confused expressions, the Tantradox glanced back to the altar. The bloody limb still lay there twitching, but the Oneirophage had grown an exact replication in its place. The Tantradox bent down to retrieve the scissors and sever this new limb as well. They rose and clove the Oneirophage's arm from the shoulder once again. It fell beside the first in a joined pool of blood. The raw red wound in the Oneirophage's shoulder began to writhe like a nest of serpents, and then, like a lizard regenerating its tail, the Oneirophage grew another perfect version of the sundered arm, an exact replica all the way down to the tiniest details of the most inconspicuous tattoos. From the back of the temple could be heard the ninefold cacchinations of Hydraman. The Tantradox cut the Oneirophage's arm off a third time, a fourth, a fifth, then flung the scissors with a loud clatter to the ground and turned to grab their ceremonial dagger. If the sacrificial demons would not cooperate, they would be eviscerated.

The Tantradox, however, in its rage and confusion, had failed to realize that none of the regenerated arms the Oneirophage sprouted were tethered to the harness. When the Siamese twins rose again, gripping their dagger, the Oneirophage's unfettered right hand shot out and grabbed Drelrei by the throat. His fist squeezed the incubus' larynx as Junisia flailed at the dream-eater with the ceremonial dagger. The Oneirophage released Drelrei's purpling throat and backfisted Junisia in the face, then wrenched the dagger from her hand and cut himself free of his bonds.

The Oneirophage and the Tantradox wrestled upon the altar, bashing each other's heads into the stone, rolling back and forth and finally falling to the ground. Chariah strained his head to watch the combat, hoping the dream-eater would extricate himself and cut him free. He had decided against possessing one of the creatures in the audience, not willing to leave his physical body vulnerable through astral projection.

The Tantradox had gained the advantage. Drelrei had a

handful of the Oneirophage's prism-plaited hair in his fist, and with a knee to the base of his spine forced him into a kneeling position. Junisia raked at his throat and face with her black fingernails, then grabbed the torch from the altar and burned the side of his face and his chest, obfuscating his tattoos with wet, black, bloody soot.

Drelrei called out to Pestilentia hovering above, then grabbed the Oneirophage beneath his shoulders and heaved him high into the air, throwing him through the opening in the temple roof. The Empress of Insects caught him in her viscous, ambrium flesh, where he immediately stuck and struggled like a sea serpent in a tar pit, sinking into the thick brown semiliquidity of one of her lower legs, wherein he would be entombed if he did not free himself.

Chariah cursed the Oneirophage. The Tantradox recaptured the dagger and used it to eviscerate the Necrodelic, slashing quickly and deeply, no longer bearing any patience for ritual or ceremony. The Necrodelic's intestines burst out like a nest of black mambas. Chariah could control every single part of his body, however, including his internal organs, and, utilizing this power, wrapped his entrails around both of the Tantradox's necks, the coils of his intestines crushing their throats like pythons. The Siamese twins leaked blood from their mouths as they hacked at Chariah's exposed viscera. The Necrodelic recoiled his intestines and rearranged them, binding the Tantradox' arms behind its back and forcing the Siamese twin demons to their knees. He tightened the entrails around their throats still further, squeezing their windpipes as though with a garrote, choking them into semi-consciousness and thus incapacitating them while he tried to free himself.

He scanned the audience again, once more considering a possession. As he dragged his crimson eye contact through the crowd, he found that he himself was the focus of someone's eye contact. Tenfold eye contact. The black eyes of Cerberus were bearing simultaneously into his own. Chariah returned the eye contact with the five-headed hellhound, and was suddenly overcome with a strong, vertiginous sense of deja vu. He had known the hellhound in previous lives. It was a soulmate.

Chariah called telepathically to Cerberus. The beast immediately responded to its ancient master, tearing free of the

Multiworm, bursting forth and dragging an entire bloody section of the monstrosity with him. Cerberus leapt onto the sacrificial altar, maintaining psychic contact with the Necrodelic all the while. An instant later, it rose up on its muscular hindquarters and ripped the ball gag from Chariah's mouth. The growling beast began tearing at the masses of tethers before being suddenly spitted on the spear of a centaur. Cerberus whined and toppled from the altar, run through from flank to flank by the weapon. Chariah sucked a fireball up from Hell, through his lungs, and spat it at the centaur, setting it aflame. Chariah breathed in the psychedelic smoke of the centaur's charred flesh, healing himself, revitalizing his dark energies, and empowering himself with evil enlightenment. The Necrodelic struggled, but still could not loose his bonds. The tethers had closed off too many of his energy points. He contemplated setting a fire that would destroy the whole temple, gallows, bonds, audience and all. It would have to be a disintegrating conflagration, else the pieces of the stone temple would crash down and cripple him.

Chariah sucked in his breath and prepared to unleash a powerful blast of flames from Hell that would instantaneously incinerate the Temples of Tantra and everything and everyone inside it except himself. His lungs glowed redly in his chest, visible beneath his black sculpted pectoral muscles as he inhaled and began drawing forth Hellfire from below. The Necrodelic began to exhale, then noticed from the corner of his crimson eyes the fallen form of Cerberus, the spear still sticking through his side. The five-headed dog lay wounded, but alive.

At the last minute Chariah tilted his head upwards and breathed the disintegrating fire through the hole in the temple ceiling. The flames rushed like screaming banshees into one of Pestilentia's upper legs and burned straight through the entire limb in less than a nanosecond. The lower part of the leg, with the wriggling Oneirophage still struggling in its ambrium, fell through the cleft in the roof to the temple floor, where it melted into a sticky golden-brown puddle, bearing thousands of preserved corpses in its viscid pools. The Oneirophage thrashed about in the scalding ambrium as it liquified, but was unable to free himself. He looked upwards and caught the Necrodelic with his kaleidoscopic eye contact.

"Set me free, death-smoker. I saved your life," the

Oneirophage hissed, his eyes spinning in their sockets.

The Necrodelic was susceptible to hypnosis in his bound and weakened state, and spat a long stream of Hellfire into the pool of ambrium. The sludgelike mass of honey, opium, amber, and ectoplasm melted, and the Oneirophage arose from its morass with steaming ambrium dripping down his body like hot candlewax.

"Return the karma," snarled the Necrodelic, "lest I transform that ambrium into naptha and smoke you where you stand."

The Oneirophage grabbed the scalpel from the altar of sacrifice and sundered the Necrodelic's bonds. Chariah untangled his entrails from Drelrei and Junisia's throats, then grabbed them by the necks and threw them violently against the rear wall of the chamber. The stone wall cracked as the Tantradox struck it. Drelrei and Junisia fell limply onto a stack of storage chests, which toppled and spilled opium and incense all over the floor.

Chariah jumped from the altar and knelt at the side of Cerberus. He placed his hands on the panting dog, then withdrew the spear from its side. He whispered a word of healing, his palms glowing red for an instant, and then the five-headed hellhound growled and jumped back to its feet, barking and howling its canine battle-cries at the Tantradox.

"You should have killed me while I was bound," said the Necrodelic to the Oneirophage. "You'll never have another chance."

"And you should have slain me while I lay trapped in ambrium. You owe me your life, and twofold at that, Necrodelic."

"Lies and games, Oneirophage. No lives have been saved or spared here, no blood-debts accrued. We are not symbiotic, you and I."

"That we are not," the Oneirophage agreed, "but we are soulmates, though dark soulmates we be."

"Then let us sacrifice those who would sacrifice us," spoke the Necrodelic in an ominous tone.

The Oneirophage smiled, his three forked tongues flickering from between his rainbow lips, and gathered up the giant scissors in his hands.

Chariah walked over to the altar and grabbed the long saw. Running his fingertips along its razor-sharp teeth until they bled, he waited for the Oneirophage to drag the unconscious Tantradox from the broken chests and piles of spilled incense and opium. The Oneirophage lifted the Tantradox over his shoulder, carried it across the temple, and dumped it heavily atop the altar. Chariah sprang onto the ichor-covered altar with a pantherish leap and landed with a splash of blood, then tied two hangman's nooses in the sundered harness dangling from the gallows.

The Oneirophage tore the black robe from around Drelrei and Junisia's shoulders and bound their hands behind their back in a complex serpent's knot that, when completed, formed the shape of a coiled cobra. Together, the Necrodelic and the Oneirophage lifted the Tantradox into the air and maneuvered their heads into the nooses. Chariah walked over to the controls in the gallows pole to draw the rope tighter, then said to the Oneirophage, "Wake them up."

The Oneirophage twirled his long-fingernailed right hand and produced the strawlike Umbilicus. He blew first into Drelrei's mouth, then into Junisia's, instantly resuscitating the incubus and succubus soulmates. The master of dreams was also a master of sleep, and could giveth or taketh either one at will. As he withdrew the Umbilicus, he sucked a single dream from Junisia's larynx, a distorted, auditory memory of the Tantradox' conversation on the Cliffs of Caine, wherein they spoke of the Soul Cleaver and the Flesh Compactor. Their voices warped into a synesthetic vision in his brain, and he beheld the imaginary weapons with his mind's eye.

The Tantradox immediately panicked when it awoke, swinging and kicking in mid-air. Chariah lifted the long saw with his right hand and placed it between Drelrei and Junisia's head, settling it in the cleft between their shoulders where their flesh had been surgically joined. With a rhythmic dragging of the saw, Chariah began to undo what the Tantradox had done.

Drelrei and Junisia screamed, cried, and begged for mercy. Chariah paid them no heed, just continued to stoically saw their flesh asunder, separating their joined shoulders, opening a wide crimson valley in their mutual chest. The Necrodelic then stepped back and let the Oneirophage take his turn. The

Oneirophage placed the scissors underneath their grotesquely misshapen middle leg and began to cut. The blades of the scissors clashed loudly together as he drove them upwards, slicing through hoof and heel, ankle and calf, knee and thigh, severing tendons, rending bone, and bloodying his arms to the elbows as he toiled. He stopped below their genitals, giving them, for the moment, a third crotch, a scarlet prosthetic groin.

The Oneirophage stepped back and held the bloody scissors down at his side. The gashed Tantradox dangled like a piece of raw meat, joined only by strings of gristle and a few pieces of bone. Drelrei and Junisia wept. Inspired by their tears, Chariah placed a talon beneath Drelrei's right eye and another beneath Junisia's left eye, each catching in the soft skin at the corners of their eyelids. He slowly dragged the two claws down their faces, opening red furrows for their tears to course through. He moved the claws to the insides of their eye sockets, and sliced another crimson groove for the tears to runnel down. He drew his hands closer together, as if in prayer, then slit the other inside corners of their eyes all the way to their chins. His talons moved closer together again, as if magnetically drawn to one another, and scratched two final rivers for their tears to sail.

With eight crimson Phlegethons canalized and irrigated in the flesh of their faces by the claws of the Death Addict, the Tantradox whimpered and struggled, their crying eyes wincing in pain, terror, and despair. Finally, Chariah brought the talons of his two forefingers together, blade against blade, razor against razor. He flicked the rest of his claws into place beside them, letting his palms hover over the Tantradox like the shadow of death. Chariah breathed in and raised his hands over his head, his ten claws forming one mighty black guillotine, its edges gleaming, glistening with slick blood, and then, with all the fury of a lightning bolt, he brought the Hellsword down, severing the Siamese twin lovers from one another completely, sundering the Tantradox from itself.

The two halves twisted violently on their nooses, spinning and swinging like fresh slabs of raw flesh on meathooks during an earthquake, dangling in a cannibal's abattoir on some seismically disturbed moon or planet. Chariah let Drelrei and Junisia hang for several minutes, their bodies trembling and seeming to spark to life when they briefly touched, only to drift away from each other's cloven halves once again. Finally, Chariah cut them down from the nooses with a flick of his claws. Drelrei and Junisia tumbled into each other's arms and collapsed into one another's gory embrace, their bleeding forms intertwining upon the altar of sacrifice. Chariah kicked their tangled bodies from the altar with one taloned foot. They landed in two quivering lumps on the floor.

"Begone with thee," the Necrodelic spoke. "Take thy humiliation and thy dismemberment and flee into your gardens, to live your lives in torture and despair, and know that when you return, with your hearts full of vengeance and your eyes bright with scorn, I shall sunder thee again, and send thy souls separately to Hell, damning you to be eternally...," the Necrodelic paused, looming over the fallen entity he had ripped in twain from atop the bloodstained altar, then breathed forth the fires of Hell over their bleeding bodies, cauterizing their wounds so that they might flee in each other's arms and be forced to live their lives as two, and in the streams of flame that burst from his blackened lips could be heard the final word of his curse, like thunder and gongs and poltergeist...

"Apart."

35

The crippled Tantradox made its way from the temple, sometimes trying to walk with one another's support and falling in a bloody heap, at other times slithering, crawling, or rolling down the aisle, then dragging each other down the stone steps and whistling for Siamese twin cockatrices to alight and bear them away. Back within the temple walls, the Oneirophage spoke to the Necrodelic in his hissing voice.

"We should have killed them."

Chariah watched with red-hot eyes as the bisected Siamese twin lovers soared off into the night on the back of their half-bird, half-serpent steed.

"I'm not through torturing them," he replied. "Revenge is a drug. It's sexual, psychedelic. It's pure black hatred, and I'm drunk on it. I wish to partake of it a while longer."

The Oneirophage watched the departure of the disjoined Tantradox through the open temple doors as well, his kaleidoscopic eyes spinning in the darkness.

As the Tantradox disappeared over the horizon, Chariah refocused his gaze upon all the creatures gathered inside and around the temple.

"Genocide time," Chariah said, dropping with feline grace and evil purpose from the altar. He was immediately followed by the Oneirophage, who still wielded the enormous scissors. Cerberus, who had been waiting obediently at the side of the altar, sprang into battle at the cue from its master, tearing into the Multiworm with all five sets of jaws, shaking his heads rabidly back and forth, tearing the conjoined vermian monstrosity to shreds with his black fangs, avenging himself upon the monstrosity that had held his leash in bondage just an hour before.

Chariah lifted his clawed hands over his shoulders and then brought them down quickly at his sides. There was a loud thunderclap, and all of the centaurs, satyrs, minotaurs, maenads, cocanaeds, lotophagi, shamans, birdmen, and beastmen in the temple spontaneously combusted, leaving behind an explosion of ashes, swirling around and around as if caught in the winds of a powerful storm.

Hydraman was exchanging headbutts with the Triskadekaminotaur in the aisle of a pew near the temple's entrance. Though outnumbered thirteen heads to nine, Hydraman had gained the advantage, raining skulls down upon the faces of the Triskadekaminotaur with a violent rhythm, a sickening drumbeat of bone striking bone that was sometimes accompanied by the shattering of a nose, the splintering of a jaw, or the sundering of a suture. Hydraman pounded the Triskadekaminotaur's heads like a musical instrument, sometimes dropping two or three headbutts simultaneously. The thirteen-headed abomination was stumbling backwards on an arching spine as Hydraman continued to rain blows. He knocked the Triskadekaminotaur onto its back and releasing a final barrage of headbutts, driving the backs of his thirteen heads against the ground. Thirteen explosions of red filled the air as thirteen skulls were encerebrated, thirteen faces melting into boneless pantomimes of themselves, thirteen brains flowing in pink puddles along the ground and spattering the walls with dripping carnelian.

Hydraman arose, his nine dragonheads bleeding, his eyes and lips swollen, his noses broken, his foreheads split wide open, and parts of his faces and body torn open by the Triskadekaminotaur's horns, to stand triumphantly beside the Necrodelic, the Oneirophage, and Cerberus.

Pestilentia and her insect hordes had followed the torn Tantradox, assisting Drelrei and Junisia with their escape and blessing them with offerings of opium before returning to the Temples of Tantra. She buzzed angrily over the aperture in the ceiling now as the battle within the temple came to an end.

"Necrodelic, in addition to betraying and slaying my sister Spidratha, you have mutilated my soulmates, the Tantradox. Oneirophage, the vendetta between your races and ours is an ancient one, and you have fueled it this night with your mistreatment of my acolytes. Before the sun rises, the two of you will be ornaments in my flesh, just another pair of fossils in my menagerie of the dead."

At that moment, Prince Scorpio burst through the temple doors, his tail streaming with venom, and charged the Necrodelic and the Oneirophage. He somersaulted down the aisle and sprang onto his hands, his venomous stinger aimed at the face of the Necrodelic. Chariah casually raised his right hand and, using two of his long talons like a pair of scissors, snipped off the dripping tip of Prince Scorpio's tail. The young scorpion sprang back onto his own open wound, sprawling in his own slippery ichor while Chariah held his severed tail up like a trophy. The Necrodelic lunged forward, and when Prince Scorpio raised his pincers to defend himself, Chariah caught each of them between a pair of claws in either hand, and like scissors chopped them off as well. As Prince Scorpio's severed chelae thrashed and pinched the air reflexively in a puddle of blood on the floor, Chariah turned sideways and struck with the same two dripping claws of his right hand with which he had severed the scorpion demon's left pincer, bringing the long razor-sharp talons of his index and middle fingers together like a pair of shears around Prince Scorpio's throat and clipping off his head.

A moment later Pestilentia rammed the temple with her titanic body, razing the entire edifice to the ground in a shower of large stones and an explosion of dust. The Necrodelic, the

Oneirophage, Hydraman, and Cerberus raced through the crumbling doors at the last moment and down the temple steps, where Pestilentia's minions, Warlord Centipedicus IV, Mistress Mantis, Madam Mantis, Mater Mantis, and the Stingmeister awaited them.

The Necrodelic engaged the gargantuan Warlord Centipedicus IV, whose hundred arms brandished a hundred different weapons simultaneously. Chariah defended himself with a furious frenzy of claws, blocking, deflecting, and knocking aside every attack with blinding speed, all the while ducking, leaping, spinning, and dodging, sometimes levitating in mid-air two hundred feet from the ground to match the colossal insect demon's towering height.

Hydraman attacked the triumvirate of mantid matriarchs, knocking the green blood from their mouths with a trio of headbutts before finding himself caught in three pairs of pincers, with three dripping mandibles gnawing on three of his faces. He detached himself from the three heads as the mantises devoured them, leaving three long throats trailing from betwixt their mandibles as they chewed upon his skulls and masticated his brains. Hydraman retreated like a lizard that leaves its tail behind in the grasp of a predator to escape, then immediately grew three more heads to replace the ones that were being devoured by the mantid succubi.

Cerberus drooled blood in ten steady streams from the corners of his five mouths, growling, barking, and lunging at Stingmeister. The wasp demon attempted to fly away but was caught by its back leg in the five-headed canine's jaws and thrown brutally to the ground, after which the hellhound continued to bash him repeatedly, raising him into the air with his fangs and then bringing him down violently, again and again and again.

The Oneirophage waited for Pestilentia to emerge from the debris of the temple, then severed the foot of one her forelegs as she flew past. Dodging the droppings of plasm falling to the ground, the Oneirophage lashed out with the battle scissors again, gashing the insectoid matriarch in the abdomen, but, this time, the blades got stuck in her flesh and the Oneirophage was carried into the air along with her, still clinging to the handles of the giant scissors.

The massive herds of animals in the fields had begun stamping their feet and trampling one another, and when a few of the Necrodelic's fireballs lighted in the grass after being deflected by the centipede warlord, they began a chaotic stampede, killing one another and knocking the battling demons and insects over in the process. Pestilentia swooped down amidst the anarchy to gather up her minions as the fires spread and the animals grew more crazed. Whereas the Necrodelic simply slashed the beasts to pieces whenever they came near him, and Hydraman kept them at bay with his headbutts, and Cerberus leapt onto their backs and broke their necks betwixt his black fangs, the insects, being more fragile and unaccustomed to fighting battles where they were outnumbered, were at a disadvantage. Pestilentia flew off with her minions safely inside the hive of her body. The Oneirophage dropped down as she took off into the skies, the giant scissors still protruding from her abdomen.

The Necrodelic, Oneirophage, Hydraman, and Cerberus spent the next several hours slaying virtually all of Elasvai's wildlife, then stood triumphant in the waning night over a massive battlefield of smoking, poisoned, perforated, broken, decapitated, artescerated, eviscerated, mutilated, and dismembered animal corpses. The carnage stretched for miles, from horizon to horizon. The stench of death was so enormous that it was visible, a black miasma rising like the mists of Erebus over the mass grave.

The Necrodelic and the Oneirophage used the glut of carcasses to satiate their addictions and heal the accretions of wounds they had suffered over the last several hours. Chariah walked among the dead like a funerary priest, breathing in the rising smoke of the immolated and cremated beasts as he traversed their ashes, inhaling the raw stuff of death which hung like a damp dark fog over the aceldama, using it to fuel his healing necromancies. His lacerations began to close, hermetically sealing themselves. Broken and fractured bones did the same, and the rib stolen by the Oneirophage regenerated itself. Chariah restored and rebalanced his energies like the vampire and predator he was, a vampire who drank the blood of his victims in evaporated form rather than liquid, a predator who devoured the flesh of his prey as gases rather than solids.

The Oneirophage likewise healed himself through the bounty of fresh corpses, plunging the Umbilicus into the skulls and faces of those who had not been destroyed by fire or mutilation, those whose bodies remained intact enough for him to plunder their insides. Imbibing their final dreams and death-visions through the Umbilicus, the Oneirophage strode through the mass grave like a mortician, performing autopsies with his sorcerous straws until he had regained his strength and vigor, until his every broken bone had healed, and every lesion, puncture, and bruise in his serpentine body had disappeared as though it had never existed.

As the first rays of dawn approached, the four demons gazed around, observing and enjoying the aesthetics of genocide. None of the exterminated animals would become the Jh'a'vyraa. Several of the species were now extinct. The population of the universe had dwindled yet again, and the end of time drew inexorably nearer.

They walked amongst the fields of corpses for a time, before coming to the edge of a cliffside upon the steppes.

"What now, ophidian one?" asked the Necrodelic.

"I have long desired to visit the Hanging Gardens of Aphrodisia," the Oneirophage responded.

"And I the Drug Topiary," spake the Necrodelic. "We should do so before the planet is destroyed."

"Farewell then, Necrodelic."

"Farewell, Oneirophage. When next we meet, it will be in battle."

The Oneirophage and Hydraman then headed south along the cliffside, while the Necrodelic and Cerberus walked north. Dzandra rose and unveiled the yellow morn. The Oneirophage transformed into Morpheus Rex while slithering along the ledge, his dark silhouette morphing from serpentine to hominid, so that he traversed the horizon on a cobra's tail one moment, and on two legs the next, his nine-headed ally following behind. Chariah and his hellhound were black figures traveling in the opposite direction, indistinguishable from their shadows as they marched, the last vestiges of night in the bright light of the topaz dawn.

Chariah could taste magnetic fields and feel them pulling on the iron in his blood as he stood at the north pole of Elasvai. The raw magnetism raised the blood to the surface of his flesh and began to pull it through his pores in miniscule droplets, a woundless bloodletting. His long black hair crackled visibly and audibly with electricity, as though it were a nest of eels, or as if an incubating phoenix were about to burst from his brain in fiery rebirth, having used his skull for an egg like a parasite.

The entire sky was filled with aurora borealis, a scintillating display of gleaming blues, purples, pinks, golds, silvers, and sparkling whites, cataracting and fountaining in endless, evanescent formations. The curved wall before him was a similar phenomenon, an eternally transforming spectrum that flowed into itself, perhaps a reflection or refraction of the aurora borealis. Or, perhaps, the aurora borealis was a reflection of it. The radiant walls rose so high into the air that he couldn't tell where they ended and the skies began. He ran his clawed hand through the wall of pure psychedelia before him, the dripping amorphous mass of colors. His hand disappeared inside the strange substance which was both liquid and light, passing through it like the hand of a ghost or an astrosome. Inside he felt the heat of a womb, the spikes of an iron maiden, and the shape of a skull. He withdrew his fingers from the shimmering barrier, glancing around for some type of door or entrance. There was none.

Placing his left hand now into the curving, ephemeral walls, Chariah began to slowly circumnavigate the Drug Topiary's continuous rampart, which seemingly had neither origin nor terminus, ingress nor egress. As he walked, his hand floated through a myriad of sensations, both pleasure and pain, sometimes simultaneously. His hand disturbed nests of vipers, scorpions, and fetuses; passed through waterfalls, ocean spray, brooks, and ponds; submerged itself in witches' cauldrons, pools of boiling acid, and volcanoes brimming with hot lava. He passed his hand over decaying corpses and fornicating lovers; over wet battlefields and mattresses; and through fire and the flaming river of Phlegethon to snow and the icy river of Cocytus. He plunged his hand into the fanged mouths of creatures that wanted to devour him, the freshly spilled entrails of sacrificial victims, and the cold phalluses and vaginas of the dead. His hand tore gently through spiderwebs and placentas; slipped in and out of handcuffs, tourniquets, and gauntlets; was given swords, battle axes, maces, and morning stars; was severed completely and later returned; was immersed in pits full of writhing maggots and razor blades. His fingers were cocooned by butterflies, suckled by younglings, masturbated by Mother Chaos, tortured with thumbscrews, severed by guillotines, and bitten off by Satan. Finally, Chariah's hand passed over his own body, the exact form, shape, texture, and temperature of his flesh and musculature, and wherever he touched the tactile simulacrum within the psychedelic wall, his external flesh could feel the touch of his palms and fingertips, and he could see visible black handprints and small red scratches appear upon his body whenever he did so.

Chariah had completely circumnavigated the psychedelic barrier and found no sign of entrance, because the entire wall itself was an entrance, something which he had been unable to previously perceive. Once imbued with this knowledge, Chariah stepped directly through the glimmering ramparts and into the Drug Topiary.

Inside, the floors were comprised of the same psychedelic substance. He could sink into it like water, wade through it like quicksand, or walk over it like terra. Before him were towering topiaries of opium poppies, sculpted into demon and animal forms, copulating, giving birth, battling, meditating, and dying. As he began to feast upon opium and poppy seeds, the sculptures began speaking to him in mantras and languages he had never heard before, their mouths moving from inside the scenery.

Cerberus had followed his master through the psychedelic entrance, and had wandered to a pool of elixir, which he now lapped up from a transmorphing shore. Chariah knelt beside his familiar and cupped the elixir in his hands, then raised them to his lips. The elixir tasted like dew and sunlight and sugar all at once, and filled his body with a cleansing, purifying sensation, healing wounds that he didn't even have. In the center of the pool of elixir was a stone fountain forming the shape of a succubus, whose eyes wept the elixir, whose lips salivated the elixir, whose breasts lactated the elixir, and whose vagina menstruated the elixir.

Walking north, Chariah found himself alongside a river of black nepenthe. He drank some and was filled with liquid darkness, as though his entire body had been hollowed, drained, and filled with outer space. He crossed a bridge of frozen cocaine with skulls sculpted into it and came into a triangle of white sand, a desert of cocaine. He breathed his scorching breath atop its surface, creating a fine layer of black and inhaling the intoxicating stimulants, then dipping his claws into the glistening grains of coca and raising them to his nostrils, breathing in pounds of the numbing drug, his heartbeat accelerating with its effects. He walked through the white desert with Cerberus at his side, leaving two trails of footprints in the sugary powder.

The entities in the opium topiaries were beginning to move, some aging and dying. Chariah came to serpentine topiaries of ganja, wherein every species of serpent writhed and struck. Some spoke to him as he devoured their brethren. He could smell their venoms, even taste them on his tongue. He could hear them slithering and hissing, feel their snakeskin on his flesh. He suckled upon the hair of maternal gorgons, drinking their poisonous milks. Curving rivers of soma splashed the psychedelic shores. Chariah followed to where they intersected with a straight stream of red wine, and drank from it, as well. Where the rivers of soma and wine met in swirling roseate confluences was where both tasted the best, and had the strongest effects. Chariah gazed down the river, and saw fountains of elixir at both ends. He could still see himself drinking at the first one, his perception of time distorted so that he watched himself cupping the elixir in his hands as Cerberus lapped up the clear liquid beside him.

Heading south, Chariah followed the crimson river of wine to a triangular desert of opium. He partook of the opium just as he had the cocaine, scorching its surface and breathing the smoke, then dipping his claws in it and inhaling it raw.

Chariah could feel the pull of Elasvai's magnetic field again, drawing the blood from his pores in small beads. Hemathidrosis had begun, as well, and his pupils were alternately dilating and constricting, sometimes synchronously, sometimes not. He walked through four sections of the Drug Topiary, each a near reflection of the others, the main difference being that two had straight rivers of nepenthe and two had wine, with the circular river of soma running through all, and two contained deserts of cocaine, while two possessed deserts of opium.

The sculptures in the walls of ganja plants and opium poppies were different, of course, and he could see, hear, feel, taste, and smell all the characters in the scenery, and their stories. He was now sweating sperm along with blood, creating a pink mist and raining infinitesimal droplets of carnelian as he walked. There were four fountains of elixirs altogether. Whereas the first had been a succubus, the one across from it had been an incubus, ejaculating the elixir. The third had been a hermaphrodite, releasing alternating jetstreams of elixir from its twin genitals in mid-air. The fourth was asexual, an androgynous deity devoid of genitalia who spouted the elixirs from the crown of its bald head.

Now within the labyrinth, the Necrodelic entered a spiral maze of morning glory, belladonna, and lotus blossoms, in every imaginable shade and hue. As he journeyed through the spiral maze, there were also several plants and flowers which he had not formerly perceived as drugs, but when he ate them, or lit them and inhaled their perfumes, he discovered that they really were and always had been. From the tranquility of hyacinth to the sexual rush of roses, the battle-strengthening effects of Venus fly traps to the near-death experiences of asphodel, Chariah felt as though must have eaten one of every species of plant in existence within the last hour.

Chariah made his slow, circular way toward the center of the gardens while sweating dreams and listening to far-off music. He ate white lotus and green lotus, and even the deadly black lotus which killed all but the most enlightened of demons. There was pink and purple and blue lotus too, and sweet berries full of psychoactive chemicals.

The spiral maze wound through the entire gardens, with rainbow bridges that parted the nepenthe rivers, soma rivers, and rivers of wine to the side as he passed. Gateways took him through the walls of ganja and opium, which along with the lotus were now coming alive at a frenzied pace, the demons and beasts carved into them now taking on their own colors and becoming more and more three-dimensional. Chariah spiraled toward the center of the Drug Topiary on a series of curving paths, until at last he came to its nexus.

The Tower of Panacea was a shimmering beam, whose light itself was a drug. Chariah stepped inside it, and it slipped over his body like a garment. Its heat was a drug too, seeping into his flesh. Now, the Necrodelic sweated his very soul. He realized that he had lost Cerberus somewhere within the gardens. The Tower of Panacea held him directly over the north pole of Elasvai. His hair began to raise and whip around him like a living entity. He could feel his entire circulatory system as clearly as he felt his face or hands, could feel the blood itself pumping through it, could even count each individual blood cell, if he so desired. He looked down and he could see all of his black inner organs. He watched the slow yogic breath of his lungs, the beating of his heart, the chemical production of his liver, the pitchlike sperm forming in his testicles, the electrical activity of his brain, and the dilations and constrictions of his eyes as they gazed forth upon themselves and his exposed insides with psychedelic X-ray vision and drugged fascination. He could see all three layers of his essence now as well, could see beneath the physical flesh and organs to his astral body on its silver cord, and below and within that astral body his black and evil soul.

The Tower of Panacea drew the Necrodelic upwards now, upwards through its swirling spectrums, its harmonious music, its sensual heat and sexual light, high into the air, so high he had no idea how far he had traveled, sweating blood, sperm, dreams, and ectoplasm, until finally he found himself levitating over the entire Drug Topiary, spinning slowly in mid-air like a star, looking over the psychedelic labyrinth he had conquered.

He could see clearly now the ancient symbols in the Drug Topiary, which had magnified and elevated his spirit to its zenith, and which made the psychedelic gardens as deadly as they were mind-bending. The amorphous psychedelic wall was more of a vertical moat, although parapets and turrets rose, crested, and fell along its surface like the waves of an ocean. The four fountains of elixir corresponded with the four points of a compass within the ramparts, one west, one east, one south, and one north, and formed the shape of ankhs. The sculpted poppies formed a square wall within the circle, and inside them were the triangular deserts of cocaine and opium. The walls of ganja formed a diamond, intersecting with the walls of opium. The rivers of wine led from each fountain of elixir, converging at the very center of the topiary, just below the Tower of Panacea, and formed the shape of a crucifix. Half of those rivers were black with nepenthe, however, and these churning atramentous streams of psychological salves and memory repressors formed a swastika, branching off in all four quarters to form sable brooks that cut through the walls of opium poppies, watering, drugging, and eroding them simultaneously. The rivers of soma formed a pentagram, with the first level of the spiral maze of lotuses encircling it. The spiral maze curved inwards thirteen times, until reaching the Tower of Panacea, upon whose zenith Chariah now floated.

The Necrodelic gazed down and saw the corpses of those that had come before him, for pleasure, enlightenment, or both, and had died within the Drug Topiary. He observed their deaths, their accidents, overdoses, suicides, and murders, observed the processes by which their flesh and souls became the topiaries in the gardens. He located Cerberus, lapping up wine and growling at phantoms. He saw himself at every point he had traversed, a continuous entity illuminating the path through the maze, Chariah after Chariah after Chariah, an infinity of Necrodelics. Chariah breathed in the serenity, and when he exhaled, the Drug Topiary underwent an incredible transformation. Every plant, every flower, every leaf were all lit by his pyromantic breath, but instead of bursting into flame, they kindled like hemp in a pipe.

The garden began to move and each section began to raise up, like the pieces of a puzzle box, forming a tiered ziggurat with his soul at the top. The walls of opium and ganja multiplied into the thirteen stories of a sacred temple. The rivers of nepenthe, soma, and wine became waterfalls, flowing over the levels of hemp and opium gardens to the fountainous pools of elixir below. The deserts of opium and cocaine became pyramids, gigantic crystal monuments of purest white and deepest black. The spiral maze became a spiral stairway, winding upwards until it reached the top of the ziggurat, and energies of every color curved upwards as well, like a serpent uncoiling, the kundalini of the Drug Topiary, which caused Chariah's kundalini to rise up over his head and strike the universe like a cosmic cobra.

Chariah crossed his legs now and rested his palms upon his knees. His third eye fluttered open, and he watched as the entire Drug Topiary coursed and flowed with cycles of energy, waterfalls pouring down the sides of the ziggurat and being replenished by the towering fountains of elixir, the white and black pyramids sparking with electricity and raw power. He hovered in outer space, directly over the north pole of Elasvai, the aurora borealis splayed majestically beneath him. He had never felt so tranquil, so real, and he knew now that he must attain the Jh'a'vyraa not only to save his soul, not only to avoid eternal torment in Hell, but to experience this same nirvanic pleasure forever.

The Necrodelic's seven black chakras whirred as they spun in place, as he himself spun, meditating in mid-air, and then the black chakras began to spin out from their energy centers and into orbit around Chariah like seven planets, rotating on their axes while he spun at their center like a sun, radiant, effulgent, filled with gravity and power to illuminate and balance his solar system.

Mother Chaos flew to the Necrodelic then, for he had penetrated the astral plane with his physical body, and alighted on his lap, perfume mingling with smoke, damson lips kissing black. She embraced him around the neck with her arms and wrapped her thighs around his back, fluttering like a butterfly and lowering herself upright onto his rigid phallus, her lotus position entwined with his, and they made love in the yab-yum position atop the ziggurat, liquid purple flowing from her body and liquid darkness flowing from his, in yet more rivers down the pyramid, double helixes of shadow and light, growing wider and wider, swelling as though with flood, until their purple and black energy poured down the Drug Topiary in one continuous ocean, which was eternally returned to them by the fountains of elixir.

They made love beyond space and time, in one continuous orgasm that lasted for eons. Finally, after an infinity of nirvana, the Dark Orgasm came, blinding Chariah, cloaking his senses, spinning him in shadows through the voids and vacuums and abysses of the cosmos, and when he awoke once more outside the Drug Topiary, he had attained greater enlightenment and blacker evil, and new powers that would manifest themselves in the days to come, making him more demonic, more lethal, and more genocidal than ever before.

37

The Oneirophage, Hydraman, two gorgons, two lamias, and the corpse of the Constrictress rode inside the mouth of Serpentikal unto the south pole of Elasvai. Through the aurora astralis they soared, the prism palace Phantasmagorika catching the shooting beams of light in its own shimmering spectrum and creating brand new colors that burst through the night skies. With rainbows arcing all around, Serpentikal flew through kaleidoscopic tunnels and over iridescent bridges to the Hanging Gardens of Aphrodisia.

The saurian spaceship landed a few feet from the fabled gardens, and the seven demons descended Serpentikal's throat to emerge before it. The Hanging Garden of Aphrodisia was composed of tiers and terraces that rose beyond the limits of vision into the aurora astralis, within which it disappeared. Its outer walls were wrapped in vines bearing grapes of every color, some larger than the serpent demons' skulls, and from these dripping grapes a moat of wine had formed around the gardens. They made their way onto the large lingham drawbridge, which protruded over the moat but reached only halfway across before abruptly terminating with a phallus tip that dripped wine from its urethra. The entrance to the Hanging Gardens of Aphrodisia was a gated yoni several feet above their heads, a constricted tunnel of labia too small for them to pass through even if they could reach it.

They strode and slithered to the edge of the bridge. The Oneirophage paused to produce the Umbilicus from the sheath of flesh in his right wrist, twirling his fingers until it appeared. He blew into the Umbilicus to elongate it, then began to sip the purple wine from the moat. Imbibing heavily of the intoxicating liquid, the Oneirophage found his body grow not only warm, but hot, as though with fever. His two penises immediately hardened into erections. The wine had an instant aphrodisiac effect, and the Oneirophage passed the Umbilicus to Hydraman, in whose claws the sorcerous straw apparatus multiplied itself ninefold, allowing him to simultaneously partake of the sweet alcoholic elixir with every dragonhead. When he had had his fill, Hydraman passed the Umbilicus to the gorgons and the lamias, who then partook of the wine themselves.

Moments later, the six of them were inebriated and entangled in a twisted mating ball, which included the preserved cadaver of the Constrictress. As they writhed in a snakepit of orgy, the lingham drawbridge began to lengthen and rise into the air. As the orgy intensified, the phallic bridge raised them to the yoni gateway high above, which itself had dilated with arousal. The large phallus began to ejaculate wine, splattering the vined walls and trellises before it, then plunged coitally into the zenithal vagina, and as orgasms were achieved, the serpent brood was delivered to the entrance of the gardens.

They rose, walked across the lingham drawbridge, and passed through the irising labial entrance. Once within the Hanging Gardens of Aphrodisia they paused to admire the towering tesserations and ubiquitous flora, picking grapes from the vines along the walls that were every bit as potent as the wines they produced. Giant fronds and ferns overlooked high terraces, while flowers, berries, and fruits bloomed on plants and vines that hung down from every ceiling like the tresses of a fertility demoness. The air was filled with clouds of pollen, visible masses that were inhaled by the thousands and which, like everything else within the Hanging Gardens of Aphrodisia, aroused the lust of those who breathed them. The Oneirophage, Hydraman, and their gorgon and lamia consorts devoured everything in their paths, from grasses and flowers to berries and fruits to seeds and spores, engaging in frequent orgies as they made their way up stairways which ascended alongside the rivers and cataracts of red and purple wine, as well as streams of amber honey, which dripped from the pleasure hives of incubus bees and their succubus queens.

After partaking of the aphrodisiac honey, they were compelled to enter one of the pleasure hives. Inside were pools full of honey and walls lined with shackles and whips. The Oneirophage and Hydraman bound the five females to the hive walls, then proceeded to flay them with the whips provided by the sex slaves of the queen bee. The Oneirophage then raped a lamia while Hydraman raped a gorgon, then the Oneirophage raped a gorgon while Hydraman raped a lamia, then both raped the corpse of the Constrictress simultaneously. Later, the Oneirophage took his turn in the chains and cuffs, simultaneously flogged by gorgons, lamias, and Hydraman alike.

After departing the pleasure hive, they made their way through tiers and terraces to a field of dandelions, whose spores were grains of cocaine, driplets of opium, and perfumed pleasuredust. The Oneirophage sodomized Hydraman while Hydraman simultaneously performed cunnilingus upon the gorgons, the lamias, and the deceased Constrictress with five of his mouths. A gorgon and lamia performed fellacio upon the Oneirophage's twin tattooed penises while Hydraman sodomized the dream-eater, and the other gorgon and lamia writhed in a lesbian mating ball nearby. The Oneirophage plunged both his penises into the Constrictress' vagina. After the dream-eater had withdrawn himself from her corpse, Hydraman took his place. The Oneirophage then proceeded to make love to a gorgon and a lamia, simultaneously, with his twin penises. The pollen, cocaine, opium, and pleasuredust swirled around them in larger and thicker clouds as aphrodisiac dandelions disintegrated beneath their bodies and thrashing limbs, penetrating their skin and orifices, intensifying lust and orgasms alike.

They finally made their way to the upper terraces, where silkworms wove lingerie for the females, corsettes that raised their swollen breasts and covered their bodies in lace while binding their hands and feet submissively. The gorgons' serpent hair rose straight up from their scalps in individual black negligees like sexual headdresses, releasing more of their venomous pheromones into the air and tantalizing the Oneirophage and Hydraman. In the middle of the topmost terrace, the zenith of the Hanging Gardens of Aphrodisia, was a raised dais with the ancient sexual yin-yang sigil drawn in its center. Upon this dais, within this sigil, the orgy continued, serpentine limbs, tongues, hair, and phalluses entangled like a Gordian knot of leviathans' tentacles, melting the silk wrappings adorning the gorgons and lamias with a combination of heat and friction.

Throughout alternating rings of analingus, cunnilingus, and fellacio, the stone dais began to shift and rise into the air. The sound of grinding stones was loud throughout the entire gardens as tantric energies seeped into the sorcerous sigil. As all seven, including the dead Constrictress, were joined and psychically bonded by seven multiple and simultaneous orgasms, the yin-yang sigil began to glow, and the ancient gravitronic mechanism was activated. The entire Hanging Gardens of Aphrodisia rotated within itself like a puzzle box, turning upside-down while it reversed its own polarities and gravities, unfolding and lengthening until it hung from the underbelly of Elasvai into outer space, freed of the South Pole and the planet's magnetic field by the tantric energies and metamorphosing into a garden which truly did hang, dangling out over the universe.

The zenith of the Hanging Gardens of Aphrodisia had become its nadir. Flowers, vines, fronds, and trees were all turned upside-down and wavered in the pull of outer space. A hail of twigs and blossoms fell into the starlit cosmos below. The Oneirophage wrapped the corpse of the Constrictress around the branch of a weeping willow, then twined a knot of inkvine around his right hand to prevent the vacuum of space from sucking him into its void. The mouths of a lamia and gorgon remained clenched around his phalluses, hanging on for life. Their weight and desperate movements not only inhibited his ability to climb back to safety but, like drowning victims, threatened to pull him down along with them.

The serpentine lower body of the lamia thrashed as she choked on his sperm, his venomous semen filling her lungs and throat and lubricating her mouth until she began to lose her grip and dug her fangs into the tattooed flesh of the Oneirophage's genitals. This brought the Oneirophage to orgasm, one which he suffused with his sorcery and discharged like a powerful pneuma. The force of his ejaculation blasted the lamia, screaming and writhing, into outer space.

The gorgon desperately held onto his upper penis, clutching and scrabbling at his scales while her legs frantically kicked at the void. Finally, her violent thrashing caused the scales of the Oneirophage's phallus to dislodge, and then the dream-eater performed a sudden ecdysis to free himself from her extra weight, sloughing off his topmost phallus' layer of integument and sending the gorgon to her doom with an empty snakeskin in her deathgrip, her serpent-hair flailing as she fell and dwindled from sight.

Hydraman, facing similar jeopardy, had held on by biting

the branches and vines above, unhinging his jaws like those of boa constrictors, and clenching his mouths around them, so that he dangled by his nine dragonheads, suspended in space. A lamia upon whom he had been performing cunnilingus now hung upside-down from his central head, her thighs wrapped tightly around his neck like a sexual strangler. A gorgon also continued to perform fellacio upon him while they hung, like a dominatrix with a sadomasochistic gallows for a sex toy. For several minutes, the trio remained intertwined, Hydraman trying to climb his way back up into the gardens, until a shower of pink lotus poured over them, stimulating Hydraman unto further heights of aphrodisia. Like the Oneirophage, he gathered and focused the energies of his body and unleashed them in an orgasm so strong that the ejaculation of his sperm blew the gorgon several feet into space, blasting her into the distance as she helplessly flailed at the cosmos.

The lamia, meanwhile, had slid all the way down to the candelabra-like base of Hydraman's nine necks and hung upside-down against his torso. As Hydraman struggled to climb to safety, her grip became more and more tenuous, until her thighs slipped from around his central throat. The lamia did a quick flip in mid-air and caught onto Hydraman's member with her fanged mouth to prevent herself from plummeting into the waiting void. An instant later, however, she did exactly that, as Hydraman discharged his phallus to rid himself of her excess weight, the same way lizards sometimes release their own tails when caught by predators. She fell with his detached genitalia in her mouth, watching Hydraman regrow a new penis even as she was whisked away with his old one clenched between her jaws.

The Oneirophage made his way back to the sigil by climbing the vines, using the corpse of the Constrictress like a grapnel at times, with Hydraman following. Both pressed on the sigil while they dangled precariously, but could not reverse its effects on the gravity of the Hanging Gardens of Aphrodisia. As showers of leaves and flower petals poured down around them, the Oneirophage emitted an ultrasonic hiss. Moments later, the Metasaur was beneath him, and he dropped into the waiting mouth of his figurehead, Serpentikal, still carrying the embalmed Constrictress with him. Hydraman released his nine mouths from the various branches, vines, and fronds that he had clamped onto and fell into the Serpentopolis, where he quickly took refuge in the coils of the labyrinthine city.

As Serpentikal turned his gargantuan head and flew the living spaceship back to the surface of Elasvai, the gravity in the Hanging Gardens of Aphrodisia returned to normal. For a moment it hung suspended from the south pole of the garden planet like the green entrails of a fertility demon's underbelly, an upside-down jungle, a true hanging garden, then reversed itself with a grinding of stone and a rearrangement of tiers and terraces, and all was as it had been before the orgiastic rites of serpentine perversion had been performed within its walls.

38

The Oneirophage prepared to resurrect the Constrictress with voodoo and necromancy. He had devoted an entire serpentorium in Phantasmagorika to her corpse. Within that serpentarium chamber he had cleaned the soot and ashes from her body, scraped away her burnt scales and grafted new patches of snakeskin onto her scorched flesh, and then stored her in a glass tank filled with cold embalming fluids, in which she floated as though on display in a menagerie of taxidermied animals. Preserved in ophidian formaldehyde-a melange of caustic venoms from acid-spewing cobras and wine distilled from the blood of gorgons, mixed together and then oxidized with the dying breath of a sacrificial dipsas-the Constrictress had neither decayed nor decomposed since her demise. The Oneirophage extracted her cadaver from the sepulchral serpentarium in which he had stored her since her death on Grytiawa, having removed her only once before, for the interlude in the Hanging Gardens of Aphordisia.

He removed the Constrictress from her aquarium-like sarcophagus, carefully lowered her limp form to the floor, and began performing ancient rites of revivification upon her corpse. He placed her in a pentagram drawn with the freshly spilled blood of sacrificial boa constrictors, then called her soul back to her body with arcane and sibilant chantings, all the while shaking dead rattlesnakes in each of his hands. With interdimensional hypnotic suggestions and the power of his dream-fueled sorceries, the Oneirophage summoned the spirit of the Constrictress back to her flesh. The Oneirophage then used the Umbilicus to resuscitate her, blowing the breath of life back into her lungs with rhythmic pneumas. Her heart restarted in her chest, her green eyelids fluttered open, and the Oneirophage had raised the dead.

Serpentikal landed near Candiru Falls. The crepitus of the Constrictress' broken bones scraped the air as the Oneirophage led her across the verdant, blooming planet. Sculpted by the Necrodelic into a giant, living pentagram, the Oneirophage had unfolded her corpse and rearranged her broken skeleton into its original form before preserving it, but the embalming fluid was neither a curative nor a remedy, and her bones remained as they had been in the moment of her demise: cracked, splintered, and sundered. In her undead state, however, the Constrictress perceived only a modicum of pain.

The Oneirophage led her like a child and a familiar to the waterfalls, where azure pools shimmered beneath the moonlight like open eyes. Within the cascading cataracts could be seen the tiny, slender forms of the black catfish, plummeting with the surging waters to the pond below, which teemed with their quill-like silhouettes. The Oneirophage waded into the swarming lagoon. The candiru shot like magnets through the currents once the Oneirophage and the Constrictress were waist-deep within the water. The stiletto-like catfish swam directly into their genitals, lodging themselves like intravenous needles in their urethras. Once inside, they clamped their fangs down upon the tender flesh therein and there they remained, like blood-drinking larvae.

The twin penises of the Oneirophage hardened, leaking tiny trickles of crimson from their tips. The pain invigorated the masochistic dream-eater. The Constrictress found herself with a wombful of the wriggling bloodsuckers, biting and attaching to her vaginal walls and membranes, swimming inside and drinking her blood from within. When there was no more room for the candiru, they dangled from betwixt her labia like a mass of slender tentacles.

The Oneirophage embraced the Constrictress, uncoiled her elongated arms and wrapped them around his body as though he were a living caduceus staff. He slipped his first penis, turgid with parasites as well as sex, its tip red with irritation, into his undead boa constrictor lover. His phallus plunged through the candirus and, with genitals infested by the acicular, piscid vampires, the Oneirophage and the Constrictress made love. The Oneirophage used his second penis to sodomize the Constrictress before shoving it into her crowded womb alongside its twin. Ejaculation was difficult due to the candiru, sometimes retrograde, turning back into his body and splashing his bladder and innards. Blood flowed from their joined sexes as they made love, tingeing the ponds of Candiru Falls with scarlet, and attracting hordes of the thirsty fish in feeding frenzies around their bodies.

The Oneirophage twirled the Umbilicus from its sheath in his wrist and impaled the Constrictress through the forehead with its tip. As they made love, he suckled upon her dreams, preserved within her brain as surely as her flesh had been preserved within the ophidian formaldehyde. The Oneirophage drank flashbacks of that fateful battle on Grystiawa, reminiscing about his home planet and the glorious war that had led to its destruction. He imbibed glimpses of Hell as well, where the Constrictress was tied to four torture racks at once and stretched for eons, until her arms, tail, and head were thinner than the candiru which infested her flesh. He devoured more dreams through the straw, and saw Satan looking on through flames as the Constrictress was forced to crush herself in her own coils. Satan laughed as he watched, making eye contact through the dimensions as he voyeuristically watched his dream-eating, serpentine progeny. The Oneirophage wilted from that incandescent and terrible eye contact and withdrew the straw from the Constrictress' skull, returning it to the small slit in his forearm before refocusing all of his energies upon his zombie lover.

As midnight crested through the starlit skies above, the Oneirophage expelled the candiru from his tattooed penises, the tattoos of Satan and serpent which covered them expectorating the parasites from their mouths while the Constrictress performed fellacio upon him, her boa constrictor jaws unhinging to encompass his genitalia the same way they would to swallow a large piece of prey, so that they could accommodate the Oneirophage's twin phalluses simultaneously. She swallowed the candiru along with the Oneirophage's powerful jetstream of sperm mere moments before the voodoo spell that had been cast upon her corpse dissipated. Her soul returned once more to the realms of the dead, leaving behind a cadaver with a belly full of water and live candiru, swimming around inside her stomach sac as if it were an aquarium.

Moments later, the Oneirophage sucked all the candirus from the pond into his Darkprism, then dragged the carcass of the Constrictress from the waters by the tail, like vanquished prey from a successful hunt, to the shores of Candiru Falls, across flowerbeds, through gardens and jungles, and back to the waiting Metasaur. The large, beady eyes of Serpentikal glared down angrily upon the Oneirophage as the dream-eater approached with the violated corpse of the Constrictress in tow. The Oneirophage slithered through the gateway in the First Serpent's torso. Serpentikal continued to glower unseen as he was commanded to rise from the ground and launch into the skies, his eyeballs two clenched fists of wrath in their sockets as he obediently soared through the night.

39

Drelrei and Junisia had retreated to the sanctuary of their birthplace, the Fiendfarms, and hidden themselves away in shame and agony. Crippled, humiliated, and sundered, they remained isolated in their laboratories and abattoirs for several days, comforting one another with tantric sex and post-coital plots of revenge, smoking pounds of opium and drinking liters of nepenthe as they healed. For the first time in years, they made love as two entities, each feeling the unbearable pangs of separation in their souls as well as their bodies, druglike withdrawal symptoms and addictive cravings for conjoinment racking their flesh like illness and poison. Weakened and feverish, sweating, shaking, vomiting, and hallucinating, their bodies covered in oozing sores and trembling with violent paroxysms, Drelrei and Junisia needed each other like vampires needed blood, like shamans needed psilocybin and peyote. Addicted to one another, the soulmates were one another's ambrosia, panacea, aphrodisiac, intoxicant, analgesic, stimulant, depressant, and psychedelic all at once. Drelrei and Junisia were one another's medicine, one another's cure for the anguish of existence, the torment of the universe, and their demonic powers were dependent upon their spiritual oneness and the conjoinment of their flesh as Siamese twins, as surely as the Necrodelic's powers depended upon the flesh he smoked, and the Oneirophage's powers depended upon the dreams he devoured.

They healed themselves with tantric rituals and medicinal drugs until they were strong enough to once again perform the sacred ceremony of conjoinment. In a rooftop garden, high atop the Stormtower, at the zenith of the Fiendfarms, directly beneath the noontime sun, Drelrei and Junisia assembled the necessary instruments, chemicals, and sacrificial victims. They lay down in the center of the circle of the ancient sigil, the male and female, yin and yang, sexual mandala that had been carved into the rooftop stone and painted red and black with blood and liquified death. The soulmates were encircled by the boundaries of the rune and an array of surgical tools, vials, jars, drugs, and drug paraphernalia. Siamese twin demons surrounded them, joined permanently together in the sexual manifestation of yin and yang, the penises of males sewn, nailed, stapled, and fused to the mouths of females in hermetically sealed fellacio, and the vaginas of those same females bound by the same means to the mouths of the males in unbreakable cunnilingus. Sexually conjoined offerings of fertility, the tantric sacrifices lay half-within and half-without the circle, forming crosses and crucifixes as they did so, which created natural wards and amplified Drelrei and Junisia's sorcerous energies.

Drelrei and Junisia filled the womb-bowl of their double pipe with squirming, yellow masses of maggots that sometimes spilled over the rim and onto the rooftop. With one simultaneous exhalation, Drelrei and Junisia triggered the automatic lighting mechanism of the pornographic pipe, kindling the living, writhing maggots inside. The maggots burned and melted, and Drelrei and Junisia inhaled their putrid smoke, breathing their essence, tasting decay and hot maggot-flesh on their tongues. The tantric demons began drifting into an altered state of consciousness as they smoked the maggots, becoming more aware, more powerful, and more real as they incinerated the acrid larvae.

Pestilentia was attracted by the rotting stench of the burning maggots and the excremental-tasting breath of Drelrei and Junisia as they exhaled the putrescent smoke. The Empress of Insects came bearing gifts of opium and royal jelly in her womb, and hovered protectively over the two demons as they copulated upon the glowing sigil. Drelrei and Junisia injected themselves with syringes full of maggots as they fornicated, jabbing the needles into their arms, thighs, jugular veins, carotid arteries, and urethras. When the maggots had all been squeezed into their circulatory systems, large fire ants, like beasts of burden, bore the jars of opium and royal jelly from Pestilentia's vagina, down her legs to the Stormtower, and deposited them around the Tantradox. Wasp demons flew from her mouth and vagina with yet more jars, these brimming with various sacrificial insects, arachnids, and invertebrates. Several minutes later, Pestilentia bade her hordes return. Chirping and buzzing a complicated insect blessing over the Tantradox' ritual as her minions resettled into her ambrium flesh, the Empress of Insects lowered herself as close to the ground as possible and gazed directly into the eyes of Drelrei and Junisia with four of her eyes.

"Have you reconsidered your battle plans?" Pestilentia asked the Tantradox. "My armies and I cannot assist you in the conditions you speak of."

"Tis the Necrodelic's only weakness," Drelrei replied. "Tis our best chance for victory."

"Very well." Pestilentia clicked one last blessing upon the Tantradox, then bade Drelrei and Junisia farewell, whirred away on dragonfly wings, and was gone.

Drelrei and Junisia drank the royal jelly, then smoked opium, ate opium, and injected opium into one another's genitals, she into his large crimson urethra, and he between her hundred blossoming labia and up into her womb like a drug-filled dildo. The demon lovers traded the syringe back and forth, successively shooting the psychedelic analgesic into all ten of Drelrei's swollen testicles and all ten of Junisia's resonating clitorises. Their pain was assuaged, their ordeal reconciled, and the two lovers copulated within the circle once more before continuing the ceremony.

One by one they emptied the jars of insects and used the living offerings to assist them in their ritual. They smoked caterpillars, butterflies, and moths for their powers of metamorphosis and rebirth, earthworms and slugs for their hermaphroditic energies, and silkworms for their binding unguents. Slowly, with large needles and long ropes of hemp, the Tantradox sewed itself back together. They drenched their flesh in the viscous slime of snails and slugs, the milk of aphids enslaved to colonies of ants, the honey of bees, the mucus of copulating earthworms, and the egg sacs and sperm packets of ticks and mites, binding their flesh with the gelid, sticky, semi-liquid agglutinations of the various species, and then smoked, snorted, injected, or devoured every last snail, slug, aphid, ant, bee, earthworm, tick, and mite whose secretions they had utilized.

Once rejoined, the Siamese twin Tantradox made love to itself. At last reunited, their orgasms carried them into a deep, intensely nirvanic state. Immediately afterwards, in a sorcerously charged state of post-coital enlightenment, Junisia swallowed a pod containing two seeds, one dark green, the other pitch black. Encoded within those spore-laden, genetimantically ensorcelled seeds were the battle plans of the Tantradox.

The Tantradox descended from the roof of the Stormtower, through the upper terraces of the Fiendfarms, and into one of their laboratories, where a red-hot forge sizzled between two surgical tables. The cerise light from the forge flickered across the shelves of vials, instruments, and preserved body parts lining the walls. Smoking fireflies, will-o-the-wisps, and electric eels from pornographic hookahs, the Tantradox began to mold large pieces of iron upon the incandescent forge with a glowing hammer and tongs. For hours, the Tantradox labored, chanting and casting tantric spells all the while. Sacrificial animals were reeled in from the hanging abattoir of the Fiendfarms' bottom level on giant meathooks. The meathooks were all interconnected by an elaborate series of chains and pulleys, and traveled along a labyrinth of grooves carved into the ceiling, a labyrinth of grooves that stretched throughout the entire Fiendfarms, connected to each level of the fortress by lifts and shafts. The hanging beasts were eviscerated as they dangled over the forge, their entrails dropping onto the hot iron and burning like gargantuan cigarettes, hissing like snakes and whipping about like unrestrained hoses before melting and disintegrating. Some of the animals were cut down from the hooks and burned alive, their flesh and blood and gore smoldering and sizzling and dissipating until they were one with the glowing forge. All the while, the Tantradox continued to hammer away at the slabs of iron.

Many hours later, the Tantradox held two new weapons in its hands: a large broadsword and a handheld iron maiden. Drelrei hefted the black hilt of the newborn sword in his cloven hands, then tested its crimson blade upon Siamese twin manticores. Drelrei raised the broadsword over his head and with one blow sundered the conjoined beasts.

The manticores fell to the ground as two creatures, freed at last from the surgeries committed upon their flesh by the Tantradox. The manticores bled and crawled around, then circled the Tantradox from either side, stalking their tormentor. Drelrei split the manticores again, one vertically from skull to tail, the other at the midpoint of its spine. All four halves remained alive, twitching and spasming. Drelrei hacked at the mutilated manticores again and again, until sixty-four bloody pieces were quivering upon the laboratory floor. When the manticores finally died, their souls went to Hell in sixty-four pieces, sundered yet surviving separately, like dissected earthworms. A wicked smile spread across the faces of Drelrei and Junisia. The Soul Cleaver had been forged, and now the Necrodelic and the Oneirophage would know the anguish of being separated and divided from one's own self, of being mutilated to the point where one lost all sense of identity. Their spirits, like those of the manticores, would be sent to Hell in fragments and morsels, bloody pieces of microscopic meat, thus multiplying their damnations exponentially. They would spend the eternity of Hell in a state of faceless, unrecognizable, torturous anatta. Their eons of evolution would be reversed, and they would devolve from demons into beasts, beasts into invertebrates, invertebrates into viruses, viruses into microorganisms. They would know the torment which the Tantradox had suffered at their hands a thousandfold. Their suffering would become the new mythology, the mythology of post-eschatological Hell.

The Tantradox turned its attention to the still-smoking iron maiden, a red and black rectangle of torture, like twin beds of nails on hinges. Drelrei placed himself against its right monolith of crimson spikes, Junisia upon its left. Slowly, the incandescent iron maiden closed around them, pressing them together until they were face to face. Its scorching spikes penetrated their scaled backs and dinosaur tails; its hot metal stuck to their skin. The Tantradox folded itself together like a butterfly, the iron maiden squeezing them closer and closer until their black nipples touched, their tongues entered each other's mouths, and Drelrei's enormous phallus pressed against Junisia's diaphragm. The iron maiden fell over, half-closed, half-open, and within its broiling, impaling confines, the Tantradox made love, the newly rejoined flesh between their shoulders, chests, abdomens, hips, and legs fusing, welding, cauterizing, and hermetically sealing itself together even further, more strongly than ever before, in the blazing heat of the freshly-forged torture device. The spikes tore puncture wounds in their backs as they thrust against one another, pain and pleasure joining into one Siamese twin entity in their conjoined bodies, culminating in a simultaneous orgasm that was at once both unbearable ecstasy and excruciating torment, nirvana and Hell in a double helix of light and darkness, sex and death, that possessed Drelrei's phallus like angry ghosts and their poltergeists, and he ejaculated fire and ice into Junisia's womb.

An hour later the ensorcelled iron maiden swung back open, like the brimstone gates of Hell. Drelrei and Junisia rose and stepped from its steaming crimson confines, their genitals dripping scorched sperm and semen, their flesh compacted in charred, gelid, oozing masses, their bodies joined in a higher, deeper, stronger state of oneness than ever before. Junisia lifted the handheld iron maiden and closed it by pressing a button on the inside of its handle. The Flesh Compactor had been born.

Drelrei retrieved the Soul Cleaver and held it aloft in his cloven hand as Junisia tested the Flesh Compactor's opening mechanism one more time. Armed with the spirit-sundering broadsword and handheld iron maiden they had imagined on the Cliffs of Caine, their body reborn, their love renewed, and their identity regained, the Tantradox prepared for one ultimate battle with the Necrodelic and the Oneirophage, one final jihad for vengeance and victory, one more armageddon in the seemingly endless procession of armageddons in the apocalyptic demon wars, with eternal damnation and infinite nirvana hanging in the balance

40

Atop the Stormtower of the Fiendfarms, as clouds began massing in the skies, Drelrei lowered a hook-tipped chain from the arm of a giant crane, pulling it down further and further with his hand, then shoved it into Junisia's vagina. Junisia devoured handfuls of eelworms as Drelrei lodged the hook deep inside her womb. When he had finished attaching his soulmate to the crane, Drelrei filled two syringes with the tiny parasites and injected them into Junisia's genitals, naval, and bloated abdomen. Meanwhile, Junisia smoked a writhing pile of eelworms from a hookah filled with hot bubbling sperm. When she had finished, she traded the hookah for one filled with boiling amniotic fluid. Junisia's stomach was growing more gravid by the second, swollen with the hordes of eelworms and the gigantic embryo gestating in her womb.

Junisia began to feel the effects of the eelworms. The vaginas of the crawling parasites were located in the center of their bodies, like the nucleus of an atom, the fulcrum of a torture device, or the sun of a solar system. Their flesh, their entire bodies, their organs, systems, and lives, all revolved around their vaginas, for it was these which were the source of their mysterious sexual powers. Now, having gorged herself upon the creatures, ingesting them with a ritual trinity of communion, Junisia had obtained those powers for herself and Drelrei. The Tantradox now possessed the black magic of the eelworm, the tantric sorcery of the eelworm, and would forevermore be part eelworm in flesh, mind, and soul.

With the instincts of an eelworm, with eelworms in her guts and dripping from her every orifice, with eelworms for familiars and eelworms for her shamanic animal-guides, Junisia began growing her vagina larger. As the birthing contractions became stronger, Junisia's vagina visibly expanded, pushing her thighs further and further apart, her labia billowing over her abdomen. Like an eelworm, Junisia's vagina was now her body's nucleus, her flesh's fulcrum, her spirit's star. Her vagina engulfed her reproductive system, growing in size until it dwarfed her entire body. Her vagina distended and seemingly detached itself from her flesh, being borne away on the gargantuan curving mass of her womb.

Drelrei pulled upon the length of chain and the arm of the adamantium crane rose high into the air, lifting the Tantradox by the hook in Junisia's womb, dangling the incubus and succubus gemini like demonic bait over the rooftop of the Fiendfarms. Below, Drelrei and Junisia observed the artificial lake they had built atop their citadel, its salty waters still and tranquil beneath the cloudy skies.

Junisia's womb continued to swell like an air bladder until its size rivaled the Fiendfarms themselves. A giant green fetus squirmed within, already larger than its parents, but eclipsed by its own birth-prison. Junisia's vagina had become a cavernous maw, an abyss dwarfing the hook that had been driven between her labia and shoved deep inside like a sadomasochistic dildo. Junisia was an eelworm demoness, an eelworm demiurge, dominated by her own sexual organs, her ballooning womb growing as rapidly as plague, as large as a rotunda or basilica, and then as massive as an amphitheater or a colosseum, before finally reaching a size large enough to accommodate the birthing mass of the leviathan mutant the Tantradox had programmed into its own genes.

Various slaves in the Tantradox' dominion, Siamese twin beasts and demons, wearing a myriad of spiked leather harnesses, saddles, yokes, straitjackets, and other such bondage devices, some leading others on leashes and studded collars, attended to their master and mistress like midwives and wet nurses, walking in single file along the arete of the crane's arm to reach them, scrabbling over the gigantic womb itself, or being raised from the sides of the Fiendfarms on circular platforms adorned with yin-yang symbols. They brought the Tantradox more eelworms, plus chalices filled with absinthe, hookahs filled with lotus, gas masks filled with cocaine, and syringes filled with opium.

With tricklings of blood and amniotic fluid running down its curved sides, Junisia's giant womb lurched and spasmed. The embryo inside rapidly and visibly metamorphosed into a fetus, the entire incubation process taking place in mere minutes. When all was ready, the creatures attending their pregnant mistress maneuvered the arm of the crane so that Junisia's swollen, hundredfold labia hung loosely over the lake atop the

Fiendfarms. The eelworm transformation of Junisia's womb and vagina, complete with miniscule Tantradox dangling like a cilia from its bulbous spherical mass, just like eelworm mothers hung by a small thread from their own disproportionate wombs, had been executed to tantric perfection. Junisia's eelworm vagina had a will of its own now, and could deliver her monstrous spawn without prodding.

The giant green head of a kraken emerged from betwixt Junisia's dripping thighs, the skull of a leviathan too colossal to be birthed by the vagina of a normal-sized beast or demon, a monster that could only have been delivered after the ancient, tantric eelworm ceremony. The kraken burst free in an explosion of placenta, amnion, and blood, and where the back of its skull should have been there was another face, identical to the one in front. As the birthing contractions continued, the conjoined nature of the krakens was slowly revealed, an exact replica of itself front and back, Siamese twin leviathans fused at the spine, a horrific Janus-monstrosity of hideous symmetry.

The Tantradox watched the birth through the translucent membranes of Junisia's womb, still dangling like a cilia from the gargantuan vagina. Hanging by the crotch, the Tantradox looked on as the Janus Kraken was deposited into the lake atop the Fiendfarms with a thunderous splash, and then sank beneath the depths in a roseate swirl of bubbles, blood, and afterbirth.

The Janus Kraken had been successfully bred and birthed, but the purpose of the giant eelworm womb was only half-fulfilled. The Tantradox now began eating, smoking, and injecting earthworms and nightworms flown to them by conjoined harpies, as well as the eggs of vultures, hawks, eagles, archaeopteryxes, phoenixes, rocs, and cockatrices, brought to them by Siamese twin slaves which walked the arm of the crane in a solemn procession, descended its long chain, and delivered their offerings to their overlords before being taken away on the rising circular platforms. The harpies sacrificed their own eggs and newborn children to the Tantradox as well. Drelrei and Junisia ingested the sacrifices, all the while singing and chanting in the ancient language of birds and avian demons. After several hours of ingesting earthworms, nightworms, and the eggs of myriad species in every stage of development and decay, three gigantic black beaks suddenly tore through the membrane of the

Tantradox' swollen womb as though it were an eggshell. Junisia's gibbous vagina exploded as the avian fertility demoness beat its immense wings and lifted into the air. Eelworms and gore rained down upon the Fiendfarms. The Tantradox was left hanging from the crane by its original womb, which now began shrinking back to its normal size. Junisia's crotch reeled her vagina back into her flesh, where it immediately reattached itself and healed. Meanwhile, the Siamese twin incubus and succubus beheld the Geryon Baal'Striga hovering above, the three-headed thunderbird which they had called forth from its infernal nest upon a darker world.

The Geryon Baal'Striga was more than half as tall as the Fiendfarms, larger than the largest roc, and blacker than the blackest crow. Its heads were the heads of giant vultures, with jaundiced and truculent eyes to match. Below those perspicacious and terrible eyes were three fanged beaks, each of which eternally masticated and ruminated things morbid and macabre. The first beak chewed on severed penises, the bloody members dangling from its mouth like earthworms, plucked from unwilling victims, former lovers, prey, and rapelings. The second and central head chewed upon a pile of the Geryon Baal'Striga's own eggs, murdering its own children as they developed with the cold calculation of a cannibalistic mother. The third used its beak to devour both its own young and the young of others, from the newborn, blind, wet squawking hatchlings it pulled from its own womb to the embryos and fetuses it pulled from the wombs of its victims in the night, to the infants and children it stole from cradles, papooses, and nests. Upon the three-headed thunderbird's chest was a cascade of beaked teats, and nests like the pouches of marsupials. The nests were full of embryos, fetuses, and newborns of all species, patterned as such that below each feathered breast was a nest, and the nests themselves rested in the cleavage of two other breasts, one to each side. There were hundreds of these black teats, each with a small beak upon its nipple that drizzled regurgitated blood and severed penises into the waiting mouths of a nestful of brood just below. Its vagina was huge and emitted the rotten smell of carrion, and every one of its feathers had been plucked from a different lover at the precise instant of their demise, thus turning black with the energy of death, after which the Geryon Baal'Striga stuck the feathers like needles and stiletto blades into its own flesh. Its feet were the feet of raptors with the hooked claws of harpies, and each talon was capable of prehensile feats as well as evisceration. Of all these hideous aspects, however, it was the wings of the avian fertility demoness which were the most awesome, and it was these that the Tantradox coveted. Their wingspan measured hundreds of feet, and the pinions themselves were as durable as adamantium, capable of beating billions of times per second and thus enabling the three-headed thunderbird to soar through the universe at supraluminal speeds.

The Tantradox rode the crane back to the circular rooftop of the Stormtower. Drelrei removed the bloody hook from Junisia's womb with a splattering of ichor. Junisia picked eelworms from her pubic hair and vagina and flicked them over the sides of the Stormtower. Overhead, the massing clouds began to roil. The Tantradox descended a stairway into the Stormtower's control chamber, then emerged from the entrance of the Stormtower onto the roof of the Fiendfarms. The controls to the crane were located just outside the Stormtower. The Tantradox seized one of the levers. The crane turned abruptly, lifted, and sank its hook into the belly of the hovering Geryon Baal'Striga. The Tantradox disappeared into the Stormtower once more. Moments later, a barrage of thunderbolts struck the three-headed thunderbird's body with terrible voltage, paralyzing it in mid-air. The crane spun the Geryon Baal'Striga's limp body so that its back faced the Stormtower. The Tantradox reemerged upon the Stormtower roof with twelve lengths of adamantium chains slung over its shoulders. Each chain was equipped with hooks and barbs the size of broadswords, and had been dipped in hot, bituminous unguents. The Tantradox swung the chains over their heads and then, one by one, released them to fly like missiles through the air. They sank into the flesh of the avian fertility demoness at different points, one in each of its three heads, one at the top of its spine, two in its upper back, one in its middlemost vertebra, two in its lower back, one just below its spine, and two in its tail. The sword-sized hooks and barbs lodged and anchored themselves deep inside its muscles and bones, and the scalding unguents fused adamantium and living tissue together into one inseparable, unbreakable mass. Drelrei and Junisia then threw the opposite ends of the chains, which were tipped with grapnels, into tiny holes bored into the underside of the crane's arm, where they stuck fast, holding the Geryon Baal'Striga captive.

The Tantradox climbed atop the crane, upon whose promontory jutted a wheel and four levers. Using these devices to control the movement of the crane, the Tantradox raised the Geryon Baal'Striga up by the chains embedded in its flesh and extended the entire contraption forward, the giant arm seemingly elongating as its hidden lengths were pulled from unseen depths within the citadel. Maneuvering the colossal machine, the Tantradox bore the Geryon Baal'Striga through the air until it dangled directly above the Siamese twin brontosauruses that pulled the Fiendfarms.

Drelrei pulled one of the levers, and a guillotine blade dropped from the arm of the crane, whistling as it fell on a long hempen rope before severing the leather leashes and reins which bound the conjoined reptiles to the Fiendfarms. The brontosauruses, finally free after years of enslavement, immediately stampeded into the distance and disappeared. The Tantradox reeled the guillotine blade back in. Once again manning the wheel of the crane, the Tantradox lowered the Geryon Baal'Striga to the ground, replacing the brontosauruses.

Drelrei and Junisia retreated back along the arm of the crane and jumped onto a nearby balcony, then slipped into an adjacent chamber and reemerged with a hundred-foot long halberd and a hundred-foot long branding iron, and an enormous, spiked choke collar draped around their necks as well. Drelrei used the halberd to disengage the grapnelled chains shackling the Geryon Baal'Striga's flesh to the crane. Guiding the adamantium tethers through the air, he then reinserted them in the metal rings studding the front walls of the Fiendfarms. Junisia welded them together with the branding iron. They leaned their long weapons against the wall, then tossed the choke collar around the Geryon Baal'Striga's throat. After fastening it around the Geryon Baal'Striga's neck with the halberd and hermetically sealing it with the branding iron, they attached a thirteenth chain to the Geryon Baal'Striga, this one linking the collar to the wall of the Fiendfarms. Finally, the Tantradox descended to the bottom floor of their citadel and walked down a short stairway to the ground. Holding a large, red-hot, sizzling, steaming, hundred-foot long battle axe, they approached the Geryon Baal'Striga. With one mighty swing the incandescent axe amputated both of the Geryon Baal'Striga's legs, and its intense heat immediately cauterized the wounds in its wake, leaving two shriveled stumps that shrank back into the demoness' feathers. The Geryon Baal'Striga screamed as its legs were severed, and instinctively began beating its wings to keep from falling to the ground below. The Tantradox hurried back inside the Fiendfarms as the fortress began to tremble and shake. The Geryon Baal'Striga's wings began beating faster and faster, and then suddenly the Fiendfarms lurched forward and the entire edifice lifted into the air.

The Tantradox emerged atop the Fiendfarms with a hundred-foot long whip in each hand, flogging the Geryon Baal'Striga's three heads to change its speed, altitude, and direction. The avian fertility demoness soared through the skies, dragging the Fiendfarms behind it like a titanic flying chariot. With its legs amputated it had been rendered an eternal martlet, and would never cease flying until the time of its demise, or the demise of time. The only landing it would ever make again would be into its own deathbed. Until then, it was the Tantradox's slave, and the Siamese twin incubus and succubus had obtained the power of flight. The Tantradox was now ready to wage war upon the Necrodelic and the Oneirophage, and then the entire universe.

41

The Tantradox flew the Megafiend from inside the Stormtower. No longer the Fiendfarms, the citadel was metamorphosing into a living spaceship. The artificial lake upon its dorsal rooftop had filled with amniotic fluid, and continued to expand and grow to accommodate the ever-enlarging Janus Kraken inside it. A system of nerves and ganglia branched through the fortress and into the shackles of the Geryon Baal'Striga, enabling Drelrei and Junisia to control the flight of the avian fertility demoness as it dragged the soaring juggernaut of the Megafiend through the skies.

Within the caudal Stormtower, the Tantradox controlled

Elasvai's weather. Long ago, Drelrei and Junisia had conquered and captured a weather warlock, bonded him psychically with Elasvai's spirit, and mutated his flesh into a living control panel through which they could create and regulate the temperature and seasons of the garden planet, as well as cause, adjust, and terminate rainfall, lightning, thunderstorms, floods, waterspouts, winds, tornadoes, earthquakes, and eclipses. Thusly had they kept Elasvai in a state of perpetual bloom and flourishment for millennia.

They adjusted the living control panel now. Its levers were fingers, phalluses, blood vessels, esophagi, intestines, tails, and bones. Its buttons were pulsating organs. The severed head of the weather warlock served as an instrumental gauge, providing oral descriptions of various measurements, levels, and conditions throughout the entire planet. Pulling on phalanges, penises, veins, arteries, entrails, esophagi, tails, and pieces of extracted skeleton, while simultaneously pressing, tapping, prodding, or gripping beating hearts, breathing lungs, digesting stomach sacs, churning livers, quivering kidneys, trembling spleens, expanding bladders, and hundreds of various glands, the Tantradox controlled the weather with a secret tactile language of applied touches, numbered repetitions, and esoteric sequential orders which they had invented long ago and were known by no one else save the severed head of the weather warlock. He interpreted these various signals by their ordered chronological tappings, musical rhythms, degrees of pressure, stimulation of pleasure and pain centers, forced glandular secretions, and various types of bloodletting, then translated them to the spirit of the planet.

The Tantradox' fingers moved across the control panel as if it were playing a musical instrument. Moments later the shadows of cumulus clouds fell across the Megafiends. Thunderheads waited to be unleashed as storms brewed in the darkening skies. Drelrei and Junisia programmed each section of Elasvai with its own individual weather pattern. Several hours, when the clouds had accumulated over the entire planet, the Tantradox unleashed the rain and headed into battle.

*

The Oneirophage imbibed the dreams of cocaine demons on the Cliffs of Caine. Albinos as white as their beloved drugs, many of them had not descended from the cliffs in centuries. A pair of Siamese twins, joined at the head, lay broken and bloodied beneath the coca plants as the Oneirophage ravished their minds. The dream-eater plunged the Umbilicus through both their skulls at once, driving the tip into the ear canal of the first until it emerged from the ear canal of the second, sucking a tunnel through their brain, imbibing their cocaine dreams and withdrawal nightmares. He saw hourglasses whose sands were cocaine, then the deserts those dwindling white granules had come from, shifting in the rhythmic wind, blowing first east, then west, then east again, and so on unto infinity. He withdrew his straw and left the cocanaeds to die, bright red blood dripping from their ears and noses and staining their lily-white skin.

Another pair of cocaine demons, joined at the hip, were ambling up the cliffside. The Oneirophage crawled behind the large stem of a giant coca plant and lay in wait for his prey, then ambushed them with a cobra strike that paralyzed them in mid-gait. These had white horns, which the Oneirophage severed with his Prismsword, then plunged the Umbilicus into the bloody holes left behind. He swallowed dreams of scales that were balanced by piles of cocaine, forever shifting up and down, their fulcrum a beating heart that palpitated with increasing rapidity as the scales swung back and forth. Turning, he saw the horns on the ground spilling cocaine in a non-stop rush. The horns had been cornucopias of cocaine, each one an unlimited stash, forever filling the conanaeds' brains with their beloved drugs.

Ascending the Cliffs of Caine, the Oneirophage found two albino soulmates dangling from the branches while joined in the sexual yin-yang position, forever welded in simultaneous fellacio and cunnilingus. Upon closer examination, he found that the lips of the male had been seamlessly fused to the labia of the female, and her pallid lips were hermetically sealed around the base of his turgid phallus. The cocaine demons had rigged up an elaborate system of coca ingestion, with the twigs, vines and roots of the surrounding plants inserted into their nostrils and the veins in the insides of their elbows, feeding them cocaine intravenously while holding them aloft in the branches above the ground as they made love. The male hung supine, the female prone above him. The bone-white addicts had strung themselves up by the branches of coca trees and given themselves a continuous supply of cocaine, a perpetual state of stimulation that had lasted for years.

The Oneirophage plunged his straw into the skull of the male, opening a new, crimson fontanel in his head to replace the one that had sealed itself after his birth. Through the gory, surgically created fontanel, the Oneirophage drank his victim's orgasm. The stolen sexual energy suffused his entire body with white lightning. He jabbed the Umbilicus all over the unpigmented flesh of both demons, sucking all the cocaine from their bloodstreams and all the sexual energy from their genitals and nervous system. The Oneirophage shuddered with paroxysms of orgasm, as though in a convulsive fit. He left the sexually conjoined Siamese twins alive, but full of bloody perforations and vampirically drained of the cocaine and hormones in their systems. With all the coca plants surrounding them now barren, the drugs sucked from their leaves and stems into the Oneirophage through the conduit of their bodies, the cocaine demons were left in a state of agonizing withdrawal, screaming, sweating, shivering, and shaking, the male's phallus now flaccid in his lover's dry and parched mouth, and she leaking blood between the cracked lips of his. They would both be dead within an hour.

Paranoid cocaine demons fled the Oneirophage as he approached. He enjoyed hunting them down and sucking the speeding dreams from their intoxicated brains, dreams with a hint of nightmare, which made them more delectable. The Oneirophage emerged onto the uppermost precipice of the Cliffs of Caine, which was also the uppermost precipice of the entire planet, and gazed out upon the Elasvaian nocturne. He watched as cumulus clouds gathered, huge thunderheads rising up like ramparts on the horizon. He could taste the moisture gathering within the clouds on his forked tongues. Storms meant rain, which meant rainbows, which meant prisms, which meant dreaming. The approaching storms were very much to the Oneirophage's advantage. Smiling to himself as the first drops began to spatter down, the Oneirophage enjoyed the scenery a moment more, then reached for the Darkprism around his neck, removed it and the necklace it dangled from, and planted it in the dirt of the cliff's edge. He stood over it like a pyrolater, lighting and then fanning the flames of a sacred fire, making sorcerous gesticulations and emitting sibilant hissing incantations, and then from out of its black hole depths grew a towering, spinning iron crucifix, the gigantic ancient artifact from the temples of Serpentikal, a relic from his destroyed homeworld of Grystiawa, which he had borne with him ever since the death of his birthplace had necessitated his exile into space. The revolving cross arose from the Darkprism, drilling itself through the night until it reached its full height. After retrieving the Darkprism from underneath it and replacing the talisman around his neck, and placing the blade of the Prismsword in his mouth and clamping his jaws down around it, the Oneirophage coiled his lower, serpentine half around the base of the monolithic crucifix and then climbed, curled, and slithered his way to its top like a bloated vine. He draped his arms over the crossbar and crucified himself on the giant spinning relic. Looming hundreds of feet above the Cliffs of Caine, and miles above the Elasvaian plains, the Oneirophage awaited the coming apocalypse with cold reptilian patience.

*

Chariah made his way from the north pole of Elasvai with Cerberus at his side, walking directly over the planet's meridian and glaring at the gathering clouds. Heading slowly south, through gardens of mandrake and forests of weeping willows, he could feel as well as hear the growl of Cerberus in response to the distant thunder. The Necrodelic held out his hand as the first drops of rain began to fall, and looked skyward with eyes like the calderas of volcanoes about to erupt. He looked at the glistening beads of water on his palm, listened to the soft ricochet of raindrops on leaves, and felt the light, dewy dampness clinging to his hair.

"Fuck," he said to himself, and continued onward.

*

On the entire planet of Elasvai, no one saw the sunrise that day except the Oneirophage and the Tantradox. The Oneirophage's spinning crucifix just cleared the tops of the cumulus clouds, and he watched Dzandra emerge from the distant horizons as he revolved. Dawn shattered across the sky like a jewel obliterated by a warhammer, glittering in the Oneirophage's peripheral vision as the giant cross spun him around. The next time he gazed upon Dzandra, it was through the eyes of Morpheus Rex.

The Tantradox had watched the sunrise hours earlier, flying over a different section of Elasvai, and followed it across the planet. They stood now upon one of the rooftop parapets of the Megafiend, the Geryon Baal'Striga flying them above the clouds as they tracked the dream-eater. As Dzandra rose over the Cliffs of Caine, it revealed in its hemisphere of saffron brilliance the silhouette of a towering crucifix, and upon that crucifix, the transforming shadow of the Oneirophage as he made his diurnal metamorphosis into Morpheus Rex. The Tantradox arrived at the Cliffs of Caine at the exact moment of dawn. It lashed its whip across the side of the Geryon Baal'Striga's face. The Megafiend lurched and hurtled directly toward the iron cross, seemingly on a collision course with the sun.

That collision course would take them directly through the flesh of Morpheus Rex as well. The Tantradox flogged their avian steed thrice about the back, spurring it to faster and faster speeds. Morpheus Rex remained on his excruciating perch and took the full force of the rocketing Geryon Baal'Striga and the weight of the entire edifice in the face and chest. The giant iron cross was blasted from its foundation and toppled heavily down the Cliffs of Caine, flattening hundred-foot coca plants and crushing cocaine demons in its wake.

The Tantradox glanced around but could find no trace of Morpheus Rex. It would be several moments before they heard a faint rustling behind them, and the Siamese twins turned just in time for Drelrei to block the Prismsword with the Soul Cleaver. Morpheus Rex spun, and Junisia raised the Flesh Compactor to block his path, using the handheld iron maiden as a shield to keep the dripping fangs of the black widow which was Morpheus Rex's left hand away from her face, then pressing the lever in its handle to make it open and close like the jaws of a rabid dragon. Morpheus Rex feinted and lunged sideways with his spider hand repeatedly, until finally he mistimed his strike and Junisia trapped his arm to the elbow in the Flesh Compactor.

Morpheus Rex maintained his sideways stance and began drifting to the right. He was just out of reach of Drelrei's Soul Cleaver. He twisted and flailed with the Prismsword, but Junisia held him at bay with subtle pushes of the Flesh Compactor. The combatants spun atop the parapet for several moments, with none gaining an advantage.

Far below, after sliding for several minutes through the fresh mud of the Cliffs of Caine, the gigantic cross suddenly came to a halt at the clawed foot of the Necrodelic. The supernatural strength of the Death Addict brought the iron tonnage of the crucifix and its miles worth of accumulated momentum to a dead stop. Beneath the cross lay the mangled corpses of dozens of cocaine demons, their backs broken and bodies mutilated. Cerberus sniffed the remains of the cocanaeds, then began tearing large chunks of meat from their bones. The cocaine in the demons' bloodstreams intoxicated the hellhound as he devoured them.

The Necrodelic reached down and lifted the enormous cross in his hands, the veins in his black biceps bulging, his chiseled muscles pressing against his skin as though they might break off of his skeleton. He waited for the Megafiend to soar overhead, then hurled the iron cross directly upwards into the skies, through the clouds, where miles away he heard the satisfying thud of the crucifix striking stone. When the crucifix fell back to the ground, it took a chunk of the Megafiend with it. As the citadel flew past again, Chariah once more hurled the cross. The crucifix flew directly upwards, broke through the floor of the Megafiend, caught more of the edifice in its crossbar, then fell directly down on the same vertical path to stick upright in the gelatinous mud. A moment later, a hailstorm of debris and bodies dropped heavily around it.

Finally, the Tantradox directed the Geryon Baal'Striga to drop beneath the clouds, and for the first time Chariah beheld the Megafiend. Its bottom story was the abattoir, but the Fiendfarms had always been terrestrial, and so the abattoir had never been equipped with any type of floor. The meathooks dangled from its underbelly, some with living beasts impaled upon them. Short stairways led to the level above. Chariah swept his gaze from the Geryon Baal'Striga to the crackling Stormtower. He watched as Morpheus Rex and the Tantradox dueled atop the Megafiend's anterior parapet, circling one another incessantly. His eyes flashed as the slaves of the Tantradox began dropping wrecking balls from the windows like nightmarish, boulder-sized hailstones.

As Chariah dodged the wrecking balls, the clouds began to spark and thunder. A rapid succession of lightning bolts gouged a labyrinth of fissures and abysses in the ground. Avoiding the deadly barrage of wrecking balls and lightning, Chariah ran to the base of the crucifix. He crouched like a panther, then jumped straight up into the air, hundreds of feet, and landed atop the crossbar. From there, it took one more demonic leap to board the Megafiend. The Necrodelic soared through the rain and alighted on one of the stairways leading to the second story. A Siamese twin minotaur charged down the steps. Chariah ducked and flipped it over his shoulder to the ground, thousands of feet below. The ten waiting jaws of Cerberus caught it like a piece of meat and the hellhound immediately began to devour it.

Chariah infiltrated the flying citadel and made his way to the parapet where Morpheus Rex and the Tantradox battled. The Dreaming Predator's left arm remained caught in the Flesh Compactor. The Tantradox was still unable to get in striking range, yet was reluctant to relinquish the handheld iron maiden and let the ophidian one slip from their clutches. Chariah appeared in the doorway like a shadow, as suddenly and silently as a spider drops through the night on a single strand of webbing. He slashed Morpheus Rex across the back with his claws, opening five diagonal lacerations from right shoulder blade to left hip. The Tantradox removed its grip from the Flesh Compactor out of necessity, for the Necrodelic's left hand was chopping downwards with claws extended to sever Junisia's hand at the wrist. Morpheus Rex stumbled backwards as the Tantradox released the handheld iron maiden.

The Tantradox turned its attention to Chariah. "Now, Necrodelic," they spake simultaneously, "you shall suffer the same agonies you unleashed upon us. Behold...the Soul Cleaver!"

The Tantradox raised the Soul Cleaver over its heads with both hands, then brought it crashing down in a sweeping arc over the Necrodelic's skull. To the shock of Drelrei and Junisia, the Necrodelic did nothing to avoid the blow, just stood stoically with his hands at his sides as the crimson blade throttled toward him. To their even greater shock, the Soul Cleaver passed right through his flesh as if he weren't there, and clattered loudly against the floor.

The Tantradox looked up with astonished eyes, then

brandished the sword diagonally, sideways, and overhand again. Each time, the crimson blade of the Soul Cleaver passed through the Necrodelic like he was an apparition, leaving behind neither scratch nor scar, nor even a ripple or mark. The Tantradox swung the Soul Cleaver wildly then, with blows that would have decapitated, eviscerated, impaled, castrated, and split from skull to crotch a lesser demon. Again, however, the Soul Cleaver had no effect upon the mysteriously impervious Death Addict. Drelrei and Junisia gazed upwards, eyes wide with fright, and the Necrodelic's igneous eye contact knocked them backwards. The Tantradox sprawled across the parapet, using their dinosaur tails and cloven hands to brace their fall.

"I'm indivisible, bitch," the Necrodelic snarled. "Pure fucking evil."

Drelrei roared with rage and leapt to his feet, dragging Junisia with him. This time he dropped the ineffective Soul Cleaver and lashed out with his fist. Chariah casually blocked the blow and grabbed Drelrei's arm in a death-grip around the wrist. He pulled the Tantradox closer and unleashed a quintet of claws upon them like a thousand machetes, a fusillage of guillotine blades, over and over, until the only thing keeping the Tantradox upright was Chariah's left hand around Drelrei's wrist. The Siamese twin demons staggered limply in his grasp, the skin of their chest hanging in large flaps and folds, their faces slashed as if by violent scarifications, a rapidly expanding pool of blood flowing out from around their cloven feet.

Chariah pulled on Drelrei's arm, trying to hold the swooning Tantradox upright. As the Necrodelic struggled to balance his adversary for a killshot, Morpheus Rex silently crept up behind the Necrodelic's back with the discarded Flesh Compactor in his hands. A reversal of fate had resulted in the Dreaming Predator wielding the weapon/torture device instead of suffering its torments. He squeezed the lever inside the handle with his black widow hand, and the iron maiden slammed shut around the Necrodelic. The flesh-smoker's hand protruded from the opening, but his radius and ulna were shattered. He released his grip on the Tantradox, causing it to stumble in the slippery pool of its own blood on cloven hooves not made for feats of balance and equilibrium. The Siamese twin demons toppled backwards over the ramparts of the parapet and disappeared from sight.

Morpheus Rex reclenched the eight spider legs of his black widow hand around the handle of the iron maiden and it swung back open. A few seconds later, the body of the Necrodelic fell out, covered with crimson puncture wounds, head to toe, front and back. He landed limply in a rapidly spreading pool of his own blood. Morpheus Rex was looking at the Flesh Compactor like a madman, his kaleidoscopic eyes gleaming, a psychotic smile on his rainbow lips.

Chariah writhed and twisted amidst his pouring plasma, raising his dripping head to glare at Morpheus Rex through the falling rain. The Dreaming Predator was bearing down upon him again with the deadly contraption. The Necrodelic reached out and grabbed the black hilt of the Soul Cleaver, which still lay on the floor where the Tantradox had dropped it. He swiveled and parried with the crimson blade, driving its point between the hinges of the handheld iron maiden. Morpheus Rex continued to squeeze its handle, but the Soul Cleaver was jammed into its gears and it would no longer open or shut. Chariah gripped the black hilt of the Soul Cleaver with both hands, one healthy, one broken, and jerked the sorcerous broadsword upwards with all his might, tearing the handheld iron maiden from Morpheus Rex's grasp and sending it spinning high into the air. The Necrodelic pirouetted suddenly, and as he spun around he brought the Soul Cleaver down with a two-fisted, overhead blow on the crown of Morpheus Rex's head.

There was a thunderclap and a flash of blinding rainbow lightning the instant the sword struck the Dreaming Predator. The eye-searing light faded just in time for Chariah to witness two bodies falling unconsciously onto their backs with a splash of bloody rainwater. One was the body of Morpheus Rex. The other was the body of the Oneirophage.

The Flesh Compactor clattered like a distant echo as it landed somewhere on the rooftop. The pouring rain was washing the blood down the Necrodelic's body, cleansing his wounds and mixing with the sanguinary streams to form a roseate puddle. The Necrodelic stood silently in the center of that roseate puddle, staring in disbelief upon the sundered bodies at his feet, not knowing which was real. Both Morpheus Rex and the Oneirophage lay as still as corpses, directly next to one another. Chariah found himself devoid of any means of comprehending the sight his crimson eyes were conveying to his blackened mind. Suddenly, truth was a force that did not exist.

Wrapped up in his philosophical vertigo, the Necrodelic left himself vulnerable to attack. The Tantradox had landed atop the back of the Geryon Baal'Striga and grabbed on to one of its chains as while sliding down the rain-slickened feathers. The Siamese twin demons climbed back up to the rooftop and pulled themselves over the parapet wall. Silently, they crept up behind the Necrodelic and kicked him in the testicles with the cloven, iron-shod foot of their disproportionately powerful middle leg. Chariah fell face-first into a puddle of rain and blood and did not move.

At the exact moment the Necrodelic's skull struck the rooftop, Morpheus Rex and the Oneirophage sat up. The Tantradox stared with the same disbelief that had gripped the Necrodelic. Like mirror images, perfectly synchronized, Morpheus Rex and the Oneirophage rose. The Tantradox attacked the Oneirophage, clawing at his face, trying to dig his eyes out. The combatants traded blows with their tails. The sounds of wet serpent, stegosaurus, and ankylosaurus tails colliding with sodden flesh were like the cracks of whips striking mermaids.

Morpheus Rex made his way across the turret and squatted over the prostrate Necrodelic like a simian assassin. With his right fist he pummeled the back of the Necrodelic's skull, then gripped him by the hair and repeatedly bashed his face into the stone rooftop. His black widow hand chewed on the open wounds lining Chariah's spine. Chariah growled, raising bubbles in the foam of rain and gore around his face. He pushed himself up, the chiseled muscles in his arms visibly straining and rippling. He surged to his feet as Morpheus Rex retreated. Chariah spun around with a wild back-handed slash that whistled through the air, but completely missed the Dreaming Predator. He shook blood and rain from his eyes and hair as Morpheus Rex gathered up the Prismsword. Chariah looked up with blazing eyes to see Morpheus Rex brandishing the scintillant blade at blinding speeds. Razor-sharp rainbows etched red spiderwebs across Chariah's flesh. Like a berserk taurean demon, the Necrodelic charged Morpheus Rex, driving through the flashing colors and the expertly swung blade and running right through the Dreaming Predator as though he were a locked gate at the end of a deadly labyrinth, a gate for which he had no key in a labyrinth whose walls were rapidly closing to crush him to a pulp, a gate to be rammed and splintered from its hinges. The force of his charge lifted Morpheus Rex off his feet and knocked him backwards through the air. Chariah went from a complete standstill to a supersonic speed in less than a second, then just as quickly came to a complete halt. Morpheus Rex sailed through the air as though he had been shot from an arbalest. He made one futile attempt to reach down beneath his back and grab the edge of the parapet wall, but Chariah had knocked him too high into the air. An instant later, he disappeared over the rim of the Megafiend. Unlike the Tantradox, he missed the Geryon Baal'Striga and its chains entirely, and plummeted to the ground below.

Chariah turned and focused on the Tantradox. Drelrei and Junisia were pummeling the Oneirophage with their spiked and clubbed tails. They drove him back against the crenellated walls, and then, with one mighty, combined, simultaneous, spinning blow of both tails knocked him backwards and over the parapet ramparts. He flipped over the tower wall, but managed to grab its edge while somersaulting backwards. He hung on with both hands, dangling precariously from the top of the turret, his belly pressed against its wet marble side. The Tantradox unleashed a furious assault upon his fingers with its tails, trying to break them so that he might lose his grip and fall. Junisia's ankylosaurus tail smashed his knuckles. Drelrei's stegosaurus tail drove stigmatas through his right hand. The black widow of his left hand panicked and detached itself from his arm. The spider crawled from the crenellation and scurried several feet down the parapet.

The Tantradox had witnessed the Necrodelic's furious assault upon Morpheus Rex as they pounded the hands of the Oneirophage, and continually looked over their shoulders to apprise themselves of his whereabouts. When they saw him pick up the Soul Cleaver and glance in their direction, the Tantradox chose to fling itself over the top of the Megafiend and regroup in the gardens far below, rather than face the Necrodelic's wrath and risk being torturously sundered from one another again.

Chariah watched the frightened Tantradox fall to the ground, dwindling further and further and then disappearing in a mass of foliage. The rain was coming down in torrents now, and he was severely wounded, mostly from the impalements of the handheld iron maiden that now lay lifeless on the ground. He needed fire, smoke, and ashes, burning flesh and immolated corpses, to heal his massive injuries. He needed pyromancy and Hellfire to unleash his full assault upon Elasvai. He had to find some way to stop the infernal rain. With Soul Cleaver in hand, the Necrodelic turned towards the Stormtower.

42

Chariah walked along the white parapets of the Megafiend, stepping carefully from crenellation to crenellation, navigating the wet and slippery ramparts. To his right an artificial lake covered nearly the entire rooftop, all the way from the anterior turret where he, the Oneirophage, Morpheus Rex, and the Tantradox had battled, to the Stormtower looming at the rear of the fortress. The rain poured down on the Necrodelic like a fusillade. Blasts of wind blew his drenched hair around his face. There were flashes of lighting and thunderclaps every few seconds as the storm intensified. Rainwater collected in his puncture wounds and stung his exposed tissues like libations of salt. Having long ago been drained of blood and cleansed by the pouring rain, these spherical marks of impalement were now windows to the jet tissues, gleaming sable organs, and ebony bones lying beneath his skin, with just a hint of crimson blood dripping through and scoring their rims. It was like an alveolated oracle for an aspirant vivisectionist, revealing the inner workings of the body in pieces, or a sexual display for a voyeuristic interniphiliac, to gaze upon vital organs, viscera, and physical processes through eyeholes drilled in flesh, and then fuck those eyeholes one by one.

The Geryon Baal'Striga flew the Megafiend erratically without the Tantradox to guide it, and the giant pool upon the rooftop of the fortress churned and sloshed, dashing the Necrodelic with ten-foot waves. During a brief moment when the lake grew relatively still, Chariah caught a glimpse of Satan's face in the water, like a rippling reflection on the surface of a pool. Satan laughed and immediately faded away, and as his image melted, Chariah detected the presence of something directly beneath it, a monster incubating in the bottom of the lake. The pool was expanding to accommodate its mysterious dweller, extending down into the upper stories of the Megafiend and simultaneously raising the parapets Chariah was walking on, the walls growing taller and taller as he made his way to the flickering Stormtower.

The Necrodelic focused the crimson lasers of his eyes upon the green mass ascending through the water. Whatever it was, it was enormous. When the Janus Kraken finally emerged from the amniotic pool, it was even more humongous than it had appeared through the reflections and refractions of the water. It arose in a chaotic tsunami that swelled over the parapets and cascaded in a miles-long cataract to the ground below. The Necrodelic braced himself as the crest of amnion rushed over him, dropping into the black lotus position, sheathing the Soul Cleaver in the stone of the citadel, spread-eagling his arms, and lodging his claws in the walls. When the tsunami had passed, Chariah looked up to see the Janus Kraken looming over him, more than one hundred feet tall. Still in the black lotus position, the Necrodelic joined his thumbs and forefingers together and spoke a susurrating mantra. He levitated as the Janus Kraken charged, rising vertically into the air until he was face to face with the leviathan.

Chariah stretched his arms out cruciform, uncrossed his legs, and unleashed a barrage of claws upon the monstrosity, carving its scales from its flesh with a frenzy of talons as he dropped back down to the parapet. The Janus Kraken, its face bloody and torn, scales flaking from its chest, suddenly rotated within the lake, presenting another side which was a complete replication of the first. This side was unharmed, however, and again the Janus Kraken charged, again the Necrodelic levitated, and again the Necrodelic shredded its scales with rapid-fire lacerations as he fell through the air.

The Janus Kraken spun again, presenting the side Chariah had first attacked, completely healed while its conjoined twin had taken its turn with the demon. Apparently the beast was part hydra, another mutant spawn of the Tantradox's genetic sorceries. The Necrodelic dislodged the Soul Cleaver from the parapet and held it for a moment, but then, remembering the way it had turned Morpheus Rex into two separate entities, was assailed with visions of the Janus Kraken becoming fourfold if he struck it with the spirit-sundering blade. He thrust the sword back into the parapet, then leapt at the oncoming Janus Kraken.

The Janus Kraken swung at the Necrodelic, swatting him from midair. The Necrodelic back-flipped and landed on the rim of the Megafiend. He jumped again, and this time, as the Janus Kraken swung at him with the opposite arm, Chariah buried his claws in the webbing between its half-formed fingers with his right hand, and simultaneously drove the claws of his left hand into the flesh of its palm. The Janus Kraken roared and tried to shake him loose, then began raising him towards its fanged mouth. Chariah looked over his shoulder as the Janus Kraken's face drew closer. Pushing off with his taloned feet, he catapulted himself from the Janus Kraken's palm, flew through the air in a high arcing backwards somersault, and alighted atop the creature's skull. The Necrodelic landed, bent on one knee, and drove his talons through the eye of the Janus Kraken. The Janus Kraken roared and reached up with both hands, but this time from the opposite direction, its arms completely rotating in their triple-jointed sockets. As he turned to meet the attack, Chariah noticed that the creature only had palms, for the backs of its hands had been fused together.

The Necrodelic launched himself into a spinning attack, a black tornado dervishing atop the Janus Kraken's head, claws outstretched to slash and sunder. The Janus Kraken's hands plunged through the deadly swirl of claws and recoiled in a shower of blood, only to swing back from the other side on hinged shoulders to pummel the twirling Necrodelic as he spun in mid-air, knocking him from its crown and into the lake below.

The arms of the Janus Kraken did not stop, however, but swung completely over its head and into the water after Chariah, blasting him with a double-handed blow. Chariah ricocheted slowly off the bottom of the lake, as though on a planet or moon of extremely low gravity. The giant webbed hands slapped him back down to the bottom of the lake again, then grabbed the Necrodelic between their palms and began to squeeze. Chariah bit through scales and blood as the Janus Kraken tried to burst his skeleton. The Janus Kraken applied unbearable pressure to the Necrodelic's body, causing fresh gouts of blood to spurt from his puncture wounds.

Chariah managed to slip both sets of claws through the narrow slits between the Janus Kraken's joined hands and tear a small hole in its scales. The water of the lake began to pour in as the opening grew. He squirted through the hard-won exit to the surface of the pool, then swam for the parapets as the Janus Kraken rose again. This time, when the Janus Kraken charged, Chariah met it with his ten claws joined into the Hellsword, opening a deep gash in its abdomen that bubbled and bled. The Janus Kraken spun, and the Necrodelic drove the point of his combined talons into its guts with an impaling strike. The Janus Kraken rotated again, and again its other side had healed and regenerated.

Just as the Necrodelic began to wonder whether to employ a strategy which would involve continually leaping from one side of the lake to the other in pursuit of the wounds he had wrought, or to direct his attack from atop the Janus Kraken's joined skulls on both sides at once, he saw the Oneirophage slithering along the parapets across from him, the ones he had originally traversed, where the Soul Cleaver remained sheathed. The Oneirophage held the Flesh Compactor in one hand and the Prismsword in the other, and began battling the Janus Kraken from the other side.

Chariah attacked the half of the Janus Kraken facing him with a flurry of claws, blasting it with overhand blows, uppercuts, backfists, tiger slashes, impaling strikes, and double-handed chops. On the opposite side of the Megafiend, the Oneirophage unleashed his own offensive repertoire of cobra strikes, venom injections, tail lashings, and blows from the Prismsword and the Flesh Compactor. Now, the Janus Kraken couldn't spin its way to safety, for it was assaulted from both sides, and it was soon a bloodied, battered, quivering pulp. Chariah had once again climbed to the top of its skull, and was driving his claws repeatedly into its brain. The monstrosity was slowed, but not yet killed. It sank back into the water to try and shake the Necrodelic loose, but Chariah would not budge, and the conjoined leviathan was forced to raise itself above the waves once more, where the Oneirophage was waiting with yet more damage to inflict. Chariah raked both sides of the Janus Kraken's face and thrust repeatedly through its eyes, but the gargantuan mutant would not die. The Oneirophage set the Prismsword aside and clutched the Soul Cleaver about the hilt, still in its surrogate sheath in the parapet beside him, and, while gripping the half-buried broadsword, called out to the Necrodelic.

"Flesh-smoker...use the Soul Cleaver."

From his perch atop the Siamese twin krakens Chariah yelled, "It will make them fourfold."

"They have but one soul," the Oneirophage hissed through the monsoon. "Remember the Tantradox. The sword shall sunder, and we shall slay."

The Necrodelic paused, a black silhouette of war mounted atop the bleeding head of the leviathan, his crimson eyes glowing amidst the gusts of wind, the torrents of rain, the explosions of thunder, and the flashes of lightning. Finally, in reply, he held out his right hand. The Oneirophage smiled and wrenched the Soul Cleaver from its pit. He lifted it and tossed it high into the air. The Necrodelic reached out and caught it by the hilt, then gestured with his head towards the Stormtower.

"Raise the crane."

The Oneirophage regathered the Prismsword and began slithering toward the Stormtower, where the tip of the crane's arm lay. As the Oneirophage made his way across the ramparts, Chariah shouted, "If this fails, I will artescerate you and smoke your still-beating heart as you look on."

The Necrodelic continued to bloody the Janus Kraken's head as the Oneirophage operated the crane. A few moments later, a great shadow fell directly over the Necrodelic. He unsheathed his claws from the Janus Kraken's skull and leapt straight upwards, landed atop the crane, and raised the Soul Cleaver over his head. For a brief instant, while lightning flickered, the silhouette of murder incarnate hung like a black hole in the sky. Then, with a battle cry that drowned out the thunder, the Necrodelic leapt, dropping as swiftly and heavily as a neutron star. He swung the sword directly through the invisible suture that bonded the krakens, ripping through the seam of their flesh and soul and falling through the bloody chasm he had wrought, two perfectly straight slabs of exposed olive muscle and pulsing organs at either side. He fell to the bottom of the lake, severing the Janus Kraken's tentacles. The vermillion blade of the Soul Cleaver, physically, had only sliced through a part of the Janus Kraken, but its sorcery did the rest, bisecting the entire Siamese twin leviathan. Both halves of the Janus Kraken fell face-first into the amniotic lake. Its vertically sundered spine rendered it motionless and paralyzed.

Chariah rose through the bloody waters and swam to the Stormtower. The liquid seared his open wounds like acid. Like a crocodile he slipped silently from currents to shore, still holding the dripping Soul Cleaver in his right hand. The Oneirophage had gone to examine the cadavers of the krakens. Chariah knew not the dream-eater's intentions, but until he abetted the accursed rain he cared for nothing else. The Necrodelic ascended the stairs of the Stormtower and entered its upper chamber. He looked once at the complicated array of organs and bones, and the severed head mumbling numbers and soliloquies to itself. The entire clandestine control panels would take days to decode. He did not look twice, merely opened his mouth and breathed a jetstream of fire over the living device. The organs sizzled and popped, bones turned to ash, and the entire control chamber incinerated around the Necrodelic.

Through the pleasant crackle of the conflagration and the assuaging smoke of cremated flesh, Chariah listened for the spattering of rain outside. There was none. Satisfied, the Necrodelic returned to the rooftops.

Hydraman had commandeered the Metasaur and maneuvered it to the side of the Megafiend. He was assisting the Oneirophage in dumping the twin carcasses of the Janus Kraken into the psychedelic moat surrounding Phantasmagorika. Chariah left them to their toil and made his way along the parapets to the Geryon Baal'Striga. He leapt onto its back and plunged his hands through the skull and brain of its second head, then dug his claws into its cerebellum and hijacked its nervous system. Through the conduit of the avian bird demoness, Chariah steered the Megafiend toward the Forest of Flesh, which had departed the lake in which it had taken sanctuary from the Necrodelic's Hellfire and once again taken root on one of Elasvai's fertile plains. Accustomed to the dragon-like ease of flight and mind-bending speeds of his bestial spaceship, Chariah flew the less-evolved Megafiend as though it were the Omnibeast, dropping altitudes and making sharp and sudden turns in a manner that spilled most of the lake from the roof, cracked the walls and foundations of the entire structure, and sent many a Siamese twin slave of the Tantradox tumbling through windows and fissures to their deaths below.

As the Forest of Flesh came into view, Chariah spurred the Geryon Baal'Striga to its maximum speed, setting the Megafiend on a collision course with the bound Omnibeast. The demon-commandeered, monstrosity-driven edifice crashed into the Forest of Flesh with an explosion of blood and flying arms, legs, and genitals. Chariah flew the Megafiend directly into his spaceship, dislodging it from its prison of living trees and gigantic bondage devices. He leapt from the back of the Geryon Baal'Striga into the waiting Arachniotics, which formed a cradle that lifted him up and bore him into the squirming underbelly of his vessel.

A moment later, the Omnibeast spun in place and soared out of the gaping void in the Forest of Flesh. Meanwhile, the Geryon Baal'Striga and the Megafiend careened through the pulpish trees, breaking the bones inside the trunks and branches, and sending extremities shooting through the skies. The Forest of Flesh cried out with millions of anguished voices. Several of the Geryon Baal'Striga's breasts were severed as it crashed, and when the avian fertility demoness smashed through the integument on the other side of the forest, it left in its wake several broods' worth of embryos, fetuses, and hatchlings impaled upon the twiglike fingers and phalluses of the trees. The wounded Geryon Baal'Striga continued to fly the Megafiend into the distance, dangerously low to the ground. Leaving behind a trail of blood, the avian fertility demoness slowly increased its altitude as it soared over the horizon.

Chariah briefly visited his meditation chamber and Bloodbong to heal his wounds, then entered the Omnibeast's cockpit and reassumed command of the vessel. He directed the Omnibeast to fly in an ellipse around the Forest of Flesh, and as it did so, the Overdragon breathed a continuous stream of fire over the trees, so that the entire mutated mass became encircled in a ring of flames taller than itself. Once the circle of containment was complete, Chariah flew the Omnibeast back over the forest in a succession of five straight lines. The Overdragon continued breathing the same stream of fire all the while. After the final path of the pattern had been flown, the Forest of Flesh was alight with a pentagram of flames, a gigantic, blazing pentagram that channeled the forces of Hell and caused the entire forest to kindle, while the flames which outlined the shape of the pentagram towered high over all the others, rising several miles into the skies, until the burning Satanic sigil could be seen from outer space and formed a blood-red constellation visible throughout the entire galaxy.

Chariah watched the Forest of Flesh burn through one of the Omnibeast's sentient scrying tubes, and saw that as the branches and trees crackled and fell to the ground they reassumed their original bodies, covering the ashen floor of the forest with a mass grave of demon corpses. Millions had been sacrificed to create the Forest of Flesh, the most massive of all the genetic and surgical abominations created by the Tantradox. They had at last been released from their tortuous purgatory, but they were being released into an eternal torment billions of times worse than that which they had suffered at the hands of the Tantradox.

The Necrodelic fitted one of the Omnibeast's umbilical cords around his nose and mouth like a gas-mask, and inhaled the smoke of the immolated demons. He lingered around the conflagration for several minutes, enjoying a pleasant surge of pyromania as he gazed with fascination upon the hypnotic flickerings of the arson he had wrought, all the while plotting the complete and total armageddon of Elasvai.

43

The Necrodelic ran at blinding speeds beneath the gargantuan shadow of the Megafiend. The claws of his right hand impaled the very air, while the Soul Cleaver in his left sundered in twain various elemental sylph demons in their ethereal and invisible lairs, for in the Necrodelic's hand the ensorcelled sword was imbued with the power to cut through the interdimensional fabric, and its crimson blade bisected the physical/astral continuum and sundered tiny portions of the two planes from one another. Chariah could hear the clatter and clanging of adamantium meathooks and iron chains overhead, could smell the fragrant aroma of meat both living and dead. He waited like a predator for the perfect moment to strike, then leapt hundreds of feet into the air and grabbed onto one of the meathooks. He swung for a moment, then hoisted himself up, to stand with one foot in the curve of the meathook and one hand gripping the chain from which it dangled. With his other hand, the Necrodelic plunged the Soul Cleaver into the white ceiling, burying it to the hilt in an upside-down sheath of stone, where it stuck fast and did not budge. Chariah then pulled himself up to the ceiling, black-veined biceps muscles rippling and bulging. He slid the talons of his feet into one of the grooves in the ceiling and dug them into the stone. The Necrodelic then let go of the chain and hung within the abattoir like a bat, upside-down, his arms crossed over his chest, and there, amongst the meathooks, concealed by bloodstained chains and dripping chunks of flesh, he waited for his prey like a meditating vampire.

*

Morpheus Rex stood atop the Siamese twin brontosauruses with their frayed and broken reins in his right hand, riding the giant reptiles across the gardens and flowerbeds in pursuit of the Tantradox. His tattooed flesh bore several bruises from a brief and vicious battle with Drelrei and Junisia, who had crashed down into a nearby meadow of lavender grass not long after he himself had fallen from the Megafiend. The Dreaming Predator had suffered an empurpled eye and split lip from Junisia's clubbed ankylosaurus tail, as well as a lacerated chest and thigh from Drelrei's spiked stegosaurus tail. The long fingernailed hand with which he directed the immense conjoined brontosauruses was covered in crimson, but the blood was that of the Tantradox, whose open wounds he had exacerbated as they fought by wrenching, prying, prodding, and ripping them at every opportunity. Drelrei and Junisia had responded by bludgeoning him with their brutal tails until the vengeful brontosauruses came lumbering over the horizon and mauled their former tormentors. Morpheus Rex had clambered onto their backs and, because he was descended from reptiles and half-ophidian, they formed an immediate psychic bond. The Dreaming Predator directed the dinosaurs to trample the Tantradox beneath the bone-crushing tread of their massive paws.

After finally extricating themselves from the feet of the

brontosauruses, the Tantradox fled across the fields on their three cloven hooves, at speeds faster than any stallion or gazelle or unicorn had ever dared. Morpheus Rex gave chase like a wildman, his prism-beaded hair streaming out behind him from atop his dinosaur steeds as they ran with their slithery, waving gait, his forked tongues flickering as he shouted incoherent battle cries and guttural animal sounds.

When the Tantradox spotted the wounded Geryon Baal'Striga, irrigating the horizon with her blood and dragging their palace, their sanctuary, the Megafiend, through the air, it was as though the citadel were a cynosure, beckoning them home. They called to the avian fertility demoness, who turned her bloody vulturine head in their direction and cried out with her three beaks, then headed towards them. As she flew low to the ground, the Tantradox ran alongside and vaulted onto the short set of stairs that led to one of the entrances. The Tantradox stopped to catch its breath on the stone steps as the Geryon Baal'Striga flew the Megafiend back into the sky, above the Siamese twin brontosauruses and the angrily gesticulating Morpheus Rex below. It was then that they felt a black hand around their ankle, and the Necrodelic dragged them kicking and thrashing into the abattoir like a trap-door spider drags its prey into its pit, a macabre polarization, an upside-down perversion, of that gruesome predatory act.

Chariah, still hanging upside-down like a vampire bat, had maneuvered through the dangling slaughterhouse by holding onto the bottom of a chain and following the grooves which had been chiseled into the ceiling for hauling meat. He reached out and grabbed Junisia's leg, then wrenched the Tantradox from the stone steps. Holding them by their outer feet, one hand around each ankle, his foot-talons firmly embedded in the ceiling above, Chariah sadistically swung the Tantradox through the air, then began dragging them inexorably upward. The Tantradox's cloven hooves clattered on the metal meathooks as they squirmed and thrashed.

Chariah bent Drelrei's knee over the curve of a meathook and violently wrenched his leg. Tendons and ligaments tore and snapped, and Drelrei's patella exploded within his very flesh. Both Drelrei and Junisia screamed simultaneously, and continued to scream while Chariah used the chains to right himself. With one foot in the smooth curves of a meathook, and his left hand gripping a nearby chain for balance, Chariah hammered Drelrei's decimated knee with the side of his hand. The Tantradox moaned, swinging painfully from its broken leg over the vertiginous, nauseating, speeding landscapes below.

Chariah etched a pentagram of blood on the Drelrei's swollen knee with a single claw. When the bloody sigil was completed it burst into flame, multiplying the agony of the Tantradox a hundredfold. The Necrodelic lifted the burning, shattered, mutilated knee upwards, jerked the Tantradox as they hung in mid-air, and drove the back of Drelrei's knee through the barbed point of the meathook. The hook impaled the Tantradox by the leg, its gleaming tip emerging from the flesh on the other side, directly in the centerpoint of the flaming pentagram. The Tantradox writhed, screaming and clutching at its knee with pain-contorted faces. The Hellfire threatened to burn completely through their broken leg. Chariah stared at the Tantradox with blazing eyes, daring it to tear off its own leg to escape, daring it not to.

Suddenly, the Megafiend rocked as though it had been struck by a meteor. The Necrodelic saw Serpentikal speeding towards the Megafiend at the last second and braced himself in the chains for the collision. All the meathooks of the abattoir swung wildly about, tangling and knotting and crashing into one another. One buried itself painfully in Chariah's thigh, but he dared not reach down and extract it.

The Tantradox swung crazily from its flaming, dripping, broken knee, hanging on by a few thin shreds of sinew that were ripping and thinning by the moment. The Geryon Baal'Striga reared to one side as the Oneirophage rammed the Megafiend with the Metasaur. Large chunks of white stone loosened and fell like boulders. A second later, the entire Megafiend fell to the ground, landing upright and intact, but laced with new cracks and fissures, much longer and greater than the cracks and fissures it had suffered in the prior battle. The front turret toppled and pinned the Geryon Baal'Striga beneath it.

The force of the crash-landing severed Drelrei's leg at the knee, leaving his amputated hoof and calf spitted upon the meathook, oozing blood and scorched pus. The sign of the pentagram was sundered and destroyed by the dismemberment, and the Hellfire immediately abated. The Tantradox landed on its back in a field of grass, the Megafiend devolving back into the Fiendfarms over their heads.

The Tantradox rose to its feet and began limping through the abattoir. The Necrodelic had disappeared back into the chains and hooks. The Metasaur was ramming the fortress again, making it shiver like earthquake and poltergeist. Warily, Drelrei and Junisia made their way through the slaughterhouse, Drelrei using the dangling chains for leverage to compensate for his amputated leg. Every rustle of iron, every flicker of shadow, made the Tantradox's skin jump. They scanned the hanging slaughterhouse with all four eyes, peering around dying beasts and large slabs of meat before continuing on. Cautiously, the wounded Siamese twins made their exit, spreading the last row of meathooks open with both hands to make one last desperate attempt at survival.

Meanwhile, the Necrodelic was crawling upside-down across the ceiling like a spider, unseen and unheard, rustling neither chain nor hook. His claws, hands, and feet made no sound upon the ceiling, and at no point was any part of his body glimpsed, not even his shadow. He did not breathe as he stalked, nor did his heart beat. He had calculated the point where Drelrei and Junisia would attempt their exit long before they reached it. As they parted the final pair of meathooks, he swung down before them like a drop of liquid night. Dangling by his fists from two chains, he slowly lowered himself in front of the frozen Tantradox, extending the full length of his black body before them with perfect muscle control, flexing his chiseled biceps and triceps, straightening himself before the four eyes of the terrified Siamese twins so that they could behold him one last time, in all his evil splendor, then dropping silently to his feet.

The Tantradox swung drunkenly from the meathook chains in their grasp and started to retreat. Chariah fixed his crimson eye contact upon them, and their four eyes began to smoke and melt. The Tantradox stumbled, entangled in the chains, then began to flee as best it could with its missing leg. The Necrodelic let them run for a couple moments more, remembering how they had bound and gagged him during those intolerable hours of dragging torture. He let their primal animal fear reach a precipitous stiletto zenith, their heartbeat accelerating to a crimson, palpitating crescendo, hormones and endorphins coursing through their veins like venom and overdoses of psychedelic drugs, and then he charged.

Chariah brushed aside chains and meathooks as he raced through the abattoir, his lips curled back over his shimmering black fangs in a silent, feral growl. He knocked aside corpses and living meat with furious intensity, leaving many on the ground in his wake, sidestepping swinging hooks with frightening dexterity as he wove his way through the labyrinth, zeroing in on his prey. The last several yards between the Tantradox and himself the Necrodelic took at a full sprint, spearing them in the chest like a black comet and running straight through them, hoisting them into the air as he did so, and then sinking his claws into their armpits to bear them cruciform through the abattoir at blinding speed.

Drelrei and Junisia screamed in terror. Chains became silver flashes, meathooks grinning madness, swinging before and behind them, each one hurtling with its sharp point extended as if it desired to be the one that skewered them. Corpses and slabs of meat became nightmarish ephemera, gruesome dripping phantasmagoria spinning insanely around their heads. The entire abattoir blurred past their dilated, frantic eyes as the Necrodelic bore them in one extended taurean fit of battering ram insanity that seemed to last for hours, yet took place in mere seconds. Meathooks swung back and forth, narrowly avoiding them but gradually coming closer and closer. It was as though they were sprinting through tunnels of falling guillotine blade that were dropping faster and faster and faster and faster. The Necrodelic ran with the Tantradox crucified on his claws until, finally, two twin, glinting meathooks hung directly in their path. The Necrodelic quickened with one final burst of speed, charging forward, drunk on death, and impaled the Tantradox on both meathooks, one through the back of Drelrei, one through the back of Junisia.

The Tantradox swung crazily from the meathooks, causing all the other meathooks around them to clash and ricochet and tangle. The meathooks dug deep into the flesh of the Tantradox, impaling them through their entrails and stomachs, severing their spines, and protruding from their torsos through their solar plexuses. Blood rained in drip-drop patterns on the ground. Trying to scream, Drelrei and Junisia coughed up blood, then vomited even more blood down their chests.

The Necrodelic stood before them with black patience, waiting for the meathooks to swing back. When they did, he reached up and seized Drelrei's genitals with his left hand. With one violent motion he castrated the incubus, ripping off his immense phallus and his ten testicles, then holding them up bleeding and dripping in his hand like a trophy. As the Tantradox looked on, swaying gently now from the meathooks, Chariah closed his fist around the severed genitals, squeezing them to a crimson pulp that leaked between his fingers and ran down his arm. When the Necrodelic opened his palm, there was nothing left of the genitals but bloodstains, dripping ichor, and shriveled strings of flesh.

As the Tantradox watched in horror, Chariah reached towards the ceiling with his right hand and grasped the hidden hilt of the Soul Cleaver, which had remained stuck in the stone of the ceiling where he'd sheathed it. He drew the crimson blade down while the Tantradox's eyes dilated even further, and they began to weep uncontrollably, for they knew the doom that was to come. Silently, Chariah gripped the handle of the sorcerous broadsword with both hands. He raised it over his head, and then brought it down with one swift, arching strike that landed between the heads of Drelrei and Junisia at the exact spot of their surgical conjoinment, slicing them in half as cleanly as razorwire and as suddenly as a thunderbolt. The supersonic speed and force of the deathstrike caused the crimson blade of the Soul Cleaver to resheath itself in the ground, just as it had been sheathed in the ceiling moments ago.

The severed bodies of the Tantradox swung wildly on their meathooks, swinging and twisting and colliding as blood and teardrops poured onto the ground. Chariah finally brought their ricocheting, dismembered bodies to a halt with his black palms. He established eye contact with each of them one last time, forever branding his face upon their souls, and then he plunged his right hand into the vagina of Junisia and his left hand into the gaping castration wound of Drelrei. With a torrent of blood his hands forced their way upwards, leaving Junisia's womb in tatters and Drelrei's thoracic cavity in shreds. His arms shot violently through their bodies, his claws tearing through every organ, tissue, and bone in their path, until the Necrodelic's arms were buried almost to the shoulders inside his prey. His fists closed around their thundering hearts, and then he withdrew his arms from their bodies in an explosion of gore, artescerating them through vagina and castrated crotch simultaneously.

Chariah held his arms out cruciform as Drelrei and Junisia died, a beating heart in each hand, and then, with his head tilted back in ecstasy, he squeezed each heart to a liquid pulp in his fists, feeling them explode in his palms. He raised his arms slowly overhead, still cruciform, so that the blood could run all over his body, and he stayed in that position for one timeless moment, deep in a meditative trance, surging with glorious black energies in the psychedelic intoxication of a vengeance exacted and a mission complete.

An eternity later, Chariah returned to his senses to find the Megafiend being rammed by the Metasaur once again, and beginning to lift off the ground. He quickly removed the corpses of the Tantradox from the meathooks, slinging Junisia's limp carcass over his right shoulder and Drelrei's over his left. As the Geryon Baal'Striga began beating her wings and the Megafiend took flight once again, Chariah was left standing all alone in the middle of the garden planet. He whistled once for the Omnibeast. The spaceship flew to his side a moment later. He spoke the word "Drakhus" and the Overdragon lifted him into its mouth with its tongue. Cerberus was waiting for him in the Overdragon's maw, cocaine-rabid, fur matted with blood, a minotaur bone in each of its five mouths. It turned and followed its master down the gullet of the Overdragon, and Necrodelic and hellhound disappeared into the Omnibeast.

*

The Oneirophage and Hydraman stood in the cavernous mouth of Serpentikal as the Metasaur repeatedly rammed the grounded Megafiend. The two halves of the Janus Kraken had been stationed in the psychedelic moat at either side of Phantasmagorika. The open flesh on their backs had adhered and assimilated into the walls of the prism palace, so that the krakens had become the second and third figureheads of the nearly-completed spaceship. Serpentikal and the two krakens took turns headbutting the Megafiend, the Metasaur continually pivoting and bashing the citadel from every angle. A brutal blow from the bruised and ensanguined skull of Serpentikal dislodged the front turret of the Megafiend, freeing the Geryon Baal'Striga, who had been pinned beneath it. The terrified, wounded avian fertility demoness frantically beat its wings until the Megafiend budged and became airborne once again. With the Metasaur following in close pursuit, the Megafiend lifted into the skies and sped away.

Traveling at greater speeds than ever before, the Metasaur quickly caught up to the Geryon Baal'Striga and cut the giant bird off. The force of their collision separated the Geryon Baal'Striga from the citadel and knocked the Megafiend into outer space, breaking the bonds of Elasvai's waning gravitational pull and spiraling into the distant cosmos beyond. At the same time the Geryon Baal'Striga plummeted to the ground and landed on its back. The sound of its wings breaking could be heard for miles around.

Removing the Darkprism from around his neck, the Oneirophage sucked the crippled Geryon Baal'Striga into the black hole pendant, then commanded Serpentikal to skim the surface of Elasvai so that he might gather up what little life remained before the Necrodelic destroyed the entire planet. While the Metasaur soared past a bloodstained field some time later, a strange glitter of crimson caught the Oneirophage's attention. He turned his head and saw the Soul Cleaver sheathed in the ground, protruding diagonally from the center of a fresh puddle of blood.

From a distance the Darkprism could only absorb organic matter, so he would have to retrieve the sword by hand. There was little time, but the Soul Cleaver was a precious bauble and powerful relic that the Oneirophage felt he must possess, in part to accompany the Flesh Compactor already displayed in his weapons gallery.

Directing Serpentikal to land the Metasaur, the Oneirophage clambered down the snake king's throat and rushed to the ensorcelled blade. He withdrew the Soul Cleaver from the ground and quickly turned to board his spaceship once more, but the Metasaur had begun lifting off without him.

With a piercing and cacophonous susurrus the Oneirophage

leapt into the sky, but the Metasaur was faster. His long fingernails scraped Serpentikal's underbelly, but he was already at the apex of his leap, hundreds of feet in the air. He whipped out the Umbilicus and swung the straw apparatus like a grappling hook. It shot through the air and lodged in the ridged scales of Serpentikal's underbelly, and the Oneirophage began pulling himself back towards the Metasaur.

Suddenly another Umbilicus, identical to his in shape and sorcerous power, emerged from Serpentikal's mouth. The alien Umbilicus quickly elongated and entangled the Oneirophage's own. A pneuma blasted through the alien Umbilicus like a solar wind, dislodging the Oneirophage's Umbilicus and sending him plummeting to the ground. As he looked up, he caught a glimpse of himself in Serpentikal's maw, and the heads of Siamese twin brontosauruses peeking from the gateway in Serpentikal's abdomen. Morpheus Rex had hijacked the Metasaur.

The Oneirophage fell to the ground as the Hellfires began. He watched the Omnibeast orbit Elasvai like a black moon, spreading flames across the garden planet. The Overdragon hurled fireballs while the Necrodelic performed his pyromancies from its sulfurous maw, raising massive conflagrations, giant firewalls, and blazing tsunamis of flame, and unleashing concatenations of spontaneous combustions and cataclysmic explosions. The Necrodelic was bringing Hell to Elasvai. Unfortunately for the Oneirophage, it looked as though this very same act of destruction was going to bring him to Hell.

The Oneirophage lay himself down in a flowerbed of blue asphodels and black crocuses and prepared to die. As psychedelic plant life blazed across the entire garden planet, the Oneirophage breathed in the perfumes of a thousand different drugs and relaxed. At peace and at one, he closed his eyes as the flames approached his body, and fainted from smoke inhalation. Thus it was that he never saw the large chiropteran shadow of Democubus descending on hooked wings through the billowing smoke, never felt the hooked hands of his soulmate cradling him against his hooked chest, and never witnessed the passing galaxies as he was borne through the cosmos to the Moons of Dread. As Democubus and the Oneirophage flew off into space, the indentation left by the Oneirophage in the flowerbed he had thought would be his deathbed slowly kindled and began to burn, forming a glowing outline of his serpentine form, which then metamorphosed into the flaming body of Satan, lying on an interdimensional funeral pyre in Hell below, laughing as he masturbated to the mass destruction, then roaring with pleasure as he came to orgasm, ejaculating magma and molten souls, the force of his ecstasy shaking the entire universe, and then Elasvai exploded, Dzandra burst into topaz supernova, and the garden planet was no more.

44

The sundered halves of the Tantradox floated within the Bloodbong. Hellfire arose from the interplanal portal on the floor, and blood began to boil, roseate steam filled the chamber, and incarnadine condensation bedewed the labyrinthine and mandalic network of twisted tubes and vessels, glass arteries and veins, that comprised the intricate flesh-smoking pipe. The Necrodelic, seated in the black lotus position with the mouthpiece of the Bloodbong betwixt his ebon lips, meditated with his crimson, glowing eyes wide open. He inhaled, the deep, slow breath of the succubus, and Junisia's skin began to crack and fissure, then blister and suppurate. The open wound left by the meathook in her back dilated, leaking blood and vertebrae into the incandescent plasma. He exhaled, the deep, slow breath of the incubus, blasting the skin from Drelrei's body, decorticating his cadaver with the hot, violent winds of Gehenna.

The skinless corpse of Drelrei floated with scarlet muscles, tissues, and membranes exposed, flayed of its entire integument by the simoom of the Necrodelic's breath. Chariah siphoned more necrodelia from the Bloodbong, smoking Junisia's eyes from their sockets and opening holes all over her body, transforming her into a bloody honeycomb of flesh. She hovered before the transparent glass of the heart-chamber like some tormented mutation afflicted with hundreds of bodily orifices, each leaking, spurting, and spraying blood, pus, and gore. A caliginous pneuma blew the lips and tongue from Drelrei's mouth, the nose and eyelids from his face, and the spaded scales from his head, back, and tail. The dislodged scales drifted along the vermillion currents and shattered against the walls and floor of the pipe. The suction-like withdrawal of Chariah's pneuma scalped Junisia, ripping the hair from her head by the roots with the skin of her face still attached, lips, tongue, cheeks, nose, eyelids, and all. Her face dissipated, leaving her scalplock to float like a drowned corpse on the bubbling surface of boiling blood. Chariah breathed out once again, and the gaping castration wound in Drelrei's crotch grew wider, slitting his torso to the sternum while two large flaps of muscle and tissue quivered around the dripping laceration, revealing the gory pit where his heart had once beat, a ragged cavern ringed by stalactites and stalagmites of severed veins and sundered arteries. The Necrodelic suckled, the force of his lungs severing Junisia's nipples like the fangs of a cannibalistic infant. He sucked even harder, ripping her breasts from her chest. Her swollen tits exploded with the sound and smell of sizzling animal fat. Beneath her ribs, the empty cavity left by her artescerated heart could be seen, her torn aorta gaping like a Hellmouth in the void. Impaling Drelrei with his breath, Chariah enlarged the gash in the incubus' torso and eviscerated him. Drelrei's intestines fell to the base of the pipe, waving about like the arms of demons burning in Hell. The Necrodelic performed cunnilingus upon the mouthpiece of the Bloodbong, and Junisia's hundredfold labia shivered and fell off, one by one, like the petals of an immortelle, the severed lobes of flesh scattering in the currents of vermillion ichor. Her ten clitorises were severed, and then her vagina was torn into a giant chasm from her thighs to her gullet, vivisecting the succubus so that all her internal organs fell from her body in a steady cortege, one by one, a grotesque parody of childbirth. Chariah ejaculated a jetstream of smoke from his mouth, blowing all the organs from Drelrei's body as well, to spin and ricochet around the heart chamber in tiny whirlpools as they joined Junisia's spilled innards. Guillotine inspiration decapitated Junisia; scythelike expiration decapitated Drelrei. Their severed heads drifted and spun, floating and sinking and then rising up through the currents again. Chariah breathed twice and ripped the tails from their broken spines. The club of Junisia's ankylosaurus tail and the mace of Drelrei's stegosaurus tail rolled through the broiling plasma. Two more breaths ripped all the remaining tissue from their skeletons, and then their bones began to unhinge and clatter to the golgotha of the pipe-chamber's floor. After the Tantradox had been completely mutilated, Chariah smoked each one of their internal organs and every single bone of their skeletons individually, in slow succession, inhaling to disintegrate those of Junisia and exhaling to detonate those of Drelrei. He saved their severed heads for last, slowly smoking their skulls and brains over a period of several hours.

After he had smoked the entire Tantradox, piece by bloody piece, the Necrodelic's eyes fluttered shut and he fell into a deeply meditative and psychedelic trance. He remembered the battles that had taken place on the now-destroyed garden planet of Elasvai, and contemplated the myriad battles yet to come. He philosophized about the singularity of his soul, the oneness of evil he had attained over billions of incarnations, which could neither be reduced nor sundered into smaller portions. He reflected upon the drug of vengeance, the black euphoria he had felt upon slaying the Tantradox, the bloody orgasm of revenge and the tantalizing games of combat leading up to it, a dark nirvana which rivaled the intoxication of betrayal he had felt upon the aceldamas of Grystiawa after incinerating Spidratha. They were each two aspects of a greater drug, the all-encompassing oversoul of necrodelia, which was his path to the salvation of the Jh'a'vyraa. Chariah now walked that long path of samsara victoriously, his crimson eyes blazing with triumph, his black brain saturated with evil, and his dark soul surging with confidence, for he was the most powerful demon the cosmos had ever spawned, the scourge of the galaxies, the genocider of a decillion races, the slayer of both space and time, the alpha male of the universe, and in his mind he had already become the Messiah of Death.

Dead Bait

RESURRECTION
By Tim Curran
www.corpseking.com

The rain is falling and the dead are rising. It began at an ultra-secret government laboratory. Experiments in limb regeneration- an unspeakable union of Medieval alchemy and cutting edge genetics result in the very germ of horror itself: a gene trigger that will reanimate dead tissue...any dead tissue. Now it's loose. It's gone viral. It's in the rain. And the rain has not stopped falling for weeks. As the country floods and corpses float in the streets, as cities are submerged, the evil dead are rising. And they are hungry.

"I REALLY love this book...Curran is a wonderful storyteller who really should be unleashed upon the general horror reading public sooner rather than leter." – *DREAD CENTRAL*

Available at www.severedpress.com, Amazon and most online bookstores

THE DEVIL NEXT DOOR

Cannibalism. Murder. Rape. Absolute brutality. When civilizations ends...when the human race begins to revert to ancient, predatory savagery...when the world descends into a bloodthirsty hell...there is only survival. But for one man and one woman, survival means becoming something less than human. Something from the primeval dawn of the race.

"Shocking and brutal, The Devil Next Door will hit you like a baseball bat to the face. Curran seems to have it in for the world ... and he's ending it as horrifyingly as he can." - *Tim Lebbon, author of Bar None*

"The Devil Next Door is dynamite! Visceral, violent, and disturbing!." *Brian Keene, author of Castaways and Dark Hollow*

"The Devil Next Door is a horror fans delight...who love extreme horror fiction, and to those that just enjoy watching the world go to hell in a hand basket" – *HORROR WORLD*

The Official Zombie Handbook: Sean T Page

Since pre-history, the living dead have been among us, with documented outbreaks from ancient Babylon and Rome right up to the present day. But what if we were to suffer a zombie apocalypse in the UK today? Through meticulous research and field work, The Official Zombie Handbook (UK) is the only guide you need to make it through a major zombie outbreak in the UK, including: -Full analysis of the latest scientific information available on the zombie virus, the living dead creatures it creates and most importantly, how to take them down - UK style. Everything you need to implement a complete 90 Day Zombie Survival Plan for you and your family including home fortification, foraging for supplies and even surviving a ghoul siege. Detailed case studies and guidelines on how to battle the living dead, which weapons to use, where to hide out and how to survive in a country dominated by millions of bloodthirsty zombies. Packed with invaluable information, the genesis of this handbook was the realisation that our country is sleep walking towards a catastrophe - that is the day when an outbreak of zombies will reach critical mass and turn our green and pleasant land into a grey and shambling wasteland. Remember, don't become a cheap meat snack for the zombies!

Available at www.severedpress.com, Amazon and most online bookstores

BIOHAZARD
Tim Curran

The day after tomorrow: Nuclear fallout. Mutations. Deadly pandemics. Corpse wagons. Body pits. Empty cities. The human race trembling on the edge of extinction. Only the desperate survive. One of them is Rick Nash. But there is a price for survival: communion with a ravenous evil born from the furnace of radioactive waste. It demands sacrifice. Only it can keep Nash one step ahead of the nightmare that stalks him-a sentient, seething plague-entity that stalks its chosen prey: the last of the human race. To accept it is a living death. To defy it, a hell beyond imagining